Scarlet Tears

Laura HERVEY

Alabaster Box Press

Text copyright © 2018 by Laura Hervey

Alabaster Box Press

Cover design and title page designed by Paper and Sage Design

All rights reserved. Published in the United States by Alabaster Box Press and Laura Hervey in 2018. No part of this book may be reproduced in any form without the author's express written permission.

ISBN 978-17325187-8-0 Trade

ISBN 978-0-692-10961-8 POD

ISBN 978-1-7325187-9-7 e-book

Library of Congress Control Number: 2018908207

Printed in the United States of America

In loving memory of

My father, Richard F. Neary

My mother, Marilyn Neary Biggs

My stepfather, James J. Biggs

Acknowledgements

Without the expertise and encouragement of my faithful critique partners, Gloria Clover, Carol Hamilton, Cindy Bingham, Ellen List, Audrey Stallsmith, Linda Turner, and Barbara Sutryn this book might never have been completed. To each I owe a debt of gratitude. Special thanks goes to my two beta readers, Jeanne Fuller and Sarah Rizzo. I would also like to thank my brother-in-law, John Carnegie, for sharing his knowledge of the responsibilities of New York State Correction Officers. I would like to thank Stacey Sowinski for her help with sections of this book pertaining the Buffalo Police Department. Thank you as well to Diane Gebel for her assistance with the descriptions of Attica State Prison. Any errors are mine, not theirs.

CHAPTER ONE

Carly Lawrence was trapped, living in a poorly plotted romance novel that had never gotten past the first chapter. She'd had several false starts, but who was she kidding? In her business, she was hardly a romantic heroine. And most of the men she met turned out to be villains. Reluctant to face reality, she'd foolishly given her heart to one Mr. Wrong after another until she believed she would never deserve Mr. Right, even if he should come along to give her more than a second glance.

But Alan Rutledge, her boss and sometimes boyfriend, made sure that would never happen. She was worth too much. In cash.

To think she'd once believed *he* was her perfect match. Why hadn't she listened to Jared or Joe? Then again, how many eighteen-year-old girls listened to their brothers or their brothers' best friends?

Standing in front of the full length mirror that had recently become unforgiving of her bouts of chocolate-cured depression, Carly allowed herself to consider for the briefest moment that she could in fact be wrong about her expectations. Maybe God did have something better in mind for her life. Something that did not leave her feeling degraded and discarded. Something precious and good.

She tapped one finger against her fuchsia-colored thumb nail to be sure the polish was dry and decided a few more minutes with her blow dryer would do the trick. Then she'd change into her short black dress with the tiny red roses. The black hid the extra ten pounds she couldn't shed. The roses reminded her of her nearly forgotten innocence. If only she could go back. Or forget entirely.

But neither option was possible. Not for her.

She was tempted to reach for the cigarette pack she kept hidden beneath her cosmetics in the oak cabinet. Her latest failed Romeo had purchased the beautiful furniture for her as a parting gift. But she didn't go for the cigarettes. She'd gained back a little of her self-respect when she'd managed to quit smoking two months ago, and she couldn't afford to give up that small victory.

As she zipped up one leather boot, then the other, her cell phone blared Sheryl Crow's "The first cut is the deepest, baby, I know …"

Carly ignored it.

Her father would leave a message. He always did, every night at the same time, at exactly 7:30. "Honey, we love you. Please, come home."

She couldn't go home, and she'd given up trying to explain that to him years ago. The person he wanted to come home didn't exist anymore.

*

Carly stepped out into the cool August night. Thank God she spotted Joe before he saw her. She scooted behind the overgrown shrubs—a fine hiding place, until her allergies kicked in. One whiff of the heady pine scent and she regretted her choice. Desperate to remain concealed, she covered her nose and mouth to muffle a fit of sneezing. Mrs. Olcott, her chatty landlady, had inadvertently alerted Carly to the fact that Officer Joseph Callahan patrolled this neighborhood, and so far, she had successfully avoided running into her old neighbor. What was he doing here anyway? Last she'd heard, he'd done a stint in the Army and won himself a Purple Heart. Made his parents proud, and her, too, when she'd read about his homecoming in the local paper.

For a nanosecond, her traitorous heart stirred at the thought of seeing him, but she shrank farther into the evening shadows and shivered in her silk wrap and summer dress that suddenly seemed about six inches too short.

What do you care what Joe Callahan thinks of you?

I don't care. Not one bit.

But she did wonder if his eyes were still as blue as a gorgeous summer sky, if they still radiated an inner confidence she could never quite attain. And if they could still make her feel as though she could spend the rest of her life exploring their luminous depths.

If only she'd never met Al.

If only Joe had seen her as more than his best friend's little sister. If only she'd had the guts to go after him. Then her life would've been entirely different.

Deep in her heart the truth echoed. Joe was a keeper.

And she'd made the wrong choice. The first in a long line of lousy choices.

"Sugar, what on earth are you doing hiding in the bushes?" asked Mrs. Zigler, the retired English teacher who'd recently moved into the apartment below her.

Heat flushed her cheeks. "I ... oh, never mind. Could you just pretend I've stopped by for tea or something?"

Mrs. Zigler's eyes crinkled in amusement. "Honey, you don't strike me as the kind of girl who'd stop for tea with an old lady."

Stung by Mrs. Zigler's words, Carly shrank away and bumped square into solid flesh. *Oh, no. Now what?* Reining in her emotions, she whirled around and adopted her most indignant air. Her eyes narrowed in an attempt to level him with a look that would have caused most men to instantly withdraw. Not Joe Callahan.

He was taller than she remembered. The hard planes of his face had completely eclipsed his boyish charm and looks. But he was devastatingly handsome. Which was completely unfair.

Still, she kept her breath even. He was, after all, just another man.

"Ma'am, I'm terribly sorry. I was just stopping by to check in on Sarah—Mrs. Zigler. There've been several burglaries in this neighborhood in the past month, and ..." He stopped midsentence, staring intently at Carly as though seeing her for the first time.

God, no. Please don't let him recognize me. She tilted her head to swing a lock of her auburn wig over her face.

"Carly? Is it really you?" His eyes shone with happiness that was quickly followed by something else. Guilt? Or regret?

She averted her gaze a moment to quiet her nerves. "It's me." *Not the me you remember, but it's still me.*

Appraising her from head to toe, Joe said, "Carly, you look—"

"So do you," she said, cutting him off. She couldn't bear his reproach. "Listen, it was great to see you, but I have to get to work. I'm fifteen minutes late already. It was great seeing you."

Wonderful. She was repeating herself. So much for the cool composure she'd developed as Elise.

"Can I call you? We could meet for coffee, to catch up."

He said it as if he didn't know she hadn't been in touch with her family for years. Surely, he and Jared were still friends. Her hands trembled, and she crossed her arms over her ribs. "That's ... probably not a good idea."

He opened his mouth to argue, but she strode off before he

could respond. Through the rhythm of her heels clicking on the concrete sidewalk, she heard him call, "Carly, wait. I need your number."

The urge to turn around and do what he asked expanded like a balloon in her chest. What could it hurt to exchange phone numbers? She halted for a second. Then the magnitude of who she'd become slammed into her with the force of sledgehammer, stealing her breath. She was one of the most sought after girls on the north side. She wasn't the girl next door who once dreamed she could date her older brother's best friend. She hurried away, the sound of his voice calling her name one last time bringing tears to her eyes.

Countless blocks down Elmwood, she caught a reflection of herself in a full length mirror displayed in an antiques shop window. She paused to appraise her appearance and didn't like what she saw. Sour lines creased her forehead, and her skin was a pallid yellow. She should have gone to the beach or tanning. Or used more cover-up. Anything to give her that fresh-as-summer look Al prized so much. A glass of champagne, maybe two, would add some color to her cheeks and help her shake her melancholy. Why on earth did she have to run into Joe tonight? He was a living, breathing reminder of the woman Carly had once believed she would become. A woman she could never be.

She pinched her cheeks until the slight pain resurrected her practical side. Roger's parties were always good money makers, but only if she kept a smile on her face and laughed at every joke, no matter how stupid. Tonight, she would do her job and do it well.

*

Seventeen days had passed since Carly had seen Joe, and she couldn't get him out of her head. At the most inconvenient times, she imagined his face fixing her with that same look of disapproval she'd hated in high school. Frustrated, she slipped on her ballet flats and fluffed her hair.

What was worse, Al knew she was off her game. He'd had complaints. Yesterday, he'd invited her to lunch at Pano's restaurant, not out of concern for her, but to warn her, his voice a low growl, "Never again. Make sure I never hear another complaint about you. Not even one."

She'd reached across the table to reassure him, but he'd pulled his hand beyond her grasp. There was nothing between them anymore but business. Apparently, they weren't even friends.

Fully aware that she needed to leave for work soon, she trudged from her bedroom to the kitchen and pulled a half empty bottle of red wine from the fridge, then filled a clean coffee mug that she grabbed from the dish drainer. Her four wine glasses were dirty in the sink, along with a collection of mugs and spoons. Tomorrow she'd have to wash dishes. In the meantime, she needed one glass of wine before she left for work. One glass to take the edge off the shame. That's all she needed.

She drank a few swallows, her frustration with Al taking her back to that first night they were together. Carly could still feel the scorch of his kiss as it seared her flesh. His hands, if only she'd had the presence of mind to stop his hands. But she hadn't wanted to, not that night or the many nights afterward.

"Remember, the day we met," Al had said, "You were the most beautiful girl I'd ever seen."

She'd blushed, believing she'd met the guy she would spend the rest of her life with.

Lies, lies, lies. How many lies had she swallowed like a ketamine-laced drink until every move she made was dictated by Al?

She gulped the rest of the dry pinot noir in two swigs. *Enjoying* wine was something you did on a date with a man who cared about you for more than a night or a week or even a month.

Her cell phone vibrated, dancing on the counter and demanding her attention. She wanted to ignore Al, but she couldn't risk his anger. Not tonight. Tonight she would make in two hours more than she usually made in an entire night. If she could hold still that long.

She emptied the rest of the wine into her mug, filling it to the brim. Then she touched her send button.

"Where the hell are you?" he growled. "We're all set up."

She yanked open the silverware drawer and reaching behind the tray, grabbed the cigarettes she'd hidden there last week. She put one in her mouth, her lips pressing against it like a kiss.

"Are you there, Elise? I said we're waiting on you."

She lit a match, held it to the cigarette, but blew it out before it could catch. How she hated when he called her Elise. "I'm here." She ground the unlit cigarette onto the flagstone floor. She'd sweep it up later. "I'll be there in twenty minutes."

"Fine. But this'll cost you ten percent."

Disgusted, she hit the end button, dropped her cell into her black leather bag, snatched her keys from the hook by the door, and headed out into the rain. She wanted to walk, so her hair would lay long and curly against her bare shoulders. Al liked that look, wild and carefree. Which was, of course, everything Carly was not. But it didn't matter what she thought about who she was or wasn't. What mattered was what *he* thought. Contradicting him was unwise. Very unwise, and painful. She'd play along, then she'd get her ten percent back for sure.

*

Every muscle in Carly's body ached, but she had agreed to a thirty-minute pose. To distract herself from her discomfort, she focused on the Van Gogh print on Al's living room wall and imagined herself drinking a mocha cappuccino at the sidewalk café on a lazy summer afternoon. Anything to keep her mind off the four artists rendering her nude form in various Conté crayon colors. Al preferred charcoal. He liked the stark, vacant feeling formed by the harsh, black lines. His friends, Peter, Amy, and Lydia were amateurs and naturally appreciated the softer lines of Conté crayons.

Carly didn't care what they used to draw her. She only wanted them to finish soon so she could collect her money and go home and soak in a tub full of the hottest water she could stand. And, of course, she wanted another glass of wine. The steam and the wine, together with a CD of Debussy would help her forget for a while what she did for a living.

The glass of wine she'd gulped down earlier had done nothing to deaden her sensibilities or her senses. "Can you turn off the air? I'm cold," she murmured, trying not to move, much, though she knew she'd be shivering soon if she didn't get warm. Who used air conditioning when it was 65° outside?

"I like the way she looks when she's cold," Amy said.

Amy was a flighty, selfish blonde without a lick of common sense under her dyed locks. Great. Al would listen to her. Of course he would. After all, the customer is always right.

"We'll be done soon," he said, evenly. "Take a five-minute break if you need to. As long as you can resume the pose."

He knew she couldn't. No model could.

At the end of the third pose, she donned her black silk robe and headed to the bathroom. Al reached for the door, holding it open and pushing her inside. "Open your robe."

Startled, she hoped her eyes didn't show her fear. Did he … had he guessed?

Hot color flooded her face as she untied the belt and let the shimmery material fall away from her belly and breasts.

"Turn around."

She turned her back to him.

He grabbed her hair, just hard enough to hurt but not so she'd cry out. She faced him again.

"Turn to the side."

She sucked in her stomach and held her breath.

"You've gained weight. Lose ten pounds before the next sitting, or I'll use Star."

What did she care if he gave the job to Star? Carly hated modeling nude. Having people stare at her naked body for two hours was worse than her escort job.

*

Since the night he'd run into Carly, Joe had driven by her apartment no less than a dozen times, sometimes while he was on duty, and other times while he was off. Those few times he'd been alone and seen her car, he'd driven by without stopping, not knowing what to say to her. But the last time had been what—three days ago?

"I'm worried about Carly Lawrence."

Harris, Joe's partner of four years, shifted his gaze from the street for a few seconds. "Have you checked the hospitals? I know you don't want to go down that road, but I've seen a lot of these girls beaten practically to death by crazed Johns—"

"She's not a prostitute." Joe shot him a steely look.

"That's not the point. One of her neighbors said she saw a dark-haired man in a suit leaving Carly's apartment. And we haven't seen her silver Focus in days."

Joe couldn't shake the awful feeling in his gut that something was terribly wrong. *God, please, let her be okay. I know I should have fought for her ten years ago when that scumbag first walked into her life.*

Harris made a sharp left into the parking lot of Erie County Medical Center. He pulled into the gated visitor lot, parked in the closest available spot, and cut the engine. "We've got a few minutes."

Stalling, Joe popped a stick of cinnamon gum into his mouth.

"Go on. Find out if she's here. You obviously care about this woman."

"You don't understand. Carly and I ... hell, there is no Carly and me. Never was. Never can be."

The older man shook his head again. "Lying to yourself shows a lack of character. You're better than that, man."

Joe wanted to say he didn't care what happened to Carly. Denying his feelings for her had become second nature years ago. "I'm just someone who knew her before ... She was something back then. The girl next door. Her brother and I are still friends."

Harris listened intently, wearing the expression he donned when collecting sufficient evidence to get an indictment.

"By the time I heard she'd left town ..." Joe stopped before he revealed what was not his secret to tell. "Look, man, you know the story. A good girl gets hooked up with the wrong guy who messes up her life."

"Just go find out if she's here. I'll wait outside," Harris said.

Joe nodded, exited the car, and sprinted through the rain to the main entrance. The silver-haired matron working the reception desk smiled. "How can I help you, Officer?"

"I need to see Carly Lawrence, please."

The woman, whose name tag read Hazel, glanced down at her computer screen. "Miss Lawrence is in ICU. Family only." She hesitated, her green eyes assessing him over the top of her designer glasses. "Unless, of course, this is *police* business."

She was giving him a way in. The way she emphasized the word police told him so, but he didn't want to lie. *Forgive me, Father.* "Yes, ma'am."

Hazel smiled. "375, Officer." She handed him a pass. "I hope you find what you're looking for."

So do I.

Joe thanked the receptionist and headed toward the bank of elevators where a young man was holding the hand of a little girl of about three. "Mommy's bringing the new baby home today, Daddy."

The father bent down to his daughter's level and hugged her. "Not today, honey. Tomorrow, they'll both be coming home."

Joe felt a pang in his heart. His own desire for a family seemed farther off than ever.

As he entered the elevator, a young couple holding hands waited to exit. They smiled briefly. It was the courteous smile of those engrossed in their own lives. Joe saw it on the streets every day.

Memories of Carly as a young girl flooded his mind as the elevator zipped to the third floor. *God, I don't know what You want me to do. It's too late for Carly and me. Why did You bring her back into my life?*

No answer came.

The smell of bleached sheets and disinfectant assaulted his senses as he walked into Carly's room. She lay motionless, her head propped up on two pillows. He quickly scanned the oxygen tube in her nose and the IV catheter taped to her left hand. He swallowed his anger at the black and purple bruises that splotched her face and arms, a harsh contrast to her pale skin.

"That bastard," Joe muttered under his breath. He half

knelt next to the head of the bed. "Who did this to you, Carly?"

Not expecting an answer, he pushed the call-button for the nurse.

"May I help you? Do you need anything, Carly?" a young woman asked via the intercom.

"I'm Officer Callahan, and I'd like to ask you a few questions."

Several moments of silence passed. "Oh. All right. Give me a minute."

Joe bent to kiss Carly's forehead. At the sound of a woman's voice behind him, he straightened quickly.

He followed the head nurse, a much older woman than the one who'd spoken over the intercom. She led him to the I.C.U. waiting room and gestured to the corner of the empty room, where they sat in two upholstered chairs staring at each other. "I'm not sure I can help you, Officer."

"How long has Ms. Lawrence been here?"

"Three days. And there isn't anything else I can tell you. If you want to know more, you will have to ask Ms. Lawrence herself. Any information about her condition is confidential."

Waiting chafed but he did need to get back to work.

*

After his shift, Joe resisted the urge to rush back to the hospital to see Carly. He'd grab something to eat, go home, and shower, then check in on her later.

He stopped at his favorite bakery. Ida's almond pastry reminded him of holidays at home before his grandmother died. But even Ida's strongest coffee didn't soothe his raw nerves. The almond pastry remained untouched on his plate. Nothing but Carly could fix what was wrong with him today, what had been wrong for a very long time. He'd just been too stubborn to admit it. Why hadn't he asked her out years ago? Then he could have saved her from all of this. Maybe.

Maybe not. Dad had tried with Mom. More than once. *Don't go there, Joe.*

Frowning slightly, Ida topped off his coffee. "I didn't burn that batch, did I?"

Puzzled, Joe set aside the morning paper. He hadn't been reading it anyway. "Excuse me?"

Ida pulled out the chair opposite him and settled in for a chat. Much to Joe's dismay. He was pretty good at anticipating people, but he'd missed Ida's maternal instincts kicking in.

How could he say just enough to satisfy her without revealing the ugly truth? "It's an old friend from back home."

"And she's in a bit of trouble?"

"More like a truckload," Joe blurted out, forgetting his intention to hide the grim prognosis. He needed to get a handle on his emotions. "Look, Ida, I can't talk about—"

"A case." She patted his hand the way his grandmother used to do. "But this one is more than a case to you, honey."

He leveled her with his most skeptical look.

"It's all over your face."

Joe was pretty sure he didn't want to know what was written all over his face, and he was just as certain Ida was about to tell him. He took a large bite of his pastry, gulped his coffee down, and rose to leave. "Thanks for your concern, Ida, and your prayers. Carly needs all the prayers she can get."

Ida nodded, her expression declaring she understood what he wasn't saying out loud. "Let me make you a sandwich before you go. You haven't been eating properly."

He shook his head. She and his grandmother would've been good friends.

"Your uniform's getting baggy."

He *had* moved his belt buckle over one hole. Acquiescing, Joe told her to make him a turkey on whole wheat.

"This city would be a great place to live if there were more people like you, Ida."

And fewer people like that animal who beat Carly.

*

Carly woke up crying. Cold tears slid down her cheeks, shocking her. *Why am I crying? I haven't cried since that first time. I didn't even cry when Al slammed me into the coffee table. And not when he beat me until merciful, black oblivion rescued me from the blows.*

Every inch of her body throbbed, ached, or stabbed with pain. Where was she? She forced her eyes to focus on her surroundings. A hospital room? But how did she get here? Al would have sooner left her to die. While he'd kicked and pounded her, completely heedless of her pleas, he'd cursed her. A dim recollection of him threatening to kill her flitted through her mind, but she dismissed it.

Carly felt around under the blankets and on top of the blankets. There had to be a nurse's call-button somewhere. She reached next to her pillow, wincing in pain, yet determined to find it. Finally, her left hand clasped the remote. She pressed the button and waited, drawing in a sharp breath and holding herself together by sheer willpower. Willpower she had. What she lacked was sense, sense enough to walk out on Al that first time he'd beat her, what was it eight, almost nine years ago now? She should have known he'd go off when she broke the news. But that didn't matter anymore. Thanks to Al, she no longer had any news to share.

"Can I help you, miss?"

"Yes," Carly said, surprised at how scratchy her own voice sounded. "I need something for the pain."

"I'll be right in."

While she waited for the nurse to bring her drugs, Carly scanned the room. She was in ICU? She'd visited a girlfriend once in ICU. She'd had to lie and say she was Star's sister.

This room with its monitors and machines had to be intensive care. Had Al really meant to kill her? Apparently, he'd nearly succeeded.

"I'm glad to see you're awake."

Carly focused on the nurse, a woman old enough to be her grandmother. Why hadn't she retired yet? Surely, she'd worked long enough and hard enough to rest and enjoy life. Doreen wore cranberry scrubs and a stethoscope around her neck. She pulled a syringe from her scrub top pocket and injected the fluid into the catheter attached to Carly's left hand.

"What did you give me?"

"Morphine. You've been on a CRI."

No way. Had the nurse really given her morphine? "What on earth is CRI?"

"Constant rate of infusion."

Carly stared at the IV bag attached to the pole near her bed. Sure enough. A label indicated her dose of morphine. She needed to set Doreen straight on the fact that she merely wanted something to take the edge off the pain. Morphine was hard stuff, and she'd made it a practice to stay away from the hard stuff. She'd seen too many girls lose everything for a fix. That's why she stuck with wine or champagne. She'd tried pot a few times, but lucky for her it made her so paranoid she couldn't function, and in Carly's line of work functioning was the major key to making money. And staying alive.

"I don't want any more morphine. Give me something else from now on. I definitely don't want a constant flow of it into my veins. No wonder I've been having nightmares."

"I'll let the doctor know" was all Doreen said.

As Carly watched Doreen recording her vital signs, a suffocating feeling of disorientation swept through her. She wasn't sure she wanted to know, but she had to ask. "What day is it?"

"Tuesday, miss."

Carly gasped. "I've been out for three days?"

Compassion flashed in Doreen's green eyes. "Yes, Miss." Then her features transformed into an impassive mask. "I'll let your doctor know you're awake. He'll be in shortly to explain everything."

Not five minutes later a man appeared at her door. Even through the morphine-induced fog, Carly recognized the down-home good looks of the boy next door. Joe Callahan. What was he doing here? Where was her doctor?

She attempted to force her eyes to focus. To avoid saying something stupid, she tried for humor. "I bet you visit all the neighborhood girls when they end up in ICU."

He crossed the room in two strides, and pulling a chair close to her head, he sat so close his spicy aftershave flooded her senses. "Only you, Carly."

His words soothed her battered soul, though she had no right to accept the comfort or anything else he might offer her. But heaven help her, she turned slightly toward him, tried to lift her hand to touch his arm, and was rewarded with a sharp pain. What was wrong with her arm? With effort, she scooted up in the bed, dragging an unexpected weight on her left leg. Swallowing her fear, she bumped it with her right foot. A cast. She was wearing two casts. One on her left ankle and another on her right forearm. Her ribs throbbed painfully. How had she not noticed sooner? Was she that out of it?

"Your wrist is broken." Anger flared in his eyes, hardening the angled planes of his face. "So is your leg and three ribs."

That explained the mind-blowing pain when she tried to move. And the morphine. Which should have taken effect by now.

"Carly, please tell me, who did this to you?"

For a second, she imagined she could tell Joe. When they were kids, she'd shared all of her secrets with him. But he was different now. She was different. Officer Joseph Callahan would not understand why Al had gone ballistic on her. She'd always had bad timing. Telling him about the baby when he was already tripping about the money she'd lost him, well that was just plain stupid. She should never have told him at all. But then, what would she have done? Gone home to her parents? Carly almost laughed, but her face hurt too much.

"If you press charges, I promise to make them stick. He'll spend the next fifteen years in prison for attempted murder."

And for murder.

"It's over and done with. It doesn't matter anymore. Nothing does," she whispered. Then she closed her eyes, hoping Joe would think she'd fallen asleep.

She waited several minutes, but his steady breathing confirmed she still couldn't fool Joe.

God, if You're listening, why didn't You just let me die, too?

"Carly, if you let that creep walk, eventually he's going to beat some other girl, and she might not—"

"Might not what? Be as lucky as me? Might not make it? That's what you were going to say, right? Listen, Joe, trying to guilt me into talking might work with someone else in my situation, but it won't work with me." She couldn't stand the recrimination in his eyes another second. Summoning all of her strength, Carly shifted her body to face the stark white wall. Maybe she should tell Joe everything. It didn't matter that Al would kill her for talking. Dying would be better than living like this.

"I'll be back tomorrow." He rested his hand on her shoulder, offering her comfort the way he always had when they were kids, as if he were another big brother. She'd had such a crush on him in those days.

But that was then. This was now. And now wasn't what she'd planned at all, and tomorrow didn't promise to be any better. "Tomorrow my answer will be the same. So let's get this over with once and for all. I did not recognize the guy who did this to me. End of story."

*

As Joe left Carly's room, two thoughts warred in his mind. One, he would put away the creep who'd done this to her. And two, he still felt something for her, something he refused to acknowledge. *God, what are You trying to do to me? You know how hard I've worked to forget her.*

Joe stopped at the chapel on his way out of the hospital. Maybe, he could pray his way through to some answers. He obviously wasn't getting anywhere with Carly. How was he supposed to protect her if she wouldn't talk to him?

CHAPTER TWO

Carly's night swirled like a dark kaleidoscope filled with torrid and terrifying images. She woke with one thought. No more morphine. She didn't care how much pain she had to endure. The hallucinations were far more painful. Especially the ones that resembled the reality of her life. Every shameful thing she'd done had come back with relentless clarity to condemn her.

A young nurse whose face still glowed with fresh innocence moved around the pristine hospital room adjusting the blinds, the covers, and finally Carly's pillows. Observing her, Carly longed to go back. Back home? Back to a time when she believed anything was possible? She steeled herself. Longings like that would kill you. Isn't that what Scarlett O'Hara had said to Ashley Wilkes after the South had been destroyed by the Civil War? Well, Carly had gone through her own civil war. With herself. And she had become the casualty. She and the babies she would never know.

A different nurse, this one wearing teal scrubs, entered the room carrying a fresh bag to replace the nearly empty one attached to her IV line.

Carly tried unsuccessfully to read the label. "If that has morphine in it, I don't want it."

The pretty nurse named Lynette frowned. "But the doctor's orders—"

"I don't care about orders. I already told the other nurse that I didn't want any more morphine. I can't take the hallucinations. They're like walking through hell."

Lynette's expression softened. "A lot of patients say that." She patted Carly's arm. "I'll get Dr. Edwards to prescribe something else for you. What number is your pain right now?"

Carly hesitated. In truth, it was somewhere between eight and nine. "Oh, about a six and a half."

*

Carly couldn't sleep. Maybe she should have asked for a sleeping pill. She'd been tossing and turning for over an hour. Her mistakes echoed in her head, condemning her with their stark finality. *This is your life. This is what you deserve. Another brutal, inescapable consequence of a lifetime of bad choices.* Harsh and unrelenting, the words pummeled her, wounding her more than Al's fists and boots had.

Her stomach had clenched. Warm fluid, unwelcome. Blood. The final verdict gushed forth. She knew before they told her. What had she been thinking? To believe, to dare to hope God would give her something so precious?

"Carly, it's me, Joe."

His faint words floated down a long, dark corridor. Joe Callahan? Impossible. She must be dreaming or delirious. He couldn't be here to see her. Not again. She was nothing to him. She was worse than nothing. She was a murderer. The evidence confronted her head-on. When he learned the truth, Joe wouldn't be able to look at her, let alone touch her the way he was doing now.

She tried to turn away, but his strong hand continued to caress her brow. She wouldn't open her eyes. Maybe then, he would leave her alone.

He clasped her hand, his fingers gently urging a response.

But she was dead inside.

"Go ..." she whispered, her voice harsh, dry, croaky, like her great-grandmother's had been on her deathbed.

If only Carly *were* dying.

That would be just. And merciful.

"Go away. Please."

His breath, warm and smelling of hazelnut coffee, tickled her nose, attesting to the unwelcome fact that she was indeed very much alive. Fighting the grittiness that kept her eyes glued shut, Carly forced her eyelids up. A nurse stood behind Joe. "Please, make him leave."

He shook his head. "Not until you tell me who did this to you."

His sharp tone penetrated her wall of defense and shamed her beyond bearing. "It doesn't matter because I'm not pressing charges."

A flash of defeat followed by anger blared in his eyes. "We'll see about that," he barked. "I'll be back tomorrow."

"Tomorrow, I will tell you the same thing I told you today and the day before. Nothing." She held his gaze in an attempt to intimidate him. "Now, go away and leave me alone."

Silent, his eyes declared that he'd seen through her.

"Officer, I must insist you leave immediately," the nurse said, finally taking charge of the situation. "It's time for Ms. Lawrence's medication. Surely, you can see she needs her rest."

Joe leaned over the bed, ignoring the nurse completely. "I'll go for now. But I'll be back to get your description of the man who did this to you. I *am* going to put him behind bars for a very long time. You can count on it."

Carly would have laughed had her face not hurt so badly. She couldn't count on anything or anyone but herself. Unfortunately, she was doing a lousy job of taking care of herself.

*

Joe pulled his pickup behind his sister's SUV just as the

kids piled out of the packed vehicle. His nieces and nephews, five in all ranging from fifteen months to eight years, were bantering back and forth, arguing over who had sprayed the grape juice box all over the back of the light gray passenger seat. His sister, Maureen, and her husband, Bob, appeared to be ignoring the whole conflict. From the sounds of it, they were having a nasty quarrel of their own. Not a very good start for Dad's birthday dinner.

Deciding to take matters into his own hands, Joe joined the fray, pulling eight-year-old Derrick off of his five-year old brother, Steve. "Hey, guys, time for a truce. Remember, today is Grandpa's special day." He'd been talking to the boys, but both Maureen and Bob glared at him. Joe smiled, knowing his dimpled grin would disarm his big sister.

"Uncle Joe is right. No more fighting," Maureen said, as she balanced the baby on one hip and Dad's favorite cheesy potatoes in the opposite hand. Baby Gwen squirmed, then flung herself backward in a failed attempt to get free. Bob grabbed his daughter in midair and tried to kiss his wife's cheek, but she jerked her face away.

"You, too, Mommy and Daddy," six-year-old Tara piped in. "Grandpa doesn't like it when you fight cuz it always makes Grandma cry."

Maureen shot Bob a scathing look.

This latest argument between his sister and her husband made Joe's gut twist into a pretzel. Maybe they needed marriage counseling. Not that it was any of his business. Even couples who were devoted to each other sometimes fought, right? Not all marriages were as harmonious as their parents'.

Beyond praying for Maureen and Bob, Joe couldn't do much. His personal experience was basically non-existent. He'd been in love with Carly once, when they were teens and everything seemed possible. Until that lowlife Alan Rutledge talked her into running off with him. Joe had let Carly go without even hinting at his feelings for her, and now he barely recognized the streetwise, brittle woman lying in ICU.

"Uncle Joe!" Three-year-old Susie tugged on his pant leg. "Carry me, please."

Joe smiled, scooped up his niece, and set her in piggyback position on his shoulders. Together, they followed the rest of the family through the house and out to the back patio where Grandpa was already grilling chicken for dinner. "Hey, Dad, happy birthday. Isn't there a rule that the birthday person doesn't have to cook?" Maureen joined in the good-natured teasing. They couldn't allow their step-mother anywhere near the grill. Last summer, she'd started the hamburgers on fire, and they'd ended up eating cold cheese sandwiches with their baked beans and potato salad. Not exactly birthday fare.

"I hear you two," his stepmother said, pretending to scold. "Lucky for you all, I can bake a mean chocolate fudge cake."

"With homemade ice cream?" Derrick asked. "I'll help you churn it, Grandma."

Leann nodded, then lavished hugs and kisses on each grandchild in turn. She glanced for a moment at Joe. He recognized that look—the arched eyebrows that asked when he was going to settle down and raise a family of his own. He could see himself as a dad, coaching little league and attending school plays and concerts. He would put his family first, if and when God chose to bless him with one.

The trouble was, how could he be sure he fell in love with a woman like Leann? A woman who was nothing like his mother.

Carly's bruised face and wounded brown eyes filled his mind until his heart constricted in pain. Was it too late? Would she even consider him in that way? They didn't know each other at all. Not anymore.

Right now, she didn't even seem to want his friendship.

Maybe that's because she only sees you as a cop.

"Joe, keep an eye on the chicken for a minute. I've got to grab more basting sauce from the fridge." Dad patted Joe's shoulder then made a fast getaway to the kitchen.

Through the sliding glass doors, Joe watched as his father swept his stepmother off her feet and up into his arms. Her soft laughter could be heard drifting through the open windows. "Put me down, James Callahan."

"Not until you kiss me."

This scene was a familiar one at the Callahan's. If Joe ever got married, he would never settle for anything less than the love and harmony his dad had finally found with his second wife.

*

"Star! I'm so glad to see you," Carly cried as the tall, slender girl rushed into the hospital room, carrying a small bouquet of roses, one red, one pink, one yellow, and three white. Her friend was easily the most thoughtful and considerate person Carly had ever met. Star obviously remembered the stories Carly had shared about her grandfather's roses and the mixed bouquets that adorned her grandparents' tables from May to October. Anyone else would have brought a boring, monochromatic bouquet. But not Star. All one color lacked zest.

After setting the vase on the nightstand, Star folded Carly into a gentle hug. "I'm so glad you're finally out of ICU. I would've come last week as soon as I heard what happened, if I wasn't so sick."

Apprehension marred Carly's joy at seeing her friend. "Should you be here? If Al finds out ..."

Star shrugged. "I don't care what Al thinks. He couldn't stop me from visiting you unless he beat the crap out of me, and then I'd be in the hospital, too." She chuckled softly, her smile an obvious attempt to ease the tension. "Elise, I have something to tell you."

Carly's stomach clenched in pain. She couldn't bear bad news right now, not when she had no idea what she would do when she was finally well enough to leave the hospital. She wouldn't be going back to Al. This last beating had finally killed any feelings she'd ever had for him. Funny, how it took several broken bones for her to see Al for the despicable snake he was.

Star was waiting. Clearly, she needed encouragement to reveal whatever was on her mind. "You know you can tell me anything, Star."

Star. Elise. Very few of Al's girls went by their real names, not even with each other. Were they all trying to shield themselves, trying to maintain something untouched deep inside? She and Star were the exception. They trusted each other enough to share their real names, though they didn't often use them.

Her friend brushed away the tears tracking down her cheeks. "I've decided to go home."

Heart palpitations overtook Carly. If only she had the courage to leave the past behind and carve out a different future for herself. Suddenly, the antiseptic smell of her hospital room stifled every bit of oxygen. Cursing her casts, Carly longed to run, to flee from the hope etched on her friend's face, to race through the hospital doors, out into the fresh air where she could breathe and think. She'd have to rip the IV from her hand, but she'd already had more pain than she could tolerate. "I'm happy for you. Really I am."

Star was crying, blowing her nose, and pulling tissue after tissue out of the box next to the bed. "Please don't look at me like that. I ... I—"

"It's okay." Carly placed her good hand over Star's. "I understand. I'll just miss you is all."

But of course that wasn't all.

Churning emotions and futile dreams rose from the ashes of her crumbled world. "When are you leaving?"

Star gulped back a sob. "This afternoon. I already bought a plane ticket."

"That soon?"

"I didn't want to give myself a chance to change my mind. I've been thinking about going home for a while. And then we heard what Al did to you."

Battling fractured flashbacks, Carly shivered.

"Are you okay?" Star asked, breaking through Carly's dark thoughts.

She managed a smile. "I'm happy for you."

Star sighed with relief. "We'll keep in touch."

Carly nodded but knew it wasn't true. Star would need to leave this life in the past completely to get the fresh start she needed. Carly would die before she did anything that caused her friend to be pulled back into their old lives. "Look in that drawer." She pointed to the nightstand. "There's something I want to give you."

Star rose from her chair, walked around the bed, and reached to open the drawer.

"There's nothing in here but a Bible."

A book Carly hadn't opened since that first dark night she'd sacrificed herself on the altar of Al's ambition. Strangled by shame, she could no longer bring herself to read the words that had once nourished her soul.

"Actually, it's a pocket New Testament with the Psalms. My old neighbor, Joe Callahan, gave it to me."

"But, but," stammered Star, "I ... I can't take that. He ... you ..."

What Star didn't say was that they both knew Carly's confusion over Joe was something she preferred to deny. Patrick was Star's missed opportunity. Joe was Carly's. One afternoon over a shared bottle of wine, she and Star had wallowed for hours in what might have been. Later, they'd dragged each other up by their fine leather boots. Unlike a lot of Al's girls, they were lucky to have the memory of a decent man who'd treated them with respect. But nostalgia was a luxury neither could afford.

"Please, take it," Carly urged, knowing Star had never read a single word of the Bible in her life. Carly couldn't do much to help her friend, but she could do this. She could offer her friend the Truth, though she herself had no idea how to take hold of it again. "Read it. Give God a chance, because it's really not about rules. It's about love." She sounded like a preacher. She almost choked on the irony. She'd turned her back on God years ago.

The skeptical look that swept Star's face made Carly fear she wouldn't accept the gift, but then Star smiled and slipped the Bible in her already stuffed shoulder bag. After a final hug and kisses on the cheeks, the younger woman whispered, "Goodbye. You're the best friend I've ever had."

*

After Star left, Carly struggled to shift her casts so she could roll over and face the window. She stared at the passing clouds until she drifted into a restless sleep. When she awoke, Joe was sitting by her side, his head bent in prayer. Wearing jeans and a blue oxford shirt, he looked better to her than all of the men in tuxedoes with their lying smiles and empty promises. Joe had never lied to her. He was a good man, reliable, trustworthy, and handsome as ever. Why had she never dared to tell him she saw him as more than her brother's best friend? The two-year difference in their ages was nothing now. If only that were all that separated them.

She laid her hand on his arm, and he looked up at her with a tentative smile. "Hello," she said.

His face was streaked with tears. He'd been crying. For her? *That* didn't seem possible. Too raw to put her feelings into words, she slid her hand down his arm and clasped his hand.

His fingers tightened around hers. "Carly, I need you to tell me who did this to you."

Joe's steadfastness, Star's courage strengthened Carly. His intense blue eyes pierced her defenses. She averted her gaze and focused on the IV taped to her left hand.

It was time. "Alan Rutledge."

"I knew it. There was always something evil about him."

Carly didn't dare look up. What Joe hadn't said—that she was a fool to trust Al, that she should have listened to Joe all those years ago—made her almost regret telling him the truth. She shrugged off his unspoken reproach.

Her course was set now.

Al would be charged with attempted murder, and Joe would do everything in his power to see Al convicted.

But what would she do now? Where could she go? Who would help her? No one from her old life would dare. Al had a lot of friends. She had no one.

Her grandmother had said that Jesus was "a friend that sticks closer than a brother." Did Jesus really want Carly after all she'd done? After what she'd become? How could He bear to look at her? She'd forsaken the truth for a lie.

But she couldn't think about any of that now. She had to deal with what was right in front of her.

Mrs. Zigler was standing in the doorway, holding a foil-covered pie plate. "I'm sorry to interrupt." After a quick glance in Joe's direction, she focused on Carly. "I thought you might appreciate some homemade cookies. Peanut butter with chocolate kisses. I hope you like them." Without waiting for a reply, her neighbor moved to the foot of the bed, obviously confident of her welcome, now that Carly was in a regular room. Unlike Star, the older woman probably hadn't been willing to pass herself off as a family member.

Joe rose from his seat and motioned for Mrs. Zigler to sit. "I was just leaving."

Carly gave him a tentative smile. Could he see the questions in her eyes? The regret? The fragile hope pushing upward through the bleak tundra of her life? Discouraged by his inscrutable expression, she lowered her head, then let out a tiny gasp as he brushed a kiss across her forehead. For a fleeting second, she imagined what it would be like to feel his lips on hers. *Foolish girl.* She slammed the gate of her heart shut. Joe should never sully his reputation by getting involved with someone like her. What would his superiors think? What would his church-going mother say? Leann Callahan served the community like an angel of mercy sent straight from heaven.

Carly didn't know what her next move would be or where her life would take her, but she did know that it would not involve a romantic relationship with the upstanding Officer Callahan.

She shielded herself with her usual mask of indifference. "I'll make a statement whenever you're ready."

A flash of hurt obscured the usual twinkle in Joe's blue eyes. He opened his mouth to say something, then must have thought better of it. What did he have to be hurt about?

"That is the procedure, right?" Carly asked, pretending not to notice Mrs. Zigler looking from her to Joe and back again.

"Yes. The department will send someone over in the

morning."

"But I thought you'd be taking my statement."

He shook his head. "Conflict of interest."

Mrs. Zigler smiled. The woman was a matchmaker.

"Goodbye, Joe. I—"

"I'll check on you tomorrow. Ladies, enjoy your visit."

Carly watched him stride out the door, glad and sorry to see him go. She was no lady. Surely, he knew that. Longing crashed over her like an Atlantic wave. His straight back, broad shoulders, and muscular arms all testified to his ability to take very good care of her. She'd dreamed about him taking on that role back in high school. Her instincts told her he was interested. But for how long?

Squaring her shoulders, she gave her full attention to Mrs. Zigler and her plate of cookies. "Thank you for coming."

Mrs. Zigler's sharp eyes studied Carly. "I'm sorry it took me so long. Joe told me you were out of ICU since the day after your surgery on your wrist. I'd have come sooner, but something always seemed to get in the way. That is until this morning during my devotions when the dear Lord Jesus whispered, *Go see Carly Lawrence today. She's ready to come home.*"

Carly drew in a sharp breath. "Home? I haven't been home in years."

"I suspected as much." Mrs. Zigler uncovered the peanut butter cookies, took one for herself, and passed the plate of tempting goodies to Carly.

She wasn't the least bit hungry, but she reached for the smallest cookie on the plate and bit into it. She smiled in spite of the anxiety that derailed her at the mere mention of going home. "These are delicious."

"Thank you, dear. I thought you might like them, so I taped a copy of the recipe to the bottom of the pie tin."

"Oh, uh ... I don't actually know—"

"You don't? Well, we can bake them together after you get out of the hospital."

Mrs. Zigler seemed in no hurry to explain her unexpected comment about Jesus. So after finishing her cookie, Carly asked, "Does God talk to you regularly?"

The lady nodded. "But not as often as I'd like. Sometimes, He lets me know exactly what He wants me to do, and other times, I figure as long as I'm about the business of helping somebody, I'm doing as Jesus would do if He were here. You know what I mean, sugar?"

Mrs. Zigler apparently was far more than a church-goer. She lived her faith. Something Carly had forgotten how to do. The fire of a blush blazed from her neck up her cheeks. She resisted the urge to cover her face.

"Are you starting to feel any better? Joseph said your doctor will probably send you on home by the first of the week." Mrs. Zigler poured Carly a cup of cold water from the plastic pitcher on the nightstand and placed it within easy reach. "Which brings me to the second reason for my visit. I'd like you to think about staying with me for a while."

Carly's mouth gaped in shock. Why? Why would she even consider making such an offer? Of course, Carly would not accept. Mrs. Zigler was a near stranger. One who merely lived in the same apartment building as Carly did. Al would come looking for her, if he got out on bail, which he probably would. Al had the contacts to find her. He had other connections, too. People who would be willing to hurt her. For a price. He had the money to pay for what he wanted. No, she needed to relocate someplace safer and less obvious than her own apartment complex.

"Drink up now. You've got to stay hydrated if you want to get well quicker. The body's over 90% water, you know."

Carly drank the water in one gulp, though she couldn't possibly be dehydrated with all the IV fluids the nurses had been pumping into her. Never in her life had she needed to go to the bathroom more than she had since she'd awakened in the hospital. And every trip was a sharp reminder of her greatest loss. But she could not, would not, think about that now. Her baby was gone, and nothing Carly could do would change that.

"You don't know me at all. Why would you trust me to stay with you?"

Mrs. Zigler patted Carly's hand as though she were a confused child. "Joe trusts you. That's good enough for me."

A half hour later, she had reluctantly agreed that when she was released from the hospital, she would travel with Mrs. Zigler to her sister's house in Bemus Point on Chautauqua Lake. Anything would be better than sitting in her apartment waiting for Al to exact his retribution. If he caught up with her, she might not survive with only a few broken bones and...

Hatred boiled inside of her at what he'd done to her baby. If God cared about her at all, Al would rot in prison for the rest of his life. In her mind, prison was better than he deserved.

CHAPTER THREE

Mrs. Zigler was filling a ceramic teapot with boiling water when Carly hobbled on one crutch into the sunny yellow kitchen. The black tea and fresh mint smelled delicious, but it was the bacon frying in a cast iron skillet on the old porcelain stove that awakened her hunger. "Good morning, Mrs. Zigler. Can I do anything to help?"

The older woman looked up from her task and smiled. Her face, aglow with warm contentment, sparked a memory in Carly's tired brain. Something about Moses' face glowing after he'd met with God. The open Bible resting on the blue-checkered tablecloth inexplicably drew Carly. Could she find answers here? Would the words still speak to her after all she'd done? Carly fingered the parchment pages.

Mrs. Zigler clearly noticed the gesture but did not comment. "Please call me Sarah. Everything's under control, so you can just rest yourself right there." When Carly didn't move, her hostess smiled serenely and pulled out a white kitchen chair made even more welcoming by two cushions in the same blue-checked pattern that adorned the windows and the table.

Carly awkwardly eased herself into the chair. Recovering in the home of a stranger for several weeks until she could get these dang casts off was a minor hardship, compared to the trouble she'd caused herself since she'd left her parents' home for a world of freedom and fun. What a fool she'd been.

She slanted a look at the open Bible. Psalm 23, one of her

grandmother's favorites. How many times had she sat on Grandma Rose's lap and listened to her read that Psalm?

"The LORD is my shepherd; I shall not want. He maketh me to lie down in green pastures: He leadeth me beside the still waters. He restoreth my soul." Carly stopped. "Why would God want to restore *my* soul?" she blurted before she could catch herself. "There's nothing worth restoring."

Sarah pivoted away from the stove. With a concerned expression, she faced Carly. "He loves you, sugar. As much today as the day you were born and the doctor placed you in your mother's arms."

Carly clamped her quivering jaw tight. Knowing she would never hold her own baby made her want to cry out in agony, but she refused to break down in front of this woman who probably had never stood face-to-face with evil, who had never been forced to do the unspeakable.

Sarah turned down the flame under the bacon, sat at the table, and placed her weathered hand over Carly's. "I don't pretend to understand all you've been through, but there is Someone who does, and He has never left your side."

Anger boiled to the surface, spilling over the boundaries of what little composure and control Carly had left. She snatched her hand away, reached for her crutch, and struggled to her feet. "Never left my side? Then why is my baby dead?"

Sarah's face paled with shock. "I didn't know."

"Joe didn't tell you?"

"Joseph told me you needed a safe place to recover. Nothing else."

"Nothing?"

"Your story is yours to tell, Carly, not Joe's, no matter how much he cares for you."

She sucked in a startled breath and gripped the back of a chair to steady herself.

Sarah's eyes pleaded. "Won't you sit back down and have breakfast with me? It's rare I have someone to share a meal with."

Carly met her hostess's gaze and saw a need far too familiar. She understood lonely men, but not a lonely old woman. What did Carly have to offer her? Their common need leveled the playing field—two lonely women with no men to care for them. Carly wasn't sure she'd ever find a man she could trust. Her judgment had been pretty lousy up to this point.

"I'll eat, but please, no more talk about God." Lowering herself into the chair, she added, "I'm sure He left me the day I left Him."

Sarah closed her eyes for a brief moment. Was she praying? The serene expression was back when she opened them again. "How do you like your eggs? Poached? Scrambled? Over easy?"

"Over medium. Runny whites nauseate me."

The older woman laughed. "Me, too."

Carly closed the Bible and reached for the morning paper. She scanned the headlines.

Nothing but violence, disasters, and betrayal. Maybe she should read the Bible after all. At least there, she'd find some good news. But she turned instead to the lifestyle section and read about girls who seemed to have their whole future smoothly mapped out. Daydreaming for a few minutes of what could never be, Carly passed the time until Mrs. Zigler set a platter of biscuits hot from the oven, eggs, and bacon, and a jar of homemade strawberry jam on the table.

"Heavenly Father," she prayed without asking Carly if she minded, "bless this house, this food, and my guest. May she learn to hope in You again and may I not say anything to keep her from hurrying to Your comforting arms. Amen."

God comfort her? More likely she'd receive a swift reprimand. Carly decided not to comment on Sarah's prayer. She might not be the young lady her mom had raised her to be, but she still had manners.

The two ate their meal in companionable silence while an instrumental CD of old-style hymns played in the background. Carly tried to dismiss memories of her grandmother singing those same songs. Her grandma had died in the fall of Carly's senior year. She'd become proficient at blocking out memories, anything that made it difficult for her to do whatever was necessary. And right now she had to figure out what her next move would be. She couldn't depend on the kindness of a stranger forever.

*

Carly was asleep in a lounge chair on the front porch when Joe climbed the steps. In the five days since he'd helped her make the move from her North Buffalo apartment to Sarah's cottage in Bemus Point on Lake Chautauqua, he hadn't been able to get Carly out of his head. It was more than their old connection, more than his desire to rescue her and look out for her.

What would Jared think if he knew Joe was ... was what? Falling for his sister? Keeping her whereabouts a secret from her family?

Joe's affection for her was irrelevant. And inappropriate. For so many reasons.

And just in case he was tempted to forget how unsuited for each other he and Carly really were, Pastor Will's adult Sunday School lesson last week had focused on the Bible's warning not to be unequally yoked together with unbelievers. Joe understood the challenges of working with his unbelieving partner, though he had no say in that relationship. He and Harris managed pretty well most days.

But Carly was another story. With her, friendship was tough enough. Anything more would be a potential disaster.

Risking his heart was out of the question. He'd vowed not to repeat his father's mistakes.

Even if Carly was ready to leave her old life behind.

The police still hadn't apprehended Rutledge. When they did, she'd have to testify against him in court, a responsibility she was dreading. Had Joe pushed too hard? Maybe. He'd seen the fear in her eyes and ignored it, insisting she press assault and battery charges against Rutledge. The guy was a parasite, a parasite who had access to enough money to post the heftiest bail the DA could ask for, which meant Carly couldn't feel safe until Rutledge was behind bars where he belonged.

She couldn't begin to think about the future until Rutledge was convicted. Maybe then she'd see that God had good plans for her. Plans that just might include Joe.

If only she'd return to her faith. Then he wouldn't have to keep his feelings under tight rein. As he stood not three feet away from her broken form, watching her sleep, her face free from pain and distress, Joe yearned to protect her from the grueling questions of the defense attorney.

But how could he protect her from Rutledge? The only way to do that was to ensure a conviction. A conviction they couldn't get without her testimony. Which brought him back to square one.

Even if there was no future for them, Joe needed to be a friend to Carly. And she needed him, didn't she? He wanted her to need him.

First things first, Callahan.

He couldn't ignore the truth. His prayers had been pretty selfish up to this point.

Carly needed to make things right with God, needed to renew her relationship with her Savior. Without Jesus, she could end up like so many other girls, emptied of all hope or happiness, arrested or dead. Joe shuddered. He couldn't let that happen to her. Even if it meant she would never care for him, he had to do anything and everything to help her back to God.

*

Carly stirred herself awake. Someone was watching her. But, instead of the anxiety and fear she expected, soothing contentment washed through her. Her eyes fluttered opened, and to her surprise, Joe was leaning against the porch railing. Out of uniform, in a pair of faded jeans and a green and blue plaid flannel shirt opened to reveal a navy t-shirt, he looked disarmingly handsome. Her breath caught, and her heart sped up. She smiled, and Joe smiled back, but his blue eyes were uncertain.

"I see you're enjoying country living."

"Who wouldn't, after living in the city for almost ten years?"

"Strange, isn't it that our paths never crossed before?"

He'd meant it as a casual remark, but running into Joe had been unlikely. Rutledge Escort Service was by all appearances as reputable as Al had originally planned. In over nine years not a single girl had ever been arrested. Al's girls didn't need to solicit business. Wealthy clients sought them out. But in the final analysis, what she did was—was the same? Was a little better? No, it was safer and more lucrative. A blush stained her cheeks as her mind flooded with unwelcome memories.

Joe laid a hand on her shoulder. "Are you all right? Can I get you a glass of water?"

She didn't have a chance to answer because Sarah appeared in the doorway carrying a tray of warm oatmeal raisin cookies, a pot of steaming tea, and three mugs. The sweet scent of cinnamon wafted in the air, mingling with that of fresh cut grass.

"What were you two talking about?" Sarah asked, positioning the tray on the end table where Carly could easily reach it. Immediately, her hostess began pouring tea for the three of them, dropping one cube of sugar into each mug. Carly was starting to get used to Sarah's attentiveness. It was almost like being home with her mother.

Joe reached for a cookie and took a mug from Sarah. "I just got here a minute ago."

Carly shot him a grateful look, needing a moment to turn her thoughts to more appropriate topics. Half listening to the easy banter between Joe and her hostess, Carly sipped her tea and bit into the best cookie she had eaten since her grandmother's death. "These are delicious. What's your secret?"

Sarah smiled, her gentle eyes warm and gracious. "Real butter, of course."

"I suppose you grind your own cinnamon, too?" Carly asked, half joking, half serious.

Sarah lifted one brow. "Not on your life. I've got better things to do with my time."

There was more to Sarah Zigler than Carly had surmised, though she should have known any woman who would invite a virtual stranger to stay in her home—correction, her sister's home—had to be special or crazy. For Sarah, hospitality clearly was more than a word reserved for Sunday dinners with friends. At first, Carly had been embarrassed to be on the receiving end of so much charity, but lately something kept telling her this place was exactly where she needed to be. If only she could figure out what her next step should be.

"Carly?" Joe asked.

He was studying her with a thoroughness that would have

been unnerving if not for the easy smile that turned up the corners of his mouth and showed his dimples. A mouth she— *Get a grip, girl.*

"Did I miss something?" she asked, forcing herself back to here and now.

"Sarah wants to know if you'd mind spending the evening with me."

Carly frowned, shook her head, and would have jumped from the lounge chair had her cast not impeded her escape. "I don't think that would be a very good idea."

"Why not? Do you have something against the Boy Scouts?" He shrugged out of his flannel shirt. The snug t-shirt he was wearing revealed the muscles of a man who lifted weights.

Carly caught herself staring. Flustered, she lifted her hair off her neck to cool down a bit. Sticky cobwebs were clinging to her brain. Had he invited her to a Boy Scout meeting of some kind? "I have no opinion about Boy Scouts. I suppose they do keep some boys from going in the wrong direction."

Sarah laughed. "You sound like me."

Joe looked from one woman to the other, his blue eyes twinkling with amusement.

Carly remembered that look.

He certainly had grown into a handsome man. Who was she kidding? He was drop dead gorgeous. Gone were the gangly arms and legs that never seemed to end. His chest and arms now rippled, probably from his working out to stay fit for his job as a cop. A cop. Joe Callahan was a cop. She'd do well to remember that. He wasn't the boy next door who'd been corralled by her brother into taking her to her junior prom when her date had dumped her at the last minute. She should not think about Joe that way. Even if dancing in his arms had been sweeter than any fantasy she'd concocted as a teen.

She resisted the urge to smile at the memory.

The years had changed them both, and police business was the only reason their paths had converged again. "I don't think it would be appropriate for me to attend a Boy Scout function. I'm not exactly the type of girl your boys should be meeting."

"My boys? How did you know I was their troop leader?"

She laughed. "Some things never change. You were always making the right choices, even back in high school, while I veered off onto other paths."

Joe's expression revealed none of his thoughts. He was a good cop. He did a lot of good for a lot of people. Becoming involved with her would only hurt him professionally, but acknowledging that didn't stop the ache in her heart, the ache to be cherished by a man she could trust. A man who could never be part of her life story.

"Carly, I don't know what you're talking about. I just need help setting up for Open House. You were always great at decorating."

She glanced in Sarah's direction for support, but instead found disappointment. Did the poor woman actually think Joe couldn't do better than Carly? She swallowed hard. She might as well set him straight once and for all. No point in leading him on. "I'm the kind of girl you bring down to the station for questioning, not to the Boy Scout Hall to help decorate."

There. She'd said it.

Anger flashed in Joe's eyes. But he didn't say a word. He nodded toward Sarah and stomped down the porch steps without even telling Carly goodbye. She swallowed a sob rising in her throat. She'd never survive if she didn't stop hoping for Prince Charming to come to her rescue. Happily ever after was for girls who'd stayed on the straight path, girls who knew what they wanted and couldn't be talked into settling for less.

That description didn't fit her.

She shivered, cold through to her heart.

"Be right back, sugar," Sarah said with a sympathetic look and disappeared into the house.

A moment later, she returned with a blanket crocheted in a rainbow of colors. Exercising great care, she spread the cozy afghan over Carly's legs and tucked it around her cold feet. Then Sarah poured them both fresh mugs of tea and patted her Bible. "You'd be surprised at the stories in here of women who felt just like you, who felt that it was too late for God to do anything good with their lives. But they were wrong and so are you, Carly." With a gentle but firm challenge shining in her hazel eyes, Sarah deposited the book in Carly's lap.

The weight of the large-print Bible pressed against her legs. Could it be true? Could God still make something good out of her tattered life? She opened the Bible where Sarah had left a postcard of a sunset over Chautauqua Lake and started reading in the book of Joshua. A prostitute named Rahab had the courage to believe God could and would help her change her life. Rahab managed to escape death, but what had she done with the rest of her life? A question Carly had been asking herself, but her speculating had brought her more heartache and disappointment than she could bear. She kept reading to the end of the seventh chapter, anxious to learn about Rahab's transformed life, but she wasn't mentioned again.

After a few moments of companionable silence, Sarah went into the house to finish making lunch, which she brought back out to the porch. "There won't be many more days to eat outside," she said, setting the table with bowls of tomato soup and plates of grilled cheese sandwiches, and crackers.

Moving from the chaise to the table, Carly's stomach growled in response. Grilled cheese and tomato soup were her favorite fall comfort foods, next to home baked goods of any kind.

Sarah took the seat opposite, unfolded a cloth napkin, and placed it on her lap. "The seasons are changing. They're changing for you, too, Carly. And for the record, Joseph Callahan is a good man."

Carly swiped the tears sliding down her cheeks. "I know. But I'm not a good woman."

Why couldn't Sarah understand that? Why did she make her say the words out loud?

*

Later that night, hiding under the blankets, curled up tight in a shell, Carly wept for all she'd once believed she could be. She'd always wanted to be a mother, but it was too late. Courage had kept her alive, but her bravery had not protected her child. What had made her think she could stand up to Al? Star had warned her that he'd be furious. He wouldn't want the baby, wouldn't believe it was his. He'd insist she have an abortion. Carly had underestimated the depth of Al's rage, and now her precious little girl was gone forever. Her stupidity had destroyed her child's future and hers with it. She would never experience the redemption her baby's smiles would have wrought in her sin-scarred heart. She would never get the chance to teach her daughter that there could be a better life for a woman.

If only Carly could go back to that day. Start over. Do everything differently.

She should have left Al years ago. He'd never cared for her, beyond the money she could make for him. How could she have been so blind? She was just another one of his girls. Dispensable. Easily replaced. Probably by a younger, more naïve version of herself. He probably already has another stupid girl ready to believe his empty promises. A girl who would never suspect, until it was too late for her, that her hero was actually a villain.

Carly bit her lip and clenched her good hand into a fist.

Stop it. Don't do this to yourself.

Her pillow was saturated with tears. She flipped it over to the dry side and whispered into the stillness of the night, "God, please. Just let me sleep."

The weight of Sarah's hand-pieced quilt pressed down on Carly like a hug, until finally she slept.

*

In the morning, her first conscious thoughts revived the bitter anguish of the night before and with it, an image of taking her own life took form. Could she really kill herself? With her eyes tightly closed, she could see the blood dripping from her wrists into the warm tub water, her life ebbing away, justice and hell awaiting her.

A sob caught in her throat. Choking back the strangling guilt, Carly struggled to a sitting position and stared at the light peeking through the lace curtains on the east windows. "God, help me. I'm lost. I don't know what to do. I ... I hate myself."

At that moment, warmth like a perfect summer day enveloped Carly.

Let Me love you.

"I don't know how. I hurt everywhere. Inside and out. And if I start crying again, I'll drown." *I won't ever be able to stop, and I'll end up in an institution. Then I'll never have a better life. Ever.*

Had God actually been speaking to her heart? Had he heard her response?

A soft rap sounded at the door, startling Carly back to her present reality. "I'm all right, Sarah. I'll be up soon. I just need a few minutes."

"Okay," Sarah said, but she didn't sound convinced.

Carly was definitely losing her edge. In the past, she'd been extremely good at hiding her feelings. She had to be, in her business. But then again, she'd never been able to hide anything from Gran either. Gran had called it the gift of discernment. That was all Carly needed, to be living with a woman who had an inside track to her thoughts.

Carly eased herself to the edge of the bed, retrieved her crutch, which she'd left leaning against the nightstand, and shuffled to the windows. Outside, doves cooed, their soft songs' intimate replies understood only by their mate. Carly ached to know what that would feel like. To have someone hold her close every night and kiss her good morning—someone to share her life with. Heaven on earth, that's how Gran described a good marriage.

Carly grimaced. Never mind a good man, why would even God want her? She was filthy. She could never try hard enough, never do enough good to make up for all she'd done wrong. Blocking out the dark memories was the most she could manage. But in the quiet moments blood still covered her hands.

"Amazing grace, how sweet the sound that saved a wretch like me ..." The words of the old hymn filtered down the hall from the kitchen. Sarah's sweet soprano blended with some guy singing tenor on the radio. The combination was almost angelic. "Amazing Grace" had been Gran's favorite. But Gran had been a saint, as sweet and innocent and full of hope and promise as her crocuses that braved their yellow and purple heads through the bitter snow. Carly was a dandelion, spreading destruction.

Better to face facts. She didn't know what life would hold for her from this point on, but it could never include a man like Joe Callahan. He needed someone unsullied, whose faith had never faltered. A girl who'd never even thought about doing the things Carly had done.

Struggling to get the yellow terry cloth robe over the cast on her right forearm, she wanted to thank Joe again for packing up all of her clothes for her. Just the thought of going back into her apartment paralyzed her with fear. He understood that, and without her even asking, he had made sure everything she needed was waiting for her when she'd arrived at the cottage. She tugged at the robe with her left hand, definitely not the dominant one, but eventually she succeeded in donning the robe. Today might be a pajama day. She wasn't planning to go farther than the front porch. She'd have coffee and toast with Sarah and then sit outside and thank God for the sunshine.

Thank God? Carly shook her head. To her surprise, she did have a few things to be thankful for. Sarah for one. And the promise of another beautiful fall day. Winter would soon snuff out the remaining flowers. An early frost was predicted for the end of the week. The geese in their V formation had been heading south for days. Carly wished she could fly away, too. From herself most of all. But the trouble was, as her former Sunday School teacher used to say, she'd be taking herself along with her.

"God, if you can do anything, save me from myself. Because I can't stand who I am."

She leaned against the armchair by her bedroom windows for several minutes waiting for an answer that didn't come.

*

At breakfast, Sarah read her Bible and underlined passages while Carly pretended to be fascinated with the newspaper. Eventually, she couldn't stand it another minute. "Why would God want me?" she asked.

Sarah's gaze flew to Carly. "Because He loves you. So

much that He gave His Son to die for you. To die even if you were the only one who would accept His gift." Sarah reached across the table and clasped Carly's hand.

That settled it then. Shuddering, she pulled her hand free of the woman's earnest grasp. "There's nothing about me to love."

"Oh, sugar, that's not true."

"How would you know? You don't know me at all. All you know about me is that I was stupid enough to let some guy put me in the hospital."

Sarah's eyes glistened with tears.

Tears for Carly? Impossible.

She grabbed her crutch and pushed herself to her feet. There was nothing more to say. No words could turn back the clock. Even God couldn't erase the past. "Sarah, I know you want to help, but—"

"Why don't you come to church with me tomorrow? I'm sure you'd hear something that would help it all make more sense to you."

Carly shook her head. The woman was persistent. And persuasive, in a gentle way. Carly wasn't used to gentleness. Cruelty and indifference she could resist, but Sarah's gentle pleas stoked the dying embers of hope in Carly's heart.

She could go to church. It couldn't hurt. After all, no one would know her as anyone other than Sarah's houseguest. No one would judge her. And if they did, what of it? They couldn't be any harsher than she was on herself. Sitting in church on Sunday morning, she'd ask God to help her. He couldn't doubt her sincerity if she made the effort to go to church, could He? She was determined to give God every opportunity because He was her last chance. Without Him she was as good as dead already. "What time do we need to leave?"

Sarah beamed with joy. "Nine thirty."

"I'll be ready," Carly said, then busied herself spreading blueberry preserves on her toast.

Maybe coming to stay with Sarah had been a good choice after all. Going to church might be another one.

CHAPTER FOUR

Sarah and Joe stood several feet away, off to the side near the sanctuary door. Snatches of their conversation drifted to where Carly leaned against the door jamb, waiting to greet Pastor Ryan, a dark-haired man who couldn't be much older than she was.

"I made up my mind a long time ago to pitch my tent in the land of hope," Sarah told Joe. "Faith and hope work hand in hand, you know."

"I'm not sure I have enough faith," Joe replied.

Carly's breath caught at the defeat in his voice. It felt like a cold October wind bringing rain with the promise of snow not far behind. And she was the storm.

"Joseph Callahan," Sarah scolded, "what you need is hope. Hope is your expectation of the blessings God has planned for you."

"I expect God to keep me going, no matter what. To stick to me because I stick to Him."

"I disagree," Sarah said, gently. "I can practice faithfulness because God is faithful."

Embarrassed, Carly tried not to listen. She was eavesdropping on a very private conversation. One that should have taken place in a far more private setting. But that wasn't the point at all. She didn't need to be reminded that she was a problem in his life. A problem he needed to put behind him.

Ignoring the pain in her armpit, she inched forward until she was third in line to speak to the pastor, behind a middle-aged couple and a young woman with a crying baby perched on one hip. A squirming toddler pulled on her other leg, struggling to free himself from his mother's steady grip. The baby's insistent cries tore at Carly's heart, and she'd have run away if she could. Instead, she bit her lower lip and gripped the crutch as tightly as she could, hoping her heart would grow as numb as her fingers.

She was an expert at blocking out pain. Usually.

At the corner of her range of vision, she saw Sarah slip her arm around Joe and pull him into a grandmotherly hug. Carly had been privileged to be on the receiving end of a few of Sarah's hugs herself. Whatever trouble Joe was having, Sarah's hug should comfort him in spite of his obvious resistance to her words.

Odd. Joe's faith was rock solid, wasn't it?

But she couldn't worry about his faith.

Not when her own was a tiny spark of light piercing the darkness of her bleak future. She was tired of walking in the dark. So tired.

Her photographs were her only substantial achievement remaining from her life with Al. Now, for the first time in years, she wanted to take pictures filled with hope rather than despair. She had boxes of candid shots she'd taken of street people, addicts, and prostitutes, many of them runaways, and some senior citizens far too old to be sleeping on the streets at night, even now, at the end of September. Shelters provided as many beds as they could, but their efforts would never be enough. Not with the homeless population swelling daily.

If it weren't for Al, she could have ended up one of them herself. But Alan Rutledge would never let his best income girl end up on the streets. He didn't even want her photographing "that population." They'd quarreled, and he'd punched her, screaming about her image, an image *he* worked so hard to create. Rutledge Escort serviced some of the richest and most powerful men in the state, and she'd been one of the most beautiful and requested escorts, and she was never allowed to do anything to mess that up.

Until she'd finally told Al the secret she could no longer disguise. He'd raged at her, the expression on his face pure hatred. She couldn't believe he'd kicked her in the stomach, a deliberate plan to accomplish what she'd refused to do.

She hated him now more than she'd ever loved him. Thinking of hurting him as much as he'd hurt her soothed her. She would take away what he valued most. His freedom. Joe said her testimony would put Al away for five to fifteen years. Five years for assault. Ten years for the wrongful death of her unborn fetus. She hated calling the baby that. The baby that she would never hold in her arms. Just like the other one.

Carly closed *that* door in her mind. She couldn't go there. Not now. And certainly not here. It was better to focus on Al getting what he deserved.

The evidence the police had gathered from her apartment should leave no doubt in the prosecuting attorney's mind that he was her attacker. The broken coffee table, the shattered vase he'd thrown at her, and the collapsed love seat proved there had been a violent struggle between them. His blood on her clothing and his blood the doctors had identified from matter underneath her fingernails would certainly secure his conviction. As soon as the police found him.

As long as Al didn't find some loophole.

Joe didn't think that would happen. Two witnesses had seen Al arriving at her apartment at 10:32 a.m. and leaving at 11:16. Sarah had called 911 when she'd arrived home at 11:10 and heard glass shattering and something heavy being thrown against a wall. Carly. He'd broken her arm then. By the time the paramedics had arrived, Al was gone, and she was clinging to consciousness. Two days later, she'd learned that the driver of the ambulance had seen Al speeding away in his silver Mercedes. The fool had left the convertible top down. No jury could find Al not guilty.

Still, the fact that the police hadn't been able to locate him kept her watching her back. He could be anywhere. He may even have left the country. But her gut told her he was nearby, maybe even watching her, waiting for a chance to persuade her with gifts and empty promises that this time he'd finally changed. Or to threaten her so she'd drop the charges against him. Predicting Al's strategies had never been her strong suit.

So she stayed on ultra-alert whenever she left the security of Sarah's lakeside cottage.

Except this morning in church, where she hadn't even thought of Al until this idle moment, waiting in line. She'd been focused on the sermon about Elijah and the widow woman. At first, Carly had listened for something that would help her figure out her next move, but the woman's story drew her. Her faith seemed as small as the amount of meal in the barrel. What had happened to her after Elijah moved on? One thing seemed certain. She'd learned that God would always meet her needs, sometimes from the most unexpected source. Safe within the walls of the quaint country church, Carly felt years of tension begin to release her body from its relentless grip. An inexplicable sense of peace in the midst of life's storms seemed not only possible but actually guaranteed for those select few with the faith to believe God's promises. Did she have such faith?

"Good morning." With a broad smile, Pastor Ryan extended his hand to Carly and then withdrew it immediately.

Carly brushed her fingers—the only part of her hand that wasn't encased in the cast—over the back of his retreated hand. Warmth sparked between them, and she caught his startled gaze. He'd felt it, too.

But he recovered quickly. "We haven't met before. I'm Pastor Ryan Edgar, and you are?"

"Staying with Sarah Zigler." Carly retreated behind her mysterious aura that had served her well these past nine years. Something about the appreciation in the young pastor's eyes set her on edge. Sarah had mentioned her pastor was single. Was he looking for a wife? That he would consider Carly for even a nanosecond was ludicrous. She almost laughed out loud. "I'm Carly Lawrence." *And if you knew anything about me, you wouldn't be looking at me like that.*

"Oh, yes, Sarah mentioned that she had a houseguest recuperating from … uh …"

Pastor Ryan's blunder, combined with his steady appraisal, unnerved her, but only momentarily. To maintain her advantage, she considered letting him flounder a bit. Instead, she took pity on him. "That would be me. We live in the same apartment building in the city."

"And Sarah thought you'd benefit from a visit to the country, which doesn't surprise me. The Zigler sisters are well-known for their hospitality."

Carly smiled. "I agree." Being with Sarah was like going on a retreat. The beautiful scenery offered many opportunities to take pictures, even though she was often confined to the front porch.

Pastor Ryan glanced behind her at the line. "I hope to see you in church again soon."

Reluctant to make any commitment, or to give him any encouragement on a personal level, Carly simply said, "We'll see. I'm not sure how much longer I'll be here."

They exchanged goodbyes, and she made her way past the remaining parishioners, working to hide her amusement. A pastor interested in her? Surely, she'd misread his signals.

Sarah and Joe were waiting for her at the door. His eyes filled with concern as their gazes met. A tender picture of Joe sweeping her up into his arms and carrying her down the patched concrete steps leaped into her head. She couldn't look into his gorgeous blue eyes for more than a few seconds without her heart pounding, but she refused to set herself up for heartbreak. The upstanding Officer Callahan was definitely not for the likes of her, either.

But that knowledge didn't stop her from inviting him to lunch. "I made homemade vegetable soup," she added to tempt him. He'd loved her mother's soup.

Sarah glanced from one to the other, then said to Joe, "I was planning to whip up a batch of cornbread with honey butter."

He hesitated, his features displaying the conflict Carly had seen several times in the past few weeks. She sensed his attraction to her, and she actually considered reassuring him that she could never be interested in him in that way, but pretending not to notice his feelings seemed easier for both of them. Denying her own was definitely best for her.

"I really need to get a few things done this afternoon," he muttered, his tone lacking the conviction of a solid no.

"I made apple pie with crumb topping," Sarah said. "You can't say no to my pies."

That settled it. Joe agreed to come for lunch, and Sarah orchestrated it so Carly would have to ride out to the farm with him in his pickup.

They had to sit much closer than she would have wanted. In order to keep her cast from crowding him as he drove, she sat in the middle of the seat next to Joe with her hip pressed against his and her legs extended toward the passenger door. Spicy aftershave wafted under her nose and stirred her unruly senses. Every nerve in her body acknowledged his nearness, flooding her battered heart with inexplicable joy.

An image of what her life might have been had she been Joe's girl in high school flitted through her mind like a hummingbird searching for life-giving nectar. But the only date they'd had was because her brother had been looking out for her.

She had to pull herself together. Joe was way out of her league. "So, you must have a steady girlfriend, right?"

He slanted a frown in her direction.

Had she actually asked him if he was dating someone? The heat radiating from her face could practically fry an egg.

"Most women aren't looking to date a cop," he said matter-of-factly. "Too much stress and anxiety."

Some women wouldn't consider dating a cop. Would she? At this point in her life, the idea was beyond ridiculous.

"Carly, I … I'd like to—"

"Sure, me, too," she interrupted before he could say the words that would change their relationship forever. "Let's stop at that roadside stand and buy a gallon of fresh pressed cider."

He schooled his features into an impassive look. "Not exactly what I had in mind. But sure."

She suppressed a sigh. "Today's a perfect day for hot spiced cider."

*

After successfully avoiding Joe's attempts get her alone, Carly had to deal with her own disappointment as he drove off in his truck. She prayed for his safety, confident that God would watch over such a good man. But what about her? If she asked Him, would God keep her safe from Al? She wasn't a good woman, but she was trying. She'd gone to church. That was a start, right? But was it enough to deserve God's protection?

Could a former prostitute become one of His favored ones,

the people God seemed almost eager to bless? Maybe, she should read more about some of those women Sarah mentioned, the ones who believed they'd gone too far down the wrong path. Carly could ask Sarah tomorrow at breakfast where to read.

Tonight, she wanted to hug her sadness a little closer to her heart. It didn't seem right that she should try to be happy so soon after the death of her baby. She hadn't punished herself nearly enough.

Maybe she should call home. Her mother would certainly give Carly an earful. Mom had always been good at reminding Carly what a disappointment she was as a daughter.

But she hadn't spoken to her mother in ten years.

She'd called her dad once at his office about five years ago just to tell him that she loved him and that she was really sorry that she couldn't come home. His reply was seared on her heart even now, after all of these years. "It doesn't matter what you've done. We love you. Come home, please. All's forgiven. Just come home."

Carly sipped the hot cider Sarah left on the end table with a plate of cranberry scones. She was heading over to church for the September pot luck before the evening service.

"Are you sure you won't come with me?" Sarah buttoned her gray wool cardigan straight up to her chin. "I don't feel right about leaving you."

Carly shook her head. "I'm too tired. Walking on one crutch with only one good arm is a lot harder than I make it look."

Sarah chuckled. "Aren't you funny? No one could ever say adversity killed your sense of humor."

Carly laughed, too, for the first time in she couldn't remember when. She was still laughing as Sarah made her way out the door with her casserole dish of baked macaroni and cheese. The dear woman had insisted on scooping out a serving for Carly and leaving it to keep warm in the oven.

A half hour later, she couldn't ignore her hunger another minute. Leaning somewhat precariously on her crutch, she scuffed her way into the kitchen. Baked macaroni and cheese was her favorite comfort food, and tonight she really needed comforting because Joe's face kept popping up in her head, no matter how much channel surfing she did. If she let herself, she could fall in love with him. And that would be another in a long list of mistakes.

*

The following morning, Carly swallowed what little pride she had left and asked Sarah to read a Bible story about a woman who had made a mess of her life.

Sarah reached across the table and laid her hand over Carly's. "Sugar, our God is a God of second chances. He wants to give you a second chance more than you want one."

As Sarah flipped the parchment pages to the beginning of the Bible, Carly inhaled a sharp breath. She didn't remember hearing much about grace or forgiveness in the Old Testament, but surely Sarah knew her Bible. Then she began to read about the harlot named Rahab who lived on the wall of Jericho. It was the same story Carly had read last week. Did Sarah know how Rahab's life turned out after she left prostitution?

But Carly hadn't exactly been a prostitute. She didn't walk the streets, but she had given herself away for food, shelter, and a place in this world. For a while, she had even managed to persuade herself that Al loved her. Too bad she hadn't known that her whole life was built on quicksand. Al didn't love her. He loved the money she brought him. Money that would stop as she grew large with their child. If only she had chosen a public place to share her news, her baby might still be growing inside her.

*

Joe couldn't lie to himself. Or to his heavenly Father. Not anymore.

He was in danger of falling in love with Carly, not with the girl he'd known when they were teens, but with the confused mixture of vulnerability and streetwise toughness that Carly had become. She was a survivor, not just because she had lived through everything that scum Rutledge had put her through. She was a survivor because she refused to give up. Underneath the tough exterior she wanted him to see, he'd caught flashes of confusion and hope in her eyes.

It was that hope he was counting on. He prayed that somehow hope would lead her back to Christ.

Because if it didn't, there could be no future for them.

Marriage to an unbeliever was out of the question. Not even to Carly. Especially not to Carly, because only Christ could heal her and set her free of all the baggage she was carrying. Joe might be tempted to lift her burdens, but that was Christ's privilege. He'd seen what trying to do God's job had done to his dad.

"Focus, Callahan."

His partner's voice cut through Joe's rambling thoughts. He gave Harris his practiced impassive stare, knowing it wouldn't fool the seasoned officer.

"I know you care for her, but man, the way you slammed your fist into that guy's face. What was that all about? Provoked or not, you'll be lucky if you don't get suspended for that move."

Harris was right. With Rutledge, it was personal. Good thing the guy had no idea of Joe's connection to Carly. Good thing the idiot had been stupid enough to resist arrest, giving Joe an excuse for his lightning left hook. It hadn't taken much.

He'd been itching for justice ever since he'd first seen Carly in the ICU. Joe's conscience squeezed his chest, tight and unrelenting, until he faced the truth. Justice had nothing to do with it. He'd been aching to pound the guy for a month. Lord knows, he'd even dreamed of putting Rutledge in the hospital.

Joe sent a silent prayer heavenward. *Lord, help me to keep my personal life and my work separate, please.*

Harris didn't say a word during the remaining six miles out to Sarah's cottage, which gave Joe time to reflect. He should have been upfront about his conflict of interest and told the chief about his past friendship with Carly. Now, Harris was angry with him. And rightly so. Partners counted on each other to keep a clear head at all times. Joe had messed up. He should apologize, but all he could think about was Carly and how she'd handle going to the station to identify Rutledge as her attacker.

And it would take more than a simple "I'm sorry, man," to restore the trust between Harris and Joe.

As soon as his partner cut the engine, Joe shoved the car door open and bounded up the steps two at a time. He rapped on the front door and waited for her to make her way through the house.

"Who is it?"

"It's me, Joe. Open the door."

He heard the chain and the old key cranking in the lock. He propped the screen door with his shoulder and waited. Carly opened the inside door, but instead of inviting him in, she yelped in surprise as she stumbled against his chest. His arms slipped around her, and he pulled her against him, in spite of the warning bells going off like an alarm in his head. Her hair smelled like lavender. Her body, soft, yielding, leaned against him until the blood started pounding in his veins. She pushed away from him with a mumbled apology, but he couldn't seem to take his hands off her waist.

The confusion in her eyes tore at his heart. He released her instantly. What had he done?

Her gaze shifted beyond him. How could he have forgotten Harris? His partner would definitely needle him about Carly now.

Carly faced them both with a steely expression. "Did you arrest Al?"

"We caught up with him late last night, trying to cross the Peace Bridge into Canada," Harris explained. "He's being detained for questioning until you come down and identify him."

CHAPTER FIVE

Carly swallowed hard. The day she'd dreaded had finally arrived. Her hands were sweating, and her heart was slamming against her still bruised ribs. The need to flee, to hide, to protect herself crashed through her until she felt the blood draining from her head. Joe caught her just as the dizziness overtook her. Leaning into the solidness of his chest and trusting the strength of his arms around her, she filled her lungs with much needed oxygen. For the second time in as many minutes, she found herself in his embrace. Nothing she'd experienced in all her twenty-nine years had prepared her for the emotions swirling through her head at this moment.

"I'm okay," she whispered. "You can let go now."

Joe ignored her. He repositioned her against his right side and slipped his arms under her thighs and carried her to the couch.

Protesting would be a waste of her breath. What must his partner be thinking? Why on earth didn't Joe think before he acted? She didn't want the other man to get the wrong impression. Ironic, right? Her being worried what some man thought about her character. It was a little late in the game for that.

"Miss, we need to drive you to the precinct as soon possible." Joe's partner spoke as if there'd been nothing unusual in her response.

But she was supposed to be stronger, her ability to conceal

her emotions refined through years of burying her feelings deep inside where no one, especially no man could see. What was happening to her arsenal? One glance at her trembling hands revealed the truth. She was afraid.

"Now?" Her voice echoed a squeak in her ears. The racing of her heart only increased her panic. She swiped her good hand across her face. Crying in front of a man—no two men—was completely unacceptable. She was losing her advantage, what little she possessed. She took a deep breath to muster her reserves. A cigarette would help calm her nerves, but she'd quit three months ago. A glass of wine—no, that wasn't the answer either.

Oh, God. I can't face Al. I don't have the right to ask anything of You. But I can't do this alone.

"Sarah can come along, if you want," Joe suggested.

"She went out to lunch with a friend." Carly checked her watch, dismayed. Sarah wasn't due back for another hour and a half.

"We'll be right there with you." Joe slanted a glance at his partner.

Carly couldn't decipher their unspoken communication. Was this the usual procedure? She didn't care one way or the other. These two men were no match for Al and his extensive network of allies. She was trapped. Whether she pressed charges or not, Al's retaliation would be swift.

Would God help her, even though she'd turned her back on Him?

"Carly, this is my partner, Officer Harris. Harris, Carly Lawrence."

The man who was old enough to be her father assessed her. "Miss Lawrence."

Unable to trust the initial kindness in the man's eyes, she steeled herself against the moment he would see her for who she really was. "Officer."

"I'll wait outside," he said.

Gratitude flashed across Joe's face. "I'll be there in a minute."

As soon as the older man left, Joe sat down next to Carly. "I know you're scared." He reached for her hand, and she let him squeeze it for a few seconds—because he needed to reassure her—then tugged her hand free.

Ignoring his hurt look, she said, "I'm not scared. I just don't know what to expect."

The pain in his expression deepened.

Would he call her out on her lie? "Tell me exactly what's going to happen when we get to the station, and I'll be fine."

Joe explained her responsibility. Unless she identified Al in a line up, he'd be free to go. While she viewed each man behind the one-way glass, Al wouldn't be able to see her. She'd watched enough television crime shows to know that much. Still, Joe's confirmation of her second-hand knowledge made her breathe more easily. On her positive identification, the police would keep Al in a holding center until his indictment before the Grand Jury. Then, it would be up to the prosecuting attorney to secure a conviction, with or without a plea bargain.

Carly looked over her shoulder to where her crutch rested against the back of the couch. Harris had obviously picked it up on his way out the door. "If you'll just hand me my crutch, I'll be ready in a few minutes."

Joe retrieved the crutch and positioned it where she could stand without assistance. His need to help her, to do everything he could for her was evident on his face. But it wouldn't do either of them any good to let him think she needed him. "I have to change."

Her gaze locked with his, and his blue eyes darkened. For a brief moment, they were teens again.

But revisiting her past crush would only weaken her resolve. "Please tell Officer Harris I'll be out in ten minutes."

Dismissed, Joe nodded and left her alone without another word.

She grabbed the pad and pen Sarah kept by the phone and scrawled a quick note. "Gone to identify Al at the police station." What time would she be back? She should have asked Joe. Hopefully, Sarah wouldn't worry.

Carly limped to her room and perused the items in her closet, frustrated that not a single article of clothing could possibly convey the conservative image she believed would confirm her innocence. She shook her head in disgust. She was far from innocent. Still, she'd done nothing to deserve the beating Al had dished out. She grabbed a plain navy silk blouse and a knee-length charcoal gray skirt. The short-sleeved blouse was too low-cut. Fortunately, prominent cleavage was not one of her assets. A floral silk scarf tied around her neck would address the problem of too much bare flesh. One black ballerina flat for her left foot and a black bootie to cover her toes at the bottom of her cast, and she was ready.

A Bible lay on the nightstand where Carly had left it last night. Her fingers grazed the worn leather. *God, if You can do anything, please don't leave me alone. I've done so many things that I'm ashamed of, but I can't do this without You.*

Focusing on her chest expanding and releasing with each breath, she waited for God to answer. Until she heard a knock at the front door. At least her heart was no longer trying to pound its way out of her chest. That was a start. She picked up the mauve wool shawl Sarah had loaned her, maneuvered it around her shoulders, tucked the ends under her arm, and positioned the crutch in her cushioned armpit. It was time to face the consequences of all of her poor choices and hope God would be merciful to her.

*

By the time they reached the precinct, Joe had managed to compartmentalize his thoughts and suppress his feelings for Carly. Temporarily at least. Harris had insisted on driving, probably because he knew Joe would be tempted to check on Carly in the rearview mirror, but the less he thought about what was going on in her head the better off he'd be. And she'd made it abundantly clear that she didn't appreciate his making their personal relationship public knowledge.

What exactly was their relationship?

She's your best friend's sister, man.

The reminder didn't help. Instead, Joe found himself shrugging off guilt. Telling her family was Carly's responsibility, not Joe's. If he told Jared he'd found her, Carly would never trust him again. Joe couldn't let that happen because, God help him, he wanted to be more than her friend. Even though the timing wasn't right, a man could hope.

Joe unhooked his seat belt, exited the police car, and opened the rear door for Carly. To his surprise, the fear he'd seen in her eyes earlier was gone. Her serene expression testified of an inner peace. He was pleased for her. Victims often felt more trepidation about identifying their assailants than that situation warranted.

Testifying in court was another matter entirely. He prayed God would spare Carly the ordeal of facing Rutledge, not to mention answering the unpleasant questions designed by the defense attorney to make the jury doubt her credibility. If only the forensic team could build an iron-tight case. Then the DA would offer a plea bargain, probably five years in prison, rather than the fifteen Rutledge would get if he were convicted.

*

Officer Harris moved to Carly's side, and the two men flanked her as they crossed the parking lot to the entrance of the police station. Conquering a wave of anxiety, she held her head high, and moved as smoothly as a woman hobbling with one crutch could. They bypassed the gruff-looking officer at the front desk, and with Officer Harris leading the way, navigated their way through a room crowded with more than a dozen policemen and women, then headed down a long hallway until they stopped before the last room on the left. He opened the door and motioned for her to enter. "You'll wait here with Officer McKenna while we assemble the suspects for the lineup," Joe explained.

Carly nodded to the young officer, relieved to be in the company of another woman. Despite affirmative action, this police station was dominated by men, and no matter how she tried to remain composed, Carly sensed their judgment. She was a victim now, but she suspected these men saw her as a prostitute, dispensable and despised. Didn't all cops believe an escort service was merely a legal front for illegal activities? Police departments looked the other way, but cops still looked down their sanctimonious noses at women like her who made their living accompanying men with money enough to pay for the very best companionship. One glance at McKenna proved female cops were no different.

If only Carly had listened to Gran years ago. Her grandmother had tried to warn Carly that Al was no good. The shiftiness in his dark eyes had aroused Gran's suspicions. But no man had ever made Carly feel so special. When his gaze locked with hers, he convinced her she was the only woman for him. What a lie that had been! From their first meeting, she'd never seen the real Alan Rutledge.

Back then, Joe hadn't actually said he didn't like Al, but she'd picked up his negative vibes. She'd ignored Joe's reactions. He was as judgmental as her brother. Jared had tried to tell her Al wasn't good enough for her, but all her friends' older brothers said stuff like that. And Al had insisted that Joe was jealous. It was the one thing Al had said that she didn't believe. Could he have been right?

"Ms. Lawrence?" Officer McKenna interrupted Carly's distracted thoughts. "The lineup is ready."

Six Caucasian men, all with similar heights and builds stood against a white wall. Carly's hand flew to her mouth to stifle a gasp. The smug look in Al's eyes brought back the terror. Excruciating pain. Shock. Shame. Despair. Her head started spinning. She gripped the window ledge and sucked in a breath.

"Look carefully at each suspect." The officer placed her hand on the middle of Carly's back, a gesture clearly meant to reassure her. "Take as much time as you need."

A bruised jaw marred Al's confident expression, but it was him. "The fourth man from my left is the man who beat me and killed our baby."

"You're sure?"

Carly shot the officer a look. A look of utter disbelief. "Of course I'm sure. I spent the last nine years of my life working for the man."

The man she'd sacrificed everything for. The man who probably believed she wouldn't have the guts to identify him as her attacker.

"Alan Rutledge beat me and left me for dead." Carly turned away from the one-way glass and moved toward the door. "May I go now?"

"After you sign some official documents, you'll be free to go."

Signing the papers was a mere formality. From the moment the doctor had told her that her baby was dead, Carly had planned to make Al pay for what he'd done.

But she would pay, too. She couldn't do anything about that. God must have decided she wouldn't be a good mother. Which wasn't surprising. She swallowed the bile rising in her throat. *Focus, Carly. Deal with what's in front of you. Now. Don't think about anything else.*

"Lead the way, Officer."

McKenna met Carly's assertive look with a flicker of condescension that someone less practiced at reading subtle emotions probably would have missed.

"Have a seat, Ms. Lawrence. I'll be right back with the paperwork."

The minute the door shut behind McKenna, Carly raised her fist to her mouth. Physical control equals mental control, and mental control equals physical control. Al said she couldn't have one without the other. And right now she needed both.

She fought against the flood of anxiety, and willing her shaking hands to be still, she gripped the crutch until her knuckles turned white. She'd figure out a way to put all of this behind her and start over. Somehow. The trouble was she had no idea what to do. At least, she had a roof over her head. Thanks to Sarah. But soon Carly would need a job. Her skills weren't exactly marketable. Unless she wanted to keep on doing what she'd been doing.

And she'd rather die.

God, help me hold it together, till I can get out of here. Don't let me cry in front of Joe again. I can't lean on him. He'll get the wrong idea, and then where will we be?

The door opened, and Joe entered the room. Without a word, he laid out several forms on the bare desk. Three pages were tabbed with sticky note arrows marked "Sign here." Carly read the documents and signed her name on each line.

Joe retrieved the papers. "Let's go." His impassive tone gave her no clue to his thoughts. Wasn't he worried about her? Dismayed, she shook her head.

"You're not ready to leave?"

Embarrassed at her lack of self-control, she averted her eyes to escape his scrutiny. The last thing she needed was to have him figure out what she was really thinking. "Sorry. My mind wandered."

His only response was to hold the door open for her until she exited the sterile room. He passed the paperwork off to Harris, who'd been waiting in the deserted hallway, and then Joe led the way through the large room crowded with desks. With as much grace as she could muster, she trudged past more police officers than she could count. Most seemed too busy to even notice her, but her palms were still sweating as she maneuvered, leaning heavily on her crutch, willing herself not to stumble.

Carly breathed a sigh of relief as they left the police station. The rain had stopped. Soft sunlight peeked through gray clouds. She scanned the sky, hoping to see a rainbow. Seconds later, she squelched her disappointment. Looking for signs was silly.

The worst was over. She'd formally identified Al. Of course, he'd try to post bail, but given the fact that he'd been apprehended trying to leave the country, the judge would certainly see Al as a flight risk. Even if he could raise the exorbitant amount, she doubted he'd be stupid enough to seek her out and compromise his case. Hopefully, he'd be more concerned with minimizing the ramifications to Rutledge Escort Service. She couldn't help smiling. She'd tried to tell him not to use Rutledge as part of the business name, but Al's pride had overruled his normally good business sense. It would serve him right if he lost their best clients. Most of them steered clear of scandal whenever possible. After it was all over, there might not be a business left. Which was perfectly fine with her.

*

Sarah was cooking dinner when Joe and his partner dropped Carly off at the cottage.

"I'm back," Carly called out, hoping Sarah wouldn't pick up on her exhaustion.

"Dinner's almost ready. I got your note. Come talk to me when you get settled."

So much for concealing her emotions. But it was okay. Sarah's concern had become a comfort Carly appreciated. Strange how things worked out. Who would have thought that a retired high school English teacher would befriend her, a professional escort?

Correction, a former professional escort. She'd starve first before she went back.

The smell of chicken and biscuits drifted from the kitchen into the front room. Carly's stomach growled in response. With the stress of going to the police station, she'd forgotten all about lunch. The aroma of Sarah's cooking roused a wave of homesickness that chipped away at the barrier Carly had erected to keep happy memories from disrupting her life.

Not that her life could be any more disrupted. She'd lost her apartment, her livelihood, and her phone. It was the first thing Al had smashed. Without her cell, she had no contacts. If she'd taken the time to back up her contacts list online, the phone company could upload her contacts into a new phone. But there was no one she wanted to call. No friends. Al encouraged cold-hearted competition among his girls, but she and Star had bonded. If Carly got another phone and kept her old number, maybe Star would call her.

But so would a lot of other people, clients mostly, and

Carly didn't want to hear from them. She'd have to get a new number. It was probably best for both her and Star if they made a clean break from their old lives.

There was one person Carly wanted to talk with. Her dad's nightly calls had annoyed her, but now she missed the sound of his voice. *Even though I couldn't talk to you, knowing you still cared … knowing you still loved me, made living more bearable.*

She picked up the phone from the end table and started to dial, then quickly slammed the receiver into its cradle. What if someone other than Dad answered? And if he did, what could she say? *Al beat me up. Because I got pregnant and refused to have an abortion. Because I was stupid enough to believe he loved me. I'm pressing charges against him because he killed our baby.* She could never say any of those things to her dad.

Defeated, she sank on to the couch, brought her knees up into a fetal position, and buried her face against the cushioned backrest. Tears she'd held at bay for hours poured down her face and slid across her cheeks. How had she ever come to this horrible place? A place from which there appeared to be no escape.

Sarah's hand on her shoulder roused Carly from her distress.

Fighting the humiliation, she whispered, "I'm sorry. I didn't mean to break down."

Her hostess shot her a teacher look. "Girl, whoever told you that crying was a sign of weakness was an idiot."

Carly stared, speechless. Her face flamed at the memory. It was the first time she'd agreed to provide perks for a client. She'd cried. The client, furious and disgusted, had left with a promise to call Al. It was the first time Al had ever punched her. She hadn't been able to successfully disguise the bruises for more than a week, which made him even angrier because she couldn't entertain clients. After that, he found ways to hurt her that left marks most people would not notice. Leaving her body undamaged—usually—he chose instead to lacerate her heart.

"It's a long story." She glanced at the framed family portraits hanging around the room. Happy smiling children and parents glowing with love for one another spoke of a security Carly had abandoned for Al and his empty promises. How could Sarah possibly understand all Carly had felt compelled to do? Looking directly into the older woman's kind eyes, Carly said, "One you probably wouldn't want to hear."

"Try me."

The encouraging expression on the older woman's face almost persuaded Carly to open up. But not quite. Not yet.

"Some other time, maybe. I'm so tired and hungry I can't think straight."

Sarah smiled, patted Carly's hand, and stood. "Let's eat dinner early and watch a movie. How about Katherine Hepburn and Cary Grant in *Bringing Up Baby*?"

Though Carly's mother loved the classics and they'd seen all of Hepburn's early stuff, Carly thought *Pretty Woman* would be a more appropriate choice, but she bit back the sarcastic reply. "I actually love Katherine Hepburn, and *Bringing Up Baby* is my favorite, after *The Philadelphia Story*."

Sarah smiled knowingly. "Aha, the classic story of a woman in love with one man and about to marry another." She disappeared into the kitchen, then a moment later swung the door open. "I invited Joe for Sunday dinner, and he said he'd be happy to come."

"That's nice," Carly lied. When would the woman stop her matchmaking?

Defeat clutched Carly's heart. Happily-ever-after happened only in the movies. Or to good girls who followed the rules, to girls who remembered that men still believed there were two kinds of women—those you married and those you used. Al had taught her that.

CHAPTER SIX

By the time Joe had stepped out of the shower, toweled off, dressed in shorts and a t-shirt, and grabbed a protein drink from the fridge, he'd changed his mind a dozen times about playing volleyball. Tonight would be the third time he'd seen Carly's brother without saying a word about her staying with Sarah in Bemus Point. He and Jared had been friends since grade school, and keeping her secret was starting to eat at Joe.

His cell blared a tinny ring reminiscent of old land lines. He grabbed it off the dresser. Drat. Bob was calling. His brother-in-law hadn't let Joe beg off last week. "Hi, Bob."

"Just calling to make sure you weren't planning to skip out on us, man. We're down one sub because Kyle's wife is in labor."

Joe suppressed a groan. "I'll be there for the game, but I can't go out to eat after." *Because I won't be able to look Jared in the eye if he brings up his sister.*

"We're planning to go to Famous Dave's for barbecue. You sure you can't make it?"

The knot twisting in Joe's gut said definitely not, but his conscience argued he couldn't avoid Jared indefinitely. "Yeah, okay."

"What's up with you? You've been distracted for weeks."

"Confidential stuff at work."

If only it were that simple. Maybe he could talk Carly into calling home. Like that was going to happen. The Lawrences hadn't heard from her in years.

*

Joe managed to avoid more than minimal conversation with Jared until after the game. They were sitting at the restaurant waiting for their food and talking about mistakes they'd made on the court. They'd lost by one point

"Sorry I missed that last return." Jared looked at each man in turn, finally resting his questioning gaze on Joe. "Dad's worried sick about Carly."

Great. Now, it was Joe's fault they'd lost the game. He straightened his shoulders, concentrated on his breathing, and waited for someone to say something. The silence felt painfully awkward, seconds lengthening to minutes.

"What's going on?" Bob's younger brother, Steve, asked. "You all haven't heard from her, have you?"

Jared's attention flitted to Steve, then back to Joe. "No, we haven't."

Joe didn't flinch, but the expression in Jared's eyes went from steely determination to a sheen of hurt, as if the other man could read the lie in Joe's silence.

This wasn't the time or place for conversation about Carly. Dave, Terrell, and Mike didn't even know her. Talking about her in front of strangers who couldn't possibly understand all she'd gone through was out of the question.

Even in private, how could Joe tell Jared that his sister had been beaten almost to death?

The whole family would want to see her, to be sure for themselves that she was going to be all right.

"That's has to be tough," Bob said. "If Tara or Susie or Gwen disappeared, I don't know what I'd do. Probably the same as your dad. Call every day and hope she'd pick up."

"That's just it. He can't even call anymore because the number's not in service."

Resisting the urge to wipe his sweaty palms on his shorts,

Joe hid his surprise that Carly had given her dad her number. "I'll see what I can find out," Joe blurted out without considering the ramifications. Guilt over betraying their whole family squeezed his heart like a vise.

Jared brightened. "Thanks, Joe. I told Dad we could count on you."

Feeling like a first-class heel, Joe said, "I'm glad to help."

He could kick himself. He'd made a promise he could never keep, not without betraying Carly's confidence in him. No matter how he looked at the situation, either Jared or Carly would be mad at him, and justifiably so. There was only one solution. Convince Carly to call her brother. She didn't want to face her parents, but maybe she'd be willing to at least let her brother know she was okay.

*

On Sunday morning, Carly woke up in a cold sweat. Fear gripped her. "It was just a dream. It's not real." She rubbed her eyes to erase the image of the car crashing into the guardrail and plunging over the Skyway into Lake Erie. In moments, both her parents and her brother had drowned in the icy cold water. "It's not true." It wasn't even physically possible for a car to go over the Skyway into water. Her parents were fine.

But she didn't know for sure. The truth was she had no idea how any of them were. Her heart ached. For years, she'd been too busy and exhausted to think much about the hole in her life—the hole she'd created by her decision to isolate herself from her family. A bitter laugh escaped her lips. Al hadn't exactly given her a choice. "It's me or them." How many times had he used that threat to control her?

Why hadn't she stood up to him?

Carly sat up in bed, used her left arm to hug her right knee to her chest, and waited for the shaking to stop. Dang the casts. This wasn't nearly as soothing as hugging both legs with two good arms. The shock of what Al had done to her swept through her anew. If anyone had told her years ago that she'd end up battered and broken with nothing to show for her life but fifteen thousand dollars in her savings account, she would've told them they were crazy. Thinking of the money made her wish she'd squirreled more away. As it was, the other girls teased her for hoarding cash when she made more in a week than some of the others made in a month. But that was then, and this was now. Now, she had to figure out what to do with the rest of her life, what was left of it.

She had too much time to think, to fret and worry about things that she couldn't possibly control, about things that would probably never happen anyway. Why had she dreamed her family had all died? Maybe because she feared she was dead to them. But that couldn't be true. Hadn't her dad called her every night for the last five years, ever since she'd had the courage to call him and give him her number, making him promise to not share it with anyone else? If she still had her phone, wouldn't he still be calling her, asking her to please come home? Thinking of him listening to a message stating her number was no longer in service caused her throat to pinch with guilt. It wasn't fair to make him wonder and worry. She should call him. Soon. She'd call soon.

A wave of nausea swept through her. What if he'd given up on her? What if he believed that the daughter he'd once loved was dead to him forever? It was true. She could never be the vivacious, optimistic girl who believed that anything and everything she wanted was within her grasp. Her past choices restricted her future options, almost as much as Al's choices restricted his. She despised herself for being so stupid. No matter how much she wanted to believe that God would help her, shame dogged her at every turn.

Maybe she'd feel differently about herself after the trial was over.

Could she really put her past behind her? Sarah thought so. And Joe … well, he was skeptical. She saw his caution and his doubts whenever she caught him looking at her, studying her. Whatever he felt, whatever he thought, didn't really matter. Not anymore.

Now, she was lying to herself, something she'd sworn she'd never do. No. That wasn't right. She was still lying to herself. She'd been lying to herself ever since Al persuaded her that the escort service would secure their future.

"If we're ever going to get married, I need you to do this for me. For us." Al pulled her close and kissed her, driving every objection from her mind. "You know how much I love you."

Flushed from his kiss, Carly wanted to believe him. The roar of Niagara Falls behind her pounded in her ears. "But an escort service? Isn't that just a front for prostitution?"

He didn't break their locked gazes. "Maybe sometimes. But Rutledge Escort Services will be upscale, catering to the rich and powerful. You'll accompany businessmen and politicians to dinners, banquets, concerts, plays, conferences. Stuff like that."

The way he put it sounded almost elegant. Dressed in fine clothes, walking on the arms of men wearing the finest suits—maybe even tuxedos, riding in limousines, providing charming companionship … Would it really be that innocent?

"I'll be able to set the limits?"

Al's eyes narrowed. "You don't trust me?" He turned, started to walk away, then shot back over his shoulder, "Forget I asked. I'll think of some other business to set us up."

Carly's heart clenched. Would he leave her here in Niagara Falls Park by herself? At eleven thirty at night? He wouldn't, would he? But his long legs had already carried him fifty yards away from her. Grateful for the bright full moon and the streetlights that lined the walkway, she raced to catch up to him. "Al, wait. Honey, I'm sorry."

He stopped but didn't turn to look at her. He was making her walk around him to see his face. His scathing expression frightened her. She felt rebuked, belittled, insignificant. Did he really love her? This wasn't the kind of love she'd dreamed of when she first left home with him nine months ago. But he was all she had, and she couldn't lose him. Where would she go if he left her? She couldn't go home.

He continued to stare her down as if she were a naughty child or a lazy servant. "Do you have something you want to say to me?"

How she hated his condescending tone. She always said she'd never let any man talk down to her or treat her like an object. She averted her face a moment to wipe the tears that had slipped down her cheek. Then she laid her hand on his arm and raised her gaze again. "I'll do it. Whatever you want me to do, I'll do it, as long as I don't have to sleep with clients."

Al smiled. Smugly—as if he'd expected her to yield.

An uneasy feeling choked her breath then passed as quickly as it came. Surely, he wouldn't want her to sleep with anybody but him. She didn't have anything to worry about.

She'd fallen asleep in the car on the drive home, and Al had carried her into the apartment and up to their bedroom. He'd made love to her, tenderly, telling her how beautiful she was and how much she pleased him, the same as he always did. He loved her, and she loved him. Everything would work out okay in the end. She'd have her little house with a wraparound porch and lilac bushes in the spring and roses in the summer. They'd have two kids—a boy and a girl—and a dog. Happily ever after would be hers *after* she helped Al establish his escort service. As soon as he hired other girls to work for him, she'd give it up. A year or two and she'd be Mrs. Alan Rutledge.

Stupid. Stupid. Stupid. You should have seen through his schemes. You crawled into bed with a rattler and then wondered why his venom slowly poisoned your life.

Carly continued to berate herself. Until a strange thought pushed to the forefront. She'd measured her worth by her value to Al for so long that she'd come to see herself solely through his eyes. When he'd cast her out, she'd labeled herself as worthless.

But was it true? Was she worth nothing at all?

Who was she if she wasn't one of Al's girls?

One of Al's girls? She laughed, choking on the bitterness that erupted from that dark place where she forced everything that threatened to shatter her sanity. For the first year, she had been *his* girl, the one he claimed as his alone, the one he said he wanted to build a life with. All of his promises were lies. Lies she'd wanted to believe because she loved him. Or thought she loved him. If only she'd had the guts to leave then, to run as fast and as far away as she could from the man who would destroy the woman she wanted to be.

The image staring back at her from the mirror above the dresser was haggard, cynical, and defeated.

She wasn't her daddy's little girl anymore. She'd forfeited her innocence for a sham. As far as she could see, it really was true that you can't go home again. Disconnected from everything and everyone she'd ever known, she had no idea what to do with the rest of her life.

God, who am I? Why am I even alive?

You are mine.

A chill rushed through her, and she shivered. If she belonged to God, what did that mean?

She deserved hell.

Heaven was for people like Sarah and Joe and her parents—people who didn't blatantly break the Ten Commandments as if there were no God at all. People who knew God was serious when He said, "Thou shalt not kill."

A knock sounded on her bedroom door.

She glanced at the bedside clock. 8:34. She'd lost track of time.

"Carly, are you up yet?" Sarah asked through the door. "We need to leave by nine fifteen if we're going to make it to Sunday School."

Reluctant to disappoint her hostess, Carly replied, "I'll be ready."

But she didn't get up. She pulled the quilt up under her chin, wishing she could shut out the world a little longer. She didn't really mind going to church. Last week, most of the people had made her feel welcome. In fact, the genuine smiles of the women, many of them in their late twenties and early thirties, surprised her with their warmth. Where Carly had expected to find judgment and scorn, she'd found acceptance, perhaps because they didn't know who she really was.

That was certainly true of their pastor. Of course, attraction often trumped good sense.

But guilt over deceiving the minister and his congregation wasn't the real reason she didn't want to go to church this morning. Six foot three with blue eyes, dark hair cropped short, and a smile framed by engaging dimples—Joe Callahan made her heart skip and her body ache. Completely unacceptable.

Maybe, she could pretend to be sick. She *had* been on her feet too much this week, and her ankle was throbbing inside the cast. She scoffed, shook her head, and maneuvered her good leg, followed by her broken one with its bulky cast, over the edge of the bed. Joe was coming for dinner, so skipping church wouldn't help her avoid him. Carly reached for her crutch, hobbled to the bathroom, opened the medicine cabinet, and took out the bottle of naproxen. She'd take two to knock out the pain, twist her way into a presentable outfit, and plaster a smile on her tired face.

Fifteen minutes later, she tottered into the sunny kitchen, breathing deeply of the cinnamon-laced air. A plate of homemade cinnamon rolls and a platter of scrambled eggs topped with shredded cheese roused her hunger. Sarah poured two mugs of coffee and grabbed a container of chocolate caramel creamer from the fridge. "I hope you're hungry," she said. "Have I told you how much I'm enjoying having someone to cook for?"

Carly smiled. "A few times. Thanks for making a hot breakfast. I get hungry before church is over if I just grab a piece of toast." Memories of Sunday mornings at home disturbed her composure. "Mom was always trying to get me out of bed earlier, but I've never been a morning person."

Sarah shot her a quizzical look.

"What? Surely, you've noticed how hard it is for me to get up in the morning."

"It's not that, sugar." Sarah placed a scoop of eggs on her plate and passed the platter to Carly. "This is the first time you've ever mentioned your mom."

Carly covered her mouth with her fingers. She couldn't take back her words. "My mom is a true saint. She expects nothing but the best from her children. To her, second best means your heart isn't in the right place. That you don't care enough to try your hardest."

Sarah frowned. "No one is perfect. We've all come short of the glory of God. Even your mother."

Come short? Carly hadn't even come anywhere near being

the best. Except at her job. Once a man had gone anywhere with her on his arm, or been *in* her arms, he never asked for another escort. To salvage her self-esteem, she'd been proud of her popularity. She'd tried to drown her shame in wine and chocolate until the revulsion subsided to a dull dissatisfaction, a disappointment with herself that was never far from the surface of her ritzy facade.

But Mom? She lived a good life. She was faithful to her husband and dedicated to her children. She volunteered at the City Mission, serving in the kitchen. She took their Labrador retriever, Sammy, to local nursing homes to visit elderly patients who'd been forgotten by their families. Mom's life brought glory to God. Carly's never could.

Sarah reached across the breakfast table and patted Carly's hand. "Are you all right? Your face is as white as a sun-bleached sheet."

"I'm fine. My ankle hurts this morning, but I took two naproxen, so I'll be fine to go to church. Don't worry about me."

Sarah nodded, bowed her head, and thanked God for the food and His many blessings, among which she actually included Carly.

Her? A blessing? It didn't seem possible.

*

"All things are possible with God," Pastor Ryan declared, his gaze resting on Carly for a second before he scanned the congregation. "Salvation is for every person who believes in Christ's redemptive work on the cross. You may think you've gone too far, that God doesn't want you anymore, but He isn't willing that anyone should perish. And that means you. Every one of you."

A sudden warmth like a cozy blanket enveloped Carly's shoulders and upper back.

"Whatever you've done, you must remember that to God

one sin is the same as all of the others. Whoever fails to keep the law in one point is guilty of all."

Could it be true? Was murder the same in God's eyes as stealing or lying? How could that be? If she'd stolen something or lied, she could make that right, but she could never undo the abortion or even her part in the miscarriage. She shifted in the pew, easing her body away from Joe. Then she found herself sitting too close to Sarah. Carly straightened her back, visualizing an imaginary barrier that kept her separate from the dear people who sat beside her.

Dear? When had she started seeing them as dear to her? For the past two weeks, Sarah had shown her more love than Carly had felt in years. But Joe was often distant, as if he were reluctant to give her the wrong impression about his friendship.

God, I can't fall in love with him. If he doesn't want me ... I don't think I could survive. Al's rejection cut like a knife to my heart. Being rejected by Joe would ...

You gave Al everything but your heart.

Her face flamed with shame. *Oh, God. I put myself through hell for a man I never really loved. Why?*

Sarah's hand on her arm penetrated Carly's grief. The pianist was playing "Just As I Am." Carly had heard that song from the time she was a little girl, but she'd never done anything that bad as a kid. Back then she could imagine Jesus opening His arms to welcome her. Now, she couldn't bear to think about all of the vile things she'd done to keep Al happy, to keep him from abusing her. At least, she'd refused to have another abortion. That counted for something, didn't it?

"Carly, are you feeling all right, dear?" Sarah asked. "You look so pale."

"I'm fine."

The congregation was filing out of the pews down the

center and side aisles toward the front door where Pastor Ryan stood waiting to greet everyone. Joe moved to the end of their pew. She and Sarah rose to follow him.

"I should have encouraged you to stay home. It's been a difficult week for you."

Sarah was right. Seeing Al again, even through the protection of one-way glass, had brought back the nightmares.

Joe turned and faced Carly. A frown marred his handsome features. "I told you not to worry. Our forensic team is very thorough. Your case probably won't go to trial."

"What if I want to testify against him? What if I want to see the look on Al's face when I tell the judge and the jury about everything he did to me?" Her stomach clenched. "What if I want to hear the jury say he's guilty? I need to hear for myself how many years in prison the judge gives him."

"No, you don't." Joe's steely gaze bore into her.

"How do you know what I want? You don't know me at all."

A wounded look flashed so fast across his face she almost missed it.

"I'm sorry." She reached out to touch him, then drew back her hand. "I didn't mean it like ... You can't possibly understand."

"Maybe not. But I've seen women in similar situations in court, and it's not pretty."

Sarah placed her hand on Carly's back. "We can talk about this later. In private, Joe."

Carly saw the second Sarah's gentle rebuke dispelled Joe's frustration.

"I only want what's best for you," he said.

That was his apology. If she wanted to let him off the hook. Which she probably should, given the fact that she had no one to blame for her outburst but herself. All of her training was slipping away with the persona of Elise. Elise would never have let any man draw her out, but Carly clearly would. The Carly Joe had known in high school had worn her heart on her sleeve. Sometimes, emotions best concealed were revealed for whoever cared enough to notice them. But Joe always said he liked her honesty. She was sincere and open to life and to people. It wasn't until Al created Elise that Carly had learned to dissemble with the best of her kind.

"I said, I only want what's best for *you*."

Al had said that, too. No. Not exactly that. He'd said, "I only want what's best for us." Hindsight revealed he'd meant best for him.

Joe was different. Could she trust him? The patient question in his eyes was impossible to ignore.

"I know you do." Her words were soft, like a kiss. She wanted to take them back, but she couldn't. "You've always been a good man." And a good friend to her brother. How must he be feeling keeping her location a secret from Jared? But she wasn't exactly asking Joe to lie for her.

He smiled. A sad smile that didn't reach his eyes. Was he reading her thoughts? Cops could do that sometimes, couldn't they?

An altogether different expression deepened the blue of his eyes. Color rose in his cheeks.

Her breath caught. "Thank you for all of your help with ... everything."

He nodded then turned away to answer an older man who'd asked him a question.

Bereft and plagued by guilt because she wanted Joe to want her, Carly waited with Sarah until the center aisle was clear.

Pastor Ryan greeted them cordially. Again, Carly discerned a spark of interest, which she sought to discourage.

"I enjoyed your sermon."

"Yes, I never tire of hearing that God views all sinners the same," Sarah said. "We're all the same because we all need Christ."

Sarah's remarks seemed more a reminder to Carly than a compliment to the pastor, but he smiled anyway. "So when do you get those casts off, Carly?"

She wrinkled her nose in dissatisfaction. "Not for two more weeks. And after that, I'll start physical therapy. I was lucky. The breaks weren't that bad considering ..." She trailed off, not wanting to share her personal business with someone who was basically a stranger, preacher or not.

His deep brown eyes conveyed his concern. "You're in my prayers."

Carly caught her breath. She hadn't heard anyone say that since she'd left home more than ten years ago. For some people, it was a reflex response, but when her parents said it, they meant they'd be praying every day until the answer came. Her dad was still praying for her. His prayers had probably saved her life. But was her mom still praying for her, or had she given up on her only daughter?

"Thank you, Pastor. I appreciate your prayers. God knows I need all of the prayers I can get."

He reached for her hand and shook it warmly. "Please call me Ryan. I'd like to stop by and visit you ladies sometime this week." His glance took in both Carly and Sarah.

"Oh, please do," Sarah said. "Can you come to supper tomorrow night?"

Supper with the preacher? Carly didn't think she was up for that.

"Tuesday would be better for me."

"Tuesday it is," Sarah agreed, already urging Carly toward the front door where Joe waited, leaning against the door jamb, his inscrutable expression sending shivers through Carly.

What was the man thinking? She used to always know what was on Joe's mind. Or maybe she'd just thought she did. Hadn't he always viewed her as Jared's pesky younger sister? There had been times he'd seemed … aware of her crush on him. And maybe amused or flattered.

He'd taken her to the prom as "just friends," but several times during the evening, he'd looked at her with an ache that stole her breath. He'd wanted to kiss her, she was sure, but he never had. Not once. Even when she'd tried to send him the message that she wanted to kiss him, too.

What had kept them apart? The fact that she was his best friend's little sister? Probably.

The day after the prom she'd met Al at the Allentown Art Festival. He'd gushed over her photographs of the big cats at the Buffalo Zoo. Alan was a master at stroking people's pride and making promises he never intended to keep. Unfortunately, she hadn't figured that out until years later.

Joe didn't make promises. He just did whatever he said he would do. What would it be like to be loved by a man like that?

"Ride with me," he said when she reached his side. Both his tone and the hard line of his mouth revealed his determination. "There's something I need to talk to you about."

Apparently, she was about to find out what he was thinking, whether she wanted to or not. "Okay. Just let me tell Sarah." But Sarah was already walking to her car, as if she took it as a matter of course that Carly would ride back to the house with Joe. She really needed to talk to Sarah about her matchmaking.

Slipping his arm possessively around her waist, Joe helped her down the stairs and across the parking lot to his truck. He opened her door for her. With his hand on her elbow, supporting her weight, she climbed into the truck without a problem.

The minute he buckled his seat belt and started the engine, she sensed his tension. Something was troubling him. That much was clear. And it had something to do with her. By the knot tightening in her stomach, she suspected that it was a problem she wouldn't want to face.

He didn't put the truck in gear. Instead, he shut off the engine and shifted in his seat to look her fully in the face. The determination in his eyes squeezed the knot in her gut tighter.

"I want you to call your brother."

Her mouth gaped. "You can't be serious. I haven't—"

"You haven't talked to him or anyone else in your family for years."

She closed her eyes to block out his pleading look. "No."

"If you don't tell them you're all right, I will."

"You will not." She glared at him with an expression that had withered stronger men than he was. "You have no right."

"No right? No right? Jared's my friend. I've known your parents my whole life. When my mom kept running off, it was *your* mother who made sure I had food to eat while my dad wasted his time searching for my mom."

Carly felt trapped. Trapped by the truth of his words. But wasn't the truth supposed to set her free?

He put his hand on her arm, igniting a reaction she fought to ignore. How long had it been since she'd felt loved and cherished in a man's arms? She pushed his hand away.

The hurt was back in his eyes. "I owe them, Carly. They have the right to know you're okay. Why didn't you tell me you'd given your cell number to your dad? He's been worried sick about you."

Dad was worried sick. What about Mom? All the warmth

Joe's touch had roused a moment ago was replaced by icy dread. But it didn't matter. Joe was more than right. She owed them. If nothing else, she owed them the simple courtesy of a phone call.

A phone call is a good place to start.

"You win. I'll call Jared."

Lines of tension between Joe's eyebrows smoothed out. His eyes glistened with tears and gratitude. "Carly, it'll be all right. I promise."

"Please don't make promises you've have no power to keep." She averted her face and stared out of the truck window at the riotous display of autumn color in the distant hills. "Just start the truck, and let's get going. I don't want Sarah to know we've been arguing. She has this crazy, impossible idea in her head that—"

"Nothing is impossible with God, Carly. You know that." He turned the key in the ignition, the truck roared to life, and they started down the road together.

CHAPTER SEVEN

Joe almost relented. He'd never seen Carly so quiet. All through dinner she'd scarcely said a word. When he offered to wash the dishes, she excused herself, claiming she was overtired. Watching her retreat, he fought the urge to go after her and tell her she didn't have to face her family alone. He'd gladly be there for her as a support or a buffer. Whatever she needed, he wanted to be. For her. For himself. Because he'd let her down all those years ago when he hadn't had the guts to reveal his true feelings for her. Surely, Jared would have preferred his sister date Joe rather than that scumbag Rutledge.

A fresh wave of regret rushed over Joe. *Lord, help me.*

Breathe. In. Out. In. Out. God is in control. God is always in control.

Sarah laid a comforting hand on his shoulder. "Do you want to talk about it?"

He tore his gaze from the vacant doorway. "I promised to wash the dishes."

"The dishes can wait. Sit."

He complied without further resistance. It was easy to see how she'd run her classroom, simply expecting cooperation. She turned her back to him, bent to remove a pan of bubbling apple crisp from the oven, set the hot dish on a potholder in the center of the table, and then took a carton of vanilla ice cream out of the freezer.

The tantalizing aroma of cinnamon and allspice brought

back memories of Sunday afternoons at the Lawrence home. Carly's mom always served a baked dessert after dinner. His lanky frame had filled out under her watchful eye, no thanks to his own negligent mother whose wanderlust broke his father's heart more times than Joe could count. He dismissed his resentment—a pointless emotion. His mother had been dead for twenty years. All of his negative feelings should have been laid to rest long ago.

But Carly and Jared had the kind of family Joe only dreamed about.

Until the day after her high school graduation, when Carly had broken her mother's heart. Her whole family had grieved as the weeks of her silence lengthened to months and then to years, which could explain why Jared chose to live with his parents. Joe still didn't understand how she could do that to the people who loved her most. And for a lowlife like Alan Rutledge.

Even now, Joe could kick himself for not asking her out again. Why hadn't he? Probably because he'd convinced himself that she'd choose Al over him.

"You were distracted all through dinner." Sarah poured purple colored tea from a china pot edged with blue forget-me-nots.

The fancy cup felt fragile in his big hand. He wasn't much of a tea drinker. He preferred coffee, especially with dessert, but he'd never tell her that. He breathed in the fruity aroma and took a sip. "This is good."

His aunt settled into the chair across from him and rested her blue-lined hands on the gingham tablecloth. "It's pomegranate blackberry. Do you want to talk about what's bothering you?"

Her patient expression urged him to confide in her. Although she was technically his great aunt, Sarah always claimed she was too young for the title. She'd been mothering him for as long as he could remember, but did he really want to burden her with his and Carly's complicated past?

Stalling, Joe spooned steaming apple crisp into two dessert bowls and topped each with a scoop of ice cream, which immediately started to melt. "I'm worried about Carly."

Sarah didn't look at him. Instead, she added an extra spoonful of apple crisp to his bowl. His eyebrows shot up. His serving was now double the size of hers.

"Don't give me that look. You've lost weight—weight you can't afford to lose." She added another scoop of ice cream. "Did something happen yesterday at the police station?"

"No. Yes. Carly needs to call her family." He hesitated, unsure how to express his concern without betraying Carly's trust. "Her brother and I play volleyball together once a week. They're all worried sick about her."

"I see. Your loyalties are divided." Sarah frowned. "And you *think* the only way out of your predicament is for Carly to let her family know what's happened to her."

"I don't see any other way," he mumbled around a spoonful of apples. The gooey dessert should be savored, not eaten with anxiety souring his stomach.

Sarah set her tea cup in the saucer and leveled him with her teacher look. "The problem with your solution is that Carly may not be ready to face her parents. Or her brother."

His aunt's words hit Joe like a punch in the gut. He'd been thinking about himself. And the Lawrences. He could relate to how they felt. He was all too familiar with what they had to face. Or not face. Joe was adept at compartmentalizing feelings he wanted to avoid. The skill served him well. Most of the time. Today wasn't one of those days. "She agreed to call her brother."

Sarah's brows knit in frustration.

"I only want what's best for her." His words sounded forced. Who was he trying to convince? Sarah? Or himself?

"What makes you so sure you know what's best for Carly? Only God does."

"Point taken."

With her characteristic grace, Sarah steered the conversation to family news surrounding Maureen and the kids' reaction to having another brother or sister soon. Joe dismissed the pang in his heart. He'd have a family of his own someday. In God's timing.

After they finished their dessert, Joe rose, cleared the table, and started to run water into a basin to wash the dishes.

"I'll do those." She pushed him toward the door. "You've got more important things to take care of."

Aunt Sarah was right. As usual.

Joe's feelings were a muddled mess. Dealing with Carly resurrected unpleasant memories of his mother. They were two different people, living with two different situations. But both women had chosen paths that hurt their families. And for what? His mom was dead. And Carly had almost been killed. He'd never understand their choices. How could he possibly advise her?

Or trust her?

He hadn't even prayed about how to handle the situation with her family. Ouch.

The Lord's gentle rebuke forced him to acknowledge the truth. Joe had committed himself, and Carly, without considering her feelings at all. So much for loving her. Trudging down the hall, he sent a silent S.O.S. prayer heavenward. Then he knocked on her door, confident that at least this time he wouldn't put his foot in his mouth.

"Come in."

Her voice sounded sleepy. Had he awakened her? "It's me,

Joe."

She opened her door faster than he supposed she could with her crutch. "I'm not up for another lecture."

He deserved that. "I'm sorry for browbeating you into agreeing to call Jared." Her startled eyes convinced him that that was exactly what he'd done. "I was feeling guilty, like I was hiding you and lying to your brother about where you were. By omission. So … what are you going to tell Jared?"

"That I'll meet him for coffee."

"Are you sure?"

She shrugged and adjusted the crutch slightly. "No. But I won't ask you to keep my whereabouts a secret any longer."

Hearing the pain in her self-reproach, he brushed his fingers in a quick caress over her hand. "I understood. I knew you weren't ready." He ached to take her in his arms and comfort her, but he stepped back. "I'll call Jared for you. When do you want to meet him?"

"It doesn't matter. Whenever and wherever is convenient for both of you." She smiled, but resignation dimmed the light in her eyes.

He'd bullied her into facing her family, and still she'd forgiven him. Just like that. Without him even asking for forgiveness. He wanted to make it up to her.

"I'm going to need a ride." Leaning heavily on the crutch, she reached her hand out to his arm. A jolt of warmth sizzled through him.

Standing on the threshold of her bedroom was suddenly intimate. Immediately, Joe reined in his need. An expert on picking up a man's subtle and not-so-subtle cues, Carly hadn't missed his reaction to her touch. Fresh anger at Rutledge pounded Joe's temples. Thankful that the creep was finally behind bars, Joe assessed the distress marring Carly's beautiful features. He really had no idea how hard this was going to be for her. "Of course, I'll drive you. I can wait in the car—"

"No, I want you with me. I need a friend because when I tell my brother ..." Her lower lip trembled. "When I tell him that his sister is—"

He put a finger over her lips. "Don't say it. Because it isn't true."

She shook her head, jerking away from his hand. "Just because you don't want it to be true doesn't mean it isn't. We both know who I am and what I've done. And soon my family will know, too. They were bound to find out eventually. I couldn't hide forever. I knew that the day I finally accepted the fact that Al was never going to marry me."

Joe swallowed hard, fighting for control. Another sucker punch. Well, not exactly. She didn't mean to hurt him, didn't know how much he wanted to be the one for her, the husband she longed for. *Stop, Callahan. You, can't go there. Neither of you are ready to start thinking along those lines. Focus. This isn't about you.*

It was too late to be Carly's knight in shining armor, but maybe Joe could erase the defeat in her eyes, give her something to hope for. He put his hands on her upper arms, the weight of his fingers slight against her sling, and held her gaze. Thank God Rutledge was too much of a scoundrel to marry her. "What was true in the past isn't true now. You can do anything you want with your life."

"Except bring my babies back." Tears tracked down her cheeks.

Babies? "You were pregnant with twins?"

She shook her head, the stricken look in her eyes revealing the truth.

Oh, no. *God, not that.*

What could he say? He eased her closer until the space

between them disappeared. Then he held her and let her cry.

*

Why had she said that? The details of her past were not his business. But it was better for him to know upfront how low she'd sunk.

Now he knows. He knows I had an abortion.

She'd seen it in his eyes—that startled mix of shock and crushing disappointment. Well, he couldn't be any more disappointed in her than she was in herself. If only she could turn back the clock and make a different choice.

She scoffed. Her? Defy Al? Not likely. Not back then.

Carly clung to Joe, sobbing against his chest, taking what comfort she could from the strength of his arms wrapped around her. "I should have listened to you."

"Shh." He pressed a kiss against the top of her head. "I should have told you the truth."

She lifted her face from his damp shirt and stared into his eyes. "You did. You told me that you didn't trust Al. I ... I thought you were just saying that because you were jealous."

"I was."

She studied his face. What was he saying? If he really cared for her, then why had he let her go so easily?

"Al was jealous of you, too. He didn't want me to see you or even talk to you on the phone. You were a threat to his plans." Realization hit her like a bolt of electricity. Al had planned all along to use her to start his escort service. And the first step in implementing his plan was to isolate her from her family and friends.

Stupid. Naïve. Gullible.

You were only eighteen.

No nineteen. And caught up in her need to hang onto happily-ever-after.

She'd brought it all on herself because she'd believed Al

loved her. What a foolish little dreamer she was. She hung her head, desperate to hide from Joe's intense regard. But he cupped her chin so that she had to meet his gaze. She closed her eyes. She couldn't look at him feeling as she did. Used up and discarded, she was of no value to any man. Except for—

"Carly, open your eyes. I'm not going to disappear. I ..."

Determined to protect herself from any more heartache, she glared at him. "You what? Understand? Know how I feel?"

"I care about you." His flushed face revealed more than his words. "I ... I'm your friend."

She pursed her lips and drew in a long breath. "That works for me."

They'd come full circle, with Joe promising friendship while sending her mixed messages about wanting but not wanting more. They were as mismatched as they'd been at the prom. No matter what he said or believed, she couldn't change who she'd become. "If you still want to be friends knowing everything about me ..."

Joe touched her cheek, and she resisted the urge to turn her face and kiss his palm. What would it be like to be loved by a man she could truly trust? She could kiss him now. It would be so easy to reach up, place her hand on the back of his neck, and with gentle pressure, urge him to lower his head until their faces were so close their breaths would mingle. If she kissed him, it would change everything. Her problems would be his problems.

He didn't deserve that.

She shifted in his arms, putting necessary distance between their bodies. He stepped away, backing slowly into the hall, but his eyes never left hers. Passion blazed in his gaze. Beneath the passion, his heart called out to her, promising her a better life if only she could somehow cleanse herself from the stain of the old one.

"Carly, I—"

"It's okay, Joe." A desperate need to reach out to him, to feel their bodies pressed together in harmony, to surrender herself to this moment swept through her. *No, I won't go down that road again.* "I'm fine."

His expression of disbelief did nothing to bolster her defenses.

"I'm going to be fine."

"I never said you weren't." His mouth hardened into a thin, grim line. "This is your second chance. And if I have anything to say about it, nothing and no one is going to mess it up for you."

*

After Joe left, Carly decided to sit outside on the porch for a while. The thermometer registered 62 degrees, but with only a slight breeze she'd be comfortable with Sarah's shawl draped over her shoulders. Reclining in the lounge chair with her foot elevated on a pillow, she closed her eyes and focused on the birds singing in the nearby maple trees, their leaves red, gold, and orange. The joyful color provided a sharp contrast to her mood. If only she could banish the unsettled feeling churning in her stomach. Joe's last words, meant to encourage her, reminded her that she wasn't exactly employable.

Maybe she could go to a community college. In high school, her grades had been good.

Could she afford tuition and books? With fifteen thousand dollars in her savings account and just under eight hundred in her checking account, she could get by for a few months. Then she would need a job, preferably one that paid more than minimum wage. Unless she gave up her apartment and moved somewhere cheaper. But where?

Going back home was not an option.

And then there was the question of what on earth should

she study? Clearly, making good choices was not her strong suit. Maybe Sarah could advise her. Or maybe there was some aptitude or interest test Carly could take online.

She'd always enjoyed photography, but the likelihood of finding a job as a photographer seemed slim. Besides, taking pictures brought her joy. If she channeled her art into making money, how long would it be before photography was just a job to her?

The very phrase "just a job" brought a sour taste to her mouth. "It's just a job, Carly," Al had said when she'd begged him to let her give it up. "It's not who you are."

But that had been the biggest lie of all.

Hadn't she been tempted—less than an hour ago—to use her skills to bind Joe to her? He'd never leave her. If they slept together, Joe would marry her. He was nothing like Al.

Hugging her arms to her chest, she gave herself to the dream of lying in Joe's arms, the two of them satiated with the delights of passion.

"No, I will not go there."

To clear her head, she turned her attention to the fading light playing on the rippling surface of the lake. Beyond the distant shore, a riot of orange, red, and yellow adorned trees that would soon lose their leaves. After a long winter, those same trees would produce new leaves—a fresh start.

She wanted a fresh start, too. Was that what accepting grace meant?

Surely, she could find another way to support herself. She did have people skills. At least those were transferrable. With modifications. She could start with general studies the first semester and then make up her mind. Whatever she chose, at least she would no longer dread going to work every day. Maybe she could start school in January. Tomorrow, she'd go online and see what she needed to do to apply to Erie

Community. ECC North was probably her best choice.

You're just avoiding the inevitable. You've got plenty of time to think about school.

She needed to figure out what she was going to say to Jared when she saw him. She should never have shifted the responsibility for making contact with her brother to Joe. Now, she'd be on edge until she heard something. Not a good idea. She needed to call Jared herself. As soon as Sarah left for the evening service, Carly would find her brother's business card and do what she should have done long ago. When she heard his voice, she would *not* hang up. She'd say hello, feel him out, and then decide if they should meet for coffee. If she could face Jared, then she could meet with her dad, too. After she'd talked to Dad, then maybe she'd be ready to see Mom. After the trial, when Al was behind bars, Carly could start to put her past behind her for good.

God, please let it be true and not just a pep talk. If You can do anything for me, give me the courage to face the consequences of my mistakes.

Sarah came outside at that moment carrying a tray with a teapot, a cup, and a dish of apple crisp. "You missed dessert, and I thought you might like some hot tea." She set the tray next to the Bible on the wicker table.

"Thank you," Carly said, but her mind wasn't on food. She'd noticed that Sarah kept a Bible in every room. Carly hoped that somewhere within its pages she'd discover the truth that would set her free. Because right now she was shackled to her sins. Everything she'd done wrong weighed on her heart and mind, and she had no idea how to move forward. Sure, she could enroll in school and go through the motions of starting her life over, but she needed more than a new career and new friends. She needed to figure out how she could become a completely different person.

Elise will always be with you. You can turn as many corners as you want, but the memories will follow you.

Carly shuddered. Was it true? Could she never escape her past?

Sarah picked up the Bible and laid it in Carly's lap.

Was the woman a mind reader? Carly shot her a questioning glance.

But Sarah only smiled. Pulling her sweater tighter around her middle, she said, "It's chilly. I'll get you a blanket." Then she disappeared into the house, leaving Carly to wonder why someone with so much energy had decided to retire.

In minutes, Sarah returned with a lamb's wool blanket, which she spread over Carly's outstretched legs. "Can I get you anything else before I head out to church?"

Carly shook her head. She hadn't opened the Bible because she wasn't sure where to find the answers she was looking for. "I still don't understand why God would want to have anything to do with someone like me. I deserve to go to hell for what I did." Saying the words aloud roused a flash of terror that threatened to consume her. Her breath hitched in her chest.

Sarah sat on the end of the lounge and squeezed Carly's knee. "Oh, sugar, we all deserve to go to hell for what we did, but we don't have to because Jesus took our place. He paid the price for the sins of the whole world. He took our punishment so that we could become sons and daughters of God."

Tears welled in Carly's eyes. "I heard the salvation message from the time I was a little girl. I went to church with my family. I even asked Jesus to live in my heart when I was about six-years-old." She covered her face with her good hand. Tears spilled through her fingers. "I knew. I knew all along what I was doing was wrong, but I did it anyway. Because I loved Al, and I believed he loved me. And then one day, I'd done so many awful things that I figured it didn't matter anymore what I did. It was too late."

"Oh, sugar, God loves you." Sarah's voice trembled with emotion. "He's ready to forgive you and bless you, just like the father of the prodigal son. That young man went off on his own and did so many things he was ashamed of that he didn't think he was worthy to be called his father's son anymore, but his father still loved him just as much as the day he left home."

Could it be true? Did God still want her for His daughter?

Sarah picked up the Bible and opened it up, then handed it back to Carly. The pages were open to Luke, chapter fifteen. "When you finish reading about the homecoming of the prodigal, look up Romans 3:23, then read chapters seven and eight. Pay particular attention to chapter seven. It tells about the struggles Christians go through trying to do what's right. Then chapter eight explains how God does it all for us as long as our heart is right. God will not let anything separate us from His love."

Carly smiled, though she doubted it was all as simple as Sarah made it sound. "I was wondering where I should be reading," Carly said, knowing she'd never remember all of Sarah's suggestions. "Thank you."

The dear woman grasped Carly's hand. "I can stay home from church if you want me to, and we can read together. That way if you have any questions, I'll be right here."

Once a teacher, always a teacher. "That's all right. You go on. If I have any questions, I can ask you over breakfast tomorrow."

Sarah stood. "Okay, if you're sure. I better get ready, or I'll be late." She grabbed the screen door handle and then pivoted to face Carly again. "I'll be praying for you, dear. It's time for this to be settled so that you can have peace with God."

CHAPTER EIGHT

Joe unlocked his front door and trudged through the house to the kitchen. He filled a tall glass with ice and sweet cider. Then he headed out back with the intention of calling Jared. Joe settled into the lounge chair on the patio, took a fortifying swig of his favorite autumn beverage, and retrieved his cell phone from his back pocket. The leaves were starting to fall from the three lines of trees framing his half-acre lot. He should probably grab the rake from the garage and begin the clean-up.

Right, man, go ahead and rake a few leaves when you should be making that phone call.

Disgusted with himself, Joe jumped up and swiped his cell screen until he came to his contact list. He touched the green phone icon for Jared's number. The phone rang three times.

"Hello."

Opting to get straight to the point, Joe said, "I know where your sister is."

"You do?" Disbelief, relief, and disappointment collided in those six words. "Where is she? How is she?"

"She's in Bemus Point with my Aunt Sarah. And she's okay."

"How long has she been *there*?"

"Since August."

"Two months! And you didn't tell me?"

Praying that Jared would understand, Joe said, "Carly didn't want you to know. She wasn't ready."

Joe heard something smash at the other end of the call.

"Ready for what? To let her family know she wasn't dead in an alley somewhere?"

The contempt in his friend's tone struck home. Joe *knew*. He knew how they felt, and still he'd left them in the dark. Hadn't he wrestled with the same anxiety and fear about his mom? "I'm sorry, man. I was caught in the middle. She wants to see you now, to meet for coffee somewhere."

"When? Where?"

"Tomorrow at Ida's? About four thirty?"

"Five o'clock would be better for me."

"We'll be there." A blue jay screeched a reprimand from a nearby tree.

"We? You're coming?"

"Carly can't drive right now." Joe considered how much he needed to prepare Jared. "Her right arm is in a cast." If he said anymore, he'd end up revealing everything.

"She had an accident?"

"Something like that. Carly will tell you all about it."

After a pause so long Joe almost disconnected their call, his friend said, "Okay. Tomorrow then."

"Jared."

"What is it?"

"Come by yourself. Carly isn't ready to see your folks yet."

*

Carly reread the precious words that told the story of the prodigal son's reconciliation with his father. With her napkin, she dabbed at the tears tracking down her cheeks. Her dad would welcome her with open arms, if she could only confront her shame and humble herself before him. Like the prodigal son, she didn't feel worthy to be her father's daughter anymore, but her dad didn't feel that way about her. Hadn't he reached out to her every single day as long as she had a phone? Surely, Dad was still waiting for her to come to her senses. But how would her mother and her brother feel? Would they resent Dad's willingness to forgive her for her stupidity and her mistakes?

She shook her head. No. Not mistakes. Sins. She'd sinned against her family and against God. And it was past time for her to make things right.

From just inside the front door, the phone rang, interrupting Carly's thoughts. She looked up from the Bible to see the sun slip below the horizon of the serene lake, then reached for her crutch, and got to her feet. She made her way through the door as the answering machine clicked on, Sarah's greeting urging the caller to leave a message after the beep.

"Carly, if you're there, pick up. It's me, Joe."

Leaning against the wall to stabilize herself, she let go of her crutch and lifted the portable phone from its cradle. "Hi."

"I talked to Jared. He'll meet us tomorrow at five at Ida's Bakery."

That soon? Carly sucked in a breath of air. *God, help me. Give me courage.*

"Honey, are you all right?"

Honey? What was he doing calling her *honey*? "I'm fine. I'll be ready by four."

"If you're sure you're all right."

The concern evident in his tone tugged at her heart. He cared for her. More than he should. He was a man she could trust. Why hadn't she realized that years ago? She'd been blinded by Al's slick charm, that's why. If she didn't stop looking back, she'd never be able to move forward.

"Are you still there?"

"I'm here. Thanks for calling Jared. I was going to call him myself tonight, but I appreciate ... everything you've done for me, Joe."

The awkward silence on the other end of the line made her a little sorry for putting her feelings out there. Something Elise would never have done. Maybe she was changing. Becoming a tiny bit more like the person she once believed she could be.

He cleared his throat. "I wish I could do more."

How could she reply to that? "Thank you."

"Try not to be too nervous, okay?"

That was easy for him to say. He'd never been a disappointment to his family. Or to anyone else for that matter.

"I'm praying for you." Joe paused. "I've always prayed for you."

Carly smiled. "Thanks. That means a lot."

They said their goodnights, and she hung up the phone feeling a spark of hope igniting the embers of her childhood faith. God could help her to make peace with her family. As soon as she made peace with Him. And with herself. She wasn't sure which would be the hardest.

Fighting lightheadedness, she grabbed her crutch. A glance at the living room clock confirmed her suspicion. She'd let the whole evening go by without eating. Not surprising, since she wasn't that hungry. She made herself a peanut butter and banana sandwich, quickly ate it with a glass of milk, and then headed outside to collect the tray and the dishes. She carried each item one at time, held between her body and the cast on her right arm. It was awkward and even a little risky, but she took her time. She couldn't leave everything outside for Sarah to clean up. Four trips back and forth and the front porch looked presentable. Last night's windstorm had blown leaves up onto the porch. Small colorful piles cluttered up two corners. If only she could manage a broom, Carly could tidy up for Sarah. If there were any light left, she could take a picture. The composition was perfect, but she'd struggle trying to hold her camera with one hand anyway.

Restricted mobility grated on Carly's independent nature, but her next doctor's appointment wasn't for two more weeks. She wanted both casts off, but that wasn't going to happen. If Dr. Mallory would at least take the cast off her arm, Carly would be able to manage much better. Maybe she could also graduate from a cast to a boot, depending on what the x-rays of her ankle showed. She definitely didn't want to deal with walking through the snow with a cast or even a boot. Sarah said the *Farmer's Almanac* predicted snow by Thanksgiving. That was still almost two months away. Surely, Carly would be fully recovered by then. Physically anyway. Her emotional healing could take much longer.

She sighed. She was so tired. Deciding to go to bed early, she poured herself a mug of milk and put it in the microwave to heat. Warm milk with nutmeg always helped her to sleep more soundly, in spite of how difficult finding a comfortable position with two casts could be.

She sat at the kitchen table and waited for the microwave to beep. Sarah had left a Bible open to Romans, chapter seven. Always the teacher, the dear lady had underlined verses 18 through 25. Carly started reading about how a person struggled to do the right thing but ended up doing the wrong thing.

She could relate to that. How many times had she known in her heart the right thing to do but lacked the courage to make the right choice? Countless times.

But if Carly could go back only once and change one decision, she would have never set foot in that dreadful clinic.

Don't think about that now.

She read to the end of the chapter and started the eighth.

"'There is therefore now no condemnation to them which are in Christ Jesus,'—*how is that possible? I feel so condemned, and that's what I've earned*—'who walk not after the flesh, but after the Spirit.'"

Carly closed her eyes and rested her head on her good arm. *Lord, I don't know how to walk after the Spirit. I've done so many horrible things. If I could do it all over, I would. Father, forgive me. My sins are so many, I hate myself. How can You stand to look at me?*

If I hadn't killed my own baby, maybe there would be hope for me …

Who condemns you? Christ died for you. Nothing can separate you from My love.

Where had those thoughts come from? Was God speaking to her heart? She turned her attention to the open Bible before her and continued to read. Every word confirmed what she'd heard in her heart. God still loved her. He would always love her. Tears of relief mingled with tears of sorrow. God forgave her, but how could she ever forgive herself?

Both of her babies were gone. How could she ever make peace with that?

*

Joe awoke the following morning with one thought resonating in his heart and mind. He loved Carly. Not as a friend. But as the woman he wanted to spend the rest of his life with.

But could he really trust her? Would she be loyal to him? Could they face their problems together? Or would she run out on him, thinking only of herself, as his mother had done more times than he could count? The blood pounded in his veins, but Joe resisted the urge to retreat. The need to protect himself had motivated him all those years ago when he should have told Carly how he really felt about her, and that same instinct surged in him now. Now that he had even more reason to doubt her.

Lord, help me remember that Carly is not my mother.

A sudden, sickening revelation surged upward from his gut. If he ran away from Carly, *he* would be exactly like his mother, a coward whose faithfulness evaporated whenever things got tough. He blew out a disgusted breath.

But he was getting ahead of himself. A relationship with Carly wasn't possible right now. They were just friends.

He was lying to himself.

God, I love her. No matter what happens. Even if Carly and I never—

He jumped out of bed and headed to his weight room to work out before taking a shower. He needed the distraction. Today was an arm day. Work on biceps and triceps and forget about Carly. Which didn't exactly turn out as he'd hoped. Strengthening the muscles in his arms only made him think about holding her.

*

Carly's palms were sweating even before she spotted Jared sitting in a booth in the back corner. He was facing the door, but she still saw him first. The moment he noted her arrival, his anxious expression disappeared. He smiled and waved her forward. From behind her, Joe whispered over her shoulder, "I'm right here. If you need me or want to leave or anything ..."

She pivoted to meet Joe's gaze and reached for his hand, which felt warm and strong in her own. "Please, sit with us."

"But your brother wants to talk to you alone. He hasn't seen you since—"

"Please?"

Joe frowned then nodded almost imperceptibly, and the knot in her stomach loosened.

But he released her hand, and she missed the connection.

They made their way through the crowded bakery to the far corner where Jared rose to greet them. His attention moved from the cast on her leg to the one on arm. "What happened to you? Were you in a car accident or something?"

Resisting a wave of shame, Carly said, "Not exactly. Give me a few minutes, and I'll explain everything."

Jared embraced her in a half hug, using so much care she felt like a broken china doll. "I can't believe it's you. You came."

She kissed his cheek, his scruffy whiskers pricking her lips. "You look good, more handsome and taller than I remembered."

"Thanks. I think." He was staring at her casts again, waiting for her to explain.

She gestured to the table behind her. "Would you mind if we sat there instead?"

Joe was already pulling out a chair for her. Having him look out for her was nice, but she shouldn't read anything into it. He had his reasons for the distance he maintained between them, and she was afraid to ask him what they were.

Always the gentleman, Joe grasped her good elbow as she settled into the chair. Jared sat directly across from her, his arms on the table, leaning toward her, his concerned expression comfortingly familiar. How she'd missed her brother! She didn't realize how much until this moment. Joe propped her crutch on one chair and then plopped down in the remaining chair. A server, who turned out to be Ida, and was obviously the owner, bustled over with a pot of coffee, but Carly opted for decaf mint tea. Her nerves were jumpy enough without caffeine. The guys accepted the coffee.

"Are you hungry? Do you want to order a sandwich or something?" Jared's tone revealed his compassion and confusion. "It's almost dinner time. I should have thought of that."

"It's okay. Maybe later. After we talk." She passed her hand over her tea to see how hot it was. The steam burned her palm. Too hot to drink. So much for her attempt to stall a bit. "Do you remember Alan Rutledge?" Stupid question. Of course her brother remembered the guy she'd run off with. "Al and I … were in business together. But we're not anymore."

The sudden unexpected weight of Joe's hand on her knee both soothed and agitated her. It was an odd gesture for a man who wanted to keep his distance, but she couldn't think about his mixed signals now.

"Do you want me to explain?" he asked.

"No, I will." Much as she wanted Joe to come to her rescue and provide a brief objective account of her life with Al, Carly needed to speak for herself. If she couldn't tell her story to her brother, how could she ever tell her parents? "The name of the business was Rutledge Escort Service, and …" Taking a deep breath, she sent a silent prayer for courage heavenward. "I was his most requested escort."

Jared dropped his cup on the table. Coffee sloshed over one teetering side, splattering the white Formica with tan splotches. He stared at her, shock evident in the twitch of his left cheek.

She had to finish. "But I'm not working for him anymore because four weeks ago he beat me so bad I ended up in the hospital."

Anger and pain flashed across her brother's face.

And I lost our baby. Our second baby. The first one I aborted because Al convinced me I didn't have any other choice. Please don't hate me. I hate myself enough for both of us.

Carly resisted the self-condemnation. She'd accepted God's forgiveness. Forgiving herself shouldn't be this hard. "I'm pressing charges." The wounded look on her older brother's face was a twisted knife in her heart. "I don't know what you're thinking. But if you're thinking that any of this is your fault, you're way off base."

He didn't respond. He wasn't even looking at her anymore. Jared glared at Joe as if he were the enemy. "Please tell me that bastard is rotting in jail."

"He's been arrested," Joe said, squeezing Carly's knee, massaging with gentle reassurance. "The district attorney is working out a plea bargain—"

"What?" Carly shoved Joe's hand off her knee. "You didn't tell me that."

Joe turned pleading eyes on her. "I just found out today. I was going to talk to you about it later. There's enough evidence to convict without your testimony."

"So what does that mean? How many years will he get?"

"Five."

Jared leaned on the table and reached for her hand. "Did Al hit you before?"

Her stomach cramped with intestinal spasms. If only she could just get up and walk out, but leaving now would only postpone the inevitable. Needing to collect herself, Carly wound the string around her tea bag and the spoon, squeezing out every drop of tea. Then she brought the cup to her mouth and inhaled the sweet mint before taking a drink. It tasted even better than it smelled. Strange to think of that at this moment. All around them, people were talking, sharing the events of their days as if nothing momentous or life-changing was happening.

A song called "Never Beyond Repair" played softly in the background. She listened to the words. She'd heard the song before on the Christian radio station that Sarah liked. Carly compressed her lips to keep from crying. How did she end up like this, as if she were too broken for even God to fix?

But that couldn't be true. God made her, and Gran always said God didn't make no junk. God wanted to help her. He would help her. He would put her life back together because she was going to give it to Him. Over and over every day, if that's what it would take.

Ida returned to refill Joe's and Jared's coffee cups and asked if she could get them anything else.

"Could you bring us menus?" Carly asked.

"Of course, dear. I'll be back in a jiff."

Joe put his hand over hers on the table. "I thought you weren't hungry."

She sighed. "I changed my mind."

Ida put three menus on the table and a few minutes later came back to take their orders.

Carly could her feel her brother's steady, expectant gaze, but answering his question required revealing details he didn't need to know. She took a slow breath and forced herself to make eye contact with Jared. "If I testify and Al is convicted, he'll get fifteen years. Five for aggravated assault and ten for the wrongful death of a fetus."

The color drained from her brother's face.

She ignored his shock. "He'll get up to fifteen years *if* the jury finds him guilty. The DA would rather not prosecute because if Al accepts the plea bargain, then the DA has a sure admission of guilt without the expense of a trial we might not win."

"And Carly doesn't have to tell her story on the witness stand," Joe added.

"All of these years," Jared said, shaking his head. "I thought you were happy. Carly, I hoped and prayed you were happy. Why didn't you call? Why didn't you tell us you were in trouble? I would have done something, anything to help you. Surely, you know that."

"You couldn't help me. Not until I was ready to give up on Al, to give up on my dreams and see him for who he really is." She glanced from her brother to Joe and back to her brother again. "I couldn't do that … until that day."

The nightmare flashed through her mind in fast forward. Could she really tell them? Did they need to know it all? Maybe not. Especially since it didn't look as if she'd get to tell her story in court.

"What day?" Jared asked, his voice catching. "The day he beat you?"

She nodded, her mind swimming with the onslaught of violent images. "I'd invited Al to my place for breakfast to tell him that I was pregnant. He was furious." She closed her eyes and surrendered to the memory.

Carly sat ramrod straight in a chair opposite Al. Gripping its beveled edge, she hoped her oversized mahogany table would provide protection from his quick temper. "I'm pregnant."

He looked up from his ham and cheese omelet. "So take care of it."

Determined to show no sign of weakness, she held his gaze. "I'm keeping this baby."

Hatred flashed in his eyes. "What!" His features contorted into an evil mask.

She jumped up, trapped between the captain's chair and the table. "It's yours. That last time we were together—"

"I'll kill you," he ground out, leaping up. His chair clattered to the floor. He stumbled over it and lunged for her.

She ran.

Desperate to escape, she raced down the hall and into the living room. Her hand closed around the front door handle. Al grabbed her hair, yanking her backward. A stabbing pain rushed through her scalp.

She twisted around and scratched his face.

His fingers closed viselike around her upper arm until she feared the bone would snap. "Do you think I care whose brat it is? You'll get rid of it. Tomorrow."

"I won't."

Searing pain fired through her pelvis and into her abdomen. He'd slammed his knee between her legs. Once. Twice. Three times, then pushed her away. She crumpled to the floor. He kicked her back, her arms, her legs. She tried to curl into a ball to protect the baby, but Al kept kicking her.

"Stop. Okay. Just stop."

He wrenched her to her feet by her hair. "Okay, you'll do it?"

Insane with pain, she shook her head.

He slammed his fist into her stomach. She stumbled. He shoved her into the coffee table, which broke on impact. A scream erupted from her throat. She slid to the floor like a discarded rag doll. Her cell phone landed inches from her right hand, and she tried to grab it, but Al stomped on the phone, kicked it out of her reach, and punted it into the wall. The sound of it shattering ended her hope of rescue.

"Planning to call 911?" He laughed, then railed on her with a string of vile names, kicking her until she feared she'd pass out from the pain. "Who do you think you are? You're nothing! Nothing but a dumb whore. That kid's not mine."

Her head was spinning. She was dying. He was going to kill her. Slowly, she got up on her hands and knees and crept away from his feet. Frantic, she crawled behind a recliner. "Stop. I'll do whatever you want," she lied.

But he must not have believed her. He picked her up and flung her against the wall. Glass shattered. Blackness closed in around her. *God, help me.*

Joe's hand on her arm brought her back to now. "Carly,

your face is so white. Don't think about it. You don't have to talk about that day."

"Yes, I do."

"You can't even talk to us about what happened. That's why I don't want you to testify."

Her brother reached across the table and covered her trembling hand with his. "I agree. If your testimony isn't needed to send that bastard to jail, then don't do it. Let us help you put this behind you."

Carly didn't want to disappoint either of them, but she didn't see how she could put it behind her if she didn't talk about it to someone. Turning it over and over in her own mind kept bringing her back to the same conclusion.

That some things could never be fixed or undone. That her past choices would always limit her options. No matter how sorry she was. No matter how much she desperately wanted to go back and do so many things differently.

She broke off several pieces of her grilled cheese sandwich and absently stirred them into her tomato soup.

"Carly, are you all right?"

She looked up from her bowl and met Joe's earnest gaze. "No. But I will be. I hope I will be."

"Of course you'll be all right," Jared declared, his tone reminding her of the way he'd always talked to her when she'd come to him with a skinned knee or a broken friendship.

"It's good to see you, Jared. I've missed you. But I'm not your baby sister anymore. That girl died a long time ago."

"What's that supposed to mean?"

She swiped at the tears sliding down her cheeks. "You don't know me anymore. And if I wasn't your sister, I'm not the kind of girl you'd want to know."

Jared got out of his seat and leaning over her, pulled her into a hug. "You're my sister. I've always loved you, and I always will love you. Nothing you've done can change that."

She whispered against his neck, "I wouldn't be so sure about that."

Jared kissed her cheek and then leaned back to study her face, but she'd said enough for one night.

"I think it's time for us to go," Joe said. "Ida, can we have the check please?"

The owner approached their table. "Sure, honey. Got it right here."

Joe took two twenties out of his wallet and slipped them under his saucer, but Jared handed one back to him. "We're splitting the check."

Overcome with exhaustion, Carly didn't care who paid for their meal.

Jared took two tens and a business card out his wallet. He placed the bills under the plate and pressed the card into her hand. "Can I call you tomorrow?" Uncertainty laced his usually confident tone. "Can I have your number?"

Fighting an irrational need to retreat behind an illusion of confidence that was getting harder and harder to maintain, Carly scrawled the number for Sarah's landline on a napkin. Maybe he wouldn't be able to read it. Then she'd never have to face her parents' disappointment.

CHAPTER NINE

Joe didn't know what to say to Carly. The meeting with her brother had gone as well as could be expected, but she looked completely rung out. When she nearly stumbled over the curb, Joe was tempted to pick her up and carry her to his truck, but she wouldn't appreciate that gesture. Not right now. She'd made herself as vulnerable as she could stand at this moment. He stayed close beside her, ready to catch her should she start to fall. Jared had parked on the other side of the parking lot. He turned to wave and called out, "I'll call you tomorrow, sis."

When Carly didn't acknowledge her brother, Joe was tempted to speak for her, but he only said, "Goodnight."

At his truck, Joe held her door and watched over her as she settled into the passenger seat. He took her crutch and laid it across the backseat of the extended cab.

"You're sure you're all right?"

"I don't know." Her voice sounded thin, childlike. "It was harder than I thought it would be."

Overwhelmed by the need to hug her, he held back. "New beginnings often are, honey. But you did the right thing. I'm proud of you, of your courage and integrity."

Her face paled whiter than before. He shouldn't have used the word integrity. She didn't think she had any. That was what did it, what made her look even more shell-shocked than the day he found her in the ICU.

Lord, we have a long way to go, haven't we?

God was silent.

Joe wrestled with his need for control, then letting out a breath he hadn't even realized he was holding, he consciously and deliberately released Carly into God's care. How many times would he need to fight this same battle in the coming days, maybe even months? Was he up for this? His faith hadn't been strong enough to bring his mother home. Could he hang in there for Carly? And for whatever the Lord might have for them?

She touched his arm, the light pressure of her fingers fanning his longing. "What's wrong?"

Reeled in by the vulnerability in her tone, Joe leaned into the car and brushed his lips over her cheek. Her sharp intake of breath made him second-guess his impulse. Could such an innocent kiss forge an unbreakable bond between them? A bond neither one of them was ready for. A bond he'd give almost anything to forge. He tore his gaze away from her mouth and looked directly into her startled eyes. "Nothing's wrong. I just got distracted for a minute."

An amused expression settled on her lovely features. She didn't buy his excuse. Police officers shouldn't let themselves get distracted. She knew that. But did she realize that she was the biggest distraction in his life? Judging by her response to his kiss, the distraction was mutual.

*

Joe and Harris left the crowded courtroom together. They'd testified against a mid-level dealer of heroin and fentanyl. The DA had enough evidence for a conviction, but his staff was still trying to bargain with Slade in the hopes of nabbing his supplier, a man known only as The Shadow.

As Joe and Harris exited the Erie County Courthouse, his partner said, "Days like this remind me why I wanted to be a cop."

"You're right about that." Slade marketed to middle-schoolers. The dirt-bag was known on the streets for his "hook'em when they're young" philosophy.

For a second, Joe flashed back. Meeting up with Slade in an abandoned building in Baghdad would give Joe great pleasure. His trigger finger twitched. Once. Twice. Eliminating terrorists was essential, especially for the safety of children. And Buffalo's children were under siege.

A check in his spirit brought him up short. Five years stateside and his military instincts still kicked in sometimes, but this was a different kind of war. Kill or be killed wasn't his mode of operation anymore. He was a good cop. But more than that he trusted God to deal with the likes of Slade and The Shadow. Redemption or condemnation was their choice, not Joe's to dictate. Still, he'd like to see them both in prison.

"I'll drive." Harris pushed past Joe and reached for the driver's door. "You're a million miles away."

Joe shrugged. "More like six thousand."

At Harris's astute appraisal, Joe added, "Just thinking about how tempting it would have been to deal with a man like Slade the Army way."

"Slade didn't have a gun on him when we apprehended him," Harris said, stating the obvious, which apparently the older man felt needed to be said anyway.

"I know you're right" Joe replied. "I just get so angry thinking about all the kids who are dying because of scum like Slade."

Harris shifted in his seat and faced Joe with a look of raw pain. His partner's twelve-year-old nephew had been killed three years ago in a drive-by shooting on the West side. Tyrell hadn't been involved with drugs. He'd been skateboarding with a friend.

"Markus, I'm sorry, man. That was a stupid thing to say.

I know you know."

"Forget it." His partner started the engine and eased out into traffic on Delaware Avenue.

Five minutes of awkward silence passed while Joe examined his state-of-mind. He couldn't escape the truth—he was relying on his own strength and neglecting the resources available to him as a child of God. The situation with Carly had pushed Joe past his comfort zone, and he'd been focusing on the storm rather than the One who waited to calm the rough seas raging in Joe's heart. He hated to admit it, but he'd neglected his personal devotions, and his current prayer life resembled the brevity of a text message.

And now his partner had paid the price for Joe's neglect.

His carelessness was completely reprehensible. On so many levels.

"I haven't been at my best these past few weeks," Joe began.

The look on his partner's face declared, that's an understatement, but he didn't say a word.

"This thing with Carly has twisted me up in knots, racked my spiritual foundation, catapulted me out of my comfort zone, made me question who I am ..."

"Wow," Harris guffawed. "That clears everything up."

Joe scowled and reined in his irritation. "Didn't you hear me say that all I have is questions?"

"Yeah. And I have the answer."

Joe stared his friend down.

"But you aren't ready to hear it."

This conversation wasn't turning out as Joe planned. He was supposed to be apologizing and reassuring his partner that he had the man's back. "But you're going to tell me anyway."

"No, I'm not," Harris replied with the patience of a man

who'd mentored many younger cops and two grown sons.

"Why not?"

"Because you already know the answer."

He did. "Okay. In the meantime, I'll do a better job of not letting my personal life affect my work."

Harris smiled—no teeth just a slight turning up of the corners of his mouth. "Good enough. But for the record, you're too hard on yourself. Being a little off in a down moment doesn't make you a bad partner."

Joe nodded, relieved but disturbed at the same time. Was he too judgmental? Too harsh with himself? With Carly? With his mother?

It was too late to do anything about his attitude toward his mom. He'd forgiven her, but not until after she'd died. He still kicked himself now and again for not saying the words to her while she was still alive. On that last day, she'd pleaded tearfully for his forgiveness, but he hadn't been able to give it. He'd been a cocky kid who judged everything in black and white and didn't have a clue how grace and mercy should operate.

He was a grown man now, and he was still figuring it out. And it was past time to get this part of his walk with Christ right. For his own sake. And for Carly's.

*

Carly struggled to rouse herself, to escape the nightmare. She sat up against the headboard, gasping and sobbing, her body racked with grief. *Oh, God.*

She hugged her good arm over her ribcage. She closed her eyes and prayed.

God, I didn't know. I didn't understand. I thought I was just making a choice that would make Al happy. Doing the only thing that made sense given everything else going on in my life.

It was ludicrous to think a prostitute could be a good

mother. And that's who I was—a high-priced call girl. No child deserves a whore for a mother. He or she would be better off not being born at all, right? Stupid. Blind fool. How could I have been so blind to kill my own baby? To let it be sucked from my body like unwanted garbage.

I … hate … myself. Lying on the cold steel table with her feet in the stirrups, Carly shivered. She tried to block out the whirr of the suction machine that would end her pregnancy in a moment. Her knees shook violently, and she bit down on her lip to keep from crying out, No, don't do it. *This isn't what I want. I want to hold my baby. Watch her grow up. Teach her how to live a good life.*

What a joke? She couldn't teach her daughter anything. Nothing Carly knew was worth passing on to her baby girl. And if her child turned out to be a boy, that would be worse. He would hate her. He'd be ashamed to introduce her as his mother. She couldn't do that to her son. Or to her daughter.

The walls of her life were closing in on her. She was trapped, and this was the only way out. But she didn't want to do it. She just didn't have any other choice. Al didn't believe the baby was his, and even if he did, it wouldn't matter. He'd made that much perfectly clear. "Having a baby now would ruin all of our plans," he'd said. "Just hang in there with me a little longer, and I'll give you everything you ever wanted." The memory of his caress on her cheek stung even now, four days later.

But she was used to being violated, conceding not only to Al but to the others, the ones who lined her pockets but stripped her soul. Her knees continued to shake, though she willed her legs to be still. She swiped at the tears trickling from the corners of her eyes.

"Are you crying?" the nurse asked, her tone razor-sharp, critical, and defensive.

The doctor moved into Carly's range of vision. His features contorted with anger. "If you don't get ahold of yourself, I'm not doing the abortion. You'll have to have it done at a hospital."

Panic exploded in her brain. Al would be furious. She had to do this. She could do this. Carly swallowed her fear, steeled her nerves, and commanded her legs to stop trembling. "I … I'll be all right. Just do it. Fast."

The intrusive, cold instruments penetrated her body, followed by the steady, much louder whirr of the machine. Her abdomen clenched in pain as tears slid down her face and puddled in her ears.

"It's over," the nurse said. "As soon as you're ready, you can get up and head into the recovery room across the hall. Someone will bring you a glass of orange juice, and then we want you to lie down for at least twenty minutes before you get dressed and leave the clinic."

Carly dragged her mind back to the present.

I don't want to think about this anymore, but I can't stop thinking about it.

God, help me. I feel as if I'm losing my mind. I don't deserve Your forgiveness. Everyone would have been better off if Al had killed me. Then no one, not Joe or Jared or my parents, no one would have had to deal with the truth, the ugly, unchangeable truth about me.

Murderer. Whore. Liar. You deserve to go to hell.

That's true. I deserve to go to hell.

She raised her arms, tried to cover her ears with her hands, but succeeded only with her good arm. Stupid cast. Stupid woman. She should have left Al years ago. No. She should've never run off with him in the first place.

But it was too late. Regrets. Remorse. Shame. Self-hatred. None of it changed the facts.

Seeing Jared had been a mistake. A selfish choice. He would have been better off believing she was dead. If only Carly had never run into Joe. Then she could have disappeared, moved to another state, changed her name, and started over somewhere else where she could pretend to be someone else. Maybe then she'd have been able to forget. Sometime. Years and miles down the road.

Her mind was spiraling into an abyss of despair. It would snap if she didn't turn off her thoughts. Now. She struggled to sit up in her bed and swung her legs over the edge. *Take a shower. Get dressed. Eat breakfast. Do normal. Be normal.*

"I am not crazy," she said aloud. Saying it out loud might make it true. Hopefully.

She reached for her crutch and started to stand. "I am forgiven."

The telephone beside her bed rang. She flinched, sank back down onto the rumpled bed.

Who could be calling so early? A glance at the clock reset that thought. It was not early. It was 10:35. Bracing herself, she picked up the phone. "Hello?"

"Hi, sis."

"Jared. I—"

"I just wanted to tell you I love you."

She paused, prayed, took a few quiet breaths.

"I said, I love you. Didn't you hear me?"

"I heard you. But you shouldn't—"

"Shouldn't what?"

"Love me. I'm a terrible sister and a worse daughter. After sleeping on it, I realize yesterday was a horrible mistake. Please don't call me again."

"Why are you talking like this? Carly, I love you. Mom and Dad love you. They were so relieved when I told them I'd found you—"

"You *told* them?" *Oh, God. I can't do this. I can't face them.* Her breathing quickened, and her heart thundered in her chest.

"They want to see you. Can I set something up?"

A wave of nausea blasted every thought from her head. "I can't talk about this right now. Call me tomorrow, Jared. Or ... next week. Yeah, next week would be better."

She hung up the phone before he could answer. She'd told him to call her next week. Why had she done that? She needed to cut them loose, not draw them into her mess.

A plan started to form in her mind. As soon as she could get these casts off, she'd leave Bemus Point. Go somewhere they'd never find her. It didn't really matter where.

Her conscience pricked her. Sarah deserved better than waking some morning to find Carly gone. But it couldn't be helped. One bad apple spread rot through the whole basket. She wouldn't let her sins spoil their lives. She could do that much good at least.

*

The smell of pot roast simmering in the oven should have peaked her appetite, but Carly's stomach churned. Why had Sarah invited the *pastor* to dinner? Did she suspect his interest in Carly went beyond his pastoral responsibilities? Dang it all. That woman was a menace as a matchmaker. First, Joe and now Pastor Ryan. Neither man was a good fit for Carly. Why couldn't Sarah see that? Both men needed a woman with a spotless reputation.

A bitter laugh erupted from Carly's throat. She had a reputation, all right. A reputation that would start the church board looking for a new pastor if Ryan Edgar showed the slightest romantic interest in a former call girl.

A former call girl. That sounded good. That was an improvement. For her anyway.

Not the best, but it was a first step toward a different life, one that she wouldn't have to be ashamed of. If only she could figure out how to support herself doing something she could tell her grandchildren about someday. Could she really make a living taking pictures? Digital photography leveled out the playing field, didn't it? Photography was more of a business and less of an art than it had been a generation before. Would the new technology make the field more or less competitive?

Her mom would urge her to pursue two careers. Always have a plan B in case plan A didn't work out.

Carly shook her head. The very idea of going to college after all of these years made her palms sweat. She'd be doing good to prepare for one career, especially since she would need to work fulltime as well. But doing what? Tempted to whine about how hard life was, Carly shrugged instead. It was her own fault. Was she woman enough to accept the consequences of her choices and choose a new path?

Three sharp raps at the front door penetrated her musings.

"Carly," Sarah shouted from the kitchen. "Can you get the door please? I'm elbow deep in flour."

Carly sighed. He was a man after all. How hard could it be to make casual conversation with him over one of Sarah's delicious dinners?

Three more insistent knocks suggested their guest's eagerness for a home-cooked meal.

"Coming!" she yelled, hoping she didn't wouldn't sound as irritable to Sarah as she did to herself.

Carly grabbed her cane instead of the crutch and thrust her good leg in the direction of the front entrance. Three steps, four more to the door. But her toe caught on the doormat at the exact moment Pastor Ryan stepped inside. Falling forward, she plunged into his arms, and he caught her against his rock-hard chest. His arms circled her waist, interrupting her certain slide to the hardwood floor. She grunted in pain as her good ankle turned in an unnatural twist. Tears pooled in her eyes.

"Are you all right?"

Mortified, she lifted her head from his chest and the pounding of his heart beneath her right ear. Their gazes met. His chiseled, flushed face revealed a mix of embarrassment and heroic pride, and his brown eyes sparkled with boyish mischief.

Dang! He *was* interested in her. And he was handsome, as good-looking as any of those snooty executive types she'd escorted around the Niagara Frontier.

"I'm fine. If you'll just help me over to the back of the couch, I can steady myself."

Ryan smiled sheepishly, released one arm from her midsection, and slid it under her thighs. Before she could protest, he'd deposited her onto the couch.

For the second time in a week, a man had lifted her into his arms and carried her with no more effort than it would take her to pick up a toddler. She was tired of playing damsel in distress to their knight-in-shining armor. "You didn't have to do that," she spouted, swiping tears from her cheeks and from under her chin.

"Why are you mad at me?" He plopped down at the opposite end of the short couch and sat sideways to look at her. "It seemed like the best plan at the time."

"I do not need to be rescued!"

Handing her a tissue, he grinned, two delightful dimples appearing at the corners of his mouth. "You don't? I'm pretty sure you'd have ended up in the emergency room with x-rays and a new cast if I hadn't caught you."

She glared at him. "I'm talking about you picking me up

as if I were a child.”

"Trust me, I do not think of you as a child." His brown eyes deepened to a shade of dark chocolate, warm and inviting.

She shivered, her body awakening to the desire apparent in his steady gaze riveted on her mouth. Hot shame flamed up her neck to her face. With lightning speed, she dropped her gaze for a few seconds, quickly recovering her composure. He was no different than any other man. She could handle him easily, squelch his interest in her with a swift cool reply. Couldn't she?

His hand on her arm sent warm electricity through her. "Carly, I'm sorry. This evening isn't starting out the way I'd planned."

She shifted to face him. The tenderness in his eyes shook her even more than the chemistry sparking between them.

"Let's start over, okay?" He held out his hand for her to shake. "I've been looking forward to having dinner with you. And with Sarah, of course."

Carly grasped his hand, and with that brief contact something was settled between them.

He did not see her as she saw herself. In his eyes, she was perfectly suitable, a woman he looked forward to getting to know. A woman whose past was forgiven.

Would he still feel that way if he knew her whole story?

"Dinner's ready." Sarah smiled at both Carly and Ryan, but Carly didn't miss the startled expression in the older woman's hazel eyes. Had she seen them shaking hands? What if she had? There was absolutely nothing wrong with the two adults shaking hands. It was a completely impersonal gesture.

Under normal circumstances.

But these were not normal circumstances. Carly flushed, averted her face, reached for her cane, and started to stand. She swallowed hard at the pain in her ankle. Maybe she did need an x-ray. Ryan's hand on her elbow steadied her, but having him in her personal space did not. "I got this."

His warm breath tickled her ear. "Don't be so stubborn," he whispered. "Let me help you."

She looked up into his warm chocolate eyes. "Sarah will get the wrong idea."

"She's gone back to the kitchen."

Carly harrumphed. "Wonderful. She probably thinks something was going on between us."

"Something was."

The determined set of his mouth flustered her, and men did not fluster her. *Get a grip, girlfriend. He's just a man. And men are all alike.*

"Not that I'm aware of," she retorted.

"If that's what you want to tell yourself."

She would not be backed into a corner by any man ever again. "The way I see it you and I are both Sarah's guests. Nothing more."

He frowned, perplexed and disappointed.

Her breath caught, and her heart beat erratically. She'd said something similar to Joe and seen the same hurt look in his eyes. Both men clearly wanted something from her. Did she actually have two good men interested in pursuing a relationship with her? Both were decent guys, attractive, and fun.

Oh, Lord, no. I can't be attracted to them both. My life is messed up enough without that.

"Joe and I were next door neighbors. He was my brother's best friend."

"I think I'd heard that. I'm not sure what that has to do with you and me."

Carly studied Ryan. He couldn't hide the slight pink cast in his cheeks. Now who was lying?

"Carly, are you all right?" Sarah called. "Let Ryan help you to the table. Dinner's getting cold."

Ryan grinned. "We're coming." He bent to pick her up again, but she backed away.

"Don't even think about it."

"Fine." His grin widened, and he wiggled his eyebrows in a comic come-on. "I promise not to carry you, if you promise to have dinner with me on Friday night."

Undecided, she hesitated. He moved into her space and slipped his arms behind her legs.

She thrust her good elbow into his chest, but their close proximity made that move completely ineffective. "Okay. I'll go out with you. Under one condition."

His warm, minty breath caressed her cheek. "What's that?"

"We go out as friends to … to get to know each other better."

Shifting to stand beside her injured leg, he said, "Now we're on the same page." He smiled down at her. "Put your arm around my shoulder, and lean on me. I'll never let you fall. No matter what."

CHAPTER TEN

After Ryan left, Carly parked herself in a chaise lounge chair on the front porch, her favorite spot. The temperature had dropped to below 50 degrees, and the air blowing across Chautauqua Lake felt even colder. Curled up in a cozy blanket, she drank in the star-studded sky. Not a cloud obscured twinkling lights or the moon, which was not quite full. The tranquil view held the promise of a beautiful tomorrow.

But peace eluded her.

The evening had passed without any further startling developments, and if it hadn't been for his whispered promise to call her tomorrow, she could almost pretend she'd imagined Ryan's flirting with her as if he'd planned all along to invite her to dinner. But her falling in his arms had provided him with the perfect opportunity to declare his intentions. Her heart skipped a beat at the memory of his words. "I'll never let you fall. No matter what."

She was used to men making promises they never intended to keep, though Ryan wasn't like the men she'd known. Why had she agreed to have dinner with him? Why start something that could only end badly? Just like every other real relationship she'd tried to have. Eventually, he would need to know the truth about her, and the fact that God had forgiven her wouldn't be enough to erase the scandal her past would cast on his life. Ryan may see her as a woman whose past was forgiven, but others might not be so generous.

A preacher, more than any other man, needed a virtuous woman by his side. One with a history of making good choices. Not a former call girl whose very existence could besmirch his reputation.

And then there was Joe.

How would he feel about her going out with the pastor?

Idiotic question. Joe would be hurt.

At this point, they were just friends, but she suspected that wasn't the way he wanted it. She'd been pushing him away since the day she'd tried to hide in the shrubbery to keep from running into him. Dear sweet Joe. From the moment he'd found her in I.C.U., he'd been there for her, as much as she'd let him. He was reliable and comfortable to be with. She could be herself, even to the point of being ornery and miserable, and Joe never changed. He was as faithful as the sun rising. She could depend on him for practically anything at all, and he wouldn't be the least put out with her requests. He knew everything about her, and still he loved her. But was he *in* love with her? Hopefully not.

Being with Ryan was different. Exciting and liberating. Because he knew next to nothing about her, Carly could convince herself that she could be anyone she wanted to be. She could be someone new. Someone better. Someone she could actually live with.

So, which was it? Could she be someone new, a new creature in Christ, or would her past dog her forever?

Joe and Ryan. How had she let this happen? She who kept a rigid rein on her feelings when it came to men.

She'd even held herself back from Al, after the abortion, when she'd finally caught a glimpse of the evil he was capable of. Why had she stayed with him? He didn't want her. He only wanted what she could do for him. And she had made him a lot of money, more than enough to start their life together, the promised one that was always just around the next corner.

She cursed the day they met, cursed herself for running off with him, for agreeing to work as an escort. Cursed herself for causing the death of both of their babies. She deserved to go to hell, but for some inexplicable reason she couldn't begin to fathom, Jesus died for her. Jesus loved her, loved her when she was utterly unlovable and undeserving. Jesus loved her when she was desperate to be loved, in spite of everything she'd done.

But she couldn't undo the past.

She would do better in the future. She had to. And that meant making wise choices in the present. Every decision made today rippled its way into tomorrow.

Scarred with regrets, she was tired of being ashamed of who she was.

Something about both Joe and Ryan had caused her to drop her guard. Neither man was a taker. That was it. Their giving nature drew her like a wounded deer to water.

Friendship with both men was possible, reasonable, and totally within her comfort zone, wasn't it? The old Carly, or more accurately Elise, would've had no trouble pursuing a close relationship with two men at the same time. But Elise didn't exist anymore. Since Carly had cried out for God's help and forgiveness, she'd sensed her identity shifting a little more each day.

More often than not, she leaned toward swearing off men altogether. She should go back to school, either here in western New York or someplace else where no one knew her, where no one would recognize her face and see Elise.

She should do Ryan a big favor and back out of their date. But she'd have to get up and go into the house to make the call. She missed the convenience and privacy a cell phone provided, but she didn't want to chance any of her former clients tracking her down. At least not until after Al was sentenced. She needed to hide out a bit longer, until she got these annoying casts off.

Besides, she was through making impulsive decisions.

The front door opened, and Sarah leaned outside. "Brr. It's mighty cold out here. Come inside. I made a pot of tea."

That sounded like a command rather than an invitation. Carly didn't mind. Maybe Sarah could help her sort out her feelings. "I'll be right there."

Sarah smiled and retreated to the warmth of the house.

Carly bowed her head, but she had no idea what to ask God to do for her. With a grunt, she pushed herself to a standing position and tossed the blanket over the cast on her arm. The dampness had seeped into her healing bones. With effort, she maneuvered her way back into the living room. Sarah had laid out the tea service on the coffee table, but the woman was nowhere to be seen.

Carly lowered herself to the cozy recliner and waited, hoping her friend would have some good advice.

A moment later, Sarah appeared with a plate of sliced apples and peanut butter. "You must be tired."

Carly was tired. Exhausted was a better word. Her ankle hurt, in spite of the extra pain reliever she'd swallowed after dinner, and she was tempted to hide under the covers and forget about everything. "I've made a horrible mess of my life." She searched Sarah's face for signs of condemnation but found only concern. "And I'm still messing up."

Without a word of disagreement, Sarah poured two cups of fragrant tea and set one near a small plate of apples on the end table where Carly could reach them easily. With a smile, her hostess settled herself on the couch, tucking her legs beneath her denim skirt. "You've changed, dear. You're letting God deal with your heart."

"Am I? I haven't changed. No decent girl would—"

"Would be interested in two men at the same time?"

Carly covered her flaming face with her left hand, tucked her chin to her chest, and let her hair fall like a veil to hide her. Liking two men at the same time meant she was still a tramp, didn't it?

Sarah knelt beside her and peered into her face, easing her fingers aside. Their eyes met in a moment of understanding.

"You judge yourself too harshly," she whispered, tenderly lifting Carly's long hair back over her shoulder.

Resisting the offered comfort, Carly averted her face from Sarah's gentle touch. "I don't judge myself harshly enough. If you only knew half the things I've done ..."

"Right now the only thing you're doing that I'm not too happy with is making me kneel on the floor to talk to you. These old knees don't want to help me back up like they used to."

Startled, Carly gathered her composure and faced her friend. "I'm sorry. I didn't think."

The sparkle in Sarah's eyes brought a smile of relief to Carly's face. She dunked an apple slice in peanut butter and took a bite. The apple was sweet, but it didn't sweeten her mood. "Did you know Ryan was interested in me?"

"So he's Ryan now instead of Pastor Ryan." Sarah wasn't smiling.

Carly felt the impropriety of her address, but the man's identity had shifted in her mind. Ryan was a man with a profession, but the profession wasn't the whole of the man. She knew that. Warmth suffused her cheeks. Lord, have mercy. Would she never be free of all her knowledge?

"I'm not criticizing you, dear. Pastor Ryan is an attractive, deeply compassionate man. You'd have to be blind not to notice him. And he'd have to be blind not to notice you."

"You knew he was interested in me?"

"I had my suspicions, but I figured I'd speed up the process by asking him to dinner."

Carly dropped a half-eaten apple slice into the napkin on her lap. "Why would you do that? I thought you liked Joe."

"I do. More than that. We're family. His grandmother and I were sisters. Marjorie was the oldest, and I was the baby, born five years after Lorraine. When Joe was a kid, he called me Aunt Sarah, but after he graduated from high school, we agreed he should drop the aunt." Sarah took a bite of her peanut butter covered apple slice and frowned. "This isn't nearly as good as caramel dip."

"Maybe not, but I can always use the extra protein."

"And I could use a few less calories." Sarah laughed then sobered immediately. Her hazel gaze revealed her concern. "Joe's always been a slow mover. Indecisive. Always waiting for somebody else to make the first move. In this case, you."

Carly swallowed a gulp of tea down the wrong way, which started a fit of coughing. This was worse than she'd imagined.

"Are you all right, dear?" Sarah asked, patting Carly's back.

"Yes. No. I'm not all right. I feel even crummier than I did before."

"Because I confirmed what you already knew?"

Carly shook her head. Sarah was supposed to say something to smooth out this complicated mess. "I told Ryan I'd go out to dinner with him this Friday."

"I'm not surprised. Ryan is exactly the opposite of Joe."

Tears welled in Carly's eyes. "Then why did you ... make it so easy for Ryan?"

Sarah sighed. "I probably shouldn't have meddled, but Ryan would've asked you out eventually. Now, Joe will have to make up his mind about you sooner rather than later."

Carly's throat clenched with her efforts to keep from crying. Joe cared for her. From the day they'd moved next door, he'd treated her like a little sister. Except on the night of her prom. But he was still her older brother's best friend. Which meant he'd been off-limits. Back then. But what about now? Now, Joe was her friend, too. Could they be more than friends? Should they?

"Did he ever talk to you about me, years ago? No, don't answer that. I can see by the look on your face he did. Oh, Sarah, why does life have to be so complicated? I like them both."

"That's just it, honey. You *like* both men. What you need to figure out is whether you can love either of them. And while you're contemplating, remember, God has good plans for all three of you."

"I want to believe that, Sarah. I really do. But somebody's going to get hurt. Maybe it'd be better if I just left."

Sarah shook her head. "Running away isn't the answer. Running away has hurt you enough for a lifetime. And you'll hurt Joe, too, if you run now."

"I never meant to hurt him." She stared out the picture window into the star-studded night, searching for answers. "When I was still in high school, we had one date. It was my prom, actually, and my brother asked Joe to take me. I never even guessed it meant anything to him until I saw him in the hospital, leaning over my bed with his heart in his eyes, begging me to tell him who'd beat me up."

Sarah added more tea to both their cups. "Honey, Joe needs to stop denying his feelings for you. If you're not the one for him, he'll meet someone else someday, but he's never looked because it's always been you."

When had Joe stopped seeing her as another sister? Why

hadn't she noticed back then that his feelings had changed? If she had, she might not have gone out with Al at all. Carly pulled a tissue from the box on the end table, wiped her tears, and blew her nose. "What should I do?"

"Give them both a chance to win your heart."

Win her heart? Sarah made it sound as if Carly's heart was worth winning. Could it be true? Did God have a happily-ever-after, loving marriage in mind for her? She certainly didn't expect a good man to want her. Because a good man expected more than she had to offer.

"Go out with them both. Make sure they each know that you're seeing the other."

"But Joe hasn't asked me."

Sarah smiled, satisfaction twinkling in her eyes. "He will. As soon as he hears about your date with Ryan."

*

Maureen was dressed in a baggy t-shirt splotched with cherry-colored, Gwen-sized handprints. His sister's brown hair was slipping out of her ponytail, and the purple shadows under her eyes testified to her tiring day. "Thanks for coming over, Joe." She pulled the door open wide for him to enter the toy-strewn living room. "When Bob called to say he had to work late, I had a meltdown."

"*You* threw these toys all over?"

The scowl on his sister's face told him his joke fell flat. Before he could ask what was really bothering her, Derrick, Tara, Steve, and Susie ran in for a group tackle.

To deflect his nieces and nephews, Joe reached out for baby Gwen, and she catapulted herself into his arms. "Unky Joe."

He planted a kiss on the top of her curly head and turned his attention to his sister. "Did you have your meltdown while you were on the phone with your husband? Or after?"

"After. In the bathroom. But Derrick heard me crying. He texted you, asking you to get over here quick."

"I sure did." Derrick smiled, clearly proud of his intervention. "Dad says when he's gone, I'm the man of the house, and I gotta look out for Mom cuz sometimes we drive her crazy."

Maureen shot her child a look that was more dubious than grateful. "Go play with your brother and sisters. I need to talk to Uncle Joe in private."

Her emphasis on the word private sent her oldest scurrying to the far corner of the room where Tara and Steve had returned to a video game.

To lighten the mood, Joe whispered in his sister's ear, "I figured the text couldn't be from you. You may be a bossy big sister, but you've mellowed a bit since high school."

She shook her head, shrugged, and released a loud sigh. "Not really. This crew takes every ounce of leadership energy I can muster, and most of the time, it isn't even close to being sufficient. What you think of as mellow is pure exhaustion."

Wasn't Leann still helping out three mornings a week? Their stepmom loved spending time with her grandkids. "Was Leann here today?"

"No. She had an appointment she couldn't change."

His sister's worried tone sent off alarm bells in his head. "Is Dad okay?"

"Dad's fine. She promised me that much, but she refused to tell me anything more."

Maureen bent to pick up an empty yogurt cup and three dirty paper plates from the floor. "Kids, I want this living room spotless in 10 minutes. I'm going to set the timer now." She made eye contact with each of her four older children. "If you finish on time, we'll have pizza and chicken wings for dinner."

"Whoopee, pizza," Susie yelled. "I call the books." Within

seconds, she was scrambling toward the piles of books that littered the floor. The older kids started grabbing stuff willy-nilly, tossing it all into a giant blue bin on wheels that normally belonged in the family room, which was actually a large playroom centrally located between the girls' and boys' bedrooms.

Amazed at the kids' quick response, Joe followed his sister into the kitchen. True to her word, she set the kitchen stove timer for exactly ten minutes. "I made a fresh pot of coffee. Want some?"

"Sure." Gwen scrambled off his lap and toddled into the living room, probably to make her siblings' chore more challenging. "Do you want me to put Gwen in her crib?"

"No, if she sleeps now, she'll be up until nine thirty at least. Steve will keep her busy while the others clean up."

Wow. Family dynamics baffled Joe. Her kids were so different, and Maureen rolled with it all. Usually. Today, something was wrong. She and Bob had had their rough spots, and they still bickered more than Joe thought a married couple should. But he'd kept his concern to himself. Up to this point. "Is everything okay with you and Bob?"

Maureen's startled expression gave Joe no clear leading as to the cause of her distress.

"You're not—"

"Of course not." Maureen glanced down at her pregnant belly and back to Joe, her look declaring he'd lost his mind. Then she set two mugs of coffee on the table with more force than was necessary. Coffee sloshed over the sides of both mugs. "Cream and sugar or chocolate creamer?"

"Whatever. Just sit down and tell me why you're so upset."

After bringing everything to the table, she sank onto the kitchen chair next to him and covered her face with her hands.

This was worse than he imagined. Joe breathed an S.O.S.

prayer, then removed his sister's wet, trembling hands from her tear-splotched face. "What is wrong?"

"I saw someone at the grocery store last night." Tears streamed down Maureen's face. "Oh, God, this can't be happening."

"Maureen, everything is going to be fine. Who did you see?"

She sobbed, choking and gasping for air. "Mom."

Joe shifted away from her, his back ramrod straight against the chair. "That's impossible. Mom died twenty years ago. You saw someone who looks like her."

Maureen blew her nose in a napkin and grabbed a second one to wipe her face. "No. It was her. She recognized me, Joe. She said I look like her. Like she did at my age."

For a nanosecond his mind shut down, then clicked into overdrive. Anger burst behind his eyes. He clenched and unclenched his fists. "Stop talking nonsense. Our mother is dead."

Maureen chewed her lower lip. "That's what she wanted us to think."

Joe leapt from his chair and backed up against the fridge. "Do you know what you're saying? Does Dad know? And Leann? What about Leann? This is going to crush them."

Maureen stood in front of him and placed her hands on his shoulders. He reached for her elbows to extricate himself, but something in his eyes must have frightened her because she let go of him, inching backward, her expression wary.

"No one knows. Not even Bob. I had to tell you first, so we could decide what to do."

As far as Joe was concerned the decision was an easy one. Forget Addie Callahan. If she *was* alive, staying away all these years certainly negated any rights she had as a mother. Or a grandmother. "Forget you saw her. Tell Bob if you have to, but no one else."

Maureen marched into his physical space, again, and leveled him with a look he hadn't seen in decades. "I can't do that. Our mother is alive. She wants to see you. And my kids."

Joe glared back at Maureen. "I have no intention of seeing her. Ever. And you can tell her that for me."

"Tell her yourself!"

"Tell who what, Mom?" Derrick asked, dumping a plastic grocery bag into the trash.

Seeing Maureen's distress, Joe placed one hand on his nephew's shoulder. "It's not important, buddy."

"But you and Mom were yelling at each other."

The boy's perplexed words tugged on Joe's heart. What could he say to smooth this over?

"Are you mad at Mom, Uncle Joe?"

Joe shook his head. "Not really. Brothers and sisters argue sometimes. You know that."

"Yeah, Tara annoys me. Especially when she tries to tell me what to do."

The sister in question bounded into the kitchen. "Mom, the living room's ready for you to check. Order the pizza, please. I'm starved."

"Go work on your bedrooms," Maureen said, her gaze encompassing both children. "I'll come check the living room in two minutes when the timer goes off."

"But you said—"

"Your mother said to clean your bedrooms," Joe ordered.

Maureen shot him a grateful look that changed to frustration the minute the kids disappeared. "Joe, you can't pretend this didn't happen. I saw her. I talked to her. She wants another chance to be a part of our lives."

His brain was going to explode. "I can't talk about this right now." Moving toward the kitchen door, he intended to duck out before he said something he'd regret. "I'm sorry, Maureen. I know this is hard for you, too." He grabbed the door knob and turned it. "I'll call you tomorrow. I promise."

CHAPTER ELEVEN

Joe was in no condition to drive, but he had no choice. He pushed the accelerator a little harder than needed to back out of his sister's driveway.

What was he doing?

Breathe, man. You're 31 years old. She can't hurt you anymore.

Pep talk. Lecture.

Whatever he called it, it didn't work. His feeble attempt to stop his world from reeling only revved his flight mechanism more. He took three deep breaths, checked his mirrors, and turned to look behind his truck before easing out into the quiet suburban street.

He had to focus. Distracted drivers caused as many accidents as impaired drivers.

It couldn't be true. Addie Callahan died in a fire on Christmas Eve twenty years ago.

He'd been eleven, his sister, fourteen. Maureen had taken it hard, weeping in her room for more nights than Joe cared to remember. He hadn't cried a single tear. He'd been glad. And relieved to finally be free of her. His mother had held their family hostage for more than five years, treating their home like a hostel she could return to when her wanderings left her burned out and penniless. She'd been in and out of their lives so many times until just the sound of her voice in the house made Joe feel as if he were drowning in despair. He hated her.

Still.

Oh, God. Forgive me. I thought I forgave her years ago.

This couldn't be happening. Dealing with Carly was challenging enough. But his mother?

Joe pulled into his driveway, shut off the engine, and grabbed his cell phone. The tight feeling in his chest wouldn't let up. "I'm not coming in tonight. I'm taking a personal day."

He never took personal days. Harris would wonder what emergency prevented his perfect attendance partner from reporting for work. Joe scrolled through his contacts until he found the number. "Harris, I'm not coming in tonight."

"Funny joke, man."

"Seriously."

"What happened?" the older man asked, all the amusement gone from his tone.

"My mother's alive."

"Alive? I thought she died when you were a kid."

"Me, too. Harris, can you talk to Matt in Missing Persons and ask him to dig into her past?"

"Sure, man. What's her full name?"

"Adelaide Marie Callahan."

"Do you know her maiden name?"

"It's Stewart."

"S-t-e-w-a-r-t or S-t-u-a-r-t?"

"I'm not sure. Check both."

"All right, man. See you tomorrow."

"Thanks. I owe you."

Making no move to exit the pickup, Joe shifted in the driver's seat. He turned the key and started up the engine, shut it off, and turned it right back on. One face in his mind brought him comfort. Carly's.

He had to see her.

But why? His feelings for her were as mixed up as his feelings for his mother.

Don't think. Just drive. You want to see her. That's enough.

Turning the radio to his favorite jazz station, Joe tried to drive without contemplating the conversation he'd have with Carly. His cell phone rang, and he swiped to see the caller's name. Dad. Ignoring him wasn't an option. With a touch, Joe sent his father the message, "I'm driving," and kept his eyes open for a convenient place to stop. He really needed to get Bluetooth for his truck. A few miles down the road, Joe pulled into a roadside stand advertising pumpkins, dried cornstalks, apples, and fresh-pressed cider. He cracked open his windows to let the cool air calm his nerves and grabbed his phone from the console.

"Hi, Dad."

"Son."

Terse conversation was the norm with his dad.

"Something going on I need to know about?" Joe asked, sounding calmer than he felt.

"Your mom wants to see you."

"I saw Leann—"

"Not Leann. Your mother."

Joe dropped the phone in his lap. Maybe Dad would think their call was disconnected due to poor service.

"Joe! Pick up the phone."

And act like an adult was the unspoken implication. Joe gripped his cell with his sweaty hand. "I heard you. I don't want to see her."

"This isn't about what you want. The four of us are having dinner tomorrow night. Be at your sister's at seven sharp."

"What about the kids? Maureen's not thinking of letting Addie see them, is she?"

"Not tomorrow, no. Bob's taking them all to a movie. Except Gwen. Leann's going to watch her."

So, everyone was in on this ridiculous scheme to set up a

family reunion. What a joke. Would Dad never learn? Addie was no good. She'd been no good as a wife or mother, and she'd be no good as a grandmother. Her promises to change were as reliable as western New York weather.

"I don't see the point, Dad. So she's back. For how long? For a few days before she disappears for another ten or twenty years?"

His father's loud exhale testified to his disgust—not with Addie but with Joe.

"I'm sorry, Dad, but I can't do this again. Not even for you or Maureen."

"Then do it for yourself."

"I don't want or need to rehash the past."

"It's your future I'm concerned with, son."

The soothing sound of giggling children penetrated through Joe's frustration. A textbook family of four was marching toward a blue minivan. The kids each carried a pumpkin almost as big as themselves. Their parents stole a glance at each other, a glance probably filled with the perfect mixture of passion, contentment, and trust.

What was he thinking? They could be on the verge of divorce. But he didn't think so. The man opened the car door for his wife and kissed her. They seemed happy.

"Joe, are you listening? I said I want to hear what your mother has to say. You should, too."

"I'll think about it, Dad. But I'm not making any promises."

Needing to escape, Joe pocketed his phone, exited his car, and moseyed into the open-air stand. A display of mixed dried flower bouquets caught his attention. One in particular contained the perfect blend of purple and orange flowers. Carly liked purple. Joe paid for the bouquet and a pint of cider.

"Nice day for a drive in the country," the cashier said as

she made change for Joe's twenty-dollar bill. "We gotta enjoy these sunny days while we have 'em cuz winter'll be here before we know it."

Joe smiled and thanked the woman whose lined face testified of a life filled with laughter. "Have a nice day, ma'am."

"You, too."

He'd been having a horrible day, but he nodded and walked to his truck with his father's words weighing on his heart. Was it true? Could his anger at his mother mess up his future?

He was being cautious, which was wise considering everything.

Considering, what exactly? His background? Carly's background?

So what if he was lonely and discontented with his life? The same could be said for a lot of people. Carly for one.

Joe laid the flowers on the passenger seat, popped open the cap on the cider, and took a long swig. What a heel he'd been.

Father, if she's the one for me, give me the courage to be the man she needs.

Fifteen minutes later, he was sitting in his truck, the engine idling, with Sarah's cottage in plain view. The old fear rose like bile in his throat and kept him glued to his leather seat.

"It's now or never, man." He cut the engine and picked up the bouquet, the first he'd ever given Carly. The first of many, if he had his way. Denying his interest all those years ago had been stupid. He'd even let her believe the wrist corsage he'd bought to match her prom dress had been her mother's idea. What if he'd kissed her that night? Would she have given Rutledge the time of day? Maybe not. Joe couldn't undo the past, but proclaiming his devotion now if she wasn't ready to take the next step in their friendship could scare her off. Or worse. Away.

If she ran, would he be the reason? Probably not. She would run from her shame and disappointment in herself. She would run from her past, seeing it as an impassable obstacle to a different future.

Had his mother run for similar reasons? Had she been haunted by her failures as a wife and a mother? Did Dad understand what Joe couldn't see? What he refused to see. Maybe.

The welcome sight of Carly stepping out with the aid of her cane onto the front porch banished all thoughts of his mother. Carly's long blonde hair lifted in the strong autumn breeze, and she struggled to gather the curly mass with her good hand. Leaning back against the door didn't provide enough stability to accomplish her goal, given the casts. She must be eager to get them off and carry on with her life. Her tinkling laughter as she surrendered her hair to the wind made him grin. Then she spotted him and lifted her hand to wave.

He was too far away to discern her expression. Was she glad to see him? His heart raced, and Joe picked up his pace. Encouraged by her smile, he mounted the steps, the flowers in his hand an offering. He stopped at arm's length from her, determined to prove his father wrong.

Joe would battle all his demons to become the man Carly deserved. He could do it for her.

Carly's gaze focused on the purple and orange straw flowers, tied with a pale tan bow. "Are those for me?"

The uncertainty in her tone caused a sharp pain in his heart. "Of course they're for you."

She raised her face to him, her eyes glistening with tears.

Before he could frame a thought, he leaned in and kissed her lips. Softly, feather light. As he moved away, a small "oh" escaped her lips. Their gazes locked, and he kissed her again. A proper kiss. The kiss of a man who'd been waiting his whole life to give his heart. And wonder of wonders, she met his passion with equal intensity. But when he ended the kiss, the look in her eyes raised questions he didn't know how to answer. Yet.

"Why did you kiss me?"

She wasn't going to let him off the hook. "Why did you kiss me?" he asked, brushing his hand over her cheek.

She shivered then steeled her features. She wasn't going to reveal her heart or her thoughts until he could convince her he wouldn't hurt her. This new Carly—the one Joe couldn't get out of his dreams—was studying him with a thoroughness that probed his motives, a skill she'd developed in her old life.

But he would have to love all of her. The woman who stood before him didn't match the image of her he'd carried in his heart all of these years, but he was looking forward to getting to know her better, if she'd let him. "I've been waiting a long time to kiss you."

*

Carly wanted to ask him what had stopped him before, but she didn't think either one of them was ready for that conversation, so she reached up and cradled his neck with her good hand, gently pulling him in for another kiss, a sweet, I'm-glad-you-kissed-me kiss. But his mouth claimed hers with a fervor that stole her breath and equilibrium.

When he released her, she laid her cheek against his chest to gather her thoughts. A simple kiss shouldn't affect her so much, she who was a master at controlling intimate encounters. But what else could she have done to let him know she was comfortable in this new phase of their relationship?

But you're not comfortable. Because he won't let you come to him on your terms.

Could she live with his terms? Joe wanted more. More than a kiss. More than her body. He wanted all of her, heart and soul. *God, help me, please. I don't know how to be the woman he needs.*

Gathering her courage, she looked directly into Joe's eyes. He loved her all right. For some people, the eyes truly do mirror the soul. Even though her pulse was racing and her mind was a tumble of possibilities, she had to lighten the mood. "Was it worth the wait?"

He raised his brows in confusion. "Was what worth the wait?"

"The kiss," she teased.

"Definitely." Joe slipped his arm around her waist and led her to the two chaise lounges at the other end of the porch. "My only regret is that I didn't kiss you sooner."

She lowered herself to the chair to stall a moment. She'd been teasing, but his reply was entirely too serious. Revisiting their past interest in each other would take them down a road she wasn't ready to travel. Yet. She smiled up at him. "You mean when you found me hiding in the shrubbery?"

He laughed. "Not exactly."

She allowed him to assist her by lifting her cast-encased leg onto the chair. He knelt down, reached across her lap for the pillow from the other chair, and positioned it under her ankle to elevate her leg. Then he kissed her nose and raised his head. Their eyes met. His troubled his expression unsettled her. Something was wrong. Why hadn't she seen it before, when he first arrived? He was too busy distracting her with kisses, that's why.

She waited until he sat in the other chair, then she pivoted as best as she could to face him. "Something happened today."

"Yep, I kissed you for the first time." He grinned, but his eyes were void of any amusement.

She shook her head, placed her hand on his forearm. "Before that. Something happened before you got here."

He covered her hand with his, brought it to his mouth, kissed her palm, and returned her hand to her lap. But he didn't answer her unspoken question. Wasn't he going to confide in her? He was staring off at the sunset, his mind the proverbial miles away from her. She knew how to meet a man's physical needs, but meeting his emotional needs was outside her realm of experience. She'd learned the hard way that Al had no emotions. At least none that she wanted to know about. And the ones she did know about, she'd done her best to avoid rousing.

Comparing the two men provided no insight. Better to leave the past behind, as much as she could.

Joe had obviously come to her upset about something. But what? "If you aren't going to talk about what's bothering you, then why did you come here?"

The wounded look in his eyes wasn't the reaction she'd hoped for. He leaped to his feet and started toward the porch stairs.

"No fair! You know I can't run after you."

He whirled to face her. "I'm not leaving. I'm pacing."

"You came here to *pace*?" Her frustration sounded insensitive.

He closed the distance between them. "I came here to kiss you."

The echo of so many others saying those same words shamed her. "Is that all? Is that all you think I'm good for? If that's how you see me—"

He kissed her again, his mouth teasing at first, then insistent.

The second he backed away she slapped him hard. "Get out! Leave me alone."

"I'm not leaving. Leaving is your specialty."

His words lacerated her last vestiges of self-respect. "Maybe. But you better go. We've already said things that are going to be hard to forget."

It wouldn't be easy to forget that first kiss, but Carly would try. As soon as she didn't have to look at him.

Joe turned his back to her without a word, and she fought against the sobs lodged in her throat. He couldn't leave soon enough. Then she could cry her eyes out over him and forget this whole night ever happened.

But he stopped at the stairs and sat down on the top step. With his head in hands, he hunched down, his elbows on his knees.

Why didn't he leave? She covered her face with her hand and swiped away her tears. Minutes passed. Twice, she checked the time on her watch and wondered what she should do. She could go inside the house, but that would be rude. The silence between them was becoming awkward. If he wasn't going home, why didn't he say something? Maybe something really was wrong.

Not sure she wanted to be the first to speak, and needing a neutral subject, she whispered, "Thank you for the flowers."

He raised his head and looked over his shoulder. "You deserve flowers. And so much more."

She shook her head. "No, I don't." She realized she was contradicting herself. Moments before she'd implied she'd deserved more, but really she'd expected more of Joe than to turn to her only for physical comfort.

Joe crossed the porch in three strides. He leaned over her and rested his hands on her shoulders until their faces were so close she couldn't miss his red-rimmed eyes. "I'm sorry I hurt you. That comment about leaving being your specialty was uncalled for. And I never would have said it if it hadn't been for ..."

She touched his cheek. "For what? Why won't you tell me what's bothering you?"

A myriad of emotions, hurt, confusion, and anger swept his face. "My mother's still alive."

Oh, God, no wonder he's so messed up. His mother ... alive after all these years?

"How's that possible?" Carly slid over to make space for him next to her on the chaise.

He pulled up a chair beside her instead, determination lighting a fire in his eyes. "I don't know, but I'm going to find out. Maureen and Dad are actually going to meet with her. Can you believe it? They want to hear her explanation."

"You don't want to hear what she has to say?"

"I've heard it all before. You know. You were there. Addie Callahan never means anything she says."

How many times during their childhood had Carly seen her brother's friend trying to hide his tears? Grateful that both of her parents were always there for her, she'd felt sorry for him, especially when they got the news that Addie was dead. At nine, Carly couldn't understand how Joe could be glad his mother wasn't ever coming home again. Now, she could guess at his relief.

"I wish she'd never come back," Joe muttered.

Carly reached over and laid her hand on his thigh to comfort him, though fighting to ignore the pleasure the contact gave her was a bit distracting. "Maybe your mother's changed."

He scowled. "That's exactly what she wants us all to think. I can't believe Maureen would even consider letting that woman anywhere near her kids."

Jerking her hand back as if she'd been burned, Carly shifted in her chair to create as much distance between them as possible.

But Joe didn't notice her retreat. "If they all think I'm just going to stand by and let Addie do to them what she did to my sister and me, they're in for a big surprise."

The biting anger of his words caused a clenching pain in Carly's chest. She was no stranger to anxiety. Slow deep breaths usually helped, but Joe's lack of confidence in his mother extinguished Carly's banked hopes. *He doesn't believe his mother can change. Which means he doesn't think I can either. Not really. Not for good.*

Her sins may be forgiven, but they'd never be forgotten. Not by Joe anyway.

"What's wrong with you? You're pale and shaking."

Telling the truth would make her too vulnerable, so she lied. "I'm freezing. I need to go inside." She swung her good leg to the floor and attempted to pull her left leg off the chaise but got it tangled up in the blanket.

"Let me help you," he said, disentangling her toes from the crocheted wool.

The touch of his warm hand ricocheted up her limb straight to her heart. The bones in her ankle may not be fully healed, but her nerves were in perfect working order. She averted her face, hoping he hadn't noticed her reaction to their brief contact.

In seconds, he was standing next to her, his right arm pulling her close so that she was leaning against him whether she wanted to or not. "I can manage."

"Maybe, but this is more fun."

She wouldn't exactly describe his nearness as fun, but they were at the front door before she could protest any further. Eager to escape the whirlwind of emotions coursing through her, she turned the doorknob. He grasped her hand and gave it a gentle squeeze as he eased her against him. Carly lifted her chin, and when their gazes met, the intense longing in his eyes stirred her own desire. He'd kiss her goodnight if she didn't stop him. Placing her palm on his chest, she shook her head and ignored the rapid beating of his heart against her hand. "I think I might be coming down with something."

"If you are, I've already been exposed." He splayed his fingers on the door behind her, effectively enclosing her in the circle of his arms. Then he kissed her, his mouth searching hers, drawing a response from her that was practiced rather than genuine.

Her conscience proclaimed her deception. Joe deserved better. But guarding her heart was a knee-jerk reaction with the judgmental types, the ones who thought they were better than her. Now that Joe was in that category, she kept the kiss flirtatious, deliberately short-circuiting his attempts to escalate their passion. The sound of footsteps inside the house gave her the excuse she needed, and she broke off the kiss.

"Goodnight, Joe."

He smiled, apparently oblivious to the emotional distance she'd erected between them. "Do you want to go out for dinner and a movie on Friday night?"

"I can't." A hot flush crept into her cheeks. "I have a date."

"A date? As in with another guy?"

"Mhmm."

He scowled, his thoughts etched on his face. How could she consider going out with another man after what had happened between them tonight?

But he understood only half of what had happened. She could tell him that his rejection of his mother made her wonder if he'd reject her too, but protecting herself made more sense to Carly.

"Do I know this guy?"

"Ryan invited me on Tuesday, and I said yes."

"You said yes to dinner with the pastor?" Joe sputtered.

"He wants to get to know me better. The new me. He isn't wondering if I'll—"

"I see."

Joe's presence in her physical space was making a difficult conversation almost impossible. "I don't think you do see. I want to get to know him, too."

"Too as in t-w-o—him and me?" He tried to smile, but it came out in a thin-lipped grimace. "You're planning to date us both?"

"Yes, but you're forgetting that until tonight there was no you and me."

A flash of understanding, followed by regret and frustration, dawned in his eyes. "Okay."

Carly almost told him she didn't need his permission, but that wasn't what he'd meant by okay. Joe would accept whatever terms she placed on their relationship because whatever attraction they may have felt in high school had developed into much more.

Schooling his features, he backed away, finally putting some space between them, space she'd thought she needed. But she missed the comfort and security of his nearness. A nearness she dare not trust until he'd resolved his issues with his mother.

CHAPTER TWELVE

"Matt was out sick yesterday," Harris explained. "So I checked the database on my I-pad and came up with nothing. Your mom hasn't been using either of her names for the past twenty years."

Joe slanted a look behind Harris. His partner heeded the unspoken signal. A moment later Ida appeared at their table. She smiled at both men as she refilled their coffee mugs, then continued on to the next table.

When the coffee shop owner had moved out of hearing range, Harris continued, "I traced Addie Stewart back to a news clip from some small town in Kansas. She and another woman, Amy Stuart, S-t-u-a-r-t, were caught in a house fire that destroyed everything they had. The report said your mom died and Amy Stuart walked away from the fire with only the clothes on her back and whatever was in her purse."

Joe almost choked on his Beef on Weck. He dropped his half-eaten sandwich on the plate. "Addie's been pretending to be Amy Stuart? Of all the lowdown, cowardly tricks. How could she do that to Dad? To Maureen and me?"

Harris stirred sugar into his coffee. "Would you like me to state the obvious?" Before Joe could respond, his partner signaled to Ida. "Could I get a piece of pumpkin pie?"

"Sure thing, officer," Ida called out as she headed to the kitchen.

"Obviously," Joe began, unable to suppress his disdain, "Addie didn't care how we felt."

"Wrong. In my opinion, your mom wanted to spare you."

"Spare us? You're giving her way too much credit."

"She didn't want you all to come looking for her anymore. So she did the only thing she could. She switched purses, leaving her purse with Amy, which conveniently contained no picture ID of any kind. And since both women had only recently arrived in town, everyone believed your mom when she said the dead woman was Addie Stewart."

Hatred for his mother churned in Joe's stomach. How could she live with herself, knowing they all thought she was dead? Why come back now, after twenty years? Why come back at all?

Harris smiled at Ida as she placed in front of him a wedge of pumpkin pie adorned with a dollop of fresh whipped cream sprinkled with cinnamon. "Why don't you have a piece?" Harris asked around a mouthful. "It'll sweeten you up."

Joe pushed his sandwich plate aside. His appetite was gone. But Ida's hopeful expression made him respond with a quick, "Sure, why not."

His cell phone vibrated in his back pocket. He stood to retrieve the phone and check the caller ID. Maureen was texting him again, pleading with him to show up at her house tonight to hear Addie's story. Disgusted, he shoved his phone back into his pocket without even considering a reply. He was more interested in what Harris had uncovered than his mother's fabrications. "What about Amy's family? Didn't anyone ever come looking for her?"

His partner leaned over the table. "Nope. Amy was an only child whose parents had died in a car accident about ten years earlier. She had no living family members. And since your mom wasn't using her married name anymore, no one contacted your dad to claim the body, so the undertaker took the cheapest route."

"Cremation?"

"You called it. By the time a resourceful reporter at the local paper discovered that Addie Stewart was Addie Callahan and informed the authorities—who contacted your father immediately—there was no body left for your dad to identify. Or in this case, fail to identify as his wife."

"Which explains why Dad didn't make a trip to Kansas to collect her remains. How easy for my mother."

"You probably don't want to hear this, but I suspect nothing has ever been easy for your mother."

Joe grimaced. "She made walking out on us look pretty easy. I never saw her shed a tear. Not one. No matter how much we all cried and pleaded with her to stay, in the morning, she was always gone, leaving Dad to clean up her mess."

The older man leveled Joe with his trademark paternal look. "I think you ought to talk to your pastor. It's time you sorted this all out and put your childhood pain behind you."

Joe harrumphed. "I might have done that ..." He paused, images of Ryan and Carly enjoying a romantic dinner together assaulting his mind. He clenched his fists under the table. "If Carly and Ryan weren't dating."

"Carly? Your Carly is dating your pastor? Now, that is an interesting development."

Joe swallowed the rest of his coffee. "I don't find this funny at all."

"Wait a minute. I thought the pastor of your church was named Bill."

"Will Stevens pastors the church I usually go to, but I've been heading down to Chautauqua Community since ..."

Harris smiled. "A little competition could be a good thing. All you have to do is show Carly you're the better man."

"Easy for you to say," Joe muttered. "You're happily

married with two grown kids.”

Happily married? Oh, no. He'd been so obsessed with his own problems, Joe hadn't given a thought to what Leann must be going through. With the first wife suddenly among the living once more, would his parents' marriage be jeopardized? Funny, how Joe thought of Leann as his mom. Leann was a better mother than Addie ever could be. And from what he could see, she was a better wife, too. Hopefully, his dad wouldn't forget that.

*

Thursday night, the phone rang just as Carly and Sarah were clearing away the dinner dishes and putting away the leftover ham and scalloped potatoes. Sarah lifted the receiver from the wall and greeted the caller. “It's for you, dear.” She hooked her foot around the leg of the nearest kitchen chair and dragged it over to the wall. With her hand covering the mouthpiece, Sarah whispered, “It's Joe. He's found out about his mother and wants to talk to you. I'll be out on the front porch enjoying the stars if you need me.”

Determined to be there for him, Carly corralled her disappointment and raised the phone to her ear. A glance at the clock on the stove confirmed her suspicions. It was too early for Joe to be calling. He'd skipped out on the family meeting. Still, giving him the benefit of the doubt was only fair. “Hi, your meeting must have ended early.”

“Before it even began.”

“You didn't go, did you?” she asked, unable to hide her frustration.

The pause at the other end lengthened. Was he angry with her for criticizing him?

“I didn't need to witness any of her theatrics. Harris filled me in on the facts.”

Carly covered her mouth and closed her eyes, then with a

quick prayer for strength, asked, "What did you find out?"

"Only that my mother stole a dead woman's identity so she could hide from her family."

"How awful! She must have been desperate."

"Yeah, desperate enough to let us all believe for twenty years that she was dead."

Carly took a deep breath and plunged ahead in Addie's defense. "She must want to make things right. I'm sure it's been horrible for her, wondering about you all, missing all of the important events in your lives. I feel sorry for her."

"Sorry for her?"

"Yes, I know what it's like to pretend everything's fine when your heart is broken."

"That woman doesn't have a heart."

"You don't mean that."

But he did. The conviction behind his words and the ensuing silence were both undeniable. And Carly couldn't lie to herself. It wouldn't help Joe. Or her. Or his mother.

No matter how hard she tried, she couldn't block out the chilling hostility behind Joe's words about his mother. He'd called her "that woman." He despised his mother and all women like her. Carly belonged in that category. Like, Addie, she, too, was a fallen woman. And in Joe's eyes, that meant he couldn't trust her. Not completely.

Yet for some inexplicable reason, he was confiding in her.

"I think God wants you to give your mother another chance."

"You think? How would you know what God wants from me?"

His ugly words were a kick in the ribs, but she couldn't stop herself from speaking the truth. "Because He's a God of second chances." Maybe saying the words out loud would convince her they applied to her as well. "I'm living proof of that."

She hung up the phone before he could reply. She needed space. He needed space. And she couldn't bear to hear him say anything else that would shatter her budding faith. Or loose the dammed up tears.

She bit her trembling lip.

She'd been a prostitute. She was a murderer who'd aborted her first baby and unwittingly caused the death of her second baby. The things she'd done were unforgivable. Who she was today was irrevocably tainted by who she'd been in the past. Thinking Joe could forget and forgive all she'd done as Elise was about as likely as him forgiving his mother for pretending to be another woman for twenty years. Traveling some roads can lead a woman so far from her dreams that finding her way back isn't possible anymore. That's how Joe saw his mother, and he may not be ready to voice it, but that's how he saw Carly, too.

Maybe she wouldn't have to worry about being attracted to both him and Ryan. The woman Joe wanted had died nine years ago on that first night she'd given her body away for a price and a dream.

Carly filled the teakettle with water and set it on the stove to boil. She dumped three chamomile teabags and a sprig of fresh mint into the ceramic teapot, retrieved two mugs from the cabinet, and slumped in a chair, her elbows on the table and her head in her hands. She needed to pray but had no idea what to ask for. Tears slipped through her fingers and puddled in her cupped hands.

Sarah's firm grip on her shoulder brought Carly back from the guilt besieging her mind. The kettle whistled, and Sarah whispered, "Hush, child. It'll all work out. I promise you."

Shifting in her seat, Carly wrapped her good arm around Sarah's waist and sobbed against the woman's chest. "He'll never forgive me."

Sarah stroked Carly's hair. "Of course He will. God has already forgiven you."

Carly lifted her face to look up at Sarah. "I know God's forgiven me." She sniffed and swiped at her tear-streaked face. "But Joe hasn't. And I don't know if he ever will."

Sarah stepped back, shocked disbelief apparent in her wide-eyed expression. "This isn't about you. It's about his mother. She's the one Joe hasn't forgiven. Yet."

"That's just it, Sarah. I'm just like his mother. Only worse."

"Lord have mercy, child. The both of you are so confused. Let me get this tea going, then we'll sit down and pray together."

Carly shook her head. "Maybe tomorrow. I'm tired. I need to go to bed."

She didn't want to think anymore. All of her thoughts were sending her deeper into the pit of despair. Free-falling was dangerous. Sleep was the best remedy. Tomorrow, in the light of day, she'd feel better. Something Ryan had said in last week's sermon pushed upward. "God's mercies are new every morning."

*

The following morning, Joe awoke to find a text message from his stepmother asking if he could join her for brunch at ten thirty. He was in no mood for another lecture from his father. Joe texted her back, "As long as it's just us." Leann did not reply immediately, so he headed to the kitchen to whip up a smoothie for breakfast. He tossed kale and strawberries into the blender with enough water to keep the blades working efficiently. Then he added protein powder, vanilla Greek yogurt, and chunks of banana. By the time, the blender had pureed the lot and crushed the four ice cubes he added at the last minute, he was wondering why Leann hadn't gotten back to him. One look at his phone and he had his answer—the whirr of the blender had drowned out his ringtones. He'd missed a call and a text from Leann. "Your dad is working. See you soon."

After drinking his smoothie, Joe opted to run a couple of miles before showering. Leaving his phone at home wasn't an option, but he wasn't ready to admit why until he'd finished the run and mounted his front porch steps. He hadn't wanted to risk missing a call from Carly. He should have known she wouldn't call him. He'd have to be a blockhead not to realize he'd hurt her. Somehow, without intending it, he'd made her feel as if he were … Were what? Lumping her into the same category as his mother?

Fool. That's exactly what you did, exactly what you've been doing ever since you learned about her connection to Rutledge Escort Service.

He considered sending Carly a quick text. "I'm sorry. I'm an idiot. Please forgive me." But she deserved a face-to-face apology, which unfortunately would have to wait until tomorrow because tonight she was going out on a date with Ryan. So much for Harris's advice that Joe prove himself the better man. If Carly were weighing them in the balance, she'd deem him a Pharisee of the worst kind, the kind that didn't even recognize his self-righteousness until he'd choked on his own foot.

He could call her. But what could he say to make things right? *Honey, I love you. Your past doesn't matter to me. I know you've changed. You're not like Addie.*

That would never fly. He would have to show Carly because she would never believe his words. He needed a plan to repair the damage he'd done, not only yesterday but on Wednesday night. She'd seemed cool when he kissed her goodbye, but exploring the reasons behind her sudden reserve was the last thing on his mind from the moment she'd told him about her date with Ryan. Joe hadn't seen that coming, though why he'd been so oblivious to the pastor's attraction to Carly was a mystery Joe would need to unravel later. Right now devising an offensive strategy to win her heart was his top priority.

But the wheels in his brain were turning in opposing directions. One minute he was tempted to drop everything and drive down to Bemus Point. The next minute he was scrambling for a way to make Leann understand his refusal to attend last night's happy family reunion. He should have run five miles instead of two. Maybe then he'd have been able to rein in his growing agitation.

If only he could skip brunch with Leann. Joe ached to see Carly, to hold her in his arms, to smell the soft floral scent of her hair, to tell her he didn't mean the things he'd said.

His phone rang, and he picked it up, hoping it was her, but when he swiped the screen his sister's name appeared. Disappointed, he kicked himself for connecting the call. "Hi, Maureen."

"I really thought you'd do the right thing."

Joe poured himself a glass of water. "What? No hello?"

"Hello, *little* brother."

Her dig hit its mark, but Joe didn't plan on giving her the satisfaction. "Good morning. Everything going smoothly at your house today?"

"I didn't call you to chat about my day," Maureen said.

In the background, the sounds of the baby crying promised this call would be brief.

"Okay, I'll bite. How was your visit with Addie? Did she tell you all about what it was like pretending to be Amy Stuart? Maybe it wasn't that difficult for her. How convenient that this other woman practically had the same last name as Addie's maiden name. And then there's the whole Amy, Addie thing—now that probably got confusing at times—"

"Mom's sick, Joe."

Whoa. This was an all-time low, even for their mother. "You believe her?"

"Of course I believe her. She has no reason to lie."

"Adelaide has no reason to lie? You have a short memory, Maureen. She's been lying to us for twenty years. Not having a good reason never stopped her before."

"I'm disappointed in you. Refusing to forgive Mom has made you bitter and just plain nasty. Give me a call when you're ready to be reasonable. In the meantime, I'll be praying for you."

Stunned, Joe took a swig of water, trying to think of an appropriate reply. "Maureen, I don't mean to make anything harder for you or Dad."

"Dad and I are fine. You're the one who's messed up," Maureen said, her tone filled with pity. "I have to go. Gwen's crying."

His sister disconnected the call before Joe could reply. It was the second time in two days a woman had hung up on him.

Hopefully, he'd do better with Leann. Reassuring her of his love and loyalty was easy. Simply showing up at her table this morning would accomplish that much, but unless he missed his guess, Leann would expect him to reach out to Addie. His stepmother was one of the most forgiving people he'd ever known, and she taught her stepchildren by example rather than through rules and demands. Leann's healthy relationship with her own father, a recovering alcoholic, was proof positive that she believed in extending grace to everyone, regardless of his or her track record.

*

"Thanks for coming." Leann kissed Joe's cheek.

He hugged her then followed her through the spotless living room and dining room into the kitchen. Joe scanned his surroundings, half expecting to see his dad. After Maureen's call, he'd braced himself for an ambush. At least Leann didn't know what an idiot he was being. The last thing he needed was for her to think he didn't trust her. She might turn out to be his only ally.

His eyes widened at the assortment of food. Scrambled eggs, fried potatoes, ham steaks, and his favorite sweet potato pancakes gave off a tantalizing aroma that made his stomach growl. Leann must think he never cooked for himself. "You didn't have to go to all of this trouble."

Leann smiled as she poured coffee. "Cooking relaxes me. You know that."

Joe took the chair opposite his stepmother. Beside his plate, she'd left the sports section of the morning newspaper. "Dad didn't read the stats before work?"

Leann scooped eggs onto her plate, and without meeting his gaze, she said, "I thought you'd like to read the paper while we eat. We'll talk after."

"Sure, whatever you want," Joe agreed, noticing for the first time that his stepmother was prepared with reading material of her own, a devotional for women.

But Joe couldn't concentrate on highlights from last night's football games or on breakfast, though the food tasted delicious. His own eggs were often chewy and sometimes charred around the edges, and his one attempt at pancakes had convinced him there was a secret to making them light and fluffy that he'd probably never learn or master.

Dang his mother for being the white elephant in the room. Any other time, he'd savor every mouthful of this feast. But not today. He sopped up the last puddle of warm maple syrup and steeled himself for Leann's plea. How ironic that the woman who'd been left to rebuild the hearts Addie had shattered would now volunteer to plead on her behalf. But plead Leann would. She could do no less. And because Joe loved her as he'd never loved his biological mother, he would hear his stepmother out.

Wearing a composed expression and a hint of a smile, she cleared the table, covered the leftovers with plastic wrap, and put them in the fridge. "Do you want to sit on the patio or in the sunroom?" she asked as if this were an ordinary day.

"It's chilly out. Let's stay inside."

Once they were seated, he in the recliner, and she with her feet tucked under her on the love seat, Leann said, "You know I've always loved you and Maureen as if you were my own, as if I'd given birth to you both myself."

Oh, boy. Joe didn't like where this was going, but he swallowed the rebuttal that rose up like a banner in his mind. Telling Leann he wished she were his mother in every way wouldn't help either of them deal with Addie's reappearance.

"You need to know that I never would have tried to take your mother's place if I'd known she was alive."

Leann was studying him. She could see what he wouldn't put into words. It had taken a while, but she had broken down the hedge of distrust that had grown like thorns and thistles around his heart. Her love created a safe haven in the ravaged Callahan family, and within the security of that refuge Joe had found a way past the pain of rejection. At least he thought he had. Until Addie decided to make an encore appearance. So she was sick. He'd been sick countless times, and she'd never been there for him. Not once. He owed her nothing.

"I don't want to overstep my bounds—"

"What? No. You can say anything to me. *You're* my mom."

Leann frowned, her forehead creased in lines of

concentration. "I was up most of the night. Between talking and praying with your dad after he came home from Maureen's, I couldn't sleep, so I came downstairs to read and pray some more." She untucked her legs and sat on the sofa, leaning close to his chair. "Joe, do you remember the verse in Micah that talks about what God requires of His children?"

He didn't remember. When he read the Old Testament, he gravitated to Psalms or Proverbs. "Trust in the LORD with all thine heart and lean not on thine own understanding" came to mind. Micah was a minor prophet. Joe didn't think he'd ever heard a sermon taken from that book. "Something about obeying the law, right?"

"No, though being under the old covenant, you'd think that would be the case, when in fact the requirements are very different from what we would expect. Shall I read it to you?"

Joe sensed this would be the preamble to Leann's argument, but he couldn't deny her, not with the sparkle of anticipation lighting up her face. "Sure, go ahead."

She picked up the Bible from the end table and opened it to a place she'd already bookmarked. "He hath shewed thee, O man, what is good; and what doth the LORD require of thee, but to do justly ..." She paused to wipe tears from the corners of her eyes. "And to love mercy, and to walk humbly with thy God."

Mercy rewrote my life. Joe had sung this song countless times.

"Please don't be mad at me, Joe, but I've got to say this because I just might be the only person you'll listen to." Tears tracked down her cheeks, but she ignored them. "I know seeing your mother again hurts you, and you don't trust her, but you have to treat her with mercy because that's what God expects from you, and it has nothing to do with what she deserves. If you're going to walk humbly with God, you have to know that none of us deserves mercy, son."

He stood and taking her hands, pulled her to her feet. Then he hugged her and whispered against her hair, "Thank you, Leann. I'll pray about what you said."

She squeezed him and patted his back. "I knew you would."

She released him, and they headed to the front door. He was turning the doorknob when she stopped him with her hand on his arm. He turned, intending to say goodbye.

"There's just one more thing, Joe. God told me to tell you that your mother has always loved you."

Tempted to grind out a denial, he shook his head. "She sure had a funny way of showing it."

CHAPTER THIRTEEN

Much to her surprise, in spite of the stress of having her cast removed that morning, Carly found herself looking forward to her date with Ryan. He was supportive and encouraging. Not judgmental like Joe. Ryan was confident without being arrogant or domineering, unlike Al. Too bad she hadn't picked up on that subtle distinction years ago. Then her life wouldn't be in such shambles.

Give yourself a break. You were a teenager. He knew all the right things to say to make you believe he'd always be your hero.

Squelching the hatred that writhed in her gut whenever she thought of Al, Carly sat on the chair in her room and bent down to unstrap the boot that now replaced the cast on her ankle. She'd been too shocked when the doctor cut off the cast to even glance at her leg. Prepared to do a thorough inspection, she lifted her skirt above her knees. The skin on her lower leg was shriveled, thin, hairy, and pale, but all that was temporary. She was young, and her body was recovering from her injuries at a faster rate than the doctor expected, though she wouldn't be getting the cast off her arm for another two weeks. Multiple breaks took longer to heal, according to Dr. Mallory. Carly needed to stop whining about inconveniences and focus on the progress she'd made. One cast instead of two was a definite improvement.

If only her heart and mind would recover as quickly as her body. Because the memories of all the shameful things she'd done kept coming back, Carly still struggled to believe she'd been made new in Christ. Forgiveness was supposed to be simple, wasn't it? Was the problem in her head or her heart? She'd probably feel differently if she hadn't grown up in the church. As a little girl, giving her heart to Jesus and living for Him seemed simple. And it had been. Until she was swept away by Al and his breathtaking good looks.

That was one reason she was excited about going out with Ryan. He didn't know anything about her past. When he looked at her, she didn't see the questions and doubts she sometimes saw in Joe's eyes. Joe knew what she'd been, and she suspected he sometimes wondered if she were going to return to that life. *Leaving is your specialty.* Did he expect her to just take off with no warning? Whether he said anything or not, he appeared to be bracing himself for her exit.

And for her rejection.

"Pretty shaky ground to build a romance on," she muttered.

She should face the facts. With Joe, the odds were definitely *not* in her favor. Addie Callahan had stacked the deck against any woman who dared to love her wounded son. Love? Carly wouldn't go straight to love—at least not the kind a couple should share. Their history was complicated. Joe was her brother's best friend. He'd been a fixture in their home for years. Sure, she'd developed a crush on him, but Joe hadn't encouraged her, except maybe on the night of her prom, when for one brief moment, he'd looked into her eyes and made her feel as if she were the only girl in the world.

A week later Al entered her life and convinced her she didn't need anyone but him.

That was another thing she hadn't noticed in the beginning. Al was controlling, intent on shaping her and later, the others, into commodities with high returns.

It was hard not to despise him. But if she were honest, she

was as much to blame.

Maybe Joe would feel differently about her once Al was in prison. Why hadn't the trial started yet? Now that her anger had dropped to a rational level, she was grateful that she didn't have to testify and bare her soul before a courtroom full of people who would certainly judge her as quickly as they would Al. The jury might believe he was a murderer who'd tried to kill her, but they wouldn't be able to forget that she was a prostitute. Some of the jurors might even think she'd gotten what she deserved. Ignoring the fear rising in her throat, she took three deep breaths. "You don't have to testify." Saying the words out loud calmed her racing heart.

Her past rippled into her present, but Carly didn't live there anymore.

Ryan saw who she was today, a woman at the beginning of her new life as a believer, a woman whose future could be wonderful. Two short months ago, none of her associates would have ever believed she'd be having dinner with a minister. She could scarcely believe it herself. Was this fresh start part of the abundant life Jesus promised to believers? She smiled, reached for her cane, and hobbled the few feet to her closet to get ready.

Choosing a conservative ankle-length brown skirt with a striped peasant top in warm fall colors, Carly considered how much better the outfit would look if she could wear *both* short, brown, lace-up boots. Dismissing her vanity, she thanked the Lord for healing her ankle. A clunky black boot with Velcro straps was a definite improvement over the cast she'd worn for five weeks. By the time she was dressed, she was humming a forgotten tune. Looking in the full-length mirror on the back of her door, she studied her reflection. The difference in her appearance went beyond her clothes. The sweetness in her smile couldn't exactly be called innocent, but her steely independence was gone.

The digital clock read five thirty when a knock on her door startled her out of musings.

"Pastor Ryan is here, dear," Sarah said through the door. "Shall I tell him you need a few minutes?"

"No, I'm ready." Carly ran her left hand through her curls and cautiously applied some lip gloss, pleased with her improved dexterity. She grabbed her crossbody purse from the dresser.

A short walk down the hall and there he was waiting by the front door. In khakis and a navy oxford shirt opened at the collar, Ryan was disarmingly handsome. Spotting her studying him, he grinned, his own gaze taking her in from head to toes. His appreciative smile made her feel more beautiful than she had in years.

"You look amazing. I especially like the mismatched boots. Quite a fashion statement, though I'm not sure it'll catch on."

The laughter in his tone was contagious. When he winked at her, she chuckled. "I'll have to remember that you like to tease." As he draped her cranberry wool shawl around her shoulders, she said, "But can you take it if I tease you back, Pastor?"

"I told you to call me Ryan. We aren't in church right now." He kissed her cheek.

The warmth rushing to her face meant he'd secured his advantage, whether he knew it or not. She could no longer shut down her own feelings at will.

"Have a nice time, you two," Sarah said, rescuing Carly from the awkward moment.

Ryan moved to her left side, apparently intending to support her as they walked to his car.

The woodsy smell of his aftershave further disarmed her as his strong arm wrapped around her back and pulled her against his ribcage. The solid presence of his hand on her waist felt too good. "I think I can do the stairs better by myself."

The doubtful expression he shot her made her question her bravado. She'd had no trouble coming up the stairs after her trip to the doctor this morning, but going down might be harder. Almost as if he'd read her mind, Ryan tightened his grip. "Nonsense. My mother taught me to be a gentleman at all times. Especially when a lady insists she can do it herself."

A lady? Now that was a stretch. How would a lady respond? Graciously, of course. "If you insist, thank you," she replied, her tone reminiscent of the charm her mother often used on her dad. Her next thought—that her charms were of another kind altogether—made her wince. Until she remembered that Christ's blood had washed her sins away.

She and Ryan successfully navigated the first three steps, but Carly was distracted, wondering if she could possibly make things right with her parents. Overcome with a longing for home, Carly's right foot overshot the last step. For one frightening instant, she was falling backward, until Ryan's arms came around her and supported her. The security of his solid, muscled chest behind her back dissolved her panic. She could get used to his attentiveness and his gentleness.

Al had used his swift reflexes to deliver blows, but Ryan was different. Though she'd never seen him lose his temper, her heart told her this man would never hurt her. Not even when he was angry.

And she would never let a man strike her ever again. She deserved better.

Ryan held her door and waited for her to get settled in the passenger seat before stowing her cane in the back. As he walked to the driver's side, she breathed a silent prayer that she would measure up to his expectations. She'd already made a good first impression, or he wouldn't have asked her out.

Still, she was nothing like the women he'd dated in the past.

Relax, Carly. Just be yourself. He likes you, the real you. You don't have to pretend to be someone else.

But years of cloaking herself in the armor that was Elise cast a lingering shadow.

Do you really think he'd like you if he knew the real you? The woman who's known more men than she can count?

Hot shame rushed to her face, and Carly squeezed her eyes shut against the ugly image that emerged to steal her happiness, an emotion she'd felt precious little of since the day she climbed into Al's Mustang convertible. Her brother's words echoed across time, "You don't have to do this, Carly. I'll—" The rest of his words had been drowned out by the blaring noise Al called music. What had Jared been trying to tell her? That he could convince Mom and Dad that Alan Rutledge was good enough for their only daughter? Not likely. Al's intentions had never been honorable. It was humiliating to admit how gullible and stupid she'd been—gullible to believe Al's lies in the first place and stupid to stay when she'd finally seen that his word meant nothing.

Ryan's hand on her arm arrested her thoughts. She'd been so immersed in her recollections that she hadn't heard him get in the car. How long had he watched her struggling with the demons of her past? Though she needed a moment to compose herself, she shifted in her seat to face him.

"Are you all right?" He peered into her eyes. "Do you need some ibuprofen or something?"

Summoning up a smile, she laid her hand over his and ran her thumb over the back of his hand. "I'm fine. More than a little hungry—"

"That I can remedy immediately." He reached in the back seat and presented her with a box of chocolates. "For the woman who has everything."

"Candy before dinner? How decadent!"

"One or two won't spoil your appetite." He snagged a caramel and popped it in his mouth. "Or mine."

She chose an oval piece encased in dark chocolate and took a small bite, savoring the delectable flavor bursting on her tongue. "Raspberry cream. My favorite. Thank you."

"My pleasure. I thought about bringing you flowers, but candy seemed like a more creative choice, since Valentine's Day is a long way off."

The mention of flowers brought back the image of Joe's expectant face as he'd presented her with the colorful straw bouquet. If only their evening had ended better. Carly might have been tempted to cancel her date with Ryan. But here she was, giving this near stranger a chance to prove himself with her, and she had no idea when she would see or even talk to Joe again.

Ryan started the engine and eased the car out onto the road. "I thought we'd drive up to Fredonia," he said, glancing in her direction for approval. "If you like Italian food—"

"Who doesn't love Italian?"

Twenty minutes later, they were seated at a cozy, family-style restaurant with red-checked tablecloths and glowing hurricane lamps for centerpieces. Carly had eaten at fancier establishments more times than she could possibly remember, but she'd never eaten any place where the sound of children's laughter was clearly accepted. In fact, this clientele appeared to be a fairly even mix of families and couples, with the occasional group of all women or all men.

Carly felt a bit out of her element, but she gave Ryan a bright smile as she opened her menu. "What's good here?" she asked, falling into her old habit of seeking suggestions from her escort. She feigned a cough to cover her sharp intake of breath, but there was no reason for her to be nervous. Ryan couldn't possibly understand the implication of her question. He was her date. Not her escort.

"Their red sauce is wonderful, so just about any pasta would be a good choice." He closed his menu and placed it where the waitress would be sure to notice it.

A baby started crying in a nearby booth, and Carly lifted her menu to hide her face as she schooled her features to mask her distress. *It's only a baby. Someone else's baby. Don't think about it.*

A blonde waitress with a perky smile and sparkling brown eyes picked up Ryan's menu.

Carly looked up from the page of desserts and beverages she'd been reading to see if he noticed the other woman, but he was focused on her.

"Are you folks ready to order?"

"I am. Are you ready, Carly?"

She handed her menu to the waitress. "I'll have the Florentine lasagna." Al had never let her order anything so fattening. He expected his girls to fit into a size four or six at most.

Ryan ordered spaghetti and meatballs. No wonder he was able to decide so quickly. He hadn't even read the whole menu.

"My mother made spaghetti every Friday night," he explained. "She's a great cook, which is why no one else in my family knows how to cook. She never let us in the kitchen."

Carly ignored her sudden homesickness. "So what do you do now that you don't live at home? Eat canned soup and frozen meals?"

Ryan ran his hand through his short-cropped brown hair and shrugged. "Sometimes. Mostly I eat out. And the ladies at Community Church ply me with food on a regular basis."

Carly laughed. "Which basically means women still believe the way to a man's heart is through his stomach."

"And you don't?"

Fortunately for Carly, their waitress chose that moment to bring a basket of warm rolls and a dish of pesto to their table. Averting her face and smiling at the younger woman gave Carly time to calm her rapidly beating pulse. "Thank you. Warm bread dipped in pesto is the best."

While they waited for their food, Ryan used his phone to check out the movies and start times at nearby theaters, finally settling on a romantic comedy—a good choice since she was in no mood for a drama. She'd lived enough drama to last a lifetime, none of which was anything she wanted to share with Ryan, so she kept him talking about himself by listening attentively and asking lots of questions. Soon, they'd finished their salads and were halfway through their entrees.

"So, you know everything about me, but you haven't told me anything about you." Ryan absently twirled spaghetti around his fork. "Where did you grow up?"

How little could she tell him and still give him the feeling that he was getting to know her? "We lived out in the country in the house my mother grew up in. Her dad and her older brother built it." She cut a bite of lasagna and lifted it with her fork. She couldn't talk with her mouth full. *Good excuse, girl.*

Ryan watched her, his expression keenly astute. Apparently, his skills as a pastor enabled him to discern her evasiveness.

"I have an older brother named Jared. He's a high school Math teacher," she offered.

Ryan nodded. "One brother and no sisters. Your house must have been quiet as a library compared to mine."

"With three younger sisters and a little brother, I suppose you would think that. It must have been hard for you to find a quiet space to do anything." *Good job, Carly. Get him talking about himself again.*

"Not really. Being the oldest meant I had more privileges *and* more responsibilities."

Carly dipped a piece of roll in the sauce seeping from between the layers of her lasagna. "So your parents expected a lot from you. How do they feel about you being a minister?"

"My mother couldn't be happier."

"And your dad? How does he feel?" Any man would be proud to have a son like Ryan. He was no prodigal.

He met her gaze in the dim light of the hurricane lamp. "My dad died three months ago, two days before his birthday."

"I'm so sorry. How awful." Carly reached across the table, and Ryan clasped her hand. The pain in his eyes rocked her soul. "I didn't know. How is your mom doing?"

"Better. Dad had prostate cancer. She'd been caring for him at home. The last four months were very hard on her." Ryan released Carly's hand, stabbed his fork into a meatball, and raised it to his mouth. "Enough about me. I want to know about you."

Carly suppressed a shudder, knowing he'd feel differently if he knew her full story. The details of her past would shock him into rethinking their friendship. "I've been staying with Sarah for the past month. She's hands-down one of the kindest people I've ever met. I don't know what I would've done without her."

"What about your parents? You couldn't stay with them while you were recovering?"

With a prayer for courage, Carly whispered, "I haven't talked to either of my parents in about five years."

Ryan's eyes widened in surprise. "Five years?"

Trying for humor, she said, "Give or take a few months. But I did see my brother this week."

Ryan placed his silverware on top of his cleared plate and slid it to the end of their table. Then he focused on Carly, his eyes searching hers. "Do you want to talk about it?" he asked gently.

"Some other time." Stacking her own plate atop his, she added, "Let's order dessert and coffee."

He smiled, and like a true gentleman, deferred to her preference. "In that case, I recommend cannoli. And if you're a coffee connoisseur, espresso."

The rest of the evening passed without any more discussion of their families. On the way to the theater, she shared her plans to go back to school, and Ryan expressed his approval of her decision to begin at a community college rather than heading straight to a four-year school. After the movie, their conversation on the way back to Sarah's centered on the believability of the plot resolution. Carly declared that the happily-ever-after ending seemed forced, but Ryan disagreed. "Love can overcome any obstacle. If two people are meant to be together, nothing can keep them apart."

If only that were true, but in her experience, true love was a dream unfounded in reality. Still, she didn't want to argue and end their date on a sour note. "I guess that happens, for some people." Reaching for the radio dial, she said, "Do you mind if we listen to some music?" Without waiting for his reply, she tuned in to the local classical station and adjusted the volume.

He seemed to take the hint that she wanted to change the subject because he suggested she might like to go with him to the Christmas concert at Kleinhan's Music Hall.

Since it was barely the middle of October, Carly was a bit startled by him proposing a date so far in the future. "We'll see."

He turned his attention from the road to glance at her. "Say yes. That way I can buy tickets tomorrow, so we'll get good seats. I like the first row balcony."

She poked him in the arm. "Keep your eyes on the road. You're making me nervous."

With his gaze fixed once more on the highway ahead, he urged, "Say you'll go with me."

She'd gone to the music hall and the theater many times before, but this would be the first time she'd attend a cultural event with a man she could care about. "Okay, first row balcony it is."

*

From the moment she'd agreed to go with Ryan to the holiday concert, Carly regretted making a commitment that far in the future. What if things didn't go well with them? What if she decided she and Joe were a better fit?

Sitting with Ryan on Sarah's front porch swing felt like a dream, as if she were living some other woman's life. But when he cupped her chin in his hand, the warmth that spread at his touch was all too real. He bent his head, and his magnetic brown eyes held her captive. Her pulse quickened as she waited for his kiss.

"I had fun tonight," he said, his fingers caressing her cheek.

For a split second, she considered reaching up, pulling his head down, and initiating their first kiss. Which is what Elise would have done.

Instead, she clasped his hand, giving him a gentle squeeze, effectively tempering their rising passion. "I better go in."

Ryan helped her to her feet, walked her to the door, and brushed a kiss across her lips. It was nothing like the kiss he'd promised with his eyes a moment before.

With mixed emotions, Carly said, "Thank you for tonight."

He smiled. "I'll call you tomorrow."

*

The following morning, Carly lay in bed, her mind gradually stirring to the point of wakefulness. She stretched her legs, satisfied that last night's walking hadn't been too much for her ankle. One cast off. One to go. She sat up in bed and reached for the Bible on her nightstand, opening it to the place she'd been reading the day before. Matthew chapter five, verse four caught her attention.

"Blessed are they that mourn: for they shall be comforted," she read aloud, letting the wonder of such mercy touch her soul with hope.

Could it be true? Would God really comfort her over the loss of her children? Even though it was all her fault they were gone? She could envision only one way that could happen. Holding a baby of her own would heal her broken heart.

Could God possibly have such an amazing plan in mind for her? Did she dare hope?

*

When the telephone rang mid-morning, Carly picked it up, expecting to hear Ryan's voice. "Hello. Good morning."

"Carly, I waited as long as I could," Joe said.

The urgency in his voice set off an alarm in her head. Had something happened to one of her parents? To her brother? Or to someone in his family?

"Joe, what's wrong?"

"I'm an idiot. That's what's wrong."

Breathing a sigh of relief, she whispered, "You scared me. I thought—"

"I need to talk to you."

"We are talking."

"In person."

"Okay, when?"

"Now. I'm parked in the driveway."

Carly shifted the living room drapes and glanced across

the leaf-strewn yard. He was standing by his car, wearing the look of a puppy who had been caught chewing a favorite pair of shoes. His distress tugged at her heart. "Give me ten minutes, and you can take me out for breakfast."

*

When Carly stepped outside, Joe was leaning against the porch post, staring at her with such anguish that her own hurt feelings receded. Had he seen his mother?

"I'm glad you came." She held out her good arm, needing to erase the distance between them. No matter what was happening between them now, Joe could count on her, but convincing him of that would be difficult.

He eased her against him in a hug that would have deprived her of oxygen had she not been wearing a cast on her right arm that kept him from crushing her against his chest. He was clinging to her and kissing her hair. "I'm sorry. You have to know I didn't mean any of those things I said."

He did mean some of those things. He really believed his mother was heartless, that her arms had never ached to hold her children. But Carly disagreed. Addie Callahan loved her family, so much that she'd believed they would be better off with her out of their lives. Wasn't that exactly how Carly herself felt about her own family until God began to show her who she could be if she could only trust His plan?

Carly squirmed in Joe's embrace until she could look up at him, expecting him to expound on his apology. But he kissed her instead, and she forgot everything but his mouth on hers and the warmth of his body seeping into her, fanning a flame of desire. Being in his arms felt like coming home, and she didn't want to stop. Joe's kisses were becoming more demanding, urging them both to a place they couldn't go. She pushed at his chest, leaned back, and broke off the kiss. A quick glance at his eyes told her she was right. Minutes before she'd needed to hold him. Now they both needed space.

Leaning on her cane, she started toward the steps. Joe was beside her in an instant, steadying her with his hand on her elbow. "Sarah recommended a little diner about ten minutes from here," Carly suggested. "Let's go eat, and we can talk."

*

Joe ordered the breakfast special—two eggs, two pancakes, hash browns, sausage, and coffee. Carly chose a Belgian waffle with fried apples. They'd managed to make small talk in the car on the way to the diner, but now that he was sitting across the table from her his thoughts were bouncing like a ping pong ball back and forth between the apology he needed to make and his nagging curiosity about her date with Ryan.

Joe blamed himself. If he hadn't waited so long to let her know how he felt about her, she would never have agreed to go out with someone else. Still, thinking of her with Ryan irritated Joe.

He and Carly had finished their meal and were on their second cups of coffee before Joe brought up his mother. "I still can't believe Addie pretended to be someone else so that we'd all think she was dead."

"You told me that over the phone." Carly folded her napkin and laid it over her plate.

Even though he didn't want her to see how angry he was at his mother, Joe kept his eyes trained on Carly's face. "There was a fire, but Amy Stuart died in that fire, not my mother. Addie stole Amy's purse and her identity."

"Why did she come back now?" Carly was studying him, no doubt looking for signs of compassion. "And what does she want from you?"

"I don't know, but everyone else wants to give her the

benefit of the doubt. Even Leann thinks I should give Addie a chance to explain."

Do justly and love mercy. He'd read that in his morning devotions. That was the second time this week he'd gotten that reminder. But could he extend mercy to his mom? Wasn't it the same as giving her another opportunity to hurt him?

Carly opened her mouth to say something then shook her head.

He could understand her reluctance to express her opinion. After all, he'd shot her down in the worst possible way. "Carly, I know it's no excuse, but having my mother show up after all of these years has messed with my head big time. What I said to you when you told me you believed God wanted me to give my mother another chance was insensitive and cruel."

"It was." Carly's glistening eyes were filled with pain, pain that he had caused.

What could he say to make things right between them? "I'm sorry I hurt you. It won't happen again. I promise."

"Let's not kid ourselves, Joe. We've known each other too long. We owe it to each other to be honest."

He hadn't been honest with her, back then or now. Could he tell her the truth? The whole truth? "Carly, I—"

"Every time you look at me, you see a woman who sold herself for a price." Scarlet shame stained her cheeks. "For a very high price, and—"

"And you've left that life behind," Joe interrupted, reaching for her hand, disappointed when she pulled away.

"That's the problem, Joe. You don't want to think it, but you can't help wondering if …" With the back of her hand, she swiped ineffectually at the tears trailing down her cheeks and sliding off her jaw. "If I'll be just like your mother, walking in and out of your life."

He wanted to tell her it wasn't true, but lying would accomplish nothing. He was botching this apology. "I never meant for my anger at Addie to spill over into our relationship."

"But that's exactly what's happened." Carly opened her purse, took out some tissues, and dried her face. When she met his gaze again, the resignation in her eyes was a punch to his gut. He dreaded what was coming but was powerless to stop it. She was going to choose Ryan over him by default. Because she didn't believe they could make it.

She didn't believe they could lay their pasts to rest. Did he?

The waitress slipped their bill onto the table and walked away. The girl must be an expert at picking up on vibes customers give off when they don't want to be interrupted.

"You're afraid to believe she's changed," Carly insisted, "because she hurt you so many times before. And if she can't change, then maybe I can't either. That's why you snapped at me. And why I hung up on you."

"Carly, please. We can work through this. I care about you. A lot. It's always been you." His words spilled out like rapid fire, just in case she wouldn't let him finish.

"No, it's always been your mother." Carly stood, and leaning on her cane, pushed in her chair. "Until you make peace with her, you and I can't be more than friends."

She was dismissing him and giving up on them. He should have known his mother coming back would bring him nothing but trouble. In one last ditch effort, he said, "But I love you."

His eyes locked with hers. He'd expected her to be surprised by his declaration, but she just looked sad. And resigned.

I can't do this without you. I'm tired of living without you in my arms, without seeing your beautiful smile, hearing your laugh, coming home to you every day. "I've always loved you, Carly. I just didn't—"

"I love you, too, but it's not enough. For either of us."

CHAPTER FOURTEEN

Joe shrugged as the ball bounced off the rim. His head wasn't in the game. Playing one-on-one with Jared made it next to impossible for Joe to think about anything but Carly. He hadn't talked to her in a week, but she invaded his thoughts and robbed him of sleep.

"What's wrong with you, man?" Jared clapped Joe on the back with unnecessary force. "You're playing like you lost your best friend."

Joe scowled, retrieved the ball, and slammed it in the direction of Jared's chest.

Jared grinned, caught the basketball, dunked it cleanly, and stared as Joe missed an easy rebound. The ball bounced onto the grass, then rolled to a stop a few feet away. "Do you want to talk about it?"

"Nah." Joe trudged off the court, heading to his car. "Let's do this another time."

Jared came alongside and passed him the basketball. "It's your ball, man."

Tucking the ball under his arm, Joe averted his face to avoid his friend's scrutiny. "Yeah, right. I knew that."

"Are you sure this isn't about your mother?"

Joe considered explaining but thought better of it. "Probably. I'm having coffee with her tomorrow afternoon. Apparently, there's something she wants to tell me that I need to hear firsthand."

"Firsthand is always better. That's why I haven't said

anything to my folks about my conversation with Carly." Jared unlocked his car, opened the driver's door, and turned back to Joe. "I haven't heard from her since I called her the day after we met at Ida's. Has she said anything to you about talking to Mom and Dad?"

Unable to hide his own frustration, Joe exhaled. "Not a word."

"Could you try to talk her into it?" Jared's expectant expression dimmed as he studied Joe's face.

"I don't think I'm the one to talk her into anything. You should probably call her yourself."

Awareness dawned in his friend's eyes. "It's Carly. She's the one you're fighting with."

"We aren't fighting. We're just friends. Not even close friends."

Jared grabbed Joe's bicep. "I knew it. I knew it all along. You always liked her. So now that you've found her again, don't mess it up. Don't let her out of your sight."

Joe pulled free of Jared's hold. "It's too late, man."

His best friend leveled Joe with his I'm-not-taking-no-for-an-answer look. "Fix whatever's wrong. You two were meant to be together. Anybody could see that, even in high school. Except for maybe you. Why you ever let her run off with Rutledge is beyond me."

Joe glared but decided to ignore the dig. "It's complicated." Staring across the park, he spotted a young couple, the guy pushing a double stroller with a baby in the back and a toddler in the front. An image of a little girl with Carly's blonde curls framing her cherub face flashed in Joe's mind then faded to nothing. "If you want your sister to talk to your folks, you'll have to convince her yourself. I'm the last person she'd listen to about reconnecting with one's parents."

"Now I get it. I'm sorry, man."

Joe climbed into the driver seat and started the engine. As far as he was concerned, this conversation had played itself out. What else could he say? Except maybe, *could you ask your sister to give me another chance?* And that Joe would not do.

*

From his booth near the window, Joe had full view of the Tim Horton's parking lot. The time on his phone was 1:40. Addie was ten minutes late. Maybe she wouldn't show. That would be typical. Addie's promises disappeared faster than the melting whipped cream on his pumpkin latte. With a disgusted harrumph, he dunked his oatmeal cookie into the coffee, then bit off half of the softened treat.

He wasn't planning to wait much longer—another five or ten minutes at most. He needed to call Carly, but she probably wouldn't talk to him. Not after the way they'd ended things. Correction, the way she'd ended things last week. After several restless nights of tossing and turning, Joe reluctantly admitted she was right. They could never have a future as long as his past invaded his emotions. And since he had no control over Addie or her choices, he would have to learn to accept his mother on her terms.

But how was he to accomplish that if she didn't even show up to have coffee with him?

He swallowed the last of his latte, shrugged into his jacket, and headed for the side door—the shortest route to his car. He was zipping up his coat against the October chill when he bumped into someone. Looking up to apologize, Joe came face to face with his mother. The uncertainty in her eyes caused him a pang of guilt, but he dismissed it. He had no reason to feel remorse of any kind. He hadn't done anything to her. Except maybe expect her to act like a real mother. One who'd done more than simply give birth to him and his sister.

"Joe, honey, I ... I'm sorry I'm late. I was at the wrong Tim

Hortons."

"That's okay. You made it. I'm still here, so …" He studied his mother. She'd aged, but she didn't look good at all. Her skin was thin and ashy pale. Obvious pain dimmed the light in her eyes. "Let me buy you a coffee, Mom."

She touched his arm but withdrew her hand quickly. Her uncertain expression, as if she were hoping he would hug her or kiss her cheek, made him feel bad, but he couldn't bring himself to extend even a token of affection to the woman who had walked out of his life more times than he could count.

Calling her mom was a surprise in itself.

Dismissing the slip as a natural reflex, he headed to the counter where the cashier was pouring coffee for an elderly gentleman leaning on a silver cane. The well-dressed man took his cup with a thank you for the cashier and turned toward the exit. With an easy smile that doubled the lines on his weathered face, he nodded to Joe and Addie. "Have a nice day, folks."

She returned his smile. "You, too," she replied, her tone conveying sincerity beyond social nicety.

"Nice days are the only ones on my schedule." The gentleman bowed his head to her then settled his gaze on Joe. "Life's too short for anything else."

The sparkle illuminating the octogenarian's eyes displayed the wisdom of years well lived. If only Joe had an hour to spare. What advice would the older man give him about Addie and Carly? With a mental sigh, Joe held the door open for the stranger to pass.

Some have entertained angels …

At the last moment, Joe called out as the man reached his car, about twenty yards from the door. "Thanks for the reminder, sir."

"Anytime, son."

Joe watched the elderly man get into his car and drive off.

When Joe turned around, his mother was waiting a few feet away, standing behind a woman holding a whimpering toddler on her left hip.

Addie met Joe's gaze. A tight-lipped frown replaced her smile. She reached for his arm and fell against him, then slipped, sliding toward the hard tile floor. In seconds, he reached under her arms. Supporting her, stunned by her lack of weight, he helped his mother to the closest chair. She sat, slumped, with her eyes closed. When she finally looked at him, she couldn't seem to focus on his face.

He knelt in front of her, assessing her condition. She was sick. But how sick? "Are you all right? Do you need a doctor?"

"I'll be okay. In a minute." Her voice was faint and thin.

She was thin. Painfully thin. How had he not noticed?

"Some tea ... might ... help."

Eager to do something, he marched to the counter and barked, "Can I get a green tea?"

The young woman bringing out a tray of fresh donuts raised her eyebrows but gave no reply.

"With honey." Joe read the girl's name tag. "Please, Sue."

He glanced back at his mother, whose cheeks had turned an unnatural cherry red against her pale skin. Returning his attention to the cashier, he added, "My mother's not feeling well."

Understanding softened the girl's features, and she placed the donuts in the case, then hurried to fill his order.

He waited impatiently, unease rippling up and down his spine. He was suddenly very grateful he'd agreed to meet Addie today. And his gratitude had nothing to do with how this meeting might change how Carly felt about him.

The cup of hot tea finally in his hand, Joe hurried to his mother's side. "Are you sure you don't need a doctor?"

Her mouth twitched into an almost smile. "I've already seen several doctors, honey."

"And?" He plopped himself in the seat across from her, leaned over the table, and grasped her free hand. Heat radiated into his palm. She was burning up but shaking with chills.

Her free hand cradled the paper cup of hot tea, as if its warmth could somehow penetrate her body and quell the shivering. "They all tell me the same thing."

Oh, God. I've seen this before. On the streets. In the exhausted faces of the homeless sick. The city's forgotten ones. Forgotten, like my mother.

Hoping against hope for a good prognosis, Joe inhaled a long breath, then released the air with a rush. "What do they say?"

She squeezed his hand. An almost imperceptible pressure on his bones.

"What's wrong with you, Mom?"

Her eyes pooled with tears and regret. "It's leukemia."

So that's why she'd come home. She was dying. For real this time. At one time, he would have been happy, would have believed she was getting what she deserved. Now ... now an ache pulsed pain from his heart through every blood vessel.

"How long have you known?"

"Almost two years."

*

Carly spent Tuesday morning registering for the January semester at Erie County Community College. She'd passed the required English and Math placement tests last week, which meant she wouldn't have to pay for any non-credit remedial courses. Since she wasn't sure what to study, she signed up for general core classes. She wanted to do something with photography, but making a living as a photographer could be iffy and might very well leech all of the joy out of taking pictures. Carly needed a reliable income. A dental hygienist, maybe? She'd give herself one semester to decide, and in the meantime, be content knowing she was making progress toward a job where she could regain her self-respect. She closed the laptop, pleased with this first step toward her new life.

Ryan was picking her up in an hour to take her to the doctor to get the cast off her arm. Next Monday, she'd be starting physical therapy. Finally. She was more than ready to regain her full mobility.

More than a week had passed since she'd spoken to Joe. She had seen Ryan three times and talked to him almost every day. Their mutual interest in art kept them busy perusing small local galleries as Carly studied the current trends in photography. She ordered the latest high-end editing software, eager to see how she could transform her favorite shots. Joy pulsed in her veins as the desire to create her own art surged upward from her scarred soul.

But that fact didn't keep her from missing Joe, in spite of the fact that Ryan had referred to her as his girlfriend, and she hadn't disagreed.

When Joe had skipped church this week, she was disappointed but not surprised. He probably saw her choice to date Ryan as another rejection. Once more she'd chosen someone else, but this time she'd met a good man, one who might cherish her, one who actually believed she was a woman of worth. In his sight, and in the sight of God and others.

Except Joe.

Joe hadn't even asked to talk to her when he'd called the house last night. "Tell Carly I'm praying for her and hope she is praying for me" was the only message he'd instructed Sarah to convey. Carly was crushed, and she scolded herself for caring so much.

Joe was giving her the space she'd asked for. If she missed him, she had no one to blame but herself. It had taken all of her willpower not to call him when Sarah slipped up, revealing the real reason for Addie's return. How was Joe dealing with his mother having cancer? The prognosis for someone in her fifties couldn't be good. Had she come home to say goodbye to her family? More than once today, Carly had picked up the phone to call Joe. She ached to comfort him, but being available whenever he needed her, knowing they couldn't be a couple, would break his heart in the long run. It would be better for them both if she kept her distance.

But it didn't really matter which man she spent time with. Neither Joe nor Ryan could help her mend her shattered heart. Only God could do that. Placing her hand over her flat abdomen, she willed herself not to cry. Crying would leave her face splotchy and red, and then she'd have to deal with Ryan's questions. Questions she had no intention of answering. At least not today.

"Face the truth, Carly. Accept it."

Her womb was empty. If she hadn't been so stupid, she'd be showing by now and more than half way through her pregnancy. How foolish she'd been to think she could handle Al. To him she was simply a commodity he owned, and her plan to keep their baby had threatened his profit margin.

Lord, please help me not to hate him. I know You expect me to forgive him, and I want to, for You. But I can't. Not yet.

Grief blew across her soul like a squall over the lake, crashing into the break walls she'd erected in her mind to protect herself, to keep her focused on the present. Resisting the pull of despair had become harder since she'd identified Al as her assailant. Knowing he was in jail didn't comfort her the way she'd imagined it would. He might be miserable, but it wasn't enough. The ache in her heart persisted. Al would get five to ten years, but hers was a life sentence. Sorrow dogged the fringes of her mind and advanced to the forefront at the slightest provocation. Last week, she'd burst into tears watching a diaper commercial.

To keep her sanity, she usually shut down all thoughts of her babies, but in unguarded moments, she dared to imagine having a family of her own, someday, when she was finally free of the consequences of her past. If only God would give her another chance to be a mother. But it was hard to hope for something that seemed so unlikely.

If she did have a baby that would mean God forgave her, right?

Deciding she'd need her own laptop soon, she replaced Sarah's on the desk in the corner of the dining room, then went to her room to prepare for Ryan's prompt arrival. Catching the reflection of her distraught face in the hallway mirror made Carly pause. She had to stop thinking about all she'd lost and thank God for what she'd gained. Ryan was a good man, a better man than any she'd ever known.

But he definitely wouldn't understand all she'd gone through with Al, and whatever she suspected Ryan wouldn't understand, she would keep from him.

For now.

They hadn't even been dating for two weeks, and their relationship wasn't official. At least not in her mind.

If things got serious between them, she'd have to tell him about being a call girl. A secret that big would destroy their relationship if she waited too long to share the truth.

How she'd earned her living wasn't the only thing she was keeping from Ryan.

Whenever they were together, Joe was another taboo subject. Whether Ryan recognized the true nature of her feelings for her brother's friend didn't matter. Not to Carly. Keeping her connection to Joe entirely separate from her romance with Ryan made sense.

Compartmentalizing her life was a survival skill she'd mastered out of necessity. Her body shuddered with unwelcome recollections. Instantly, she slammed that door in her mind shut. No one would ever call her Elise again. Her mind might be periodically plagued with memories of her old life, but her heart was new, cleansed of her scarlet sins by Christ's death.

The house phone rang, jarring her nerves. Which was why she continued to postpone getting a new cell phone. An unexpected call could be anyone, but thank goodness, not Al or one of his friends. There was no reason for her to be afraid to answer the landline. Joe had made sure her whereabouts were kept out of all public records. He'd even started a rumor that she'd left the state for Pennsylvania or Ohio. No one knew for sure where Elise Smith had gone. Since the district attorney's investigation had yielded enough physical evidence to prosecute Rutledge without Carly's testimony, anybody who cared probably assumed she'd wanted to get as far away from her former boss as possible.

The phone continued to ring. Could it be the DA's office calling to tell her she'd have to testify after all? Would facing Al in the courtroom and testifying against him make it easier or harder to forgive him? Her palms started to sweat. She breathed deeply to muster her poise and picked up the receiver. "Hello."

"Hi. I didn't think you'd answer."

Joe. The sound of his voice erased her anxiety, but the vulnerability in his words tugged at her, magnifying her need to be there for him. "I'm glad you called. How are you?"

"I miss you."

Those three honest words stirred the memory of their recent kisses, kisses that had taken them both by surprise. Magnetic and infused with longing, Joe's confession fanned a spark of doubt. What was she doing? How could she expect to be happy if she didn't have the courage to follow her heart? "I miss you, too."

"I can be there in an hour."

Feeling trapped and confused, Carly slumped in the chair. "Ryan's on his way. He's driving me to the doctor."

"Oh. Tomorrow then?"

Joe's forced casual tone started a wall behind which they would both hide, if she didn't say the right thing. But what was the right thing?

"Umm, maybe." She paused a few seconds, wanting to ask about his mom but unsure how her concern would be received. "Sarah told me—"

"That I was praying for you?"

"Yes. No. About your mom."

His silence was palpable, proof that Carly had made the only decision they could live with. "I shouldn't have brought her up. I'm sorry."

"No. I'm the one who's sorry. Please, can I take you out to dinner tomorrow?"

"It's Ryan's birthday tomorrow." The impossibility of it all pressed on her, robbing her of oxygen. "We're going to a family dinner at his mother's."

Joe didn't reply. What had she expected him to say? *I didn't know you were that serious.*

Don't go out with Ryan anymore. Give me another chance. Joe would never say any of those things.

Why on earth had she committed to a dinner with his mother so soon in their relationship?

Carly gripped the phone as if her life depended on his next

words. "Joe? Are you still there?"

"Yep."

"I'll call you soon and ... we can go for coffee or lunch. Okay?"

"Yeah, sure. Whenever. Give me a call when you're free."

Somehow, Carly found her voice to say goodbye. Heedless of the tears streaming down her face and dripping off her jaw, she hung up the phone. She pulled a tissue from the box on the table and dried her face.

Had she made a horrible mistake? Should she have been more patient with Joe, trusting that he would eventually deal with his bitterness? If only he could give the past over to God, but her own experience was teaching her how hard that could be. Releasing the past was a painful process in which she made a few steps forward and then slipped back two. From where she sat, Joe didn't want to begin the process at all. If his mom didn't have cancer, would he be willing to even talk to her?

"That's not fair. He met her for coffee before he knew about the leukemia." Audibly reprimanding herself restored a measure of objectivity. Now wasn't the time to sort out her feelings for Joe.

Carly grabbed another tissue, blew her nose, and glanced at her watch. Ryan would be here in ten minutes. She needed to wash her face and brush her hair. And she needed to sit down with her Bible because her conversation with Joe made her question her plan. Was it fair to continue to date Ryan to see if she could care for him as much as he obviously cared for her? As much as she cared for ... Joe?

Sarah had been right about one thing at least. Carly's decision to date Ryan had forced Joe to reveal his love for her, but Sarah hadn't counted on Addie returning. No one could have predicted that a woman presumed dead for almost twenty years would walk back into her family's lives. But

Sarah's other assumption—that Carly would discover which man she could truly love—hadn't panned out. Had it?

"Ryan is a good man. A relationship with him is safe and comfortable. And free of baggage. But Joe ..." Talking to herself wasn't helping. *Lord, help me. Safe and comfortable sounds good, but is it enough to build a relationship?*

Determined to clear her head before Ryan arrived, she headed to the bathroom to get ready.

*

Carly was brushing her teeth when she heard Ryan's car pull into the driveway. His muffler announced his presence. He'd planned to take it to the mechanic this morning, until her doctor's appointment got moved up a day. He'd immediately rescheduled his appointment, explaining that taking care of her took priority over car repairs. She hadn't been a priority in anyone's life since she'd left home two days after her high school graduation. Ryan made her feel cherished and protected. She could definitely get used to the emotional security he provided. Especially because there were no strings attached.

With Al, everything had strings attached until she'd felt strangled to death.

Her naiveté still stung. God was right. Al had wounded her pride. But he hadn't held a gun to her head. Her choices were her own. Ultimately.

Lord, thank You for forgiving me. Please help me to stop beating myself up and to forgive myself.

Ryan knocked on the front door, and Carly turned her wrist to read her watch. Eleven fifteen. He was right on time, as usual. She hadn't meant to depend on him so much, especially since they weren't officially a couple, but in her defense, her limited experience left her clueless about what to expect in a normal relationship.

Sure, she'd managed to meet a few nice guys over the years, mostly at art shows or bookstores. But none of them had hung around long once they found out what she did for a living, and Al had always made sure they found out. The scorn in their eyes when they asked her if it was true was always the same. It didn't matter if she'd dated them for two days or two months, they never called her again. That was something she never understood. Men paid her for company and sex, but *their* actions were acceptable, or at the very least excusable, while hers were reprehensible.

Great-grandma had been right. For men, there are two kinds of women—the kind you marry and the kind you'd never take home to your mother.

But Ryan *was* taking her to meet his mother, even though his interest in Carly wasn't public knowledge. Why was he so invested in their relationship so soon? Elise would keep her guard up. Should Carly?

He knocked a second time on the front door. She swallowed around a painful lump lodged in her throat as she hurried down the hall. The boot slowed her pace a little, but it wasn't nearly as cumbersome as the cast had been. Still, by the time she reached the living room, he was knocking again and calling her name.

When she opened the inside door, the sight of him standing in the morning sunlight made her heart race. Handsome even in a bulky parka, he looked prepared for an early winter storm. Had she missed something in the weather report? She frowned.

His warm brown eyes gazed at her with concern as he pulled both doors closed behind him. "Are you all right?" He tucked a curl behind her ear, sending a shiver of awareness through her.

Breathless, she could only nod. She wanted to grab his

hand and hold it against her cheek. She loved it when he cupped her face with his big hands and kissed her like nothing mattered in the world but the two of them.

Unfortunately, other things mattered.

His current job.

Her former job.

But she pushed the obvious from her mind. "Of course, I'm all right. I … will be as soon as you—"

On cue, he lowered his mouth to hers and kissed her hello. She kissed him back, her response more playful and sweet than passionate.

After a moment, he ended the kiss but kept his arms wrapped around her waist and gave her a reassuring smile.

This man was definitely reliable. A keeper for sure. In his embrace, she felt precious and fine, a woman to be treasured for a lifetime. She didn't exactly believe in love at first sight, but he obviously did. His eyes, his smile, his lips on hers, his arms holding her securely against his muscled chest, all revealed his heart. Could she trust him?

"Good morning. Are you ready to get that cast cut off?"

She grinned. "More than ready." Hugging him back with two arms would be so much more fun.

And dangerous.

But she was a master at knowing where to draw a safe line. Ryan might not know, but she did. The problem would be convincing him that the boundary line was his idea. No, it would be far better to restrict the physical side of their relationship to short hugs and kisses that did no more than take her breath away. That way she could gauge the level of passion smoldering in his eyes and keep their affection within acceptable bounds.

She leaned in close and kissed his cheek. "Let's go. Time's a wasting, as my great-grandmother used to say."

Ryan smiled, the sparkles in his chocolate eyes drawing her in. "What else did your great-grandma say?"

Carly's breath caught in her throat. "Too many things to remember right now. Dr. Mallory is waiting."

There may be two kinds of women, but tomorrow Ryan was taking her home to meet his mother for the first time, and on his birthday of all days. Would Carly pass Mrs. Edgar's litmus test, whatever it was?

Carly Lawrence, you're a new creature in Christ, and Ryan is a preacher of the Gospel, a man who lives by faith and not by the law. And it's just dinner.

She steeled her features and pasted a smile on her face. "Do you think we could stop at the mall after lunch? I'd like to get started on my Christmas shopping."

"Shopping?" He shot her a look of pure panic that puzzled her, until she remembered that he had three younger sisters. "Why do you need to shop today? Christmas is two months away."

"Don't worry. I know exactly what I want. You can wait in the food court if you want. I'm sure you have a book in the car, right?"

He nodded, relief smoothing out the frown in his brow. "The doctor's office, lunch at your favorite restaurant to celebrate, and on to the mall. My whole afternoon is all yours."

CHAPTER FIFTEEN

Joe spent the whole afternoon cleaning his apartment, doing laundry, and stewing about how quickly Ryan Edgar had managed to take Joe's place in Carly's life. Definitely not the way he wanted to spend a Saturday off. She said she missed him. She'd told him she loved him. But she hadn't wasted any time replacing him. Joe dumped the basket of clean laundry on his bed and started to fold it. "You have no one to blame but yourself. And you're acting like a jealous teenager."

The rebuke stung, but what could he do? Push his way back into her life? Prove himself to be the better man? He'd already tried that and failed.

He could pray. And wait.

Waiting gnawed at him, mostly because the longer he waited the more likely Carly would fall in love with Ryan. He was a good man, one without baggage that would hurt her. Unlike Joe.

His baggage was obvious to everyone. Apparently, it always had been. But he'd been unwilling to acknowledge it. Until now.

He was trying with Addie. He'd met her for coffee three times in the last two weeks.

Every time he saw her, she looked frailer. The leukemia was back in full force after a six-month remission. The doctors wanted to try a bone marrow transplant, but his mother had no living siblings. Her children could be a possible match—

there was a one in twenty chance, according to the latest research he'd found on the internet—but with Maureen pregnant, Bob wouldn't even discuss her being tested. That left Joe.

He could do it. He was healthy. He had enough personal time available to complete the procedure and take a few days off to recover. He'd be sore after the extraction of bone marrow from his pelvic bone, but that didn't matter at all. His dad was right. The real problem was Joe's attitude. His bitterness was a poison in his veins more deadly than the leukemia destroying his mother's body.

Forgiving Addie was the answer—the first step toward all he was hoping for himself, for his family, and for Carly. It was past time for him to let go of his anger. But how? Was it as simple as making a decision—*I, Joseph Callahan, resolve to forgive my mother and to stop being angry at her for things that happened years ago.*

That declaration had almost no effect on his feelings. Maybe he needed to say it out loud. "Lord, I resolve to forgive my mother and to stop being angry at her for the past. I know this is what You require of me. Help my feelings to line up with my decision." He set the laundry basket on the bed and caught his reflection in the mirror. He looked the same, except the lines between his eyebrows weren't quite so pronounced. Slow progress was better than no progress.

Now, if only he could hear God's clear directions for how to proceed with the women in his life. Joe could certainly be there for Addie, even if Carly had steeled her heart against him.

Fighting the despair that threatened at the thought of forever losing the woman he loved, Joe absently dropped stacks of clothes in their proper drawers and headed into the kitchen to see what he could scrounge up for dinner. He opened the refrigerator door to find only a jar of mayonnaise, a single hard-boiled egg, a package of cheese, and a moldy hot dog roll. When had he shopped last? Two weeks? Three weeks?

He grabbed the egg, peeled it over the garbage can, and ate it standing over the kitchen sink while staring out at the bare trees in his backyard. Snow was forecast by the end of the next week. Other years, Sarah would have closed up her sister's lakeside cottage by now and moved back to North Buffalo. It didn't take the skill of a detective to figure out that his great-aunt had been delaying her return to accommodate Carly.

Now that Rutledge had been transferred from Wende to Attica State Prison, Carly could relocate without being afraid her former boyfriend turned boss would try to find her. His high-priced attorney had cut a deal with the DA, just as Joe had anticipated. The owner of Rutledge Escort would serve ten years, rather than the maximum of fifteen possible with a conviction. Joe was relieved Carly didn't have to testify against the scumbag who had almost killed her, but when would it truly be over for her?

Did she still blame herself for the miscarriage? Did she cry out her grief on Ryan's shoulder? The thought of her in another man's arms sucked the air out of Joe's lungs, but when he sloughed off his jealousy and reasoned like the astute cop he was known to be, he couldn't help concluding that Carly had told the young pastor nothing at all about her past as Rutledge Escort's most sought after call girl. When she finally did confide in him, how would the man respond if he were looking for a wife who had never been involved in anything remotely objectionable?

Once again, Joe found himself prepared to protect her like another brother would, ready to come to her aid should the man she'd chosen break her heart. He didn't relish the role, but her happiness had always been more important than his own. It still was.

How was she doing now that she'd started physical therapy? He'd resisted the urge to inquire about her emotional state, but Sarah had casually mentioned driving Carly to her first physical therapy session. Admitting that he clearly had ulterior motives when he'd arranged for Carly to stay with his great-aunt pinched his conscience, but information, however limited, was better than knowing nothing. He'd endured ten years of that.

Maybe he could talk Carly into going out for dinner. See what her plans were. Help her find an apartment. Any excuse to see her. He pulled his cell phone from his back pocket and opened his contact list, then touched the icon for Sarah's number before he could change his mind. The phone rang and rang until her answering machine picked up. Joe hung up without leaving a message.

He clenched and unclenched his fists several times. If Carly was out somewhere with Ryan, Joe had no one to blame but himself. But constantly reminding himself of that unfortunate fact made him feel more defeated.

And anxious for her.

Resigned to eating alone, he grabbed his car keys from the kitchen counter. Fast food didn't appeal to him and sit-down dining magnified his loneliness. Wegmans was his best choice. He could always find something delicious and healthy in the grocer's selection of prepared foods. He'd eat first and then grocery shop, taking care of both tasks in one stop. He was midway through his meal of pulled pork, twice-baked potatoes, and roasted vegetables when his phone rang. He didn't recognize the number. "Callahan, here."

"Hi, Joe," Carly said, her tone hesitant, as if she wasn't sure he'd want to talk to her.

"Hi. I didn't recognize the number."

"I bought a new cell phone today. Since there's no chance of Al getting out of prison any time soon, I figured ..."

His protective instincts roared to life. "Just be careful who you give your number to. Don't trust anyone who knew you as Elise."

She sighed. "You're right. So that means I can share my number with about five people."

Joe smiled. He liked the idea that he was one of the first people she'd contacted, so much so that he didn't even want to ask her if it were true. "I'm glad you called. How is your leg and your arm?"

"No more casts, hopefully for the rest of my life."

If he had his way, no one would ever hurt her again. But Ryan would be responsible for looking out for Carly. Unless they ...

"I played basketball with your brother on Sunday. He said he hasn't talked to you since the day after we met for coffee."

She didn't reply.

"Are you still there?" Silently, Joe prayed she wouldn't shut him out. "Jared asked me again about you talking to your parents."

"Look, Joe, I want to see them. I'm just not ready."

Nearly a month had passed since she'd talked with her brother. Jared's frustration was more than understandable. Joe considered asking Carly when she would be ready, but he wasn't exactly moving at lightning speed with his own family, so he opted to change the subject. "I have tickets to a concert two weeks from tonight. Will you go with me?"

He held his breath waiting for her to answer, his heart pounding with anticipation.

"Okay, as long as you understand that we can't be more than friends."

Was there still an unspoken "until" at the tail of that remark? Or had her relationship with Ryan …? Joe would not go there. Not yet. Today, he would settle for seeing her on her terms. "Friends can go out to dinner and a concert and maybe dessert after. I know how much you like your chocolate."

She thanked him for the invitation, and his world was instantly brighter despite the dark November night. "I'll be looking forward to it. I'll pick you up at five o'clock."

*

Joe sat at his sister's kitchen table and waited while she put Gwen down for a nap. He dunked another of Maureen's ginger snaps in his coffee, then popped it in his mouth, savoring the spicy bite of cloves and ginger. His sister could bake treats to rival the finest bakery, a skill she had definitely not learned from their mother. Where Addie was deficient, Leann excelled, but to be fair, their stepmother had trained to be a pastry chef, and she'd gladly taught Maureen everything she knew about baking. The timer blared, and Joe stuffed his hands into oven mitts before opening the oven to retrieve the next tray of cookies. He'd eaten four of them by the time his sister rejoined him in the sunny kitchen.

After a quick glance at the cookie sheet, she raised her eyebrows in mock disapproval. "I take it you didn't eat breakfast."

He laughed. "Who would when they could eat your warm cookies?"

Maureen refilled both their coffee mugs then sat in a chair directly across from him.

"You didn't come here to eat my cookies. Or to share my decaf coffee." She laughed at her own joke, a trait she'd had for as long as Joe could remember.

He dipped a warm ginger snap—his fifth—into coffee that no longer tasted as good now that he'd learned it wasn't high-test. He added more sugar and stirred it with the sugar bowl spoon.

She scowled. "So do you want to tell me what's going on?"

Why was he stalling? His sister would approve. "I'm going to do the bone marrow transplant for Mom."

Maureen's mouth gaped, and the cookie she was eating fell into her lap.

"Don't look so shocked. You're making me feel like a heel."

She shook her head. "No, it's just that … I'm surprised. Mom isn't exactly your favorite person, and there's a lot involved in a bone marrow transplant. The chances of you being a match are next to nothing. And—"

"I know the odds," he said, cutting his sister off before she could verbalize the prognosis.

"I'm going to be tested this week. If I'm a match, there's a good chance Addie can beat the cancer. I need to do this for her." *And for me.*

"I have to ask you." Maureen started to tear up, then a broad smile brightened her tired features. "What brought about this sudden change in your attitude toward Mom?"

He sighed then decided to reveal the truth. "Carly did."

"Carly Lawrence? She hasn't been around in … what, almost ten years?"

"About that." His phone vibrated on the table. One quick glance told him the text was from Carly. They'd been texting every day since she'd gotten her phone. He flipped his cell over so Maureen couldn't see Carly's name on his screen.

Understanding dawned in his sister's eyes. She had seen. "You were sweet on her in high school. I always wondered why the two of you never got together. Something to do with Jared maybe. Then, I heard she'd left town with some—"

"She's back and staying down at Lake Chautauqua."

"Not in Bemus Point?" Maureen's probing look nailed him.

He tried to school his features, but heat flooded his face.

"You're kidding me? She's staying in Bemus Point? With Aunt Sarah? That's pretty convenient for you."

Her teasing hit its mark. Why had he brought Carly into this discussion? He gathered his empty mug and scrunched napkins, then trudged to the sink. "I came to ask you to pray with me for Mom. Nothing more, okay?"

Maureen was standing behind him, the gentle pressure of her hand on his shoulder conveying her concern. "Are you sure you don't want to talk about you and Carly?"

Keeping his back to his sister, Joe mumbled, "There is no me and Carly." Unless he counted multiple daily texts that sometimes morphed into long sharing-their-day talks.

Perching on her toes, Maureen leaned around his stiff shoulder and planted a kiss on his cheek. "That's something else I'm going to pray about."

*

Carly had never been this nervous. Except in the beginning, those first few times, when she'd been with total strangers. Blushing with shame at the memories, she resisted the urge to hide her face with her hands and rubbed her stomach in hopes of calming the tsunami threatening her intestines. But all her attempts at a silent pep talk failed to dissipate her growing anxiety. She almost wished that she and Ryan had spent *his* birthday with his family as they'd originally planned. If only his nieces and nephews hadn't given his mother the stomach flu, then this first meeting would be over. What if Ryan's mother didn't like her? Or worse, didn't approve of her?

Not wanting Ryan to pick up on her anxiety, Carly resisted the urge to clench and unclench her hands. She reached across the console and patted his arm as he made a right-hand turn into his mother's driveway.

Situated at the end of a long asphalt road lined with pine trees, Ryan's childhood home was a stately Victorian painted in pale blue with ivory trim. Dressed in a sleek navy dress that touched the tops of her shoes, his mother waited on the front porch to receive her oldest son.

"Ryan, honey," she called out. "I'm so glad you could make it."

Glancing quickly in Carly's direction, Ryan reached for her hand and clasped it in his steady grip. As they mounted the stone steps together, Mrs. Edgar's gaze surreptitiously assessed Carly and seemed to find her deficient—not at all the sort of woman she'd planned for her son. Carly's palms instantly began to sweat. Ryan squeezed her hand twice for reassurance. She straightened her back and returned the older woman's appraisal with a measuring look of her own. In a nanosecond, Carly saw what she was up against. Elizabeth Edgar was exactly the kind of woman Carly would never want for a mother-in-law—the kind who wasn't willing to give up her place as the most important woman in her son's life.

"Happy birthday, Mother." Ryan kissed both her cheeks, then stepped back and wrapped one arm around Carly's waist, pulling her to his side in a familiar gesture that roused a flash of disapproval in his mother's eyes. "Carly, this is my mother, Elizabeth Edgar. Mother, this is Carly Lawrence, the amazing woman who has captured my heart."

So much for him giving his mother time to adjust. Men!

Mrs. Edgar extended her hand, her manicured nails flashing a sparkling red more appropriate for the Christmas season than early November. "Pleased to meet you, Miss Lawrence."

Taking the older woman's hand and giving it a firm shake, Carly replied, "Nice to meet you, too, but please call me Carly."

Mrs. Edgar didn't need to know how uncomfortable Carly

was with being referred to as Miss. To her, Miss suggested a purity she had lost a long time ago, though Christ's blood had washed her spirit clean. He saw her just as if she'd never sinned—Sarah's words—but Carly still struggled to see herself like that.

A moment of confusion registered on the older woman's face. "Carly. Carly Lawrence. Have we met before?"

Carly shuddered at the possibility. It couldn't be. She'd attended several banquets for local businessmen in recent years, but surely she'd never met Ryan's mother.

Ryan linked one arm in Carly's and the other in his mother's. "Let's continue this discussion inside, ladies. You're starting to shiver, Mother."

Grateful for the distraction, Carly searched her memory for an image of Elizabeth Edgar. Nothing. She had definitely never met the woman before tonight. "Some people say we all have a twin somewhere," Carly said, hoping the cliché would distract rather than convict her.

"Perhaps," Mrs. Edgar said as Ryan hung their coats in a cedar closet just inside the front door. "I seem to remember meeting a young woman at a business function several years ago. Your face reminds me of her. What was her name? Elaine? Ellie? Elise? Yes, her name was Elise."

Every ounce of oxygen leeched out of Carly. She stumbled backward into Ryan's solid chest.

"Are you all right, sweetheart?"

She wasn't. She'd heard of people with an uncanny knack for putting together names with faces of people they'd only met once. Why did Ryan's mother have to be one of them?

Ryan studied Carly, probably noting her dilated eyes. That was the one witness to her fear she'd been unable to control.

"I'm fine," she lied, hoping they didn't notice how

breathless she sounded. "My ankle gave out."

The second the lie escaped her lips she regretted it. Ryan swooped her up into his arms and carried her into the nearby sitting room. Carly's face flushed hot. "I'm fine. You don't have to carry me. I'm perfectly capable of walking." Placing her lips against his ear, she whispered, "You're embarrassing me in front of your mother."

Ignoring her concern, Ryan gently positioned her in a Queen Anne's chair with an ottoman supporting her weak leg. Then he dropped to one knee, unzipped the boot, and carefully freed her foot to check her ankle. The touch of his warm hands against her cool skin soothed her nerves, but his attention heightened her embarrassment. "Please don't fuss. I'm fine."

"I don't feel any swelling." He raised his face to hers, the concern in his eyes eclipsed by a glimmer of teasing as he replaced the clunky boot and zipped it back up, then lowered her foot to the floor. "I guess you can walk to the dinner table." Getting to his feet, he addressed his mother, "Carly is recovering from a broken ankle. And a broken arm."

Resisting the temptation to avert her eyes, Carly met Mrs. Edgar's gaze directly and saw what she expected to find— curiosity bordering on suspicion. But the woman, obviously well-schooled in social etiquette, asked no questions.

Moments later, the house was full of laughter and voices as Ryan's younger brother and sisters with their spouses and more children than Carly could keep track of all greeted the family matriarch to wish her a happy birthday. Calling on her own social graces, Carly managed to be cordial as she was introduced to each member of Ryan's family. She even remembered all of their names, a skill she'd honed in her years as an escort. But *she* wouldn't remember their names years later, especially if she never saw them again.

Whenever she wasn't part of the conversation,

apprehension snaked up her spine. She'd never been introduced to the Edgars, but that didn't mean Elizabeth hadn't seen Carly on the arm of one of her husband's associates. She would need to tell Ryan soon. Before his mother added two and two and came up with Rutledge Escort Service.

*

Ryan held her coat as Carly slipped her arms into the fur-lined sleeves. She couldn't wait to get home. As the evening had worn on, she'd taken a chill that was more mental than physical, though her composure never faltered. She'd laughed and smiled at all of the right times and even held Ryan's youngest niece on her lap. Holding a newborn snuggled against her bare shoulder was almost more than Carly could bear. The sweet, clean smell of baby, together with the absolute helplessness of the infant in her arms made Carly want to weep with despair. But she'd tamped down her emotions long enough to escape to the bathroom where she gave herself a stern but silent lecture that brightened the bleak winter in her heart.

Ryan lifted her hair over her coat, sending an altogether different shiver through her. His fingers grazed her neck as he straightened her collar, and she trembled. He kissed her cheek, and she caught a whiff of his woodsy aftershave.

"You were wonderful tonight. My whole family was enchanted with you."

If only that were true. What could she say that wouldn't be an outright lie? The expansive foyer was closing in on her. "That's nice."

"Nice?"

Apparently, he had no idea what this evening had cost her. He couldn't read her at all, couldn't see through her carefully constructed facade. Joe would have known the instant something distressed her. And that distressed her even more because she'd be tempted to confide in him.

You're not being fair. How could Ryan understand when you've told him nothing? And talking to Joe about this would be all wrong.

Ryan raised his eyebrows, his eyes questioning her.

He'd obviously asked her something, and she'd zoned out. "I'm sorry. What were you talking about?" she asked, struggling to ground herself in this moment.

Smiling, Ryan held open the mahogany door for her. "About my family, and how much they like you."

This was important to him, but she'd spent the whole night saying the appropriate thing, and she was exhausted with trying to please everyone.

He took her arm, and they started down the steps, her relying more on his support than on the cursed cane.

"Are you all right?"

Averting her face, she replied, "I'm tired is all."

"Too tired to stop somewhere for coffee?" He opened her car door and waited for her answer as she settled into the bucket seat, clicked her seatbelt in place, and reached past him for the handle to pull the door shut.

Her gaze caught his, his desire obvious in the bright moonlight, but all she could think about was his mother watching from the front window, trying to decide if Elise and Carly were the same person. When Ryan bent into the car and moved in to kiss her, she stopped him with her palm flat against his chest. "One of the kids could be watching out the window." *Or worse, your mother.*

He frowned, straightened to his full height, shut her door, and rounded the car to the driver's side. He started the engine without another word.

Until they were out of sight of the house. Then he pulled

over onto the shoulder and put the car in park. "What's going on?" He laid his hand on her knee. "And don't say nothing because I won't believe you."

A believable lie popped into her head. She blurted it out. "Being with your family tonight forced me to face how much I miss my own family."

And suddenly, it was true.

But condemnation pressed like a lead sinker against her heart, and tears welled in her eyes. She turned her face to the side window. *God, I'm sorry for lying. I'll tell him the truth. Soon. But not tonight.*

Ryan gripped her shoulders. His powerful hands massaged through her coat to work out the knots of tension. She winced but refused to cry out. Her pain was her business.

When had she started again pretending to be someone she was not? She twisted away from his strong, but gentle touch and found herself inches from his mouth. "Ryan, I have to tell you something."

He covered her lips with his, silencing her words, and she gave herself to the love and passion he offered. If only for a moment, she wanted to believe she could still be the right woman for him.

But heat coursed through her body, roused by his deepening, demanding kiss. It would be so easy to …

To what? Forget her convictions and ruin everything?

She struggled in his arms, and he released her instantly.

The loss of his warmth and comfort brought fresh tears.

"I'm sorry. I didn't mean—"

She stopped his words with one finger over his mouth. "Don't apologize. If anyone needs to apologize, it's me."

He frowned, disbelief creasing lines between his dark eyebrows. "You didn't do anything wrong. Now or in the driveway."

Not tonight she hadn't.

Unless she counted lying about her ankle and what was really bothering her—lying about how she used to earn her living. And making him believe she was someone she was not. Yes, she was a new creature in Christ. But she was more Rahab than Mary. What would Ryan do when he found that out?

"Can you take me home, please?" She met his questioning eyes. "I have a headache."

"Of course. But first ..." He reached into the glove compartment for a bottle of pain reliever, then grabbed an unopened water bottle from the backseat, and handed them to her before starting the engine and pointing his car in the direction of Sarah's house.

His caring made her feel even worse.

*

About eleven Joe gave up looking for a text from Carly, but he couldn't help wondering about her evening with Ryan's mother. No matter how the birthday party had gone, Carly probably didn't want to talk to Joe about it. But knowing that only increased his anxiety. He fell asleep praying for her. "Carly needs You, Lord. She's been hurt so much already." Joe continued to lie on his back with his eyes closed, his heart pouring out pleas for the woman he loved until he dozed off.

His alarm clock was blaring its awful beeping. Joe flung his arm backward and made contact with the snooze button. Seconds later, he was on his feet, heading to the shower. Time to face this day.

Thirty minutes later, he arrived at the station for a special meeting to debrief the members of his precinct after the shooting death of one of their own, a young rookie who had come back from maternity leave only last month.

*

On Friday afternoon, Joe stopped at a local lab to have his blood drawn to type his HLA. Before he found out about his mother's leukemia, Joe had never even heard of Human Leukocyte Antigens. What he knew now gave him a glimmer of hope. The odds—one in twenty children would match a parent identically—didn't stop him from wanting to investigate the possibility. If his bone marrow could help his mother fight the cancer ravaging her body, then Joe would gladly donate. In the meantime, Roswell Park was searching the national donor registry for a possible match. Addie could still go into remission again without the transplant, but with the transplant the doctors could increase the intensity of her chemotherapy treatments, possibly eradicating the cancer for good.

The nurse drawing his blood was obviously gifted at her job. Joe hadn't felt more than a slight pinch when she inserted the needle. "How long before I can find out if I'm a match?"

The young woman smiled. "I can't answer that question for you. I advise you to have your mother contact her doctor in a few days."

So much for following through with his plan without his mother's knowledge.

Tomorrow, Maureen and Bob were having a party for Susie's fourth birthday. Everyone would be there. Bob's parents. Dad and Leann. And Addie. It would be their first family event since his mother's return. Hopefully, having Leann and Addie in the same room for the first time wouldn't be too awkward for either of them. Or for Dad.

But that wasn't Joe's first concern. He needed to get his mother alone for a few minutes to tell her about his intention to become a bone marrow donor for her.

CHAPTER SIXTEEN

A cluster of bright pink and purple balloons decorated his sister's mailbox. Had she invited someone other than family members to Susie's party? Hopefully not other four-year-olds. Joe didn't mind kids. He enjoyed his nieces and nephews, but he was in no mood for the escalated volume of a house full of children on sugar-highs. He recognized all of the cars parked in the driveway but one, which was probably Addie's. There was still room for two more vehicles, but Joe opted to park along the curb across the street. He'd rather not block anyone in, especially his mom, who might need to leave early if the birthday party got to be too much for her.

After knocking several times on the front door without anyone greeting him, he simply let himself in. The festive scene before him erased any hope he had of talking to his mother about the bone marrow transplant tonight, but shifting gears had never been easy for him, especially where his mother was concerned, and telling her he'd been tested had been uppermost in his mind all day. Even if his HLA markers didn't match hers, Joe wanted her to know he'd tried. Maybe it was his way of letting her know he forgave her without actually saying the words.

That's not good enough, Callahan. What if she doesn't make it?

He refused to go there. She had to recover. Maureen and the kids needed her to recover. He needed her to recover. Now that she was back in their lives, the thought of losing her again, for good this time, knifed his heart.

What exactly was he expecting her to do? Make up for all of the time they'd lost because she'd decided other things were more important than her family?

Joe gave himself a mental smack upside the head. This was not the time or the place to reopen old wounds. Susie deserved tonight to be all about her. Turning four was a big deal for a little girl. And it had to be confusing for her to suddenly have three grandmothers.

Joe spotted the birthday girl on the other side of the room, sitting in the rocker on Addie's lap. The two of them were reading his favorite childhood book, *The Pokey Little Puppy*. With nods and brief hellos, he acknowledged the other members of his family as he navigated his way across the crowded room to greet Addie and Susie. He planted a kiss on the top of her curly head. "Happy birthday, sweetheart."

She rewarded him with a smile that highlighted her dimples. "Did you bring me a present, Uncle Joe?"

From behind his back, he produced a brightly wrapped box adorned with a pink and white polka-dotted bow. "Of course I did. Do you want to open it now?"

His mother shot him a look, glanced over his shoulder to where he'd last seen his sister, and mouthed the word "later."

To his surprise, Joe did not bristle at her directive. He smiled at her instead, then backpedaled with his niece. "Oh, yeah. I forgot. You have to wait until Mommy and Daddy are ready to take pictures of you opening your gifts."

Susie nodded, her expression serious. "And I have to wait until after everyone sings 'Happy Birthday' to me, and we eat cake and ice cream."

"We're having dinner first, aren't we?" Joe asked, directing his question to his mother.

Addie smiled. "We've been waiting for you."

Her comment was a simple statement of fact, devoid of any rebuke. Leann would have nailed him with a look that demanded an explanation for his tardiness, but Addie was treading carefully with him. Joe sighed, unsure what to do about the awkwardness between them.

Deciding he'd better offer to lay out the food on the sideboard, assuming his sister had planned a buffet, Joe said, "I'll go help Maureen." Then, without second-guessing his reasons or her potential reaction, Joe kissed his mother's forehead, and whispered in her ear, "I love you, Mom. I'm glad you're here."

As he straightened to his full height, he caught her gaze and was startled by the sheen of moisture in her tired eyes. She opened her mouth to reply, but her lips trembled with emotion.

She bit her lower lip. "Me, too, honey."

With those three words, everything shifted. He'd made the decision to forgive her. Now, he felt he really had.

Joe headed into the kitchen, where the ladies were bustling about from stovetop to fridge to oven, attending to food in various stages of preparation. Leann was stirring a thick cheddar cheese sauce for the broccoli. Bob's mother, Rose, carried a cookie sheet of stuffed mushrooms from the oven to the center island, where Maureen was already arranging an assortment of hot finger foods. Joe snagged a mozzarella stick and dipped it in marinara sauce before popping it in his mouth. His sister gave him a playful swat on the arm. "Did you come in here to help or to sneak food?"

He grinned. "You wound me. I came to help."

"Great, then you can slice the roast beef." She gestured to the far counter, which was crowded with roasting pans and covered casseroles. "And then you can tackle the ham."

"Your wish is my command, fair sister." He bowed with a

flourish of his right hand.

Maureen arched her brows. "What is wrong with you?"

How could he explain? He'd never realized how much his unforgiveness had weighed down his heart. He shrugged his shoulders, not ready to talk about what had happened until he'd said everything he needed to say to Addie. "I'm happy we're all here together."

Maureen and Leann exchanged glances. Apparently, neither of them missed the significance of his declaration. Either the women in his life were extremely perceptive, or he was entirely too transparent, which he'd never been accused of in the past. On the other hand, Maureen, Leann, and Dad had all called Joe out, urging him to get over his bitterness against Addie so that he could get on with his life. Now that he had taken their advice, he shouldn't be surprised when they noticed the change in his attitude.

Joe was halfway through slicing the roast when Bob came in the kitchen to check on their progress. He wrapped his arms around Maureen's expanding waist and kissed her neck, causing a pink blush to rise in her cheeks. "Stop. Your mother is staring at you."

Bob laughed and whispered something in Maureen's ear that made her giggle.

Watching their exchange, Joe missed Carly. Her absence was painful and entirely his fault. If he had heeded his family's advice sooner, Carly would be here with him, sharing in Susie's birthday celebration, but the woman he loved had chosen Ryan over him because she couldn't bear to wonder if Joe would always be waiting for her to walk out of his life the way his mother had.

He was an idiot.

He squelched the frown that threatened to spoil the atmosphere. He'd figure out a way to persuade Carly that she could trust him with her heart. If God meant them for each other, God would make a way where there seemed to be no way, just like the song promised. Joe needed to have faith. More than any other time in his life, he had to trust that God was in control, no matter how out of control things might seem.

*

Standing at the kitchen sink, washing the handful of dishes after her dinner of tomato soup and a grilled cheese sandwich, Carly regretted turning down Sarah's invitation to attend the ladies' Friday night Bible study. Her mind simply would not be quiet. Being in the company of others would have silenced the litany of reproofs in her head.

It wasn't being alone that was the problem. She was used to being lonely. From the moment Al had started Rutledge Escort Service, the focus of their relationship had shifted from personal to business, though it took years for her to face *that* unpleasant truth. He was an opportunist, and she was beautiful. Even now the possibility that she'd only been a commodity to him from the very beginning haunted her. Maybe that's why Joe had always despised him. And why her brother had done everything short of locking her in her room the day she'd packed her bags and announced her intention to leave with Al. She shook her head at her foolishness. How could she have been so stupid? Jared and Joe had never lied to her, yet she'd chosen to believe Al, whose promises meant nothing to him.

Worst of all, she'd ignored her conscience, rationalizing her choice because she and Al were planning to get married.

But all that was in the past. A past that kept eclipsing her present and her future.

Why hadn't she gone to the Bible study tonight? She might have heard something that would have helped her figure out what to do next. For starters, she needed to learn how to stop berating herself. Jesus had died for her sins. He'd paid the ultimate price. There was no reason for her to continue to punish herself. So, why couldn't she stop? She'd asked God to help her forgive herself. Why wasn't He answering that prayer?

Maybe because she was still thinking about what she deserved.

If she and Ryan weren't dating, she'd talk and pray with him until God lifted this burden. Sharing a romantic relationship with one's pastor definitely had its drawbacks.

Carly wanted to call Joe in the worst way. In the two weeks since she'd bought her cell phone, they'd talked several times, but he'd kept their conversation casual, which was okay because sharing her spiritual struggles with Joe didn't seem right. Ryan would see it as inappropriate and unnecessary. On the other hand, Joe was the only person who knew the whole ugly, bitter truth about her. He was a good listener.

And God help her, she missed him. She was looking forward to going to the concert with him tomorrow night, though she hadn't told Ryan about her plans. He would not understand her needing any man but him.

Still, admitting that she needed anyone, especially Joe, felt strange. For most of her life, he'd been just her brother's friend, another guy telling her what he thought was best for her. She'd been miffed at the two of them ganging up on her, nagging her with all the reasons why Al couldn't be trusted. Would she have listened if they'd given her a little breathing room to figure things out for herself? Maybe. But Al had made sure she spent every waking hour with him, probably so she'd have no time to rethink her decision.

God, it doesn't matter anymore. Please help me to stop torturing myself with what ifs. What if I'd never left with Al?

What if I'd refused to have the abortion? What if I'd gone home years ago?

Carly took her hands out of the dishwater, dried them quickly, swiped the screen on her cell phone, and navigated to Joe's number. She wanted to call. She shouldn't call him. It wouldn't be fair. She plunged her hands back into the sudsy water and tried to think.

For the past eight years, she'd confided in no one. Sure, she and Star had commiserated with each other, especially after a really bad night with a client. Contrary to what some people believed, streetwalkers weren't the only ones who got beat up. Men with a lot of money to spend and even more pride often displayed great skill in hurting a woman without leaving a single mark that could be seen by the casual observer. And Al had always been a casual observer. He wanted his merchandise in pristine condition—his words not theirs. But he never looked beyond a quick glance at their arms. And their faces, of course. Al expected his girls to report anything serious, specifically, anything a little cover-up couldn't conceal. He kept a list of offenders who were no longer granted escorts, with or without fringe benefits, no matter how much money they were willing to lay on the table. But the list was a short one.

Carly shuddered at the memories. After that first time, she'd gone home and thrown up everything she'd eaten that day, her body and soul repulsed by what she'd submitted to. How could she have sold her body? She wasn't a whore. She'd grown up in a Christian home. Her conscience begged her to stand up to Al. But she'd ignored the warning to flee that rose from deep in her spirit.

Lord, thank You for getting me out, for forgiving me and giving me a chance at a new life.

But in order to start her new life, she had to lay her old

life to rest, and that meant doing more than just forgiving herself. She needed to make things right with her parents. She scoffed out loud. How ironic! Here she was judging Joe because he couldn't reconcile with his mother, and she had yet to even call her parents.

Or tell Ryan about her past.

Before his mother made the connection between business social functions and Rutledge Escort Service. Before she realized that Carly not only looked like Elise but was in fact the same person.

If Carly didn't tell him herself, Ryan would feel betrayed when he found out. And he would find out eventually. She couldn't let him be caught off guard and unprepared for his mother's caustic disapproval. Within moments of meeting her, Carly had recognized Mrs. Edgar's emphasis on appearances. For her type, being gracious did not extend beyond what she considered socially correct. Having her minister son involved with a former call girl was about as far from socially correct as anyone could imagine.

Frustrated, Carly scrubbed the pot with more muscle power than was necessary, rinsed it, and set it in the drainer. She dried her hands and applied two squirts of Sarah's favorite pumpkin spice lotion. Then, before she could change her mind, she marched to her bedroom, found the purse she'd carried the day she'd met Jared at the coffee shop and dug through the contents until she found her brother's business card.

"Lord, let this be the right choice. Not just for me. But for my family, too." She picked up her phone and keyed in Jared's cell number. It rang. Once. Twice. Three times. Then four.

Should she hang up? Wait for his voicemail? Call back later?

"Hello. Jared Lawrence speaking. Who's calling, please?"

"It's me, Jare."

"Carly," he whispered. "Is it really you?"

"Yes. Why are you whispering?"

"Because Dad is in the next room reading *The Wall Street Journal*."

Right. Jared was still living at home, paying off his school loans. She'd forgotten. She sucked in a deep breath, and before she could change her mind, said, "Ask him to come to the phone."

"You want to talk to him? Are you sure? What about Mom? Are you ready to talk to her, too?"

"Jared, please stop hammering me with questions. Just hand your phone to Dad." Carly could hear their voices but couldn't make out what they were saying. Her palms were sweating so much she almost dropped her cell.

"Hello. This is Sean Lawrence."

Her breath caught in her throat, and her prayers barraged heaven. "It's me, Dad. I want to see you. And Mom."

"Carly! Oh, honey, it's been so long. Where are you?"

The emotion in his voice broke her heart. "Dad, I'm sorry. I never meant to hurt you. Any of you."

"It doesn't matter now. As long as you're okay."

It did matter. More than her father could possibly imagine. "Dad, I need to explain. But not on the phone. Can I see you? And Mom?"

"Can you see us? Honey, not a single day has gone by that we haven't prayed to hear your voice, to see you again."

In a matter of minutes, her father had arranged for Jared to pick her up and bring her to their house for Sunday dinner. They said their goodbyes, he disconnected the call, and Carly released a long sigh. In less than 48 hours, she would be sitting in her parents' living room telling them how far she had drifted from all they'd tried to teach her. And the story of her life would be worse than anything they may have imagined.

Had she made a horrible mistake?

She could still back out—see them without confiding the horrid details of her miserable life with Alan Rutledge. Dread cloaked her heart in fear. Fear of being rejected, abandoned, disowned.

Lord, I know You love me. But I need my parents' love, too. Please. I can't bear to see them look at me with disgust.

Carly reached for the Bible on the kitchen table and opened it to one of her favorite passages and read until her heart quieted.

"Your Word says You'll be with me, God. With Your help, I can do this. I *have* to do this."

*

Before she'd even had her first cup of coffee, Ryan's ringtone interrupted her morning shower. Should she answer? She hadn't told him about her plans with Joe. Ignoring Ryan's call wasn't an option. He'd only call back in an hour or so, as soon as he had a spare minute. Shoving the shower curtain aside, she reached for her cell where she'd dropped it on top of her towels. "Good morning, I'm in the shower." She sensed the blush flaming his face. His embarrassment would cut this call short. "What's up?"

"Mom wants to know if we'd like to come over for dinner."

Thank You, God. "I can't. I have plans, remember?"

"I don't. But, okay, I'll tell her we'll see her on Thanksgiving."

Carly backed up far enough in the bathtub that the sound of the water hitting the shower curtain would remind Ryan that he was talking to her while she wasn't wearing any clothes. "Is there anything else you need right now because I need to rinse the shampoo out of my hair?"

"No, um, I'll see you tomorrow." The blush was back. She

could hear it in his voice.

"Enjoy dinner at your mom's and tell her I said hello."

*

Joe arrived fifteen minutes early. Carly was fussing with her unruly curls, attempting to tame them into submission with a new leave-in conditioner that Sarah had picked up at the hair salon. As he greeted his aunt and the two began to laugh at something Carly couldn't make out, she dismissed the warm feeling that rushed through her body at the sound of his voice. She frowned at her flushed face. Her hands were shaking, making the whole hair process more complicated than it needed to be.

This was Joe. They were old friends going to dinner and a concert. It wasn't a date.

Ryan had no cause to be jealous. She should have been upfront about her plans for tonight. Trying to make Ryan think they'd had a conversation he'd forgotten was dishonest. That was reason enough to feel guilty. *I'm sorry, Lord. I just couldn't get into a conflict with him today, not when I'm going to talk to my parents tomorrow.*

Besides, other than the Christmas concert, Ryan had no interest in classical music. She and Joe had both played in their high school orchestra, first and second chair violins. Tonight's concert would feature a harpist and a classical guitarist. She and Joe were going as friends, friends who shared a common interest in chamber music. Carly squirted her favorite perfume on the palms of her hands and rubbed the fragrance into the soft skin at her throat and wrists. Inhaling deeply of the heady fragrance, she groaned. Wearing perfume on a night out might be second nature for her, but Joe could easily get the wrong impression.

*

Carly paused in the kitchen doorway, her smile indicating

that she had no idea how captivating she looked to Joe. Her long blonde curls spilled over a brown V-neck sweater, and a print skirt of some flowing material hugged her legs. He was so used to seeing her with the cast that he'd forgotten how gorgeous her legs were. And satin smooth. A distant memory from high school unfolded. Their legs accidentally brushing against each other under the Lawrence dinner table. His instant denial of their connection the second he'd seen Jared's questioning appraisal.

Joe inhaled a sharp breath, rose from his chair, and stopped several feet away from her. Dismissing the urge to hug her and hold her close, he dragged his gaze from her shapely form and back to her sparkling brown eyes. She didn't know the effect she was having on him. Did she? How could she not know, with her experience? He frowned. That wasn't fair. She'd changed, but expecting her to have amnesia when it came to men was ridiculous and … unrealistic.

She leveled him with a blank stare that concealed her thoughts. But he wasn't fooled.

She didn't miss much either. Maybe she should think about becoming a cop herself. "You look stunning."

Her smile returned. In seconds, she closed the space between them, kissed his cheek, and whispered, "You look awesome, too."

Succumbing to her enticing perfume, he enclosed her in his arms, his fingers catching in her silky curls and drawing a soft breath from her. Her body fit so perfectly against his that he could almost forget she was dating Ryan. But not quite. Joe released her, backed away, and faced his great-aunt. Sarah's knowing smile proved he wasn't fooling her either.

"We should be going." He emptied his half-full coffee cup into the sink, taking a moment to collect himself. Dinner and a concert with a friend—that's what he'd promised her. It didn't matter that he wanted so much more.

The kisses they'd shared haunted his dreams. In just a month, he'd increased his muscle mass by twenty percent trying to work off his frustration.

*

After the concert, Joe had barely turned the key in the ignition before Carly reached over and placed her palm on his thigh. Her fingers were ice cold, thank goodness. He tensed. She withdrew her hand, and he shifted to see her face. She was trying to smile, but her lips were trembling. Tears tracked her cheeks. He wiped them away with his thumb. He needed to kiss her, but what she needed mattered more. "What's wrong? Why are you crying? I'm sorry about the lullabies. If I'd known—"

"It's okay. Grief's a funny thing. Sometimes, I have to dig my nails into my palms to keep from sobbing in public. Tonight, I let myself imagine what might have been. I was fantasizing about rocking my baby while "Brahms' Lullaby" soothed us … both to sleep. Until I remembered that my babies are gone because of me." She turned her face toward the passenger window. "If remembering them didn't make me cry, what kind of a woman would I be?"

Joe had no idea what to say to ease her pain. *God forgives you? You can have other children someday.* He touched her shoulder, gently turning her until their eyes met.

"I called Jared. I'm going to tell my parents everything tomorrow."

Adrenaline surged through Joe. "I'll go with you."

One look at her widened eyes told him he'd said the wrong thing. She needed to do this alone. Unless. "Is Ryan going with you?"

She shook her head twice.

Joe released the breath he hadn't realized he was holding.

"Jared's picking you up?"

"At your aunt's house, right after church."

Her brother would look out for her, but every fiber of Joe ached to be by her side, to pour his strength into her so she could survive the most difficult conversation she'd ever have.

Carly reached for his hand and squeezed it tightly. "Will you pray for me?"

"I've never stopped."

CHAPTER SEVENTEEN

No way was Carly ready to see Ryan. Why hadn't she asked her brother to pick her up before church? Ryan would expect her to go out to lunch with him after the service. Spending Sunday afternoons together had become their routine in the past month since they'd started dating.

But even if she weren't going to see her parents for the first time in ten years, she'd be looking for a way to postpone the conversation looming over her head.

"Coward," she said aloud as she typed a quick text explaining that she was going to her parents for dinner. She tapped send, then realized Ryan would think her message was abrupt, possibly even rude, so she sent him a second message promising to call him later tonight. Even that didn't calm the hornets buzzing in her stomach. The possibility that she'd end up telling her parents and Ryan about her past in the same day caused a wave of nausea to rise up into her throat. She swallowed hard. Ryan would have to wait. After Jared dropped her off, she would text Ryan that she had a headache and would call him tomorrow. Her plan gave her a measure of control over what would certainly be an unpredictable day. It probably wouldn't even be a lie. The mere thought of telling her parents that their daughter had been a prostitute caused shooting pain behind her eyes.

Lord, help me get through this day, please.

Carly made her bed and then jumped in the shower. She relished the pulsing hot water massaging the tension out of her shoulders. She closed her eyes and let the water streaming over her face mingle with her tears. Would she never be free of all she'd done as Elise? If only the water could wash her clean of her past. Then she could start fresh.

But Christ's blood had done that for her. In her heart, she believed she was "washed in the soul-cleansing blood of the Lamb," but her mind kept reminding her of every shameful thing she'd ever done. Instinctively, she scrubbed harder with the loofah sponge, trying to wash away the memory of being touched. Not for the first time she wondered who she despised more, the men who used her or herself for allowing them to take her body in exchange for money and expensive, useless gifts. At what cost had she permitted herself to be violated? She'd given herself away and gotten nothing of lasting value in return. Worst of all, she'd lost her babies.

If only Carly could turn back the clock and start over, she would listen to Jared and break off her relationship with Al instead of following him who knows where. She would welcome the affection in Joe's eyes.

Carly rubbed her fists over her eyes and started to sing, "I know it was the blood for me ..." She sang through the whole song, the inspired words making her feel stronger and more valuable, at least in God's eyes. Whether she'd feel as cherished after she told her parents the truth would depend on their willingness to forgive her.

*

With his mother's hand gently gripping his left arm, Joe stepped through the sanctuary doors, his eyes scanning the congregation for Carly and Sarah. They were seated in Sarah's usual place in the second pew on the right. Carly's head was bent, her forehead pressed against her folded arms, which were resting on the back of the polished pew in front of her. Was she praying about talking to her parents? Probably. He hoped she wasn't still plagued with guilt from her past. He was ashamed to admit, even to himself, that he wanted her to be praying about her feelings for him. As unlikely as that was. He gave himself a mental punch. Thinking about their relationship today was pure selfishness. Her reconciliation with her parents was far more important.

Still, he wanted to be nearby in case she needed him.

Tempted to lead Addie down the outside aisle along the row of stained glass windows directly to the vacant pew behind Carly, Joe debated. He didn't want to be a distraction to her, or to Ryan, either, though his feelings for his rival were not benevolent. But, rather than joining Maureen and her family for their service as he had for the past two Sundays, Joe *had* chosen to bring Addie *here,* so Carly could see with her own eyes that he had forgiven his mother. That meant sitting where the woman he loved would be sure to see him at some point.

Addie looked up at him, her eyes questioning his hesitation. Making a snap decision, he started down the outside aisle but stopped three rows behind Sarah and Carly. She'd be sure to notice them at the close of the service, when his presence would not interfere with her focus on the Lord.

But what if her mind was more on the pastor than the message? Jealousy knotted Joe's stomach and knit his brows in a frown. The possibility that Ryan might actually be the better man for Carly threatened to squeeze every drop of blood from Joe's heart. *Lord, help. I love her so much.*

Joe resisted the thought that if he really loved her he would respect her choice and let her go. He sensed he wouldn't have to give her up, though she and Ryan were clearly a couple. At the moment. Always the strategist, Joe renewed his determination to wait patiently. He'd make sure that Carly knew she could rely on him. Then, if something happened between her and Ryan …

Of course, that approach hadn't worked in the past, when Joe had convinced himself that his best course of action would be to wait for Carly to recognize Rutledge's true character.

This time, she'd picked a man of honor.

Lord, maybe coming here wasn't such a good idea after all.

His mother placed her frail hand over his. "Are you all right?"

Joe favored her with a reassuring smile then directed his attention to the platform at the front of the church where the choir was gathered. The music director nodded to the group, and the song service began, encouraging Joe to center his thoughts on his relationship with the Lord, but Carly's beautiful soprano voice soon drew his gaze to her long blonde curls, and he found himself thinking about running his fingers through those silky tresses and kissing her soundly. Clearly, sitting behind her was not his best idea.

During the final chorus of "Leave It There," Pastor Ryan strode to the pulpit and opened his worn Bible. He greeted the congregation with a smile, which irked Joe. The man looked decidedly happier than he had in September, before Carly had become a regular parishioner. Beautiful and compassionate, she did have a way of making a man feel as if his life was better with her in it. If only she believed that about herself.

Hindsight is definitely twenty-twenty, Callahan.

"Please open your Bibles to Philippians, chapter one, beginning with verse three." Without being prompted, the congregation stood in unison, listening while the pastor read verses three through seven. Then he besought the Lord's blessing on the service and directed everyone to be seated.

Joe redoubled his efforts to keep his eyes off Carly and on the pastor, or better yet on his Bible.

"Today, I'd like us to focus on not only how we see

ourselves in Christ but on how we view others. Too many times, believers stop short with verse six and miss the message of verse seven," Pastor Ryan said as he wrote the Scriptures references on a white board propped on a wooden easel to the left of the pulpit. "The promise that God will finish the good work that He started in us brings great comfort, particularly when we're plagued by frustration and disappointment. This is especially true when we know we're at fault. But many times we forget to apply that same grace and mercy to others."

The faint smell of his mother's citrus perfume wafted up to Joe's nose. He wanted to reach over, clasp her hand in his, and beg her to forgive him for all the times he'd failed to see her the way God saw them all—as works-in-progress being changed a little at a time in the Potter's patient hands.

Joe met Pastor Ryan's gaze, and they exchanged a brief look of mutual respect that transcended the tension caused by their affection for the same woman.

The moment passed, and the pastor surveyed the whole congregation. He held up a second Bible. "Let me read it to you out of the Amplified. 'And I am convinced and sure of this very thing, that He Who began a good work in you will continue until the day of Jesus Christ [right up to the time of His return], developing [that good work] and perfecting and bringing it to full completion in you.' And now verse seven: 'It is right and appropriate for me to have this confidence and feel this way about you all ...'"

The remainder of the sermon roused frequent exclamations of "amen" and "that's right, brother" as Pastor Ryan exhorted the people to encourage and uplift one another rather than to pass judgment. "Just as none of us were without sin when we came to Christ, no one can say he or she has reached perfection, so in the end, no one has a right to condemn or reject another believer. As the saying goes, I'm not what I want to be, and I'm not what I ought to be, but I'm not what I used to be, praise God."

*

Tears slid down Carly's cheeks, cooling her face. Overwhelming gratitude for God's deliverance filled her heart. She was not who she used to be, and she would never be that person again. Elise was gone forever. God had given her a new start and a brand new identity as his daughter. She was loved for herself. No longer would she be an ornament or an object for some man's pleasure. She wasn't sure what her future would hold, but from deep in her soul welled up the comforting knowledge that God's plans for her would always be good.

Without a word, Sarah slipped her several tissues, and Carly dried her face as Ryan closed the service with a prayer reminding the congregation that every process of salvation, including sanctification, depended on the believer's faith in the finished work of Christ. The music director started singing "What Can Wash Away My Sin," reinforcing the pastor's message.

At the last bar, Sarah was on her feet before Carly. The older woman squeezed Carly's shoulder to get her attention. She tried to stand, but Sarah stopped her with all of her one hundred and twenty-pounds, then bent to whisper, "Joe's here. With his mother."

Carly's mind whirled with questions. Why hadn't Joe mentioned last night that he was coming back here to church today? And why had he brought his mother? Addie's presence could only mean one thing. He was sending Carly a message— that his past would no longer interfere with their relationship, that she could count on him, no matter what. Her heart sped up. Happily-ever-after images flitted through her mind. The two of them holding hands, strolling through the park, listening to music, perusing the local galleries, pushing a baby carriage. No way. She would not go there.

Believing in Joe's fragile trust was too risky. Wasn't it?

For a nanosecond, she considered slipping out without talking to him or Ryan. She didn't want to deal with either man right now, but when her eyes met Joe's, she could no more ignore him than stop breathing. Of their own volition, her feet carried her to where he stood waiting, his face animated with expectation. His barely contained eagerness took her back to their high school days. She'd seen that longing look a few times, whenever Jared had left them alone and Joe had dared to drop his guard. If only she'd known then what was so obvious now.

A flood of guilt about her evening with Joe brought her back to reality. Going to dinner and a concert with him had been a big mistake. She'd told herself since her argument with Joe that she was dating Ryan exclusively. The new her wanted to be loyal to one man.

"Hi." Joe's fingers grazed the back of her hand, his blue eyes alight with love for her. "You look beautiful."

Uncomfortable with the blush that crept up her neck and cheeks, Carly brushed a lock of her unruly hair over her shoulder. "Thank you." To avoid his magnetic gaze, she made eye contact with his mother but ignored the question in the older woman's expression. "It's nice to see you again, Mrs. Callahan."

With a firm handshake, Addie replied, "It's Stewart now. Leann is the only Mrs. Callahan. At the moment."

Carly couldn't miss the implication. One day Joe would marry, and there would be two Mrs. Callahans. Refusing to analyze the wave of sorrow that threatened to overtake her, Carly decided a change of subject was in order. "How are you feeling, Ms. Stewart?"

"Please call me Addie. I'm a little tired, but my blood counts were pretty good at my last visit. My oncologist is still hoping to do a bone marrow transplant. Then he can slam me with a mega dose of chemo." Pausing, she glanced up at her son. "Joe insisted on being tested, even though the chance of us being a match is almost zero."

He smiled at his mom, then his eyes met Carly's. He looked pleased by her surprise, but she knew he wouldn't consider doing a bone marrow transplant simply to prove something to her. The absence of any tension between Joe and Addie was a clear indication that he'd done exactly as Carly had asked. He had finally made peace with his mother.

A flash of envy marred her happiness for him, and she wasn't sure if it was caused by her anxiety about seeing her parents, or by her fear that he'd waited too long to lay the past to rest for his new outlook to have any positive impact on his relationship with her. Joe could still tug at her heart, but she'd envisioned a possible future with Ryan. She dismissed the memory of Joe holding her hand as he prayed for her conversation with her parents. He *was* a good friend. And she was attracted to him, which was only natural considering how long they'd known each other, but they both carried too much baggage. With Ryan, she could be the woman she knew God wanted her to be. Committing to Ryan made sense.

"Are you okay?" Joe rested his hand on her arm.

She shifted away from his touch. "I've been on edge all morning, wondering what Dad's going to say, imagining Mom's face when I tell her."

"I can still go with you, if you want."

Carly ached to accept, but Ryan would never understand. "I ... no. Just pray for me."

"Always."

Sarah, who hadn't added a word to their conversation,

interjected, "We need to get going, Carly. It was very nice to see you again, Addie. I'm sure both Joe and Maureen are happy to have you home."

Carly couldn't miss Addie's distress, but she couldn't discern whether the pain in the older woman's eyes was emotional or physical. Regret made a nagging companion in the best of circumstances, and best certainly didn't describe this situation. Addie took her son's arm and started toward the door where Ryan stood in his usual place greeting members of the congregation. Joe pivoted, and over his shoulder, whispered to Carly, "I'll call you tonight to see how it went with your folks."

Grateful for his support, Carly smiled, drawn by the love in his eyes. Needing to break their magnetic connection, she turned to Sarah. "Do you think we could sneak out the side door? Ryan seems pretty busy talking, and I don't want to make Jared wait alone at your house."

Sarah's furrowed brow was a clear indication of her skepticism or disapproval or both.

Carly hastened to add, "I'll text Ryan in the car. He knows I'm having dinner with my parents today." She had texted him, hadn't she? She'd meant to talk to him about her plans, but time had gotten away from her.

Excuses.

"All right," Carly groused. "I'll tell him."

Sarah smiled. "I'll meet you in the car," she said and headed out the side door.

Offering a series of mumbled apologies, Carly made her way past the line of people leaving the church directly to the second spot in line. A young teenager new to their church was chatting with Ryan. When she caught his attention, he thanked the girl for attending and smiled over her shoulder at Carly. Clasping her hand with a look that said he'd rather kiss her, he asked, "How did you like the sermon?"

"It seemed very appropriate, considering."

"Considering what?" His brown eyes studied her with uncanny discernment. "Is something going on that I should know about?"

Carly tried to smile but knew without even seeing her reflection that her lips were stretched in tight, thin lines. "I'm going to my parents' house for dinner."

"I seem to remember getting a text that said something like that."

His sarcasm tinged with betrayal was a slap in the face. "I meant to call you."

Ryan bent close and whispered in her ear. "I understand you're nervous about seeing them, but I would have gone with you."

He couldn't hold her hand while she talked to her parents, but his breath on her face brought a shiver of awareness and a longing to be cherished and protected.

It was horribly disconcerting to be so affected by two men. Two very different men that she cared for a great deal. Maybe she hadn't changed as much as she'd hoped. Or as much as she believed she should have.

"I'll let you know how it goes. I'll call you tomorrow." Avoiding his reply, she headed toward the door.

Without a backward glance, Carly exited the church. Two questions pressed on her already stressed out brain. If she could choose, which man would she rather have beside her when she talked to her folks? And why wasn't the answer obvious?

*

Carly trudged through the dusting of snow to her parents' backdoor. Jared was right behind her, prepared to catch her should she lose her footing on the slick asphalt driveway. He was a good brother. She'd forgotten. When he'd opened her car door, he'd offered to hold her arm, but for some reason she didn't want to examine, she needed to enter her parents' house on her own power. Pride probably. How ironic. She had nothing to be proud of.

She entered the mudroom with one prayer. *Please, Lord, help me.*

The second she opened the kitchen door, her dad enclosed her in a bear hug. She'd forgotten the security of her father's arms about her, her head resting against his chest, hearing his steady heart beating beneath her ear, making her feel as if nothing could hurt her as long as he was near. If only she'd been as steady in her love for him. Loving Al had meant rejecting her father and everything he stood for. Leaving with Al had broken her dad's and her mom's hearts. How could she have done that? It had all seemed so simple back then. Now ... now she faced the truth. She'd given up her family for nothing more than a fairy tale turned nightmare.

"Carly, girl," Dad said against the top of her head. "Thank you."

Pushing against his chest, she raised her face to him, her stomach twisted in knots. "Thank you? I haven't done one thing to deserve your thanks."

Her father's eyes, filling with tears and lined with wrinkles she'd probably caused, were almost her undoing.

"Thank you for coming back to us," he said, his gaze taking her in as if she were his greatest joy.

"Yes," her mom agreed. "Thank you for coming home."

Carly extricated herself from her father's embrace and faced her mom.

"Your dad never gave up hope."

Not knowing what to say, Carly stared, startled by her mother's appearance. She looked about twenty years older.

Her dark, shoulder-length hair was streaked with gray, and her once bright, violet eyes were dimmed by the storms of life, storms Carly had caused. Mom was thin, too, about fifteen pounds underweight given the gaunt look of her hollowed cheeks and the sharp projections of her collar bone.

"I wasn't so sure you'd ever be back."

Carly crossed the kitchen to where her mother stood ramrod straight against the double sinks. Miles and years separated them. How could Carly close the distance? Especially when the story she needed to tell could create an impassable chasm as wide as the Grand Canyon. She stopped arm's length away from the woman who had dried all of her childhood tears. Carly waited, daring to hope against hope.

Her mother opened her arms, and Carly fell into them. They both sobbed, Carly murmuring apologies and her mother insisting that the only thing that mattered now was that their daughter was home.

Jared cleared his throat. "Mom, Dad, why don't you and Carly go sit in the living room? I'll make a fresh pot of coffee. Carly has a story to tell you."

Disengaging herself from her mother's hug, she shot her brother a grateful look. Leave it to Jared to keep things on track. Nothing could be gained by delaying the telling of her disgrace.

The living room looked pretty much as she remembered it, except Dad had replaced the old television with a flat-screen TV that filled the east wall. He'd been watching football, but her mother reached for the remote and switched off the power. Carly sat on the couch, and Mom started to settle in next to her, but Carly leaped up. "Dad, please sit with Mom. I'll take this chair. I need to look at you both when I ..."

Jared brought out a tray with four mugs, a pint of half-and-half, a sugar bowl, and a plate of Mom's cut-outs in the shape of turkeys, each one decorated with precise details. Carly had almost forgotten that Thanksgiving was this week. Would her parents still feel thankful to have her home when they learned the truth?

Her brother bent down near her ear and whispered, "Wait for me, sis. The coffee's almost done."

Dad searched Carly's face for some clue to what could have her so distressed. The questions in his eyes were obvious. Why wasn't she relieved and happy to be home at last?

But Carly was a prodigal daughter, and she had no idea what to expect.

Jared left for the kitchen and returned with a carafe. He poured everyone's coffee and added whatever they wanted. The silence in the room was painful, and the tight feeling squeezing Carly's chest made her wonder if she could hold the mug her brother offered her without dropping it on the plush beige carpeting. Jared took up a place behind her chair and laid a hand on her right shoulder for support. "Start wherever you want," he said, "and take as long as you want."

Taking as long as … No, that wasn't the plan. No details. Just the bare bones.

"Mom, Dad, I …" She gulped back a sob, hid her face in her hands, and let the tears flow unchecked. How would she ever get through this?

"Honey, you're frightening your mother. Please, tell us what's wrong."

Clinging to God's mercy, Carly forced a deep breath of air into her lungs and met the concerned gazes of her parents. "I've done things, terrible things, and if you don't want to see me—"

"Joe found Carly in the hospital, in ICU." Jared squeezed her shoulder, his voice filled with a strength she didn't possess at that moment.

God, give me words.

"Al tried to kill me."

Dad jumped to his feet, growling, "I'll kill the bastard," but Mom pulled on his arm, urging him to sit back down and listen.

"He did kill our baby."

The shocked white expressions on her parents' faces wiped all thought from Carly's mind for a nanosecond, but then she hurried on with, "The baby I was carrying died from multiple kicks to the abdomen and back. That's how the doctor explained it. But I know my daughter died because I was stupid enough to believe that some part of Al still loved me." She paused, clenching and unclenching her hands in her lap. "But I don't think he ever loved me. He only wanted to use me to start his business. A very lucrative escort service."

"No," her mother wailed, "God, no."

Dad slipped his arm around Mom's trembling shoulder and drew her up against his side.

"Jill, let her finish."

Horror and grief clouded her mother's eyes. If only Carly could make this easier for Mom, somehow. Blurting it out, fast and furious would be best for everyone.

But all she could manage was a whispered, "For nine years, I was a high-priced call girl, a prostitute for rich and powerful men." The words left a vile taste in her mouth. For a second, Carly feared she'd vomit, but she had to tell them everything. "Al promised me that Rutledge Escort Service would make us enough money that we could buy a house in the country, get married, and start a family. But it was all a lie. He never loved me. It took me years to admit that he was only using me. Just like he used all of the other girls."

Her mother rose, and in one lurching motion, fell to her knees at Carly's feet. "Oh, honey. I'm so sorry. I should never have let you go off with him."

Carly touched her mother's tear-streaked face. "There's more, Mom."

Her own tears were falling so fast that she could scarcely breathe. She wanted to crumple into a ball and hide from the ugliest, most unforgivable truth—a reality she could never escape. The truth that would haunt her for the rest of her life. "I was pregnant one other time, back when I was answering the phones and escorting without, you know … Al insisted that I have an abortion. He said it was the only way he could guarantee our future." She wiped the moisture from her face with both hands, instinctively trying to scrub away the shame. "Not long after, I found out what he meant, what he expected me to do for his best clients."

"I'll kill him." Dad's face was red with suppressed rage.

"He's in prison, Dad," Jared said. "For the next ten years. He pled guilty for attempted murder and the death of an unborn fetus."

The silence in the room threatened to choke the life out of Carly. There didn't seem to be anywhere to go from this point in the conversation, but she had to ask the question that would determine her next move.

First, she met her mother's gaze, then raised her face to her father's. "Can you ever forgive me?"

Within seconds her whole family had pulled her into a hug that eased her fears.

With his strong hand, Dad lifted her chin. "Of course we forgive you. We love you. Nothing can ever change that."

Carly's lower lip trembled. She bit it, the slight pressure calming her nerves. "Mom?"

Mom looked up at Dad, their gazes locked in unspoken messages only they understood.

"I forgive *you*, honey." Mom ran her thin hand down the

length of Carly's hair. "I love you. But I'll never, ever forgive that monster for what he did to you."

That Carly understood too well. She was having a difficult time forgiving Al herself. Knowing that God expected her to forgive as she'd been forgiven didn't erase the anger that welled up from deep in her heart. The pain of her poor choices rippled, touching the lives of everyone she loved and those who chose to love her still. In spite of the fact that she was an ex-prostitute and a murderer.

For murder was exactly what she'd done. Al may have pressured her into having the abortion, but she'd been the one who stayed in the room when she'd wanted to flee. Flee to protect her baby's life and her own.

Oh, God, why didn't I run?

The need to go back and do so many things differently suffocated her. But that horrible day—she'd give anything to be able to do it over.

"We'll get through this," Dad said, "together." His gaze met each one of them in turn, falling at last on Carly. He pressed a kiss to her forehead, the way he'd always done, every single night of her childhood.

But she wasn't a little girl anymore, and her daddy couldn't fix everything. Could God restore all they'd lost? His Word said so. But how was that possible, when some things could never be undone?

CHAPTER EIGHTEEN

Carly was quiet on the long drive back to Chautauqua. What had begun as light flurries when they left Lancaster swiftly became blowing snow that reduced visibility to a few car lengths ahead as they headed further south. Jared kept his gaze on the road, both hands gripped on the steering wheel, and the radio playing low. A country love song came on, and she tapped the scan button until she found the classical station. She was in no mood for cheating songs, even if the heroine told her loser ex to get lost and stay lost.

Today had gone as well as Carly could have hoped. Her parents forgave her. They asked no questions, settling for whatever she was willing to share, which wasn't much. Mom and Dad were grateful to have her back in their lives again, and they were all looking forward to sharing Thanksgiving together for the first time in ten years.

But Carly felt uneasy. It didn't take much thinking to pinpoint the source of her anxiety. She still had to tell Ryan. Telling him wouldn't be so bad, but then he would have to tell his mother, and Carly was absolutely certain that Elizabeth Edgar would urge her son to break off his relationship with any woman of questionable background. Carly could almost hear the matriarch say, it's only a matter of time before someone recognizes her, and then what will people think of a minister dating an ex-prostitute?

Too bad Carly hadn't factored in his mother's influence or his father's former business associates. If she had, maybe she'd … what? Refused to become emotionally involved? Kept their relationship to strictly friendship? Made some excuse to avoid dating Ryan at all?

"Are you all right?" Jared asked when the snow stopped and the sky shone clear with a smattering of stars.

"Yeah, I guess."

"I thought Mom and Dad handled everything well."

"Yes, better than I'd dared to hope." Even she could hear the distress in her voice.

"Is this about Joe?"

Startled, she said, "No. Yes. Him and Ryan."

"The pastor you're dating?"

Carly swallowed her surprise. "How do you know about him?"

"Joe told me."

"Of course." Joe would talk to Jared.

"Are you mad? Don't be mad at him, sis. He only—"

"Please don't say it. I can't deal with anything else right now." Especially not hearing her brother confirm her suspicions about how long Joe had cared for her. Not now when she'd made her decision to be faithful to Ryan.

A few moments later, Jared shot her a quick glance. "What do you want to do about Thanksgiving? Do you want me to pick you up?"

Hopefully, she wouldn't need a ride. "I think Ryan will come with me." But truthfully, she had no idea if he'd be willing to give up his family Thanksgiving in order to meet her family. Or if he would even want to see her anymore once she told him everything. "I'll let you know by Wednesday morning."

*

Joe had checked the time every twenty minutes or so since seven o'clock. The Italian sausage sub loaded down with fried peppers and onions was not sitting well on his nervous stomach. It was 8:55, and Carly still hadn't called. His heart hurt for her, but his need to be with her would only complicate her life more. Had she said she would call him? Or had he told her he'd call her?

He grabbed his cell just as it started to ring. Her name popped up on the screen, and he connected the call before the third ring. "Hi, beautiful."

"Hi to you, too."

She sounded calm. Maybe a little subdued. Which was perfectly normal considering what she'd had to do today.

His arms ached to hold her, to draw her close and protect her from anyone who would dare to hurt her. The Lawrences were good people. They'd been heartbroken over the disappearance of their daughter, and Jared had assured Joe that they would welcome Carly home in spite of, and maybe even because of, all she'd endured. "How did it go with your folks?"

"They forgave me. They're both angry at Al. I knew they would be. But it's hard enough for me to get past my own unforgiveness. I really can't help them with that part."

Neither could Joe. The monster didn't deserve forgiveness. He deserved … Joe shut down that thought. "At least he's in prison, and he'll be there for a very long time."

"That's what Jared said, too."

She gave Joe a brief summary of the conversation and ended with, "Thanks for praying for me."

"Anytime."

Joe wanted to do more than pray. With every fiber of his being he longed to be the one who held her, soothed her fears, and dried her tears. "Carly, can I take you out for lunch tomorrow?" He had to work second shift, so he could make it back to the city in plenty of time to meet Harris at the station by three thirty. "Say around noon?"

Her long sigh was his answer. "I'm having dinner with Ryan at six o'clock. I have to tell him. Before he finds out from someone else."

"Someone else? Who could he possibly know that would know anything about your past?"

"His mother."

"His mother? How could that be?"

"Once, about a year ago, at a local businessmen's banquet, she saw me."

"She what? You don't mean—"

"No, she hasn't exactly made the connection. But she remembers seeing a woman who called herself Elise."

Lord, no. Not like this. This could get so ugly, and there was absolutely nothing Joe could do to protect her. He wanted to pound something. The image of Al's face complete with his signature cocky grin came immediately to mind.

"Tuesday, then," Joe said, keeping his voice even with some effort. "I'll pick you up at noon, we'll go to lunch, and then to the mall so you can start your Christmas shopping."

If she still felt like shopping.

"We'll see. I'd rather not make any plans right now."

"Okay, I'll call you on Tuesday morning." But even if she didn't want to go anywhere, he would insist. She'd need the distraction. Maybe he'd take her to a sad movie, and she could cry on his shoulder without admitting ... Admitting what? That she'd fallen in love with another man who'd broken her heart?

After they'd said goodnight, Joe prayed for Carly and for himself, because God help him, he really didn't want things to work out for her and Ryan.

*

Carly prayed herself to sleep. She awoke several times

during the night, at three, at four, and again at five thirty. Disturbing dreams in which she was being chased by an unknown assailant left her shaking and covered with sweat. The last time she was crying in her dream and when she woke up, her face was streaked with cold tears. She sat up in bed and switched on the lamp on her nightstand. Reaching for her Bible, she opened it to the Psalms and read until she felt herself drifting off to sleep, but as soon as she lay back down, she continued to toss and turn.

By the time her alarm clock blared its annoying buzz, her legs were twisted in the blankets. If only this day were over. Then she'd know how things were going to be with her and Ryan. He was a good man, and she was pretty sure she could be happy with him. But could he be happy with her? He hadn't told her he loved her. And if he didn't love her, his first loyalty would be to his mother. No matter how much he cared for Carly. No matter how much chemistry they shared.

She reached for her phone and started to call him, then changed her mind when she noticed the time. Seven o'clock was too early. He'd be in the shower or spending time in prayer. She could wait another hour at least. Then she'd call him. Waiting until dinner would drive her crazy. Meeting for lunch would be so much better. Hopefully, he'd be up for the change in their plans.

Carly swung her legs over the edge of the bed and knelt down to pray. Bowing her head, her forehead pressed against her interlaced fingers, she thanked God for allowing her to reconcile with her parents. Joy welled up in her heart. She'd missed the unconditional love of her family, and now, wonder of wonders, God had made a way for her to be part of their lives again. Would He make a way for her and Ryan to discover what they could be together?

Perhaps not.

"Father, maybe his mother is right. Maybe I'm not cut out to be a pastor's wife. Whatever happens today, give me wisdom and the strength to accept it as Your will for me, and for Ryan."

As usual the hardest part of praying was getting her mind to quiet down. Hearing God speak to her heart so that she could distinguish a thought as an idea specifically from God was a skill she had yet to master, but she did feel decidedly more peaceful when she rose to her feet. No matter what today would bring, God would be with her. He promised to never leave her or forsake her.

Ryan had made no such promise.

If he wanted to end their relationship, she would graciously accept his decision. Still, her heart clenched at the thought of losing him. He had made her feel treasured and beautiful. Plenty of men had made her feel beautiful and desirable, but none had ever cherished her as Ryan did.

Except Joe.

Maybe she and Ryan weren't meant to be. If they were, would she still be thinking about Joe?

Her cell phone vibrated on the nightstand, and she swiped it to read the text message. "I'm praying for you. If you need me, anytime, I'm here for you." Joe.

He had always been like another brother, until he'd transformed overnight into the hunkiest guy in the senior class. But she'd still been Jared's little sister. Too bad she hadn't known about Joe's feelings back then. Two years wasn't that big of an age difference. How ironic that she'd had a crush on him when he'd had feelings for her, too.

And now, they were trying to be just friends.

Her friendship with Joe didn't bother Ryan, but she hadn't exactly told him the whole truth. He still believed Joe was her brother's friend, looking out for her for Jared's sake.

If she and Joe were only friends, why hadn't she told Ryan

about the concert?

Her thoughts were spinning, spiraling in directions she didn't want to go. She could be loyal, and she had to focus on telling Ryan her story. She gathered her stuff and headed to the bathroom to shower. Then she'd have a cup of coffee, maybe two, before she sent him a text to ask him to come over for lunch instead of taking her out to dinner.

*

Sarah had only been gone ten minutes when Ryan pulled in the driveway. Carly knew exactly how much time had passed because she'd been pacing from the front window back to the kitchen to stir the potato soup simmering on the stove. The homey aroma of corn bread baking in the oven filled the house. The atmosphere was decidedly domestic, and her plan was to keep the conversation light until after lunch, but with her stomach clenching in painful knots, Carly didn't know how much she could actually eat.

With a quick prayer, she hurried to answer Ryan's knock. She opened the inside door at the exact moment he opened the screen door, letting in an unseasonably warm November breeze. Questions flashed in his eyes, and she managed a token smile. He brushed his hand over her cheek, tucking her hair behind her ear with one smooth movement. She welcomed his reassuring touch as he wrapped his arms around her. When his lips met hers, she could feel his restraint and decided to follow his lead. His lips moved from her mouth, and he brushed a chaste kiss over her forehead as he broke off the hug. His eyes met hers, and he studied her with an intensity that made her wonder if he could see her soul. Did all pastors have the ability to read people so well? She supposed so.

Instinctively, she moved toward the kitchen, putting more distance between them. Preparing herself for this painful conversation would certainly be easier if he didn't pick up her distress so quickly. In the past, she'd had no trouble concealing her feelings, but maybe that was because other men she'd known hadn't cared enough to notice.

"Are you all right? How did it go with your parents?"

Her cheeks burned. "As well as could be expected, considering what I had to tell them."

Ryan touched her shoulder, then slipped his arm around her waist, urging her to his side.

Uncertain, she looked up at him. Anxiety swept his face. Was he hiding something? Had his mother figured out that Elise and Carly were the same person?

No. If he knew, he wouldn't be this calm. And he'd confront her directly.

Breathe, Carly. Forgiveness is his business. He'll forgive you. You can do this.

She leaned her head against his strong shoulder for a moment, savoring the scent of his woodsy aftershave.

In the kitchen, the wonderful smells of her favorite winter meal greeted them. Maybe telling him here wasn't the best idea after all. The atmosphere was decidedly intimate, if not comfortable, but she hadn't wanted to tell him at a restaurant because she was pretty sure she'd end up crying and drawing unwanted attention to herself.

Unwanted attention.

She knew all she ever wanted to know about that. Her breath caught in her throat, and she swallowed hard, hoping Ryan hadn't felt her tension.

"I hope you're hungry."

"Starved," he said into her ear, standing so close behind her that his breath on her cheek disturbed her hair. She longed to rely on his strength and find security in his arms, but after today there'd be no guarantees of that.

Without turning to look at him, she said, "Hand me those

bowls from the table, please."

He obliged, moving aside to give her the space she needed, but his sheer male presence in the room continued to distract her. Willing her hands to stop shaking, Carly ladled the potato soup into the bowls, and he placed them on the table.

"Anything else I can do for you? Like maybe another kiss?"

A nervous laugh erupted from her throat. "No, I think we're good." But were they?

She smiled her practiced smile, the one that gave others, and even sometimes herself, the illusion that she was in control. "Have a seat." She bent to retrieve the corn muffins from the oven, then dumped them into a towel-lined basket, which she placed on the table next to the honey butter she'd whipped that morning. The meal was a favorite one handed down from her grandmother, and everything was perfect.

Except her.

Today she was going to tell Ryan just how far from perfect she was. Why had she ever agreed to see where their relationship could go? Even if she didn't factor in his mother, the congregation would surely disapprove.

"Do you want your coffee with lunch or after?" Her words came out calm and controlled, and for that measure of grace she was thankful.

"Sit down, Carly." Ryan reached for the water glass at his place setting and took a drink. "I'll have coffee after. With dessert."

She frowned. She'd forgotten about his sweet tooth. So much for plying him with food.

There were a few chocolate chip cookies in Sarah's cookie jar leftover from the ladies Bible study. That would have to do. Sitting in the chair across from him, Carly tried to dismiss the irrational thought that she was going before the Inquisition. She and Ryan had only been dating for about six weeks. If he didn't want to see her anymore, she'd survive. Survival was a skill set she'd mastered long ago. But discovering again that a man she believed loved her actually didn't love her at all would be painful.

Could her already broken heart withstand the blow?

Ryan reached for her hand and met her gaze briefly, his eyes searching hers. Her skin tingled at his touch, and she clasped his hand firmly, trying to convey more confidence than she felt. Then he bowed his head, and she closed her eyes, grateful for a quiet moment free of his scrutiny. Until his prayer for the food ended with, "And help Carly not to be nervous about whatever she has to tell me. Help her to remember nothing is as bad as it seems. Amen."

If only that were true. She doubted he'd feel the same way by the end of the afternoon.

While they were eating, Carly succeeded in steering the conversation to safe subjects by getting Ryan to talk about his plans for additional outreach ministries during the Christmas season. The congregation would be making visits to several local nursing homes, and the church board would organize teams to help out at the Buffalo City Mission, serving food and sorting and boxing donations for needy families. And, of course, they would put on a live Nativity play two Sundays before Christmas, a tradition started by Ryan's predecessor.

Carly especially looked forward to helping out at the nursing homes. If Ryan decided he still wanted her by his side.

Twenty minutes later, he'd polished off two bowls of soup and four muffins to her one bowl and one muffin. "That was the best potato soup I've ever eaten. And corn muffins with honey butter—a man could get used to eating like a king." He grinned at her, his brown eyes gleaming with mischief.

Smiling, she rose to clear the table and make a fresh pot of coffee. Ryan turned the water on, added dish detergent, and started washing the dishes. She hated to spoil this cozy domestic scene, but she couldn't wait any longer. Her chest was tight with anxiety. "I'll do those later. Why don't you take a seat in the living room, and I'll bring your coffee as soon as it's done."

Ryan shot her a questioning look but left the kitchen without an argument.

Staring at the coffee dripping into the carafe, Carly inhaled several deep breaths, willing her heart to stop its furious pounding. She could do this. She'd told her parents. She could tell Ryan, too.

But unlike her family, he had no obligation to her. They'd made no formal commitment to each other.

The final gurgles of the coffeemaker signaled the end of her brief reprieve. She poured the fragrant brew, methodically added cream and sugar to his mug, and arranged chocolate chip cookies on a dessert plate with several dark chocolate kisses in the center. Then she put everything on a tray with a stack of napkins. When she set the tray on the coffee table, Ryan was checking his email on his phone. He reached for her hand and pulled her down next to him on the couch before she could react. "When are you going to tell me what's bothering you?"

His tender words brought tears. She blinked, averting her face, but he cupped her chin in his strong hand and gently turned her so that she had to meet his eyes.

"You're crying. Something's really wrong."

He touched her shoulder, and she jumped like a startled child and retreated to the other side of the room. She would never be able to tell him with his concerned gaze locked on her as if he would do absolutely anything to relieve her distress. She paced the room twice, snatched a tissue from the box on the table near the front door, dried her face, and dabbed her nose. Then she forced herself to sit in the chair farthest from the couch. Perched on the edge of the cushion, Carly took a deep breath and prayed for courage. "You're going to be really shocked by what I have to tell you, and I should have told you from the very beginning." She pressed her hand against her pounding heart. "I hope you can understand why I did the things I did. Things I'd do almost anything not to have done at all."

He started to stand, and she stopped him with her hand up, palm facing him like a traffic officer. "Sit there. Please. I can't tell you if … if you're too close."

Ryan complied, but his rigidly alert posture meant he was prepared to go to her if she needed his comfort.

But would he want to comfort her? Would he even listen to the whole ugly story?

"After I graduated from high school, I moved out of my parents' house." Heat flooded her face, but she resisted the urge to cover her cheeks with her trembling hands. "With a guy."

A startled look flashed across Ryan's face, then he composed his features and waited.

"I thought we were going to get married, but I was wrong about that. I was wrong about a lot of things. I believed Al when he said he loved me and that we were a team nothing could ever separate. But he didn't want a wife. He wanted—" She swallowed the bile that rose in her throat. "An employee."

Ryan shook his head. "I don't understand. What kind of business was he in?"

Say it fast, Carly.

There was no point in dragging this out, but what if he didn't let her explain? "He said we could get married as soon as we made enough money for a down payment on a house." She could still hear his voice in her head after all of these years. He was so persuasive. When Al pulled her into his arms, he held her as if he never intended to let her go. But what she had thought was love was only possessiveness. And she was his most prized possession.

Ryan's eyes bored into hers, willing her to clear up the confusion that swept his face at her words. "But you didn't get married, did you?"

She shook her head three times. "Al made it seem as if he and I were partners working together for our future. I was very uncomfortable, even a little panicky, when he first told me what he wanted to do, what he wanted me to do."

Just say it, Carly. God, help me to say it.

"Al wanted to start an escort service."

The pain in Ryan's eyes made her drop her gaze to her lap, but just for a few seconds. She had to see his reaction to know where she stood. "I was his first girl. Six months later there were fifteen, all of us handpicked to please a select group of clients with very diverse tastes. At first, I only accompanied clients to social engagements, business banquets, the theater, concerts, things like that." Memories flooded her mind, and Carly gave herself a mental shake to free herself from their cloying effect. She had to focus on this moment. Carefully considering her words, she continued, "But then Al set me up with one of his most powerful and prestigious clients, and ..."

In a nanosecond, Ryan crossed the room. His hands gripped her shoulders as he leaned close to her face. His expression was a mixture of anger, frustration, and disbelief. "You can't mean what I think you're—"

"Before I ... could figure a way out, I was ... I became ..." She closed her eyes to gather her courage. When she opened them again, she was sure Ryan did not want her to finish her story, but he had to hear it. All of it. She was close enough to kiss him.

The kiss of betrayal.

"I was a call girl for almost nine years. I left Al in September when he beat me up so bad I ended up in the hospital."

The grief that swept Ryan's face sliced her last hope that they could somehow move beyond her past. His hands dropped to his sides, and he backed several feet away from her. He was a man who wanted to be the only one for his wife.

Why didn't he say something? Anything at all would be better than the eerie silence.

"Ryan, I'm sorry. I'd give anything to start my life over and make different choices." But she had started her life over, as a believer forgiven by God.

The sheen of moisture in his eyes startled her. She could only imagine the conflict raging inside of him. He deserved better. She should have told him at the very beginning, given him the freedom to choose whether to become emotionally involved with her or not.

"Your broken arm and your broken leg, he did that to you?" Ryan knelt before her, then let his hand travel in a slow caress down her arm.

Carly wanted to lean forward into his embrace and accept whatever comfort he was willing to offer, but she couldn't afford to give way to what might be futile for both of them. "Al had a horrible temper, but, of course, I didn't know that in the beginning. I was so naïve. Joe never liked him, and neither did my brother, but I refused to listen to either of them. I was swept away by the fairy tale, adored by a man who promised me the world." She laughed. "Ironic, considering I ended up feeling as if I were living in hell."

Ryan pulled her to her feet and into his arms. Holding her in a protective embrace, he kissed the top of her head, and with his lips still resting against her hair, he said, "It must have been horrible for you."

He had no idea. But he was trying to be sympathetic. And he hadn't rejected her. Yet.

She raised her face from the security of his chest and his heart beating steadily against her ear. "There's more I need to tell you."

"No. You don't. It's in the past. Forgiven and forgotten." His tone suggested he was trying to convince them both.

"Please, sit with me so I can tell you everything. Everything you need to know about me so that you can decide if you still want there to be an us."

He unlocked his arms from around her lower back, and she sat on the couch, knowing he'd insist on being near her. He settled so close that his thigh pressed against her leg, and she was thankful her legs weren't shaking with nerves like that dreadful day. He took her hand and rubbed his thumb over her knuckles. "Before you say anymore, you need to know nothing you've told me changes how I feel about you. Except that now I think you're the bravest woman I've ever known to have the courage to walk away from all of that and rebuild your life."

She touched his cheek. She couldn't help herself. He was offering her a life beyond anything she'd ever imagined, a life she could never deserve, a life that should belong to a girl who'd made all of the right choices and hadn't destroyed her reputation.

He pressed a tender kiss against her lips. "It'll be all right. I promise."

She wanted to believe him. A tear slipped unbidden down her cheek. "I was pregnant when Al beat me. I lost the baby. His baby."

Anger darkened Ryan's eyes. The same anger she'd seen in every man's eyes when she'd told them. Joe. Her brother.

Her dad. Ryan's mouth tightened into a thin line as he fought to control his emotions. She'd seen that reaction before, too. She waited for him to process the horror of what had happened to her.

"Are you all right now?"

He meant, could she have more babies? "I'm fine. I'm still sad." *And I probably always will be.* "But I'm fine."

If only this was all she had to share, but he deserved to know how low she'd sunk in her desire to please a man who had never cared about her. Stupid, horrific decision that she'd regret for the rest of her life. A decision that defined and limited her.

How could he possibly understand? She didn't understand. Sometimes, she convinced herself she'd been bullied by Al into the abortion. But in the end, the final, irrevocable decision had been hers. She'd lain on the surgical table and submitted to the procedure that killed her baby. She'd chosen the mirage of Al's love over her baby.

She was a murderer. Nothing she could ever do could change that. Nothing.

"There's one more thing you need to know." Her gaze riveted with his, she whispered, "Nine years ago, I had an abortion. Al insisted. He said it was the wrong time for us to have a baby. We'd just started the escort service three months earlier. And I wasn't, you know, not until later."

The color drained from his face.

Was there a limit to what even Ryan could forgive? She couldn't blame him if there were. Believing in forgiveness and extending forgiveness should go together, but in her case, it couldn't be easy for him. Life was sacred to him. It was precious to her, too. If only she'd recognized the truth before...

"Not a day goes by that I don't regret what I did. Sometimes, the memories are an open, bleeding wound."

Absently, her hand moved to her stomach and her empty womb. Afraid to see disdain marring Ryan's handsome features, Carly stared out through the front windows to the choppy lake a hundred or so yards beyond the road. The storm outside was nothing compared to the one raging in her heart. "Other times, I limp through my day, because no matter how much it hurts, there's nothing I can do to make this right." She would have felt better, if she'd been able to deliver her second baby safely, but she'd failed to protect that baby, too.

Ignoring the tears rolling down her cheeks, she sucked in several long breaths. "If you want to leave now, I understand."

Ryan laid his hand on her leg and gave her knee a gentle squeeze. "Why would I do that to you?"

Carly whirled to face him, to read the emotions and the intentions behind his kind words. "Because this is way more than what you signed on for when we started dating."

His response, enclosing her hands in his, brought fresh tears. Tears that he brushed gently away with the pads of his fingers. "I love you, Carly Lawrence. Nothing you've told me today could possibly change how I feel about you."

"How can you say that knowing the kind of woman I was? I can't possibly be what you're looking for. Who you've been waiting for."

"None of it matters. It's all in the past. It's forgiven and forgotten." He took her hands in his again. He exhaled a deep, definitive breath. "No one needs to know."

No one needs to know? Was he kidding? There would always be a chance that someone might recognize her and remember Elise. "Your mother recognized me."

"She told you that?"

The anxiety in his voice sent her heart into an irregular rhythm. "No. But I saw her struggling to make the connection."

His impassive reaction revealed nothing of his thoughts. Perhaps, he really did believe her past wouldn't affect them. If only that were true. Maybe, she should dye her hair, but she was too pale to be a brunette, and she couldn't imagine herself as a strawberry blonde.

If the truth was supposed to set her free, then why did she feel as if she would spend the rest of her life trying to hide who she once was?

Was Ryan ashamed of her past? If he was, she certainly couldn't hold it against him. She was ashamed, too.

"If your mother recognizes me, other people you know, people we may meet—"

He covered her lips with his index finger, stopping her words. "If that happens, we'll deal with it. Together."

CHAPTER NINETEEN

After Ryan left, Carly didn't want to think. She needed to relax. Her nerves were wound so tightly that the left side of her neck ached. She knelt in front of Sarah's entertainment center and scanned the shelves for a Christmas movie. Classic romantic comedies, such as *White Christmas* and *Christmas in Connecticut* tempted her, but today she couldn't muster up the energy to hope for her own happy ending. She chose *It's a Wonderful Life*, her family's favorite, though her own life felt far from wonderful.

The sun was setting over Chautauqua as George was running through the streets of Bedford Falls. By the end of the movie, Carly was sobbing, not only for George but also for herself. George realized that his life was valuable because he had made a difference in so many people's lives. Would Carly ever make a difference in anyone's life? She wanted to believe that God could work the most wonderful miracle of all—that someone's life would actually be better for knowing her.

When her cell phone rang, interrupting the end of the movie, she dreaded seeing Ryan's number on the screen. "I can't talk to him right now." She let it ring and trudged into the kitchen to make a cup of tea. The phone rang again, and an unfamiliar number popped up.

"Hello?"

"Honey, it's me, Mom."

Carly released the breath she hadn't even realized she was holding. "Hi, Mom. I didn't recognize the number."

"This is my cell. Is everything all right? You sound upset."

Could she confide in her mother, after all these years of having no one she could truly trust? "I told Ryan this afternoon."

"How did he take it?"

"Okay, I guess. We're still together. For now."

"Did you ask him if he wanted to join us for Thanksgiving dinner?"

She'd forgotten all about Thanksgiving. Part of her hoped he'd prefer going to his mother's over sharing the holiday with her family. "I'll call him tonight or tomorrow morning."

"Will you two be spending part of the day with his family?"

"I hope not."

"Honey, I thought you said things are okay with the two of you."

"I did. He said we can face whatever happens together, but—"

"What do you mean whatever happens?"

"Mom, we're bound to run into somebody who remembers me. It's inevitable."

"Oh, Carly, you can't know that. You can't spend your life looking over your shoulder. Though your sins be as scarlet, they'll be as white as snow."

Carly sighed. "If only it were that simple. I know God's forgiven me, but other people aren't always ready or willing to forgive."

Her mother's reply was a mumbled prayer that God would protect her daughter and give her peace.

"I love you, Mom. Tell Jared I'll let him know tomorrow night if I need him to pick me up on Thursday afternoon."

Carly disconnected the call, forced herself to eat a bowl of soup, and tried to read her Bible, but she simply couldn't concentrate. No matter how she searched, nothing banished the scene playing over and over in her mind. Elizabeth Edgar's withering disdain as she confronted Carly about her sordid past spurred her into flight mode.

"Lord, take away this fear, please. I'm in Your hands."

Feeling her heart begin to unclench, she trudged to the bathroom to get ready for bed. It was barely seven thirty, but she was exhausted. She climbed between the flannel sheets, grateful that she was free of the cumbersome casts that had made every movement so challenging. No matter what happened between her and Ryan, she could see God's hand at work in her life, and for that mercy she was extremely grateful.

She composed a quick text letting Joe know she was okay and looking forward to having lunch with him tomorrow, then she closed her eyes and prayed sleep would come quickly.

*

Joe read Carly's text. It was very brief, too brief for him to read between the lines. One thing was obvious. She and Ryan were still a couple. Apparently, the man lived what he preached. He hadn't judged Carly or rejected her. Which was good for Carly and not so good for Joe.

Lord, if she's really meant to marry Edgar, help me not to love her anymore. I can't get her out of my heart without Your help. I don't even want to try.

*

Harris pulled into the parking lot of a local gift shop. A shoplifting call had come over the radio. He was out of the car before the engine slowed to a stop. "Are you coming, Callahan?"

Joe unbuckled his seatbelt and jumped from the squad car. "Yeah, I'm focused."

The shoplifter was a fifteen-year-old female, but sometimes young girls were so hysterical that listening to them gave him a headache. It seemed as though they believed if they cried hard enough, the store manager would decide not to press charges. In Joe's experience that never happened. But it was pointless to try to tell that to a teen girl. Hysteria moved them past the point of reason every single time, especially if they'd never gotten caught before. It was going to be a long night.

*

The next morning Joe called the doctor's office promptly at 9 a.m. to check on the results of his HLA test. Hearing the nurse practitioner voice what he'd already suspected, that his HLAs did not match his mother's, was no shock. Joe was not a possible bone marrow donor. He managed to force a thank you past the lump in his throat. Five minutes later, he was in the shower, tears rolling down his face, the familiar fear of losing Addie rushing in as if he were still a little boy who didn't understand why his mother was leaving him again. Only now, he was a thirty-one-year-old man, and she wasn't leaving. She could be dying. And like always, there was nothing Joe could do.

Except pray.

He asked God for more time. For another chance at a relationship with his mother that was stable and happy. To dance with her at his wedding. To see the joy on her face when she held his first child. To see her smiling face at every birthday and holiday gathering.

But what if none of that fit with what God had planned for Addie?

Joe scrubbed the tears from his face, finished his shower, shaved, brushed his teeth, and pulled on a pair of jeans and a black thermal shirt. He stared at his reflection in the mirror. He had the look of a man about to lose everything. "Lord, restore my hope because right now hoping against hope is my only option. For Mom and for Carly."

A glance at his watch told Joe he had just enough time to stop at a florist and pick up a red poinsettia for Carly and maybe a white or pink one for Sarah. When a man wants to please a woman, he can never go wrong with flowers.

Leann's advice.

His stepmother had been an amazing blessing to their family. She had managed to erase the lines of grief that had creased his father's face and to replace them with laugh lines around the man's eyes and mouth. She had taught Joe that some women could be trusted to keep their word and to hang in there with a man through good times and bad.

Why hadn't Joe remembered Leann's faithfulness when he'd first found Carly again? Instead, the pain of his mother's wanderlust had entirely eclipsed any happiness Leann had brought to their lives. And he'd given Carly the message that he didn't trust her.

Would he get another chance to prove to her that he knew she was nothing like his mother?

Maybe. If something went wrong in her relationship with Ryan.

But if that happened, she'd be hurt again. And Joe didn't want to see her hurt. He'd give anything to protect her. Specifically, to be the man entitled to protect her.

He shook his head to dislodge the tangled thoughts. He locked his front door and headed to his car, noting the dusting of snow on the road and the sidewalks. Taking it slow on the side streets until he reached Walden Avenue, he detoured down Transit to the florist to pick up the poinsettias. He chose a deep red for Carly and a white-edged pink for Sarah. By ten thirty, he was on Route 86 heading to Chautauqua. Thankfully, the highway was bare, because the traffic was heavier than usual, probably due to Thanksgiving travelers seeking to beat the Wednesday rush. Wouldn't it be nice if Carly would move back toward Buffalo? She was planning to start school in January. Maybe she'd move back with her parents until she could find a small apartment near the community college. He hadn't asked her if she was going to the north or south campus. He'd ask her today. If he remembered.

And if she wasn't too upset over her conversation with Ryan. Jared had already confirmed things had gone well with her parents when Joe called to cancel their game of one-on-one, so Carly should be at peace about that.

Joe gripped the steering wheel, annoyed at his mounting frustration. Wanting Carly to be his wouldn't make it so. He would have to fight for her.

Patience. Timing is everything in matters of the heart. His grandmother's sage advice to both him and Maureen when they'd reached their teen years. Grandma Callahan didn't believe in pussyfooting around the truth. And for her, that meant telling her grandchildren that finding happiness in this life depended entirely upon one's faith in the providence of God. Nothing more and nothing less.

But he had been patient.

No. That was a lie. And his grandmother would never tolerate lying to oneself, which she believed was just as bad as lying to someone else, and often worse.

For a while, he'd been patient. But about two years after that scumbag Rutledge pulled out of the Lawrences' driveway with Carly riding beside him, Joe had given up entirely. He'd decided he and Carly weren't meant to be and had buried his feelings deep in his heart. Only in moments of extreme weakness or danger had he allowed himself to remember how much he loved her. Whether she'd felt anything for him was not something he pondered. What would be the point? She'd made her choice.

Now, he was stuck again playing a supporting role while another man claimed her heart and her hand. Joe was tired of being like another brother to her.

Man up, Callahan.

The ember of hope fanned by her smile that day he'd discovered her hiding in the shrubbery refused to go out. Surely, she'd felt their instant connection.

Maybe he should tell her again. Maybe this time she would believe him.

Did he dare risk his heart one last time to win the one woman he wanted to spend the rest of his life loving?

*

With a troubled heart, Carly ended her call with Ryan. He'd ignored her subtle hint that she'd prefer spending the entire day with her family since this would be their first Thanksgiving together in years. Why hadn't she simply told Ryan what she wanted to do? Instead, she'd listened like a meek mouse as he'd outlined the logistics of sharing the holiday meal at two homes. Just thinking about seeing Elizabeth Edgar again made Carly's palms sweat with anxiety. His mother would recognize her eventually, and the more they saw each other, the sooner that day would come.

Fighting discouragement, Carly sank into her comfy bedroom chair and covered her face with her hands. *Lord, what should I do?*

Trust Me.

Of course she needed to trust God, but could she really make herself completely vulnerable? She'd done that with Al, and in the process, given up her convictions.

But this was different. Trusting God was simply acknowledging His sovereignty and recognizing that all His plans for her were motivated by His perfect love. All Al's plans for her had been motivated by money.

But could she reasonably expect God to protect her from the inevitable consequences of her own poor choices?

"Lord, I trust You. Help me to trust You more. A little more every day."

Saying the words aloud made them more real and quieted the nagging whisper, *It's only a matter of time.*

If and when her past caught up with her, Ryan had said they'd face it together, but could he really deal with the shame and embarrassment? Or would he leave her behind, deeply apologetic, and perhaps regretting his lack of courage?

Whatever happened with Ryan, God would be with her. Fear beat again at the doors of her mind, and Carly focused on a verse she'd read that morning in the Psalms. "What time I am afraid, I will trust in God."

Determined not to borrow trouble, she rose from her chair, checked her hair, grabbed her purse from the dresser, and headed into the living room to wait for Joe.

Ever faithful, he arrived exactly on time at eleven o'clock. His truck in the driveway was a welcome sight, and as he marched to the front steps carrying two potted plants, the smile on his handsome face quickened Carly's heart and brought a smile to her own lips. Spending the day with Joe would be relaxing and fun—a chance to forget about her worries over Ryan's mom.

Joe entered the house without knocking, one plant tucked in the crook of his arm, his left hand firmly gripping the other flower pot. "Good morning, beautiful."

At last glance in the mirror, she did *not* look beautiful. Not even pretty. But through Joe's eyes she'd always *felt* beautiful. Her brother's best friend had always told her she was the prettiest girl in school. Why hadn't she realized he wasn't just being nice?

But it didn't matter. She needed to stop looking behind

her. No one—not even God—could change the past.

"Thanks for the compliment. I didn't sleep well last night, so I know I look haggard." She reached for the plant in his hand, her skin tingling where their hands touched. The urge to kiss him flitted through her mind, and a blush born of pondered delight warmed her cheeks. To dispel the image, she quickly shook her head, her hair catching in the petals of the crimson poinsettia. Joe caught the wayward tresses in his free hand, his gaze drifting to her mouth. Carly suppressed a tremble. They shouldn't. Even thinking about kissing him again made her feel guilty, as if she were cheating on Ryan.

Two large plants formed a convenient or inconvenient barrier, depending on how she wanted to spin the situation. At this moment, every nerve in her body pulsed with the need to feel the security of Joe's strong arms around her.

She averted her face, marched away from him, and set the gorgeous twelve-inch poinsettia on the end table farthest from the door. Why was she fleeing? This was just Joe. She'd known him for as long as she could remember, and though she'd never appreciated him, he was willing to be her friend when he clearly wanted much more. He'd never turn his back on her, no matter what anyone said about her.

Could she say the same thing about Ryan? If ever the time came when he saw her as an impediment to his ministry, he would choose his life work over her, and she wouldn't blame him. If she'd learned one thing from her disastrous past, it was the simple fact that God's plans were always better than anything she could imagine on her own. God's plan for Ryan was for him to be an effective pastor and preacher. That much was certain.

A relationship with her could become a liability overnight. Carly was equally certain that Elizabeth Edgar would never let that happen.

"The dark red one is for you." Joe touched her arm, sending a wave of awareness through her. Why did her body respond immediately to the briefest contact with this man?

"The pink and white one is for Sarah." Electricity sparked from the gentle pressure of his hand on her upper arm in spite of the long-sleeved sweater Carly wore.

She took a deep breath and faced him, not caring if the blush had not yet faded from her cheeks, not caring if he noticed how he affected her. "You picked well. Both of them are beautiful, but the red is stunning. Thank you." Standing on her tiptoes, she brushed a fast kiss over his lips, but before she could retreat, he wrapped his arms around her upper back and pulled her close. She tucked her head and nestled against his muscled chest. His heart was pounding an urgent rhythm. He wanted to kiss her, really kiss her. She knew it as sure as the solid hardwood floor beneath her feet. Placing a hand on each side of his narrow waist, she gave him a gentle push and extricated herself from his arms.

"I'm starving. Can we go eat now?" she asked, the words coming out in a nervous burst of energy as she snatched her coat from where she'd draped it over the couch. She headed out the front door before he could protest.

Before they did something that muddled her life even more.

In Joe's defense, the awkwardness between them was her fault. She was giving him mixed signals. She had to stop. Now. She was Ryan's girl, and he deserved better from her.

If only she could rein in her traitorous heart.

All the way to the restaurant, Carly turned one thought over in her mind. If she loved Ryan, would she be having these feelings for Joe?

As he parked the car and walked to her side to open the door for her, another thought slithered into her brain. What if, because of her past, she was incapable of being faithful to one man? She swallowed hard, fighting against the self-recrimination. She couldn't change the past, but the present and the future could both be different, with God's help. *Lord, I can't control my feelings, but I can control my actions.*

No more affectionate kisses between friends.

Because she and Joe were—were what? More than friends? Already closer than friends should be?

Sarah had advised Carly to discover which man she could love. The trouble was she loved them both. But how could she possibly love two men at the same time? A normal girl who'd lived a normal life would never find herself in such a heart-wrenching predicament.

But she hadn't lived a normal life, and maybe she never would. In any case, Carly had no idea what normal should look like. With Al, she'd gone from fairy tale to fantasy to nightmare and barely escaped with her life. Had she slipped back into fairy tale mode again? Ryan had all the makings of a prince charming, but she definitely wasn't the princess his mother had envisioned. Carly doubted happily-ever-after was in their future. Still, she wasn't ready to give up on the possibility. Not without giving Ryan a chance to prove himself.

Which probably meant she shouldn't be spending so much time with Joe.

He opened Carly's door and shot her a quizzical look. "Are you all right?"

Carly couldn't lie to him anymore, but she couldn't exactly tell him what was bothering her. "Not really." She sighed then gave him a half-smile. "But I will be."

Offering her his arm, he said, "Let's walk a bit."

"Okay." The prospect of walking in the warm sunshine cheered her. As she tucked her hand in the crook of his arm, the tension in her shoulders slid away. For a second, she considered that simply being with Joe made her feel better, but she rejected that assessment.

Joe led her past Main Street shops and across the street to a park behind the library. Wanting to savor the day, Carly stopped on the varnished wood bridge that spanned the creek circling the island park. The water shimmered and glistened as a shower of reluctant red and gold leaves drifted to the surface. "It's beautiful here," she said, looking up at Joe.

"Not as beautiful as you are." His fingers grazed her cheeks, and she drew back.

Averting her face a moment to suppress and conceal her response, "Joe, I … we …"

His hand on her shoulder urged her to turn and face him. "You're with Ryan. I know. I tell myself a half a dozen times every day. But my heart won't listen to my head. I have always—"

Carly laid a firm finger against his mouth. "Don't. Don't say anymore."

Joe jerked away from her, marched off the bridge, and headed down the path so fast that she had to run to keep up. She grabbed his right arm. He whirled around, eliminating all but a few inches of space between them. The anguish in his eyes knifed her heart, and she swallowed a painful gasp of air past the lump in her constricted throat.

"I can't expect you to understand, but I have to try with Ryan, to give him a chance to be the man I need, to see if God can work things out for us."

Taking her by the shoulders, he leaned so close she could smell his cinnamon gum.

"Then why are you here with me?"

Her lower lip trembled, and she bit down to steady herself in the face of his raw emotion.

His eyes held her captive. "It's a fair question. I think I

deserve an answer, don't you?"

God, help me.

The tears flooded her eyes and ran down her cheeks.

Joe pulled her into his arms, and she didn't even try to escape his embrace.

"I'm sorry, honey. I didn't mean to make you cry. Being just your friend seems impossible, but if that's what you need right now, that's what I'll do."

Pushing past the shame clouding her thinking, she framed the question she had no right to ask. "Can you give me until the end of the year to figure out where Ryan and I stand?" She raised her face to his, awaiting his answer. "Please?"

"If I say yes, then what?" he replied, frustration weighting down every word.

"I don't know. I know I need a friend right now."

Disbelief and disappointment dimmed the summer blue of his eyes, but he squeezed her in a quick, friendly hug. Then he released her, captured her hand, and led her back along the same path. "That means romantic walks in the park are a definite no-no. Let's go eat lunch, so we can hit the mall before the after-five crowd makes shopping a chore."

Carly smiled, surprised but relieved that he'd accepted her terms so readily. *I should be happy. I have a great boyfriend and an amazing friend.*

The problem was she wanted both in the same man.

CHAPTER TWENTY

Joe wanted to shake Carly. How long would she continue to deny the chemistry that surged between them? He saw her blush and understood her desperate need to put physical distance between them. So why did she keep drawing him in with her soulful looks? The better question was why did he let her?

She'd asked for time to figure things out with Edgar, and Joe had agreed. Competing with the minister for her affection didn't sit well, but Joe had let her walk out of his life without a fight before. "And look how that turned out," he muttered.

Carly looked up from her Beef on Weck sandwich, her brown eyes softly questioning. "Did you say something?"

Not wanting to lie, he opted for a truth—maybe not the truth of this moment, but a truth nonetheless. "I'm thankful for how your case turned out. I was hoping the DA could gather enough evidence without you taking the stand, but having Rutledge accept a plea of guilty without going to trial ... Well, that's a miracle even I didn't dare hope for."

Carly frowned. "I wonder what happened to the other girls."

Joe popped a loaded potato skin in his mouth, buying time to consider his answer. He swallowed the last of the appetizer, took a long drink of iced tea, and wiped his hands on his napkin. Instinctively, he reached across the table and let his fingertips briefly caress the back of her left hand. He resisted the urge to intertwine their fingers and withdrew his hand. "I didn't want to tell you, but Harris figured you'd find out eventually."

"Harris?"

"My partner."

Her eyes widened with fear. "Joe, what did you hear?"

"It's not what I heard. It's confirmed. Rutledge had been prepping some guy named Davison to take over. It seems your ex planned to expand into real estate and wanted to clean up his image. Rutledge Escort Service is now Davison Dates."

Devastation clouded Carly's features before she covered her face with her hands.

Joe tried to stop himself from reacting to her distress, but his heart trumped his good sense. He captured her hands and drew them away from her face, but she pulled free. Whatever she was thinking, he wanted her to know she wasn't alone. "Talk to me, Carly. Do you know Davison? Are you worried he might try to contact you?"

She shook her head. "It wouldn't matter if he did. I'm never going back to that life."

"So, you do know him?"

She frowned, her brow furrowed in tense lines. "Liam liked my friend, Star, but she was always smarter than me. She knew a snake in the grass when she saw one." Carly scoffed. "So Liam's running things for Al. I'm not surprised. They've been friends since grade school."

"If you're not afraid that Davison will look for you, then what's bothering you?"

She shrugged. "You'll think I'm naïve, which is pretty ironic, but I was hoping no one would take over the escort service. I wanted the whole operation to shut down permanently. If I had never agreed to help Al ..." She averted her face and focused on stirring salt into her ketchup with a French fry until it broke in two.

Her frustration hung in the air between them.

"Carly, look at me." He waited until she met his gaze. "It's not your fault that other women got involved. Everyone's responsible for their own mistakes. God doesn't hold you accountable for what the other escorts decided to do after Rutledge was sentenced."

"Okay, I guess. I want to believe you. But the other girls followed my lead." She smashed a French fry into the salted ketchup. "When I caved, no one else dared to stand up to Al."

Anguished regret laced her words, and Joe wanted to rise to her defense, but he couldn't be her champion. Any comfort he could offer would be temporary. "Then tell God you're sorry and let it go. God forgives you, but you won't be free until you forgive yourself."

Carly smiled. "You sound like a preacher."

His brows knit into a scowl. Was she comparing him to Ryan? Who was Joe kidding? Of course Carly compared them. Whether she admitted it or not, one day she would have to choose. Unless Ryan broke her heart. Then Joe would come to her rescue. Again. This time he would never let her go.

Carly reached across the table and touched his arm. "I was kidding. And for the record, I know you're right. But forgiving myself is more difficult than I ever imagined."

"It'll get easier," he said, drawing back from her touch. "When you realize that no one is perfect. We've all fallen far short of who we should have been. Myself included."

*

Carly cut their shopping trip short. She bought a soft wool scarf for her mother and a gift card for Dicks Sporting Goods for her brother. She had no idea what to get for her dad.

Hopefully, Mom could give her some ideas.

On the drive back to Bemus Point, she and Joe listened to an instrumental Christmas CD. Being together without talking should have been awkward, but she found herself drifting in a state of quasi sleep, meandering from one daydream to the next. Until suddenly the face of the man in her imagination became Joe. Joe in a tuxedo. And she was wearing … She straightened in her seat to shake off the image.

Her cell phone vibrated in her lap, and she keyed in her password to read the text. Ryan, confirming that he'd pick her up at one thirty for dinner at his mother's. Carly did not reply. Texting Ryan while she was riding in the truck with Joe seemed weird. Besides, she had no idea what to say. Could she bow out without hurting Ryan's feelings? Probably not.

Not unless she were too sick to go. Then she'd miss seeing her own family.

For years, Thanksgiving had been a day off for her. She'd sleep late, read, watch television, and eat Chinese take-out in her pajamas. She never answered her phone. Not even for Al, who always insisted on joining his family for a traditional Thanksgiving celebration, to which Carly had never been invited. Not once in ten years. His deliberately excluding her from every holiday gathering with his family should have clued her in long ago. She meant nothing to him.

I guess we all believe what we want to believe. No matter what the evidence shows.

Joe turned into Sarah's driveway. "What are you going to do tomorrow?"

Try to figure out how to avoid Ryan's mother. She couldn't say that. "I'm going to help Sarah make up Thanksgiving baskets to deliver to several neighbors who may not be able to afford the usual stuff. Cranberries, yams, potatoes, gravy, stuffing mix, fresh turkeys."

"Turkeys, too?"

Carly smiled, pleased to be making a difference. "Sarah gets a list of names every year from the local senior center.

This year we're putting together a dozen baskets and delivering them all by 10 a.m."

"A dozen?"

She shot him an amused look. "What are you, a Polly parrot?"

Obviously ignoring her question, Joe raked his hand through his hair. "Where does she get the money to buy all of that stuff?"

"Donations, mostly. Then she kicks in the rest herself."

Joe shifted in his seat and retrieved his wallet from the inside pocket of his jacket. He pulled out a bill and handed it to Carly.

She took it, her mouth agape. "This is a hundred dollar bill."

"Yep." Joe shut off the car and opened his door. "Tell her I'll give her another hundred next week. And if she needs more than that, I want you to find out and let me know. I'd ask her directly, but Sarah isn't likely to be straight with me."

Joe circled the car and opened Carly's door. His gaze fastened on her mouth, but he looked away before she could get to her feet. When he offered her his arm, his expression was unreadable.

"Joe, I'm sorry. I don't know what else to say."

*

Say you love me. Say dating Ryan was a mistake. "There's nothing to be sorry for." Joe held her gaze so she'd know he met every word. "We're fine."

But the look in her eyes said they weren't fine. And being what she needed was more than Joe could manage. His self-control stretched like a tight rubber band, he held the front door open for her and watched her walk inside.

"Aren't you coming in for coffee?"

"I can't." He turned and started down the steps. Over his

shoulder, he said, "Call if you need me. Day or night."

He could feel her disappointment like cold November rain hanging in the air.

*

Carly didn't want to cry, but the sobs clogging her throat demanded release. Now that she'd given her heart to the Lord, life was supposed to be easier, wasn't it? The urge to run after Joe surged through her muscles, but she kept her feet moving in the opposite direction. When she reached her bedroom, one glance at her distressed reflection in the mirror confirmed her confusion. The sound of the truck engine as Joe drove away mocked her. "God, what I am supposed to do? Why won't You show me?"

A soft knock sounded on her half-open door. "Carly?"

Sarah was home. Where was her car? Not in the driveway. She must have pulled it into the garage.

"May I come in?" Sarah's voice was soft with concern.

Carly pushed the door aside, not caring if Sarah saw her tears.

"Honey, what's happened?" Sarah took Carly's hand and led her to the bed where they sat together for a moment without speaking. "Is it Joe? Or Ryan?"

Carly jerked her head to the side and faced her friend. "Yes! I can't go on like this. I thought I'd changed, but maybe I can't change." *Maybe I'll always be Elise.*

Sarah laid her hand on Carly's thigh. "What happened today?"

"Joe loves me. He wants me to break it off with Ryan. But I—"

"He said that? I thought he'd give you time to decide."

"No. Yes. He didn't say that, but that's what he wants me to do. I wondered if he was seeing me ... differently, even back in high school." Startled at the regret that laced her words, she took a deep breath to settle herself. "I asked him to give me until the end of the year to figure things out with Ryan."

Sarah's expression was open and gentle, without any condemnation. "What do you need to figure out?"

No point in denying the truth. "Whether Ryan can live with the repercussions of my past."

"I see. What makes you think that there will be repercussions?"

"Ryan's mother recognized me." Shame burned Carly's cheeks. "She said I reminded her of a woman she'd met at a businessmen's banquet. A woman named Elise."

"Elise?"

"Elise was the name I went by when I was working." Carly stared at her clenched fists in her lap. "Eventually, Mrs. Edgar will figure out who I am."

Sarah touched Carly's arm. "Who you *were*."

Looking up into the older woman's kind face, Carly almost believed it would be that simple. "Either way it turns out, someone's going to be hurt. Joe or Ryan. Joe's right. I need to choose between them. It's not fair of me to expect Joe to be just a friend, waiting, indefinitely, when he wants so much more."

"And what do you want?"

"I wish I knew. I want to be with the man that God wants me to marry, so I don't mess up my life again."

Sarah wrapped her arms around Carly in a grandmotherly hug. "Don't you worry. God knows your heart. And He is watching over all three of you. You just need to have faith."

Carly moved out of the comforting embrace. "Faith to believe what?"

"Faith that God loves you. And Joe and Ryan. Faith that everything will work out the way it is supposed to."

*

Joe and Harris were five hours into their shift when a text beeped in on Joe's cell. As a general rule, he didn't take personal calls or texts while he was working, but this one was from his sister. If he'd been driving, Joe wouldn't have checked his phone at all. Thank God he did. The message was a knife in his gut. "Mom's at Roswell. Get here ASAP."

Oh, God, please. Not now.

Joe keyed in a quick reply. "Working. Be there by seven thirty."

Harris slanted Joe a concerned look. "What's wrong? Your tension level just went through the roof."

"It's my mom. They took her to Roswell."

"When?"

"I don't know." Joe shot off a second text. "How long has she been there?"

Maureen's reply was instantaneous. "Since about 3."

"She was admitted about an hour ago."

"Call your sister," Harris ordered as he pulled the squad car into a Tim Horton's parking lot. "I'll grab us a couple of coffees."

It had been a quiet night. Which was good in one way and bad in another. Time would drag until the end of their shift. Joe needed information before then.

Maureen answered on the second ring. "Joe, where are you? Mom's asking for you."

"How bad is it?"

"She collapsed. When she came to after a few minutes, she called 911. The ambulance brought her to Roswell. One of the EMTs called me because I was the last person on Mom's recent call list. Bob and I got here about twenty minutes ago."

"What's going on?"

"They're running tests. We haven't heard anything yet."

"Text me the minute you hear anything. Anything at all.

I'll get back to you as soon as I'm able."

Joe disconnected the call, praying the next three hours would zip past. He wanted nothing more than to be at his mother's side.

When Harris returned with their coffees, he asked, "Is she going to be all right?" In the pale light of the street lamps, his partner's concern mirrored his own.

"They're doing tests." Joe sipped his hot coffee, ignoring the heat rushing down his throat. "Let's switch. I need to be doing something. I'll drive the rest of the shift."

Harris nodded. Without another word, they exchanged places, and Joe headed the car east on Hertel Avenue. The city was quieter than usual, but then again it was the night before Thanksgiving, a time to be home with family. Which was exactly where Joe wanted to be, with Carly at his side at the hospital with Bob and Maureen, waiting for news about their mom.

He didn't have much to be thankful for tonight with his mom back in the hospital and Carly preparing to spend the holiday with Ryan. At least she wouldn't be alone. Or worse spending the day with Rutledge. Prison was too good for that scumbag.

Pray for your enemies.

Joe wanted to reject that thought. It was a tough command, especially for someone in his profession. But right was right, no matter how he felt. His feelings would catch up to his convictions later. So he prayed for Rutledge. And for Ryan Edgar, though the pastor could hardly be considered an enemy. A rival, yes. An enemy, no. Especially if he made Carly happy.

An hour later, Joe was making a left turn onto Delevan when a domestic dispute call came over the radio. They'd answered a call at that address last week. By the time they'd arrived, the guy had calmed down and his wife had apologized for calling 911, insisting that she'd overreacted. Tonight could very well be more of the same, but domestic violence often escalated when a man believed the woman wouldn't press charges.

In less than three minutes, Joe parked in front of the plain brick two-story with its newly painted porch. He and Harris hurried up the steps and pounded on the door. "Police!"

Instantly, the inside door flew open, and a woman appeared with a baby straddling her left hip and an overnight bag in her right hand. Her left eye was already starting to swell, and blood was dripping from a cut on her lower lip, which was also bruised and swollen. Surprisingly, the baby wasn't crying.

For a split second, Joe flashed back to Carly in the ICU. Rutledge had nearly killed her. Joe's heart pounded, adrenaline racing through his body. Then he took two deep breaths, drawing on his training. *Focus, man. Here and now.*

"Ma'am?" Harris asked. "Is your husband on the premises?"

"No, he ran out when I called 911. I have to get away before he comes back, but he took our car."

Harris nodded, reaching for the overnight bag. "Is there anything else you need for yourself or the baby?"

She shook her head. "Not now. I can't stay here another minute. Riley might come back and—"

"Where's your baby's car seat, ma'am?"

Panic swept the young woman's battered features, then a light shone in her defeated eyes. "The new car seat is in the front closet. Bailey was getting too big for the newborn one."

Joe retrieved the car seat, and in minutes, they were all buckled in the police car. After a brief discussion, Harris persuaded the young mother to press charges. She argued that she'd be safe at her mother's house, but he convinced her that for the next few days at least she'd be safer at a women's shelter where her husband wouldn't be able to find her.

Two hours later, after they had finished writing up their reports for the night, Harris asked, "Do you want me to drop you off at Roswell or go back for your car?"

Fighting exhaustion, Joe considered his offer. "Yeah, drop me off. I'll get someone to take me back to the station later, after I find out how Mom is." He met his partner's concerned gaze. "Harris, thanks. In case I haven't told you lately, I'm glad you're my partner."

*

Joe held his mother's hand and stared at the monitors displaying her vitals. Heart rate, respiration, and blood pressure were all within normal ranges. Addie was sleeping peacefully. Except for the ashen pallor of her skin, the IV drip in the back of her hand, and the whirr of the machines, he could almost convince himself that nothing was wrong with her.

But the intern on duty had brought the expected news. His mother's white blood cell counts, low from her last round of chemo, had left her vulnerable to infection. She'd collapsed from dehydration caused by persistent vomiting and fever. Intravenous fluids with a course of antibiotics should resolve the effects of the infection, but the course of chemotherapy would have to be suspended temporarily, which meant she would not be able to receive a bone marrow transplant should a match be found. Anxiety prickled down Joe's back. Timing was critical, but there wasn't a thing Joe could do for his mother but pray and wait. He was more than willing to pray, but the waiting rankled. This was supposed to be their first Thanksgiving together as a family in more than twenty years. The number of things that did not turn out as he expected boggled his mind.

Maureen and Bob had left the hospital shortly after Joe arrived at eight o'clock. Explaining that Leann would be anxious to get the turkey in the oven, Dad decided to go with them, leaving his car for Joe to use. At this point, picking up his truck today wasn't important. He didn't plan to make it to Maureen's house for dinner. Since he was the only one without a family of his own, he was the logical choice to stay with Mom.

Around nine o'clock, an intern wearing a blue lab coat entered the room. He stood in the doorway a moment, reading over a chart. Joe set his half-empty coffee cup on the nightstand, got to his feet, and crossed the room in two strides.

"Can I help you, Officer?"

Joe extended his hand. "My name is Callahan. This is my mother."

The doctor gripped Joe's hand in a brief, firm shake then took in his police uniform in one glance.

"I'm not here on police business of any kind. I got off work at seven and came right here."

An almost imperceptible smile crossed the doctor's face. "Your mother's white blood cell counts are up slightly from last night. Her temperature is normal, but her condition is still serious. I'd like to test her bone marrow to determine if her blast cell counts are up."

"And if they are?"

"Counts above 5 per cent mean your mother has relapsed."

"What do we do then?"

"We start a more aggressive chemotherapy program in preparation for a bone marrow transplant."

Joe stared at his mother's ashen face, completely relaxed in sleep. "But I thought that wouldn't be possible with her being so sick."

At the pressure of the doctor's hand on his arm, Joe

pivoted. They were nearly the same height, and the compassion in the other man's eyes made Joe draw in a sharp breath.

"I received news yesterday morning. A perfect match has been found for your mother. The donor, a resident of Chicago, is standing by to fly to Buffalo as soon as your mother is cleared for the procedure."

Joe squelched his impatience. "When do you think that will be?" His tone sounded much calmer than he felt.

The doctor's expression didn't change. "We should be able to project a transplant date in the next few days."

"Really?"

The faint sound of his mother's voice ignited the faith sparked by the doctor's news. In seconds, Joe was sitting on the edge of her bed and leaning over to kiss her cheek. "You had us all so worried."

Addie scanned the hospital room, her eyes displaying her confusion.

"Everyone went home a couple of hours ago. Maureen, Bob, and Dad came as soon as the EMTs notified her. Dad left me his truck. Leann spent the night with the kids."

Addie smiled, but the regret in her eyes was unmistakable. "That was nice of her. I guess your dad picked a keeper this time."

Joe sucked in a sharp breath. "Mom, don't–"

"If you'll give me a few minutes alone with your mother," the doctor said, completely nonplussed by Addie's personal comment, "I need to examine her."

"I'll go down to the cafeteria and grab some breakfast." Joe exited the room before his mother could reply. His cell vibrated in his pocket, overshadowing the rumbling in his stomach. Standing in front of the bank of elevators, he checked his phone. Someone had sent him a text. Probably Maureen wondering how Mom was doing.

Joe boarded an elevator then put in his password incorrectly two times. Maybe he was hungrier than he thought. He entered it the third time successfully. Carly's name led off his text log. Just seeing her name stirred the longing he'd tried for years to suppress. For a minute, he imagined reading the words, "I love you."

Get it together, man.

He drew in a deep, steadying breath then read her message. The text actually said, "Happy Thanksgiving. You're on my mind and in my prayers."

She was on his mind, too. Too much and too often.

The elevator doors opened, and Joe followed the signs to the cafeteria. With a quick glance at his options, he headed for the grill and ordered a three-egg omelet with ham, cheese, and mushrooms and a side order of hash browns and whole wheat toast. While he waited for the cook to prepare his food, Joe sent a reply to Carly. "Happy Thanksgiving to you, too. My mother's in the hospital. Please keep her in your prayers."

Ten minutes later, he was halfway through his breakfast when his cell phone started bouncing on the table. Carly was calling him. "Hi. Good morning." *Beautiful, you have no idea how much I wanted to hear your voice* was what he wanted to say. Instead, he said, "Thanks for calling."

"How's your mother?" she asked, her tone tender with concern.

"She has an infection. They have her hooked up to an IV that's pumping her full of fluids and antibiotics."

"That's good, right?"

"Yes, and the sooner the antibiotics work, the better. The hospital's found a match."

"For a bone marrow transplant? That's great news."

"Yes, it is." Joe pushed his plate aside. "Thanks for your

prayers. I'm glad you called, but I need to get back to Mom. I'll keep you updated."

"Joe, I … I'm happy things are going so well between you and your mom."

Sadness tinged her words, reminding him that if he had reconciled with his mother sooner, Carly might be here with him right now.

"Enjoy your day with your family," Joe said, "and tell Ryan I said hello."

After they said goodbye, Joe swallowed the last of his coffee, cleared his table, and headed back to the elevators. He still needed to clear up a few things with his mother.

*

He prayed for wisdom, before quietly opening the door to her room. Joe sighed at the sight before him. His mother lay on her side, her left arm resting on a pillow tucked to her chest. She was snoring softly. He considered keeping watch over her, but the boxy chair next to her bed looked horribly uncomfortable. One glance at his watch and his decision was made. It was past ten thirty, and he'd be more of a help to his mother if he went home to sleep a few hours in his own bed. Their conversation would have to wait.

CHAPTER TWENTY-ONE

"This conversation can't wait." Elizabeth Edgar's tone was imperiously insistent. "Ryan, you've always been the sensible one in this family. It simply doesn't make sense for you to be dating a woman whose past is—"

"Mother, who I date is *my* business. Not yours."

"Do you know anything at all about her life before she came to live with Mrs. Zigler? I'm sure I've seen her before."

Carly flattened her back against the hallway wall and inched away from the kitchen door. If only she could make herself invisible. Willing her heart to stop racing, she wiped her sweaty palms on her skirt. She should retreat. Join the others in the living room. Duck back into the bathroom. Anything but stand in plain sight where Ryan would discover her the second he left the kitchen. He wouldn't want to believe she'd been eavesdropping, but his mother wouldn't be that generous, and Carly didn't want to give the woman more ammunition to use against her.

Ryan's voice was so low. Why didn't he speak up? Carly strained to hear his reply. Was he sharing her story with his mother? Bile rose into Carly's throat. She swallowed hard and pressed her palm against her churning stomach. Escaping to the nearby bathroom, she prayed he would say nothing. Not yet.

Elizabeth Edgar was incapable of understanding how any woman could possibly end up selling herself to keep a man. She had certainly never known the kind of man that would ask that of a woman. Carly stared at her ashen reflection in the gilt-edged mirror then bent over the sink to splash water on her face. For a moment, she considered feigning illness but dismissed the idea. She'd been many things. A liar wasn't one of them.

She shuddered. That wasn't true. For years, she'd built her life on a foundation of lies.

God, forgive me. Please help me get through dinner.

*

Carly settled into the bucket seat next to Ryan. The car was comfortably warm, thanks to his thoughtfulness in starting the engine a full ten minutes before they needed to leave. The radio station was playing Christmas favorites from her childhood, stirring up memories that added to her melancholy mood. Frank Sinatra singing "I'll Be Home for Christmas" brought tears to her eyes. That one had been getting to her for years. She tilted her head toward the window and leaned her cheek against her gloved hand, confident that the fabric would absorb any moisture and conceal her distress.

Ryan reached across the leather seat and let his palm rest on Carly's thigh. She shivered at his touch. Had he seen her crying? "That wasn't so bad, was it?" he asked, lingering at a stop sign.

Clearly, he didn't suspect she'd overheard his conversation with his mother. She should ask him about it. After all, being grilled by his mother couldn't have been easy for him. And that was only the beginning. His congregation would have questions, too. Did he love Carly enough to withstand widespread disapproval?

Wanting to trust him, she shifted in the seat toward him. His brows knit with concern. He cared enough to ask how she handled the visit, but could he handle the truth?

You're not being fair. He promised that whatever

happened, you would handle it together.

But what exactly was the truth? That *she* couldn't handle widespread disapproval? That overt disapproval would make it even more difficult for her to slough off the old image of herself that kept condemning her? She refused to get into this now.

Ryan bent close. The tender look in his chocolate eyes made her feel cherished. Could she unburden her heart to him?

He brushed a kiss across her lips. "Hmm. Peppermint. My favorite." He smiled, obviously expecting a smile in return, as if a kiss could fix everything.

Her lower lip trembled. Elise had never cried, but Carly couldn't seem to rein in her emotions. Not since the miscarriage. If it wasn't Thanksgiving, she would've asked Ryan to drive her back to Sarah's, but she wanted—no needed—to see her family.

Three short honks sounded. In the side view mirror, Carly spotted a man in a red pickup truck preparing to lay into his horn again, but Ryan pulled out into the intersection, short-circuiting the other guy's response. Her boyfriend gave his full attention to the road, and Carly thanked God for the reprieve, praying she could get herself together enough to avoid arousing questions that would end in a discussion neither of them were ready to have. A discussion that could lead to the end of their relationship.

She wasn't ready to give up on them. Or on the person she could become if they stayed together.

Was she?

Remembering his mother's words, Carly shuddered beneath the dread crushing her heart.

It was only a matter of time until Elizabeth Edgar would back her son into a corner.

*

Carly and Ryan found Dad and Jared watching football in the family room. After brief introductions, all three men were sitting, leaning forward, elbows on their thighs, ready to reprimand players for every mistake. Carly looked from one to another. Each man's gaze was riveted on the flat screen TV that filled one wall of the room. Had they all forgotten she was here? Apparently.

"I guess I'll go see if Mom needs any help."

No one replied to her comment. Carly shrugged and headed to the kitchen.

Standing at the gleaming counter, her mother was beating whipped cream into fluffy mounds. Carly recalled the last time she'd tasted homemade whipped cream. She'd made it herself for Joe's 20th birthday berry pie. His hand had brushed hers when she'd handed him his plate.

She'd managed to ignore the electricity surging between them that night. Her promises to Al had weighed heavy on her mind.

Guilt. That was it.

I shouldn't have been feeling anything for Joe, so I told myself I didn't. Lord, I lied to myself, didn't I?

"Carly, are you all right?" Mom crossed the room and brushed a lock of hair from Carly's cheek. "You look pale. You're not sick, are you?"

"I'm fine." Carly reached for the coffee pot and poured the heavenly scented hazelnut brew into one of her mother's snowman mugs. "Being with Ryan's family was exhausting."

Mom handed her a spoon heaped with whipped cream. "Try this in your coffee."

Carly swirled the sweetened cream, watched it melt, and then added another dollop. "Shall I make you a mug?"

Mom nodded, waited for Carly to fix another coffee, and

then put the bowl of whipped cream into the refrigerator. Mom took a seat at the kitchen table. "Do you want to tell me what's bothering you?"

Uncertainty dimmed her mother's eyes, a sign that it cost her something to reach out to a daughter she barely knew. That fact alone caused a pain-filled frown to deepen the lines on her tired face. Carly couldn't leave her hanging. "Ryan's mother doesn't like me. She suspects something … unacceptable. I remind her of someone. She hasn't figured it out yet, but several years ago she saw me at a business conference."

"Oh, honey. I'm so sorry." Her mother reached across the table and brushed her manicured fingertips light as a butterfly over the back of Carly's hand. "What are you going to do? Does Ryan know?"

"Yeah, the day I told him about my past, I mentioned that his mother almost recognized me." Carly took a long swallow of coffee for fortification. "He thinks that whatever comes up, we'll handle it together." A tear slid down one cheek. She swiped it away. "But he's wrong. We won't be able to handle his mother."

Or his congregation.

Mom's eyes widened in surprise, not at Carly's declaration, but at the fact they'd been overheard.

With her back to the door, Carly couldn't be sure who had entered the kitchen, but she felt his presence. Her breath caught in her throat, and she swallowed hard as she pushed the chair 45 degrees, then stood on trembling legs. "Ryan, I …"

He stared at her, his mouth a grim line.

Why didn't he say something? He was clearly upset, most likely by her lack of confidence in him. Why was the trust between them so fragile? Was it her fault? Or his?

Mom moved to the cupboard above the coffee pot and took

out three mugs. "I'm sure your dad sent Ryan for coffee, right?"

"I volunteered." He nodded, his gaze resting on Carly. "I missed you," he whispered in her ear.

Missed her? She'd been in the kitchen less than twenty minutes. Apparently, her efforts to conceal her distress had failed. He was hovering. And disappointed in her.

Not a good combination.

"Let's go for a walk." It was a command, not a request.

She bristled but kept her voice even. "What about the game?"

"I'm not a huge fan of football."

Mom chuckled. "Don't say that out loud in this house. Jared will flip."

Carly sighed with relief. Her mother had always known how to lighten the mood. She'd thank her later.

Ryan pulled Carly's chair out, and she got to her feet. "I guess I would like to walk off your mother's delicious dinner so I have room for pie."

Glancing out the windows above the sink, Carly noted that the snow had stopped. Mom's cardinal thermometer registered 30 degrees—not too cold if they bundled up. Her folks kept a stash of scarves, hats, and mittens in the mudroom. She could give orders, too. "Grab our coats from the front closet and meet me in the mudroom."

"Mudroom?"

Carly gestured to the door on the opposite end of the long kitchen. He'd never heard of a mudroom? Clearly not. She almost laughed aloud at the thought of Elizabeth Edgar having a mudroom in her house. The Edgar children certainly did not come inside with mud on their shoes or their boots. Again, Carly wasn't being fair. Her apprehensiveness was making her uncharitable. "It's a little room at the back of the house. We use it on rainy days so we don't track mud through the house."

Ryan nodded. "Makes perfect sense. I wonder why every house doesn't have one." He tossed the last remark over his shoulder as he headed off to retrieve their coats and boots.

Mom opened the mudroom door. "Carly, I'm sorry Ryan overheard what you said about his mother. If I hadn't asked you to talk about what was bothering you ..."

She clasped her mother by her shoulders, astonished again at how frail she was. "I'm glad you did. It's been a long time. I've missed talking things over with you."

A startled look flitted in her mother's eyes. In a heartbeat, Carly found herself in her mother's comforting embrace. Neither said a word. Carly didn't let go until Ryan showed up with their stuff.

With a grin, she handed him a Buffalo Bills hat, scarf, and mittens.

Mom laughed. "We'll make a fan out of you yet."

Ryan smiled, shook his head at them, and helped Carly into her coat.

Within minutes, they were heading down the street, heedless of the two inches of snow covering the sidewalks. Carly didn't know whether to be grateful for Ryan's steady hand on her elbow or distressed at the high-handed way he'd insisted they go for a walk. She breathed a silent prayer. She might as well be the first one to speak. "I know you heard what I said about your mother." She stopped under a streetlamp and twisted to face him. "But what *you* don't know is that I heard what your mother said about me."

Ryan paled. "I sensed you were upset about something. Why didn't you tell me in the car?"

"I didn't want to spoil Thanksgiving for you, but you and I both know your mother is going to flip out when she finds out what I used to do for a living." She harrumphed. "Boy, is that ever a misnomer. I didn't have a life."

"Carly, don't think about that. It's over."

She shook her head. "You don't understand. I may not work for the escort service anymore, but your mother knows people who travel in the same circles that I did."

"But we don't travel in those circles."

"Ryan, please. If one person recognizes me, your mother is going to—"

"Going to what? Tell me I can't see you anymore? I'm not a teenager."

"Your mother is going to see me as a liability you can't afford. Being seen with a former call girl will tarnish your reputation and your good name."

Ryan captured her face in his gloved hands. "I don't feel that way about you." He lowered his head to kiss her.

She should move away, but standing in the glow of the street lamp, a flurry of delicate snowflakes swirling about them, Carly needed this moment. She stood on her toes and kissed him until their kiss banished the cold from her lips and the panic from her heart.

Ryan pulled away first, clasped her hand, and started them strolling down the street, past an occasional house already lit up with Christmas lights. They walked three blocks then turned around to head back. Her dad would be eager for pie and Mom's whipped cream.

Maybe she was worrying for nothing. She'd committed her life into God's hands. Surely, He had a good plan for her.

And if Ryan were part of that plan, Elizabeth Edgar would adjust. Eventually.

*

Joe held the ICU door open for Maureen. His sister carried a plate with two slivers of pie, pumpkin and pecan. Addie sat propped up in bed, a magazine open on her lap. Her face lost its tired cast as she smiled at Joe and Maureen. "I didn't expect to see you two today. Why aren't you with your family, Maureen?"

His sister bent and kissed Mom's forehead. "Bob is keeping the kids busy playing board games. Joe and I didn't want you to be alone all day on Thanksgiving."

"We brought you some pie," Joe said, relieved to see a little color in her cheeks. "I hope you like pumpkin or pecan." For a second, resentment reared its head. He should know what kind of pie his own mother preferred.

Her puzzled frown put a smile back on his face. "The kids ate all of the apple."

Maureen set the paper plate on the bed tray and positioned the tray over Addie's lap. "Do you want some now?"

Joe smiled as his ever-prepared sister pulled a plastic fork from her purse.

Addie took two bites of each pie then sighed with pleasure. "I'll eat the rest later."

Sitting stiffly in the straight back hospital chair, Joe listened to his sister and their mother discuss what the kids wanted for Christmas until his patience wore thin. "Has the doctor been in?"

Addie cast him a confused look. "Not since this morning. Why?"

"Because I want to know how the bone marrow test went."

Addie and Maureen exchanged amused glances. "Joe, the hospital staff isn't going to do that kind of a test on Thanksgiving." His sister's expression declared he should have been able to figure that out on his own.

"The test is scheduled for tomorrow at 10 a.m." His mother's matter-of-fact tone suggested she'd had more than her fill of medical procedures over the last two years. "I know this is hard for you, Joe, but I've learned to view each day as a gift. Tomorrow isn't guaranteed to anyone, whether she's cancer-free or not."

The color fled from his sister's face. "Mom, don't."

Addie covered Maureen's hand with her own. "Don't what? Have faith that God's timing is best?"

Maureen shook her head. "I didn't mean it like that. It's ... we just got you back."

Joe's heart skipped out of rhythm. For years, years they could have shared together, his mother had been too busy with her own life to care about them, to be there for them. But all of that was past. What counted was right now. His mother was right about that.

"We want you to beat this, Mom." He sat on the edge of the bed opposite Maureen. "We need you."

Addie's eyes glistened with tears. "I know. I ... I'm sorry I missed so much with both of you."

"Don't think about it," Maureen pleaded.

A memory flashed in Joe's mind—his sister crying on her wedding day, missing her mom in spite of Leann's capable and attentive mothering. "We can't do anything about the past, except put it behind us." He should know. He'd been shackled by his own bitterness for far too long.

Her eyes filled with regret, but Addie managed a smile. "I love you both. I've always loved you. And I intend to spend the rest of my life making up for all the pain my selfishness caused you."

Maureen was crying freely now, and Joe pressed his lips tightly together. Addie spread her arms wide to enclose them both in a hug. "Can you ever forgive me?"

"Oh, Mom," Maureen said, "I forgave you years ago, even before we thought you were dead. I know you would've stayed if you could."

"Honey, that's the worst part, I could have stayed. I chose

to leave. Over and over. And I have to live with the consequences of that."

A quiet settled over Joe. "Mom, I forgive you. You did the best you could. Thank you for being with us now."

Loving someone took faith and patience, more than Joe could muster on his own. Thank God he'd finally figured that much out. If God ever gave him another chance with Carly, Joe wouldn't rely on his own strength to love her the way she deserved.

*

Carly slept late the day after Thanksgiving. Black Friday shopping was not for her. Sarah had been willing to drive her to the McKinley Mall in Hamburg, but being jostled by the crowds was not Carly's idea of getting into the holiday spirit. She and Sarah planned to make Christmas cookies after lunch and then order a pizza for dinner.

Shocked at the time, Carly stared at the bedside clock. Nine thirty. How could she have slept so long? Stress. That's what. A long hot shower was what she needed. That and a cup of Sarah's strong coffee with peppermint mocha creamer.

Following the sound of Christmas carols coming from the radio, Carly wandered into the kitchen where Sarah was already mixing the dough for anise cut-outs in a big bowl. "I thought we were going to wait until after lunch." Carly poured a tall mug of java. She stirred in the holiday creamer and dropped a slice of rye bread into the toaster.

"I decided to get a head start." Sarah brushed flour off her apron. "This way we can start cutting them out sooner."

Carly spread butter on the hot toast.

Sarah frowned at Carly's meager breakfast. "There's leftover pumpkin pancake batter in the fridge."

"Let's save that for lunch." Carly plopped down in a chair across from Sarah then dunked her toast in her coffee and savored the first bite. Hungrier than she'd first thought, she finished eating in record time. She grabbed a Clementine from the fruit bowl of fruit. With her attention focused on peeling the citrus treat, Carly confided, "I don't think it's going to work out with Ryan and me."

Sarah shot her a look of disbelief but didn't respond. She picked up the oversized mixing bowl, made a spot in the refrigerator for the dough to chill, poured herself a cup of coffee, and then returned to the table. "What makes you say that?"

"His mother doesn't like me."

Sarah wrapped her hands around her coffee mug. "She didn't *say* that?"

"Not in so many words. But it's obvious she doesn't think I'm in the same class as her or her son."

Sarah's brow knit in a frown. "What does Ryan say?"

"That whatever happens we'll face it together." Carly drained the last drops of her coffee. "He's being naïve." She twisted her napkin, unwound it, then twisted it again.

"Do you love him?"

"Of course I love him. He's a wonderful guy."

Sarah studied her, hazel eyes searching for answers Carly had yet to discover. "Do you love him because he's wonderful, or do you think he's wonderful because you love him?"

Carly released a soft chuckle. "That sounds like a line from Rodger and Hammerstein's *Cinderella.*"

"It is … a bit. But it's still a valid question."

Carly rose from the table and carried her dirty dishes to the sink to give herself a moment. What was Sarah getting at? Ryan Edgar was a great guy, a guy any girl could fall in love with. She should love him. But did she? Truly love him? Love him so much that she couldn't imagine her life without him?

Apparently not.

Because she was already imagining what she would do if he ended their relationship. If she were in love with him, wouldn't she be planning what she'd do to keep him, rather than preparing for him to leave her?

Was she borrowing trouble? Where was her faith in God's good plan for her?

She wanted to believe Ryan loved her enough to weather the inevitable repercussions of her poor choices. But he simply didn't understand that though God may view her as a new creature living a transformed life, some men, and women, too, were of the opinion that girls like her never changed. And that they didn't deserve a chance to even try.

Thank You, Father, that's it not about what I deserve, but about what Jesus did for me.

Still, some mistakes simply could not be undone or made right. She'd lost both of her babies because of her stupidity, and she'd never be able to make that right. She had to live with the reality that her babies were dead. One at her hand. The other at the hand of his father.

She swiped at the tears chilling her face.

Sarah's hand on her shoulder was her undoing. Carly twirled on her heels, fell into the older woman's arms, and wept. Sarah didn't say a word. She let Carly cry it all out until her grief was spent. For now.

After a few minutes, she raised her face, backed away, and met the other woman's kind eyes. "Ryan thinks he loves me. But he loves the person he imagines I am. Or maybe the person he wants me to be. He says I should forget the past, but I am the woman I am today in spite of my past *and* because of my past. Ryan doesn't understand that."

"But Joe does."

Carly inhaled a sharp breath.

"Does Ryan know you're still seeing Joe?"

Heat rushed into Carly's face, spreading down her neck. "I'm not *seeing* Joe. We're … friends." She couldn't bear it if Sarah thought less of him. For Joe's sake, she rushed to his defense. "He and my brother have been friends so long that Joe's practically family. He accepts me. No matter how badly I mess up."

Sarah put up her hand, flour sprinkling to the floor. "You misunderstand me. I was the one who told you that you needed to figure out which man you could love. I'd be a hypocrite if I criticized you for continuing to spend time with my nephew."

Carly sank into a chair. With her elbows on the table and her chin resting in her hands, she sighed. "Then what are you saying?"

"Joe knows you're seeing Ryan, but you haven't told Ryan about your friendship with Joe, have you?"

Carly shook her head. "He thinks Joe is just my brother's friend. My relationship with Joe is complicated. Ryan wouldn't understand."

Sarah flipped through a few pages of her cookbook. Then she looked up at Carly. "He would if you and Joe are only friends. But if you're more than friends, well, of course Ryan wouldn't understand *that*."

She was Ryan's girl, but she didn't want to give Joe up. Was he more than a friend? What did she want from him? If things got ugly, he was the one she trusted. He would let her lean on him without expecting anything in return.

Could she say the same about Ryan? He was pressing for a commitment she wasn't ready to make.

If Joe hadn't seen his mother every time he looked at Carly, would she have been dating him and not Ryan? She would never know. Joe's bitterness toward Addie had made loving Carly a risk he wasn't willing to take. Was she with Ryan just because she couldn't be with Joe? If it were true, what kind of a person did that make her? A dishonest one. A liar of the worst kind. The kind that couldn't even tell herself the truth.

Carly pushed back from the table. "I need to go for a walk." Maybe alone, outside, walking beneath the rare November blue sky filled with feathery clouds, she could pray and figure out what she should do. She cared about both men, loved them, respected them, and …

She should be in love with Ryan, but was she? And if she wasn't in love with him, did that necessarily mean she was in love with Joe? He'd told her he loved her, but was he prepared to build a life with her in spite of her past? And his?

Carly had given her life to the Lord, asked for His guidance and His will. So why was she still so confused?

CHAPTER TWENTY-TWO

A half hour later, Carly marched up the porch steps and grabbed the snow shovel.

Walking always calmed her, and since she'd recommitted her life to God, made her more aware of His presence and His voice. But today the only sound was the crunching of the crisp snow beneath her boots. Even though she'd managed to squelch the noise in her own brain, the Holy Spirit was silent.

Frustrated, she attacked the four inches of packed snow that had fallen last night and now covered their walkway. Push, thrust, bend, throw. Repeat. And repeat again. And again. Her breath came in quick puffs in the frigid air. Beneath her down parka, sweat trickled down her back from the exertion.

Why wasn't God making His will plain to her?

Maybe because she really could envision herself married to Ryan. Being one half of a respectable couple appealed to her. What would it be like to be completely free from the shame of the past? Would she at last feel validated because she'd been deemed worthy to be the wife of a preacher? Ryan was a man who'd guarded his actions as he'd guarded his heart. He was dedicated to helping others no matter how far they'd strayed from God's best plans for their lives. She'd be proud to be his wife. But would he always be proud to be her husband?

At least, she could empathize with those who felt they'd gone too far for God to want them. Surely, her compassion was worth something. Weighed in the balance, she wouldn't be found entirely wanting.

Be realistic. You'll never measure up to the standards a congregation would expect from the pastor's wife.

If Ryan weren't a minister. If his late father hadn't been a high profile businessman. If his mother approved of her.

Too many ifs. And too many buts. Maybe she should make a list of pros and cons.

A laugh erupted from her throat. Pros and cons could never tell her what was in her heart.

She looked up at the sky that had gone completely gray in the last fifteen minutes. "Why won't You help me?"

*

Another half hour later, Carly gazed with approval at her work. The driveway was clear to the road, completely free of snow, and sprinkled with rock salt. She'd accomplished a lot, but she was no closer to knowing her own mind. She trudged up the porch stairs and into the house.

The smell of fresh-baked cookies tickled her nose. Sarah had started baking without her. Carly shed her winter gear, left her boots in the tray near the front door, and hurried to help.

The kitchen resembled a bakery. Three different types of cookies were in various stages of preparation. Sarah had already begun frosting the cut-outs. Green trees adorned with colored sprinkles and bright yellow stars dusted with red sugar were drying on sheets of parchment paper. Mexican wedding cakes cooled on racks. A bag of chocolate kisses lay near a mixing bowl filled with peanut butter cookie dough. Her capable hostess deftly rolled the dough into balls and tossed them into a bowl of granulated sugar before lining them up on a cookie sheet, and flattening each one with a fork.

"Oh, my," Carly exclaimed. "I didn't realize I was outside that long."

Sarah smiled. "Did you figure anything out?"

Shaking her head, Carly reached for the peanut butter cookie dough. "I didn't intend to leave you with all of this work. Do you want to take a break while I finish these?"

"I would like to get off my feet for a bit. I'll just finish frosting the snowmen and the bells." Sarah reached for the small bowl of blue frosting and started on the stack of bells. She looked up from her task a moment later. "I forgot to tell you. Your phone rang twice while you were gone."

Carly spotted her cell where she'd left it on the counter next to the toaster. Trepidation tripped through her veins. Ryan had probably called to see if she was feeling any better. Or maybe Joe wanted to know if she'd had a nice Thanksgiving with her folks. Chiding herself for her anxiety, Carly picked up her phone just as it rang again. She didn't recognize the number, but she accepted the call anyway.

"Hello?"

"Hi there, sexy. Miss me?"

The phone slid from her hand and crashed to the floor. She squatted to retrieve it, then demanded, "How did you get this number?"

"Now, is that any way to greet the man you were supposed to marry?"

"Don't ever call me again."

Carly hung up, then quickly checked her missed call log. One was from Jared and the other was from Ryan. At least Al hadn't been blowing up her phone. She stared at her hands, shaking from fear's adrenaline rush. She should have known he'd try to contact her eventually.

"Are you all right, dear?" Sarah asked. "Your face is as white as new-fallen snow."

Carly covered her eyes with her hands, then dragged her fingers over her cheekbones and down her face as if she could wipe away the shudders shaking her thin frame. "That was Al. I ... I don't know how he got my number." She strode across the kitchen toward the living room then turned back to face her friend. "I need to call Joe."

"Of course. He'll know what to do." Sarah bent her head and mouthed a quiet prayer asking God to give Carly peace in the midst of this new storm.

But how could she have peace when Al could barge back into her life whenever he chose?

Joe answered her call on the second ring. "Hi. I was just going to call you."

The warm welcome in his greeting brought instant tears, which she ignored. "Al," she choked around a sob clutching her throat. "Al just called me. Joe, how did he get my number? What am I going to do? I told you he'd never let me go."

"Carly, listen to me, honey. I don't know how he got your number. But we'll make sure he doesn't call you or contact you again. Get in touch with the phone company and have them block the number. On Monday morning, I'll file for a restraining order—"

"I don't need a restraining order. Can't I just go on my parents' phone plan and get a new number?"

"You could, but with a restraining order if Rutledge so much as sends you a postcard, he'll be in violation. He won't want to jeopardize his chances of getting early parole for good behavior."

"What? What do you mean get out early?" She gulped back more sobs.

"Honey, that's years down the road. Are you still crying?"

"Of course, I'm still crying. I just talked to the man who tried to kill me." *And pressured me into having an abortion.* She sank onto the couch, tucked her legs beneath her, and clutched a pillow to her chest. "Can you come over?"

"I'm on my way."

One look out the front window, and Carly regretted asking Joe to drive down. Snow swirled in a dervish of white, making it difficult to see the house across the street. *Lord, keep him safe on the roads, please. And forgive me for needing him so much.*

*

Joe was surprised that the highway was still open. Traffic crawled at a rate of 25 mph. Joe switched on his four-way flashers. By the time he parked in Sarah's driveway, he'd had to pull over to knock the ice off his windshield wipers a half dozen times. Grateful he always kept a duffel bag with a change of clothes in the car, he made up his mind that he'd not be heading back to Buffalo tonight. Aunt Sarah's second guest room with the tiny twin bed would have to do.

Carly met him at the front door. Her face was scrubbed clean of any trace of crying, but her pupils were wide with fear. He pulled her into his arms, forgetting that his jacket was covered with snow. She smelled like peanut butter cookies and floral shampoo, and he wanted to kiss away all of her troubles. He kissed the top of her head the way a brother would and set her from him. "Tell me you're all right."

"I am now." She grabbed his hand and led him to the couch. She sat, attempting to pull him down next to her.

He resisted. "Let me get out of these wet things." Turning his back to her to gain control of his riotous feelings, he kicked off his boots and left them in the tray by the door, then hung his coat, hat, scarf, and gloves on the rack to dry. When he turned around, Carly was standing so close he bumped into her. She grabbed his arm to steady herself.

From behind her, Sarah entered the living room carrying a tray of coffee and cookies. Her expression was unreadable. Did she approve of him coming? More than likely his great aunt believed Carly should have called Ryan instead. Why hadn't she?

"Pizza won't be here for another hour, and I figured you'd be hungry after that long drive." Sarah set the tray on the coffee table then headed back into the kitchen, leaving him alone with Carly.

He stirred creamer into his coffee and ate three cookies before tasting the steaming brew. Finally, he asked the question running through his mind the whole drive down. "Why do you think Rutledge called you today, after all this time?"

Carly stared into her coffee mug then raised bleak eyes to his. "Today was our special day. Al always spent Thanksgiving with his family. I think he felt guilty leaving me alone on the holiday, so the next day was always just the two of us. No business engagements. He didn't even take any calls. Every year, he'd promise it would be the last time we'd be apart for the holidays. He was always promising me a spring wedding. I can't believe I believed him. Ever."

Against his better judgment, Joe laid one hand on her leg and squeezed her knee. Even through her jeans, heat rushed into his palm. He drew his hand back and kicked himself for the hurt look that settled in her eyes. She was no stranger to rejection. He could see that, too.

"If I hadn't been so naïve, I would never have had an abortion. Or the miscarriage." She averted her face but not before he saw the shame that tortured her heart.

He took her in his arms then because he didn't know what else he could do to ease her pain. She sobbed as if she could never forget what she'd done. He rubbed one hand down the length of her hair, and with the other, he massaged her back in slow circles as tears streaked his own face.

Lord, I love this woman. Help me not to scare her off.

When her trembling stopped, Joe whispered against her hair, "Are you … better?"

She raised her face to his, and nodded, but her eyes held the same guilt and confusion assailing him. "Yes." She scrambled to her feet and headed toward the kitchen. "I'm going to see if Sarah needs help finishing up the cookies. Why don't you turn on the television and check on the weather report?"

Joe smiled, grateful that the most recent wave of grief had passed. He didn't expect her to get over her babies anytime soon. Part of her would always grieve their loss. But maybe having another child … with him … in time …

He had never imagined himself married to anyone but Carly. And he needed to tell her that. Soon.

Joe pointed the remote at the TV and switched the station until the news came on. The meteorologist was predicting twelve to eighteen inches by morning. Good thing he had tomorrow off.

*

Stretched out on his back on the soft twin mattress designed to support a child's weight, Joe stared with dismay at the play of shadows on the ceiling caused by the neighbor's light posts. Why didn't Great Aunt Ellie have double-insulated, light-blocking drapes? Blaming his insomnia on the lack of darkness was easier than acknowledging the truth. Every nerve in his body was aware that Carly lay asleep in her bed next door. He should have never given in to Sarah's arguments about the hazards of driving home. Or packed a bag so he could stay overnight. Battling with the snowstorm would've been easier than wrestling with his desire for Carly.

Lord, help me get some sleep tonight, or I'll be no help to her in the morning.

*

Carly rolled from her back to her side. She'd been tossing and turning for over an hour. Longing for the elusive escape of sleep, she considered switching on the light and reading for a while. The image of herself lying beneath Joe, arms and legs wrapped around his back caused a rush of shame to burn her face. *Lord, no. I … don't let me think about him like that. Please.*

If only she were innocent and naïve. But she could never be that girl again.

Ryan was wrong. Forgetting the past was impossible. How could she possibly forget what she'd already experienced? Yes, Ryan would be truly shocked if she were to confess the direction of her thoughts tonight.

But what was more shocking was she'd never had those thoughts about Ryan.

Then again, he'd never slept in the next room.

Carly scooted up in bed, stuffed the extra pillow behind her back, turned on the bedside lamp, and opened her Bible. She read aloud from the Psalms, her voice a whisper, until her eyes started drifting closed. Then she put out the light, wrapped her arms around the extra pillow, and sighed as sleep claimed her at last around 2 a.m.

*

Joe found the freshly ground coffee and filters in the cupboard above the coffeemaker. He started a pot, then stood in front of the kitchen sink and watched a pair of cardinals eating seeds from a bird feeder Sarah had hung in the bare branches of a lilac bush. The image of Carly crouching in the shrubbery last August brought a smile to his tired face.

He should've asked her out for lunch that day. He'd been a fool to let her get away.

If he hadn't been so caught up in his own issues, maybe he could have protected her. If she'd confided in him about the baby, he would have helped her get away from Rutledge, and her baby would be alive today.

If she had let him help her. If he'd been able to convince her not to trust Rutledge.

If Joe had told her years ago how he felt about her, maybe she would never have gone with Rutledge in the first place.

So many, too many ifs.

The floral smell of her perfume invaded his senses, alerting him to her presence. Standing close behind him, Carly was the biggest temptation he'd ever faced. He'd give almost anything to forget everything and take her in his arms, to soothe away her fears and put a smile on her face. Her soft hand on his bare arm was almost his undoing.

"Good morning," she said, her voice still husky with sleep.

He sidestepped, putting necessary distance between them. "Good morning to you, too. The snow's stopped, and I heard the plows come through about ten minutes ago, so I should be able to head out right after breakfast."

Disappointment flashed in her eyes, then she composed her features into an unreadable mask. "Of course, you need to get going. I'll whip up some scrambled eggs and sausage." She turned her back to him and started gathering ingredients for breakfast from the refrigerator.

She was good at erecting walls. That might work with some people, but not with Joe. She was used to protecting herself, used to counting on no one, but she'd come to depend on him, reluctantly at first. Given her past, trusting men didn't come easily.

Why *did* she rely on him so much? Why wasn't she turning to Ryan? Maybe things weren't as serious with them as Joe had imagined. Maybe this was his opportunity.

He decided to fish a bit. "Have you told Ryan about Al's phone call?"

She dropped an egg on the counter, and it slid to floor, smashing into a sticky mess on the linoleum.

He snatched a rag from the sink and bent to help her. He swiped the mess in a quick circular motion, then looked up. Mere inches separated their faces. Her mouth opened in an O, and before he could stop himself, his lips met hers. The kiss was quick, and they broke apart from the electric shock of the contact. He stumbled to his feet then reached one hand down to help her up. An apology was on his lips, but he refused to apologize when all he could think about was kissing her again.

*

"I … I shouldn't have done that," Carly said, not knowing who had initiated the kiss. She should apologize, but she'd be lying, lying because she wanted to kiss him again, really kiss him so she'd know for sure if the passion blazing in his eyes meant what she suspected. That he was crazy in love with her, enough to move heaven and earth for her. Because she was … Was what?

The same as always.

No, she'd changed. She would not betray Ryan. None of the women she'd met at church struggled with remaining loyal to one man. Was Carly capable of that level of fidelity?

She certainly hoped so because someday she wanted a family of her own. If God would see fit to give her another chance at motherhood.

"Carly, please don't blame yourself. You asked me to give you time, and I agreed. I had no business kissing you."

How did he manage to read her very thoughts? "And I had no business responding. But I did, and I'm sorry. It won't, it can't happen again. So let's just forget it happened, okay?"

When he didn't answer, she decided to interpret his silence as agreement.

She cut a chunk of butter and set it in the frying pan to

heat while she scrambled a half of a dozen eggs. A few minutes later, she passed Joe the loaf of bread. "Would you mind making the toast while I cook?" she asked without meeting his gaze. Developing her domestic skills had never been high on her priority list, but Sarah was a patient and capable teacher. "I'm afraid I haven't mastered the fine art of getting everything hot and ready at the same time."

"Carly's far too modest," Sarah interjected, tightening the belt of her robe as she stepped into the kitchen. "Why didn't one of you wake me? I can't remember when I slept past seven o'clock."

Carly felt a hot blush staining her cheeks. She hadn't even thought about knocking on Sarah's door. She'd been grateful for the time alone with Joe.

After breakfast, Sarah said goodbye in the kitchen, leaving Carly to walk Joe to the front door. "Thanks again for driving out last night in the storm. You really are a great friend. Better than I have any right to expect."

Joe brushed a lock of hair that had fallen over her left eye. She shivered at the contact, and he drew his hand back quickly. His eyes said he was sorry, sorry that he couldn't seem to stop touching her. "I'm glad I could be here for you." His voice caressed her heart. "You can call me anytime. Day or night."

Moved, Carly stood on her toes and brushed a fast kiss across his cheek.

He enclosed her face in his hands, and she ached to kiss him, but it wasn't desire she saw in his eyes.

"Do something for me?" he asked, his tone somber.

She was afraid to ask him what he wanted from her.

"Get a restraining order. It makes sense. The guy almost killed you."

She shuddered at the memories. "You're right. If Al tries

to contact me again, I'll get a restraining order, but right now, I ... I don't think it's necessary." As long as she didn't have to see him or hear his voice, she wouldn't be afraid.

"It's your decision, but if he so much as sends you a postcard ..."

"I'll ask for a restraining order. I promise."

There wasn't anything else to say, but she was reluctant to see him go. To erase the disappointment in his eyes, she wrapped her arms around him and hugged him for several minutes until her conscience pricked her. He was her best friend, not her boyfriend. She dropped her arms and stepped back with a smile she hoped would smooth things over between them. "Text me when you get home so that I know you made it safe."

He grinned. "Anything to make you happy."

*

"You know I'd do anything to make you happy, Carly, but this fundraiser is very important to my mother. She started this foundation to support prostate cancer research to honor Father's memory. We have to attend." Ryan pushed his plate to the edge of the table, his signal to the server that they were ready for the check.

Normally, she wanted dessert, but today Carly was trying to quell the swarm of anxiety roiling in her gut. She had exactly thirteen days to figure out a way to avoid The Xavier Edgar First Christmas Ball. "I know it's important to her and to you, too, Ryan, but I—"

"You worry too much. You'll be charming as always."

Charming and memorable were two words clients always used when they requested the pleasure of Elise's company. Dyeing and straightening her hair might be her best offense against being recognized. Maybe she could pull off dark brown with streaks of auburn. Green contacts would complete the disguise. Ryan would think she was being paranoid, but the man had no idea how extensive her contacts were in the western New York business community.

Maybe she'd get lucky and contract a debilitating case of the flu. For now, she'd settle for changing the subject. "My parents have tickets for *A Christmas Carol* at the Alleyway next Friday night. Do you want to go to dinner with them before the performance? My brother, Jared, is bringing a date, and we'll all be meeting her for the first time."

Clearly impatient to leave, Ryan set her empty plate on top of his and signaled the server, who promptly brought their bill. "Next Friday? I thought you said the tickets were for this Friday." He pulled his credit card from his wallet and tucked it in the leather folder, then looked up at her, his brown eyes full of frustration. "I have a wedding to do."

Hiding her disappointment behind a practiced smile, she considered her response. "I'm sure Mom can find someone to use your ticket."

He reached across the table, clasped Carly's hand, and started massaging her palm with his thumb. "Thanks for being so understanding. We need a joint planner to keep track of all of our responsibilities. I'll pick one up for us the next time I'm in Barnes & Noble."

Feeling claustrophobic at the mere thought of Ryan having a visual account of all of her activities, Carly pulled her hand free. "I need to use the restroom before we leave." Thankful for the excuse, she navigated her way through the crowded restaurant, grateful for a few minutes alone to conceal her annoyance.

*

The Canalside ice skating arena was crowded with ice skaters of all ages by the time they arrived. Carly hadn't been too sure her ankle was ready for the rigors of ice skating, but with an ace bandage wrapped snugly beneath her wool sock, she felt steady on both feet as she and Ryan glided hand-in-hand across the smooth ice.

An hour later, the cold had seeped into her bones. Her arm and her ankle both ached at the site of the breaks. She frowned and steered Ryan off the ice and toward the refreshment counter. "Let's get some hot chocolate. I need to sit awhile."

But sitting wasn't the answer. After they'd finished their sweet beverages, Carly stood to leave, and her ankle turned, making her wince. A moan escaped her lips. So much for her plans to walk along the harbor and photograph the lighthouse. She tried to stand and cried out again.

"I think you're done for today."

Ryan was right, but she didn't appreciate him belaboring the obvious. Tempted to grumble at him, she bit back her retort. Why was she being so harsh with him? It wasn't his fault his mother's ball was sure to be Carly's day of reckoning.

*

"Mom's bone marrow transplant is scheduled for 9 a.m." Maureen gave Joe a big sister look that said he'd better be there to see Addie before she went under the anesthesia.

He wouldn't consider being anywhere else. He'd scheduled two days off, Thursday and Friday, just in case she needed him nearby. By Friday evening, he expected her to be recovered enough that he could take advantage of Jared's offer to be Carly's escort for dinner at Pano's before the play. He hadn't seen *A Christmas Carol* since high school. The truth was he'd been a bit of a Scrooge himself ever since his mother's so-called death on Christmas Eve, years ago. His step-mother loved everything about Christmas, so after she and Dad got married, Leann made sure the holiday was both fun and well-grounded in the true meaning of the season. But something had been missing for Joe.

The spirit of forgiveness.

It wasn't until he'd forgiven his mother that Joe comprehended the connection between the baby in the manger and the Savior on the cross. Christmas meant so much more to him now. He'd even managed to forgive himself for letting Carly slip away not once but twice. But if God gave him a third chance, Joe would move heaven and earth to make her his wife.

Maureen grabbed his sleeve and jerked his arm. "I'm talking to you, little brother, and you haven't heard a word I've said."

A sheepish flush crept across his face and down his neck.

"Only one woman can make my brother blush." Maureen poked his chest with her index finger. "Carly Lawrence. Bob mentioned you'd seen her recently."

Regretting his failure to emphasize confidentiality to his brother-in-law, Joe pasted on a smile but said nothing. He punched the "up" button on the elevator, which caused the door to slide immediately open.

By the time they reached the surgical ICU, trepidation threatened to strangle Joe's shaky faith. At the sight of Addie's frail form curled up on the bed, Maureen let out a soft gasp. He captured his sister's hand and squeezed it with more assurance than he felt. Mom stirred and rolled over onto her back, giving Joe and his sister a clear view of the dark shadows beneath their mother's eyes, the purplish gray a sharp contrast against her pale skin. The mega-doses of chemo necessary to prepare her body to receive the bone marrow transplant had left her weak. The scrubs they wore over their street clothes, including booties covering their shoes and masks on their faces were all precautions to ensure as germ-free an environment as was humanly possible.

"Should we wake her?" Maureen whispered.

"I'm awake." Addie opened her eyes and struggled to a sitting position. Joe rushed to adjust the bed and plump the pillows behind her back. He planted a kiss on her forehead then moved aside to let his sister hug their mother.

As soon as he caught his sister's attention, Joe mouthed the words, don't you dare cry. Angling a wobbly smile in his direction, Maureen pulled a straight-back chair next to the bed. He lowered himself into an uncomfortable vinyl chair in the far corner and half listened as Maureen chatted about her children's eagerness for school to be out and the Christmas festivities to begin. She'd never been sick with any of her other pregnancies, and her older children expected her to do everything associated with Christmas, including carpooling the neighborhood kids to various skating and sledding parties—a regular Saturday activity that left Maureen so exhausted that Bob put his foot down, which led to him being in charge of transporting and chaperoning kids between the ages of eight and eleven. "The kids don't understand why I'm so tired all of the time, but ever since the beginning of my eighth month, I barely have enough energy for the necessities. I don't know how I'd manage without Bob's help."

"You married a good man," Addie said. "Like your dad."

The wistful regret behind those words struck Joe. She was truly sorry for her choices, but no matter how remorseful a person may be, some choices simply could not be undone, and the consequences were irrevocable.

That's how Carly feels.

Was that his thought? Or was God trying to tell him something? If it were true, how could Joe help Carly? Did she even want his help? Her boyfriend was a pastor after all, and he should be able to help her. If the man could be objective. Which Joe doubted. According to Carly, Ryan expected her to be able to forget her past, but her grief was too new and too raw to forget. Why didn't the other man understand that? Joe would never expect her to simply move on with her life. She'd suffered two great losses, losses she believed she could have prevented. Joe understood, because he blamed himself, too.

CHAPTER TWENTY-THREE

Addie's bone marrow transplant had proceeded according to her doctor's expectations. The man seemed cautiously optimistic, but Joe wanted more facts. "What happens next?"

"The only thing to do now is monitor your mother for signs of GVHD, graft-versus-host-disease, which happens when the body rejects foreign tissue. I've prescribed medication for your mother to weaken her immune system, which usually prevents this reaction. Ms. Stewart came through the procedure well, but she needs rest. I suggest you go home and do the same."

Joe had spent the night before the transplant sleeping curled up in that awful chair at his mother's bedside, if he could call the snatches of dozing off only to wake up with cramps in his arm, his back, and his legs sleeping. "If there's any change in her condition, someone will contact me immediately?"

"Certainly, Mr. Callahan." The doctor's glance flicked to his watch and back to Joe's face. "If you'll excuse me, I need to complete my rounds."

Joe headed down the hall to the bank of elevators and met his sister. His eyebrows lifted in surprise.

"I knew you wouldn't leave unless I took over." Maureen unbuttoned the buttons on her coat, at least the ones that still closed over her very pregnant belly.

Joe suppressed a chuckle. His sister would not appreciate him laughing at her expense. This was her sixth child, and he'd heard her say she felt like a beached whale. "Actually ..." Joe yawned. "I was headed home. I have plans tonight, and I didn't get much sleep."

His sister's smirk meant she recognized his evasive maneuver.

"The Lawrences had an extra ticket to the theater, and Jared asked me if I wanted to go in—"

"Instead of who?"

"Whom."

"Whatever. Just be careful, little brother. You've been down this road before."

Note to self. Never tell Bob anything ever again. "Carly and I are just friends."

"That may be what she thinks, but it's not how *you* feel."

"Maureen, go see Mom. I can take care of myself."

That wasn't exactly the truth. He was in way over his head, but there was nowhere else he'd rather be. If he didn't give Carly his all this time, he'd never be able to live with the consequences. Loving someone meant taking risks. His dad understood that. He'd gone after his wife again and again. He'd never given up on her. Not until she faked her own death to set him free.

Joe released a deep sigh. His mother had had her reasons, reasons he hadn't even glimpsed as a little kid. Everything made more sense now.

Maureen stepped up on her toes and kissed his cheek. "I'm praying for you."

He wrapped his arm around her shoulder and with the other hand patted her watermelon-sized middle. The baby kicked against his palm, and an image of Carly big with his child flashed like a sweet dream in his tired mind. "Thanks, sis. Don't stay too long. You and that new niece of mine need plenty of rest."

Maureen smiled. "I won't. Dad and Leann will be here at one o'clock to relieve me."

Not for the first time since Addie's reappearance, Joe's heart surged with pride at his step-mother's graciousness. "Text me if Mom needs me."

"Mom will be fine. I'm going to make sure she knows you're on a date."

"It's not a date."

*

"You're going on a date with Joe Callahan?" Ryan growled. "It's not my fault I can't go with you. You can't expect me to postpone a wedding just to go to the theater with you."

"It's not a date." Carly tried to keep the irritation from her tone. "Jared gave Joe your ticket. That's all."

"That's all? He'll be escorting you."

Tamping down the irrational burst of anger at his choice of words, Carly took a deep breath and tried again. "Six of us are going to dinner and a play. That is not a date."

"Your parents, Jared and his new girlfriend, you and Callahan. That sounds like a date to me."

She was tempted to retort, *I'm sorry I told you at all.* Instead, she soothed, "You have no reason to be jealous."

But that wasn't exactly true.

"Tomorrow we can shop for a dress and a tux for your mother's Christmas ball." Carly would be lucky to find something this late. She should never have waited until a week before the fundraiser. It didn't matter that she'd rather be anywhere else. Well, practically anywhere else. This was important to Ryan, and she was Ryan's girl. But reminding herself of that fact didn't make his possessiveness any more palatable.

"Why don't you pick me up about eleven, and we can go to lunch first and still have plenty of time to dress for dinner and the concert?"

"I can't. I haven't even started on my sermon. I have appointments all afternoon. Getting everything done by the time I need to pick you up at five is going to be a challenge."

She should be disappointed that he didn't want to spend the day with her, but she wasn't. Ryan's impatience made shopping a chore. "Oh, well, I'll get something that will go with your basic black tie. You do have a tux already, don't you?"

"Yes. Listen, Carly, don't have too much fun at the play without me, okay?"

So they were back to that again. What was a safe reply? She settled for, "Of course not."

Relieved when he finally hung up, Carly muttered, "Well, that was an unpleasant conversation." Good thing her bedroom door was closed. She certainly didn't want to get into this with Sarah, not so much because she expected her friend to be critical, but more because she was feeling guilty enough already.

Lord, I need to choose. Why aren't You helping me?

Maybe she needed to wait and see how it all played out, but this was her second chance at a decent life, and she had no intention of making a total mess. She'd done that before. In spades.

*

If it's not a date, then why are you so nervous? She massaged the conditioner down the length of her hair, one small section at a time, then let the hot water soothe her tense shoulders for several minutes before rinsing the conditioner out and finishing her shower.

Thirty-five minutes later she was dressed in a black velour skirt topped off with a scooped neck, sparkly red sweater. Tall black leather boots with sensible heels wouldn't have been her first choice, but her ankle had been acting up ever since the recent bout of sub-zero temperatures. She sprayed her favorite floral scent on her wrists and rubbed some behind her ears and over her midriff. Then she selected a simple necklace in links of varying sizes and several gold bangles for her wrists. Twirling her hair around her fingers one last time to tame her curls, she assessed her appearance in the full-length mirror. Her nails were painted in the exact shade as her sweater. She looked good. Presentable and pretty. Nothing suggesting that she was trying to impress … anyone.

"Joe's here," Sarah called down the hall. "You about ready?"

Knowing this moment shouldn't matter so much, Carly calmed her nerves with slow, deep breaths and paused at the entrance to the living room. "I'm here."

Joe shot her a look of approval that belied all of her attempts to convince herself that she didn't care about his reaction. Her traitorous heart skipped out of rhythm for a brief moment as she stood entranced by his welcoming smile.

"You're the most beautiful woman I've ever seen."

Her smile wobbled, but she managed to reply, "That's the best compliment I've ever had."

The instant the words escaped her mouth one word echoed in her brain. Betrayal. She'd told Ryan he had nothing to be jealous about. She'd lied. *Lord, forgive me. I didn't mean to lie. I just didn't want to hurt him.*

The questions in Joe's eyes jolted her back to this moment. "Are you okay?"

"Of course." Having him accompany her had seemed innocent enough when Jared told her he'd asked Joe to take the extra ticket. Ryan had insisted it was date, but Carly had wanted to believe she and Joe were going as friends only. Until this moment.

The love in his eyes drew her in. There was nowhere else she'd rather be.

Except in his arms. Heat tingled her cheeks as she remembered the quick kiss they'd shared in the kitchen.

His smile broadened. "Are you ready, honey?"

"Sure. Yeah." She should tell him to stop calling her honey, but she didn't want to.

"Good. We don't want to keep your family waiting." Joe held out her wool coat, and she slipped her arms into its luxurious warmth, grateful the weight shielded her from the electric touch of his hands on her shoulders. "I left the car running so it would stay warm for you." He lifted her hair, and she shivered in response and jumped away to pick up her scarf and gloves from the table.

If Joe noticed her reaction, she didn't want to know. What was wrong with her that she could react with almost equal intensity to two men? Her body responded to them both, but she was beginning to realize that her heart was another matter entirely.

*

"You're very quiet tonight," Joe said after ten minutes of driving in silence. He turned his head slightly to evaluate her expression, but in the dim light of the setting sun reading her was difficult. "Are you going to tell me what's wrong?"

She tugged her gloves off and flexed her hands. Then she busied herself smoothing her skirt over her knees, accenting the lovely shape of her legs. Her silence intensified his concern, but pressuring her for an answer would only make her clam up completely. Drawing on his skills as a cop, he waited, his body relaxed and still, his eagerness to know completely hidden behind his impassive features. He waited so long that he started to wonder if she were going to confide in him at all.

"Ryan didn't want me to go with you tonight." She stared straight out the windshield. Her face masked her feelings as thoroughly as he hid his.

"He didn't?" Joe could understand why.

"He said this was a date."

Her voice, barely a whisper, revealed uncertainty and something else Joe couldn't identify. If he hadn't been driving, he would've reached over and captured her face in his hands so he could search her eyes for the truth. With a quick prayer for guidance, he asked, "*Is* this a date?"

"Of course not. We're just going out with my family. You and Jared have been friends forever. How could it be a date?"

When a man loves a woman, and he takes her out to a nice restaurant and the theater, it's definitely a date. Did it really matter that they were going with two other couples who happened to be her family? "If you say so. We can *call* this dinner with your family."

She shook her head.

Dang his excellent peripheral vision. He wracked his brain, searching for something to say to soothe her, but he couldn't think of a single thing. Changing the subject might help. "Are you all registered for classes in January?"

She reached over the console to turn down the heater and the blower. "Yeah. I'm taking general stuff—Math, English Composition, Biology, and Photography."

The smile in her voice warmed his heart. Going back to school was the right choice for her. But photography? She'd always carried a camera back in high school. Their art teacher had told her she had an eye for composition and lighting. Had she continued taking pictures? "Any idea what you'd like to major in?"

"I'm not sure yet. Maybe dental technician. People will always need to get their teeth cleaned."

Joe had trouble picturing her scraping plaque off people's teeth for the rest of her life.

"Have you kept up with your photography?"

"Some. A lot of my photos are pretty depressing."

"Really? I remember your work differently. Bright with possibility and wonder."

She let out a small laugh. "That was before I found out how hard a lot of people have it."

He understood. He'd seen much he wanted to forget—in combat and back in the States. Buffalo's homeless population seemed to grow every year, and the poorer neighborhoods were often infested with predators of all sorts. "I'd like to see your recent work."

She laid her hand on his arm, her need for reassurance tugging at his heart. "Are you sure? I tried to capture the suffering of people who feel hopeless and forgotten."

The implication was he wouldn't like her view of the world. But he wasn't surprised. She'd felt forgotten herself. He'd seen it in her eyes when she was lying in the ICU, blessed to even be alive. The trouble was she hadn't seen it that way. With her baby dead, she'd had nothing left to live for. But she was a survivor. Like his mom.

"I never forgot you." *I never stopped loving you.*

A moment passed. Then she said, "I'm sure you have a lot of memories of Jared's pesky younger sister."

"I never once thought of you that way."

"Not even when Jared made you take me to the prom?"

Joe maneuvered the car so that he could parallel park between a BMW and a Mercedes less than a block from the restaurant. Then he shut off the engine and turned in his seat to look at her. "That's what you think happened?" He shook his head. "No way. The only thing your brother did was let me know that punk kid had dumped you. I didn't even let Jared finish his sentence. I sprinted to your house so fast to ask you out before somebody else did."

Her beautiful eyes processed his words. An easy smile parted her pink lips. He leaned in to kiss her, and she stiffened, tense lines knitting her brow. He laid his hand on her cheek, his fingers caressing her silky skin. "I won't rush you."

She turned her face and pressed a kiss on his palm. "Thanks for coming with me tonight, Joe."

"There's nowhere else I'd rather be."

*

The next morning, Carly awoke with a stuffed up nose. Her throat hurt so bad she could barely swallow. No way was she up for going to the holiday concert with Ryan tonight. She didn't even know if she could talk on the phone, but he would flip out if she sent him a text message. Shopping for a dress for Elizabeth's Christmas ball wasn't going to happen either. Maybe Carly could find a suitable gown in her closet. Surely, she had something conservative enough. Mentally surveying her wardrobe, she decided either the midnight blue velvet gown with the princess bodice or the sleek cranberry satin A-line would do. Both dresses were festive enough for a holiday function and with her black pearls and her hair in an upsweep … Wait a minute.

She'd planned to color her hair brown with auburn highlights. If she got up the nerve to make such a drastic change. With hair as light blonde as hers, pretty much any other color would constitute a drastic change. She rolled over and pulled the blankets up to her chin. She'd think about changing her appearance tomorrow. Or the next day. Right now, she hurt all over, and sleep would be the best medicine, but first she needed to call Ryan and tell him she was too sick to go to the Christmas concert tonight. Maybe he could take his mother instead.

*

Unfortunately, she didn't feel any better on Sunday morning, though she'd spent most of Saturday in bed, reading and sleeping off and on, until in desperation, around seven o'clock, she'd jumped in the shower, counting on the hot steam to clear her sinuses. After that, she'd fallen asleep sometime before nine and surprisingly slept straight through.

A knock on her bedroom door prompted her to check the time on her bedside clock. Seven forty-five.

"May I come in, dear?" Sarah called through the door.

Carly tested her voice with a scratchy, "Yes." When Sarah failed to respond, Carly climbed out of bed to open the door. The dear lady was carrying a tray of tempting breakfast foods.

"You're spoiling me." For reasons Carly couldn't articulate, having someone bring her breakfast in bed made her feel loved and cherished. The soothing aroma of coffee and homemade cinnamon rolls wafted to her nose. She could smell at least, but her throat still hurt. Hesitant to be a bother, she asked, "Could I have tea with honey and lemon instead of coffee?"

Sarah frowned. "I should have thought of that myself. Get back in bed and start on your scrambled eggs and cinnamon roll before they get cold." She waited for Carly to comply then positioned the tray over her lap. Snatching up the coffee, creamer and sugar, Sarah said, "I'll be back in a jiffy," and dashed away before Carly could even thank her.

Ignoring the eggs, she reached for a roll, but the first bite of the warm cinnamon treat was a disappointment. Apparently, her taste buds were out of commission today. Oh, well. Maybe the tea would revive her sense of taste. She finished the eggs, knowing they'd taste disgusting cold, then moved the breakfast tray aside and picked up her Bible where she'd left it on the other side of the double bed. She still wasn't sure where to read to find the answers to her questions, so she opened the book to a random page in Luke. Her gaze centered on part of a verse in chapter twelve. "Ye are of more value than many sparrows."

Instantly, she closed her eyes. *Lord, I know You say I'm valuable, but after all I've done, please just make me useful. Give me something to do that I'm not ashamed of.*

Forget your past.

But, Lord, that's impossible. All I do is remember.

Sarah's hand on her shoulder startled Carly. She swiped at the tears trickling down her flushed face. She was tired and sick. Now, she could add weepy and unobservant to her list of ailments.

"Can I do anything else for you before I get ready for church?" She set the teapot on the nightstand and the full cup of steaming tea on the tray.

"Please tell Ryan I'm sorry I missed church."

"You're not going to call him?"

"I called yesterday to tell him I was too sick to go to the Christmas concert with him. He bought those tickets in October. When I suggested he take his mother, he was annoyed." Carly sipped her tea to soothe her throat.

"That doesn't seem like Ryan."

"He might've been more understanding if he wasn't still mad about my going to the theater with Joe. Ryan insisted that was a date." Carly struggled to keep the irritation from her voice. "He wouldn't listen to me when I tried to explain."

Sarah sat down on the end of the bed and waited, her kind face free of any condemnation.

"Maybe it *was* a date. I didn't mean for it to be a date, but Joe and I ... well, we ..." She paused, searching for the right word. "Fit."

"I see."

Aching to resolve the romantic turmoil she'd caused by her interest in the two men, Carly ignored the accusing voice in her head reminding her there are two kinds of women. "I want to be the woman Ryan needs, but I don't think I can. He needs a girl who's grown up in the church, who … who's never, you know." Her cheeks heated with shame.

Sarah placed a firm hand on Carly's forearm. "Why don't you let him decide what he needs? You have a great capacity for empathy, a very useful quality in a pastor's wife."

She'd asked to be useful. Would her awareness of how desperately she needed forgiveness make it easier for her to persuade others that God would forgive them, too, if they only had the courage to ask? Would Ryan be willing for her to share her testimony with others?

Or would he insist her past be forgotten, never to be spoken of, even between them?

If that's what he wanted, could she stand to live in constant fear of exposure? Because that's what would happen if she tried to keep this secret. Hadn't the woman at the well run into town, telling everyone who would listen that Jesus had told her everything she'd ever done? She hadn't tried to hide her past. "I don't think Ryan understands me or what I need."

"What do you need?"

"I don't know, but I can't pretend that I was never a prostitute." *I have to accept my past and move on.*

*

Joe decided to stop in the chapel before heading upstairs to see his mother. Grateful to find the small, sparsely furnished room empty, he settled his tall frame into a front pew and bowed his head. In just a few months' time, his life had been turned upside down. No. Right-side up was closer to the truth. Letting go of his bitterness toward his mother had changed all of his relationships for the better. And seeing Carly again made him ... made him what? Believe that God had a good plan for him that included more than work? Definitely. He wanted more than the police force. A home and a family of his own topped the list.

But he'd come in here to pray, not to take stock of his life.

Lord, thank You for finding a match for Mom. Thank You that her body has accepted the transplant. But most of all, thank You for giving us another chance to be a family. You are a God who promises to restore and redeem, to bring something good out of suffering and heartache. I'm sorry it took so long for me to figure that out, Lord. Please help Mom and Carly see how much You love them. Help them believe that You have good plans for their futures. And, Father, thank You for letting me be a part of it. Please.

Footsteps echoed on the polished wood floor. Instinctively, Joe twisted slightly to glance over his shoulder. "Jared. What are you doing here, man?"

Jared's eyes gleamed with purpose. "Harris texted me where to find you. You haven't answered any of my calls."

"You only called twice. Once yesterday afternoon and once this morning. But you're right. I should have called you back. I'm just not ready to talk." He met his friend's piercing gaze with a steady one of his own.

Jared sat down on the pew and waited. After a few minutes, he said, "Let me buy you a coffee."

Joe couldn't blame his friend for his persistence. Jared may not have had much opportunity, but protecting his sister was a responsibility he'd never shirk.

"I need to check in on my mom. I'll meet you in the lobby in twenty minutes."

*

After several minutes of Joe trying to deflect Jared's questions about the sparks flying between him and Carly, his friend spread his hands wide in a gesture of defeat. "She belongs with you, Joe. I can't believe you don't know that yet."

Stalling, Joe dunked his donut in his coffee and took a bite. What could he say in his own defense? He'd made up his mind to fight for her, but he was waiting … for what? A signal? For her to break it off with Ryan entirely? "It's complicated."

"Really? That's all you have to say? Just tell her you love her, man."

"I already did." Joe rose to his feet, picked up his cup, and drained the last of the coffee.

"It wasn't enough."

Jared stood, too. "What do you mean it wasn't enough?"

Resisting the regret battering his heart, Joe decided to admit the truth out loud. "She said she thought I believed she'd be just like my mother. She couldn't live with that, so she started dating Edgar."

Jared's features scrunched in a frown. "You don't think that anymore."

Joe shook his head. "Not even a little. Mom and Carly are two very different people."

"So, tell my sister you're over your trust issues."

"She knows. She's with Ryan, and she has to make up her mind if she wants to stay with him. Her feelings for me make her feel guilty and confused."

But Joe hadn't exactly given her the space she'd asked for. He taken advantage of every opportunity to be close to her, taking her hand as they walked into the theater, leaning shoulder to shoulder, whispering in her ear, his lips grazing her cheekbone, his thigh pressed against hers, her light floral perfume tempting him to kiss her. And he would have, if she'd given him the slightest chance.

She'd wanted to kiss him, too. He'd seen it in her eyes. But that wasn't all he'd seen. She was afraid she hadn't changed. Joe refused to be a part of making her feel that way.

*

Carly studied her reflection in the bank of mirrors as the young stylist fluffed her curls into delicate swirls. The brunette locks framing her face made her appear unnaturally pale. She'd hoped the auburn highlights would soften the contrast between her ivory complexion and the hair color she'd chosen. No such luck. If anything her new hair color made her stand out even more. But it was too late to go back to blonde. The party was in three days. Maybe if she washed her hair sooner than the stylist recommended the color would fade a little. At least her eyes were brown. Brown hair, brown eyes was a natural combination. If only her face didn't look so washed out. She could try tanning. Concerned about skin cancer, she had always avoided the tanning beds, though Star and some of the other girls went tanning regularly during the winter months. With Carly's luck, her skin would turn a freakish orange. Tanning wasn't the answer. Makeup would have to do. "Can you suggest a foundation color that would make my face, well ... make it look like this is my natural hair color?"

Wearing makeup a shade darker than her skin tone complemented her new hair color, but the young woman staring back at her didn't look familiar. Which was the whole point. She should be happy, but her mouth was set in a grim frown. Just because she didn't look like herself didn't guarantee that no former client would recognize her at Mrs. Edgar's fundraiser.

"That's much better, but your eyebrows need to be darker," the stylist advised. "Then you'll be happier with the change. I'll be happy to do it for you."

Carly scoffed. "I miss my blonde hair already."

"But you said you wanted a dramatic change." The stylist concerned tone seemed more for herself than for Carly.

"I did. I just didn't realize—"

"I can add more highlights or take off three or four more inches so it hangs just below your shoulders, if you want."

"No, I'll be wearing it up on Saturday night, so the length won't matter, but go ahead and do my eyebrows."

The stylist's features relaxed once again, but she had no cause to worry. Carly wasn't the type to complain to the management. That much she'd learned from Al. She'd become an expert at making the best of whatever hand she was dealt.

But she didn't have to manage on her own anymore. God would help her, wouldn't He?

*

Not wanting to shock Sarah, Carly pulled her hood up to hide her dyed hair. She hadn't counted on the wind knocking her hood askew and whipping an auburn lock into her eyes as she opened the car door.

For a split second, Sarah's mouth gaped, then she said, "I love your hair."

Carly buckled her seatbelt. "You don't have to be polite. I know it's a drastic change, and Ryan's probably not going to like it. If I hear him say one more time, 'Whatever happens, we'll deal with it,' I'm going to scream."

Sarah put the car back in park and shifted in her seat until their eyes met. "If you don't want to go to the dance, don't go."

Carly released a long sigh.

"Ryan will support your decision. If you're anxious—"

"He would let me off the hook if this was any dance, but it's a memorial fundraiser to honor his dad." Carly struggled to keep the frustration from her tone. "Ryan wants me with him."

"But surely he trusts your instincts."

"If only that were true. He says I need to have more faith." Apprehension settled in her stomach, and she swallowed the bile rising in her throat. "I know I'm forgiven, but God didn't promise me that I'd never run into a former client."

Sarah captured Carly's hand and squeezed it gently. "Whatever you decide, I'll be praying that God gives you wisdom and strength."

Carly blinked back tears. She needed all of the prayers she could get.

CHAPTER TWENTY-FOUR

Joe wanted to see Carly. And kiss her. Why hadn't he kissed her when he had the chance? For that matter, why hadn't he kissed her whenever he could? Because he hadn't wanted to pressure her into breaking up with Ryan.

Had Joe been wrong? They hadn't spoken since their night out with her family, and he'd lost count of the number of times he'd brought up her number on his phone, but he'd never followed through. She'd call him when she was ready to talk. That's what he kept telling himself, but five whole days had passed without a word from her.

His daily visits with his mother helped pass the time, and Joe found himself enjoying getting to know her better over Scrabble games and crossword puzzles. Best of all, Joe had heard the doctor's good report for himself. His mother was cancer-free and could go home as soon as her white blood cell count reached normal levels.

Unable to tolerate the suspense another minute, he typed a text message to Carly. "Are you okay? I'm worried about you," then deleted it. Days off were supposed to be relaxing. But not when all his energy went to trying *not* to think about the woman he loved.

He shrugged into his down jacket and rifled through two weeks' worth of mail strewn on the table until his fingers stumbled upon his keys. "Might as well start my Christmas shopping." A glance at the calendar confirmed his suspicion.

Christmas was less than two weeks away. Joe hated elbowing his way through crowds of last minute shoppers. He'd made that mistake once, five years ago, when his sister had only three kids. Never again. He was a power shopper. Get in and get out. Buy exactly what Maureen had put on his list for his nieces and nephews then pick up restaurant gift certificates and movie coupons for Dad and Leanne, and Maureen and Bob. Finding something suitable for his mother would be the real challenge. The last Christmas present he'd given her was a blue and green candy dish he'd made in art class. She'd taken it with her that final time she'd packed up. Did she still have it?

He texted her, asking for suggestions. "Anything you pick will be perfect. Love, Mom," was her reply. No help there. More than likely his mother would be in the hospital for at least another week, and when she did go home, she'd need to restrict her activities. She loved to paint. A trip to the art supply store might give him some ideas. Acrylic paints, brushes, and canvases might be a suitable last resort.

Halfway through purchasing the items on his list, another text message beeped in, this one from Carly. He grinned at her smiling face framed with reddish brown curls. So she'd done it. He wasn't surprised she'd taken matters into her own hands. Her anxiety about running into someone who'd known her as Elise was understandable. Unfortunately, the color change probably wouldn't matter. Carly's warm brown eyes were unforgettable. Still, she needed all of the encouragement she could get. And more than a text message could convey. He tapped the green phone icon and made the one call he'd been aching to make all day. "Hi, beautiful."

"Joe, does it look okay, really?"

He wanted to tell her she'd look gorgeous no matter what color she dyed her hair, but that wasn't what she was asking.

"If I'd never met you before, I'd still know you'd colored your hair, but I'm a cop, remember? We're trained to pay close attention to details." He took a deep breath before telling her what she didn't want to hear. "Some of your former clients may still be able to recognize you."

Her long, painful sigh twisted knots in his gut. "If you're not comfortable going to this function, tell Ryan you don't want to go."

"You know I can't do that. He thinks I'm being paranoid."

Joe shifted his bulging shopping bags from one arm to the other and waited, not wanting to press her into sharing more about her relationship with the other man than she intended.

"Do *you* think I'm paranoid?"

"No, I think you're being realistic." If she wasn't willing to tell her boyfriend that she didn't want to go to the Christmas dance, there wasn't anything else Joe could say, except, "If you need me, anytime, you'll call, right?"

"Knowing I can count on you means a lot, Joe."

Their agreement to be just friends, at least until the end of the year, chaffed. Friendship was not what he wanted, but he'd be what she needed. He loved her that much.

*

The main banquet room sparkled with colored lights twinkling on elegantly decorated Douglass Firs set up in all four corners. Hurricane lamps dressed in pine greens, holly, and red satin ribbons adorned the thirty or so tables strategically placed to allow for after-dinner dancing in the center of the spacious room. Near the far exit, a gray-haired gentleman in a silver tuxedo played a medley of traditional Christmas carols on a grand piano. Carly sucked in a breath. If this was all they were planning for music, most of the dances would probably be slow. And slow meant dancing too close. Especially if the man wasn't Ryan.

Or Joe.

But neither could protect her tonight. Joe wouldn't be here, and Ryan didn't understand what could happen. More than anything, Carly dreaded any man presumptuously tapping on Ryan's shoulder, expecting to cut in on a dance.

Suddenly, the well-fitted bodice of her navy satin gown seemed immodest for this occasion, though many women in the room wore similar styles. Why hadn't Carly bought a simple black gown that would conceal her curves? At least her silver lace wrap covered her shoulders and décolletage, providing some protection from the dreaded look. The one that saw a scarlet "A" tattooed on her breast proving her virtue should be exploited rather than protected. Why had she agreed to come tonight? Ryan should have understood why this whole night was impossible for her.

A warm hand on her bare arm startled her. She whirled to see who had touched her.

Ryan studied her with tender concern. "I didn't mean to scare you."

She tucked her hand in the crook of his arm. She averted her eyes. "You didn't. I'm fine." It wasn't exactly a lie. Being fine wasn't a feeling. It was a decision she'd made in many situations, most worse than this by far.

"Can we sit down, please?" Standing up, she was more likely to be noticed, spotted by someone she'd rather avoid.

Ryan nodded and led her to a table too close to the front of the room, where a podium waited for someone—probably Elizabeth Edgar—to make a speech.

"Do we have to sit here? Couldn't we sit back farther?" At his raised eyebrows, Carly despised the fear in her tone and wished she could recall her words.

"Mother wants us all to sit together."

By all, he meant all of the Edgar children and their

spouses. The fact that his mother made Carly feel decidedly unwelcome in their family circle had escaped Ryan's usually astute observations. Maybe he was ignoring his mother's censure. Carly wanted to give him the benefit of the doubt.

What would Elise have done tonight?

At the unbidden thought, her breathing slowed. *Be calm and poised. And above all, keep your emotions hidden.*

The person in control of every situation was the person in control of herself. How ironic Al's words were. And designed to what? Placate her? Delude her? It didn't matter now. Now, Jesus was with her. At this very moment. *Lord, help me get through this night.*

Ryan pulled out a chair and waited for her to be seated. Carly gathered the satin folds of her dress together so the delicate fabric wouldn't get caught up in the chair legs when she sat.

He chose the seat at her left side, then leaned close, and whispered in her ear, "Thank you for coming with me tonight." His breath was a subtle caress on her face, and his signature woodsy scent stirred her senses. He kissed her cheek. "I know this isn't easy for you. Tomorrow, we can do whatever you want. Bake cookies. Watch Christmas movies. Whatever you want."

She acknowledged his thoughtfulness with a smile. "That's sweet, but you'll be working on your sermon all day tomorrow." Mildly disturbed at the relief that accompanied her words, she rested her hand on his arm for a moment. "You can make it up to me next week."

*

Carly made it through the delicious four-course meal without incident. She'd learned long ago which utensil to use for each item placed before her, so table etiquette wasn't an issue. Ryan's oldest sister, Madeline, and his cousin, Shelby, kept the dinner conversation going with tales of their children's attempts to discover where their parents had stashed the Christmas presents. Alyssa and Danielle, Ryan's younger sisters shot each other looks that suggested they didn't want any children quite yet. Their husbands' expression conveyed similar attitudes, but Madeline and Shelby didn't seem to notice. Her husband, Tom, appeared genuinely happy to be the father of four kids under eight-years-old. Ryan's brother Cal smiled at his wife, Joy. They were expecting their second child in February.

Carly laughed in all the right places and tried not to feel sorry for herself. Surely, she'd have a child of her own someday, perhaps in a year or two. Succumbing to hope, she let her mind drift a moment. To her shock, the man standing next to her in her imagination wasn't Ryan but Joe.

Squelching her guilt, she gave her date her best practiced smile. It wasn't his fault she was beginning to suspect they weren't right for each other.

Ryan patted her knee under the table. "I have to dance the first dance with my mother, but after that, I'm all yours for the rest of the evening," he said, low enough that only she could hear above the chatter in the room.

Carly didn't mind not dancing. On the dance floor she'd be more vulnerable than sitting at the table with his family. She'd tried explaining this reality to Ryan and had failed. She wouldn't bring it up again.

The minute she finished her coffee and tiramisu, she excused herself to go to the ladies room before Mrs. Edgar gave her speech. As Carly navigated her way through the increasing number of guests milling about, she carried herself with the bearing of a well-brought-up lady—another skill she'd mastered under Al's tutelage. A mocking voice in her head whispered, Fake. She resisted the devil's lie. *Lord, I need*

You.

The elegant restroom was crowded, too, but thankfully, Carly saw no one she knew. After using the facilities, she gave her appearance one last look in the full-length mirror. Her navy satin gown hugged her ribcage, accenting her figure perfectly. If she wanted to be noticed. Which she did not.

Reluctantly, she exited the sanctuary of the ladies room and stepped into the dimly lit hallway. If only this night were over. In the past, she would have reached for a glass of wine to soothe her nerves, but tonight she was determined to lean entirely on Jesus for strength. She drew in a long breath and released it slowly, deliberately relaxing her shoulders.

Let me cross the banquet room, Lord, without meeting anyone I know, please.

I will never leave you.

Clinging to that truth, Carly put one foot in front of the other. Then with her back straight, she glided across the polished hardwood floor, her skirt moving in a gentle flow against her long legs. She scanned the room, searching for Ryan. He was escorting his mother to the podium.

Was there enough time for Carly to rejoin his family? Several other people were also making their way back to their seats, so Carly hurried her pace and slipped into her place beside one of Ryan's brothers-in-law just as Elizabeth's voice rang out clear and true. "Welcome. Thank you all for coming tonight. The holidays are filled with so many festivities and obligations that my children and I are truly grateful you have set aside this time to remember Benjamin and help us raise money for prostate cancer research. According to the American Cancer Society, one in every seven men will be diagnosed with prostate cancer at some point in their lifetime." Elizabeth paused, her gaze encompassing everyone in the room. "This fact makes funding further research a high priority for all of us."

When Ryan's mother ended her short speech with a thank you to all of the guests for their generous contributions, Carly felt only admiration for the woman's courage. Her husband hadn't even been dead a full year, and yet she had delivered one of the most persuasive appeals Carly had ever heard, and in her capacity as an escort, she'd attended scores of fundraising events. Not surprisingly, the entire room echoed with resounding applause as people all over the room rose to their feet. Standing with Ryan's family, Carly relaxed a bit.

A hum of conversation mingled with the piano player's rendition of "Baby, It's Cold Outside," as a man's hand settled on the small of Carly's back. She shuddered at the unfamiliar tentative touch, so light, as if the owner suspected his contact might be unwelcome. Drawing on a strength beyond her own, she turned to face the presumptuous man who believed it was okay to invade her personal space.

The satisfied smile that split his face didn't quite reach the well-dressed man's dark, penetrating eyes. "I thought that was you, Elise. You changed your hair color, but I'd still recognize you anywhere." His gaze devoured her from head to foot as if she were a commodity he could purchase at will. "I wasn't surprised to hear you'd left Rutledge behind. Bad business, that. I thought the guy had class, but ..." The man's cloying fingers grazed Carly's jaw, and she flinched as she struggled to remember his name. Backing a few steps away from the table to prevent the Edgar clan from hearing her conversation, Carly forced herself to look into the man's cold eyes. Jonathan Harrison. He'd persuaded Al to fire a new escort who'd been less than cooperative. A formidable enemy, Harrison enjoyed exacting revenge. Her skin crawled with memories she'd blocked out until this moment. Swallowing her fear, Carly backed up several more steps, bumping into the edge of the next table.

"Why aren't you working for Davison? His operation is more upscale, more in line with your special qualities."

"You have me confused with someone else, sir." Carly pivoted and started to walk away.

His hand gripped her elbow, halting her escape. She stumbled, nearly losing her balance in the low heels. *Courage, Carly.*

He whirled her around, jerking her toward him until mere inches separated their bodies. "I am not confused. You may have changed your hair and your name, but you look as beautiful in that dress as I remember. And I remember you look stunning without—"

"I don't care what you think you remember." She ground out the words. "I'm here with Elizabeth Edgar's son, Ryan." With feigned confidence, Carly backed away from the sardonic expression darkening the man's eyes. "So if you'll be kind enough to excuse me ..."

"You *have* changed. Whoever would have believed you'd be the escort of a preacher?"

Heat rose up her throat and into her face. "I'm his girlfriend."

Harrison laughed a full belly laugh. People turned to stare. Had no one noticed their confrontation before? Perhaps not.

Carly's gaze swept the room in a frantic hope Ryan or someone from his family would be heading toward their table, but the entire Edgar clan stood waiting together near one of the Christmas trees, where a photographer was setting up a tripod to take their picture.

"Hoping to be rescued by your knight in shining armor?"

Harrison's triumphant tone sent shivers racing down her back. "Do I need to be rescued? I thought you were a gentleman."

He reached out and caught her upper arm in a painful grip that was sure to leave bruises.

"That preacher can't possibly know the first thing about pleasing you. If you're not going to work for Davison, perhaps you and I can make exclusive arrangements. Maybe with an apartment in Manhattan and a six-figure salary."

She flexed her fingers. Oh, to slap that smug look off his face. But that would only draw more attention. Carly yanked her arm free of Harrison's hold and stumbled into Ryan, who caught her and set her on her feet. His left eye was twitching with controlled rage leveled at the man standing behind her. "It's time for you to leave."

"You must be Elise's date. I'm an old friend." Harrison had the gall to extend his hand to Ryan.

Ryan's arms remained rigid at his sides. He clenched and unclenched his fists. "I said, it's time for you to leave. Unless you'd like Ms. Lawrence to bring assault charges against you."

Carly slanted a glance at her left arm, which bore the purple marks of the man's fingerprints.

Harrison sputtered, his face sallow and slack, and without a word he strode away as if his reputation had been compromised rather than hers.

Ryan opened his arms, and she collapsed against his solid chest, grateful for his strong arms keeping her upright. Tears stung the backs of her eyelids. She whispered, "I need to go home."

His hand stroked her back. "Walk with me." He led her out of the banquet room, down the carpeted hall, and into a sitting room with two Queen Anne chairs and a settee. Carly sank onto the brocade-covered loveseat, and Ryan sat next to her, his knee just touching hers.

"Are you all right?"

She released a shuddering breath. "No, I'm not." She covered her face with her hands and hunched over, but she didn't cry. Ryan slipped his arm around her shoulders and drew her close, but his embrace didn't erase the renewed shame brought on by Harrison's insinuations. The man believed she could still be bought. With a high price, but with a price nonetheless.

You have *been bought, with the precious blood of Christ.*

Carly let the comforting words of the Holy Spirit begin the healing process in her soul. What Harrison believed did not define her. Her identity as a daughter of God could not be stolen from her because nothing could ever separate her from His love.

"You can't leave yet, can you?" She whispered the words, keeping her eyes on the photograph of an English country garden on the wall opposite the settee. "Not without explaining to your mother."

Ryan cupped her chin and turned her face toward him. "Do you want to tell me what happened?"

She nodded. "Harrison thought he could set me up with an apartment in New York, pay me a six-figure salary, and basically own me for as long as I ..." She swallowed hard. "Pleased him."

"Oh, honey. I'm sorry. If I'd have known—"

"What would you have done? Stayed with me the entire time? That's not realistic, and we both know it. This is just what I thought would happen. I tried to tell you I didn't want to come here, but you didn't believe me."

"I'll do better next time." He captured her hands, enclosing them in his. "I'll protect you."

She wanted to tell him it would be enough, to assure him his words brought her comfort. But wanting something to be true didn't make it so. "Do you think your mother would mind if you left?" At his frown, she added, "Just long enough to drop me off at my parents?"

"She'll ask questions, and what's happened is none of her business."

Carly wished she could buck up for the rest of the function, but her hands were still shaking. "Tell her I'm feeling nauseated. That's the truth."

"I'll come back and get you after—"

"No, Jared can drive me home." Either that or she'd spend the night at her folks. She didn't really want to see Ryan again tonight, and she was too exhausted to think about what that meant.

*

The moment Ryan pulled up in front of her parents' house Carly recognized Joe's truck parked behind her mom's compact car. Her brother's truck was the same shade of blue. Did Ryan notice the difference? Apparently not. Without a word, he climbed out of the driver's seat, rounded the car, and opened her door for her. "I'm sorry about tonight." He kissed her cheek. "Call me if you need me."

She let him hug her, recognizing his need to feel close to her. "I'll be okay now. I'll call you tomorrow for an update on the fundraiser."

He started walking her to the side door, but the beginning chords of "Amazing Grace" alerted them to an incoming call. She halted her steps to wait while he retrieved his cell from his pants pocket.

"It's my mother."

"Go ahead and answer it," Carly said, grateful that Ryan wouldn't accidentally run into Joe. The last thing she needed tonight was a tense confrontation between the two men.

Ryan raised his gaze from the phone and faced her with a distressed expression. Divided loyalties? Guilt? "I wish I could stay here with you, but …”

“You need to get back.”

Ryan brushed a kiss across her forehead. “Thank you for understanding.”

And she did. More than he suspected. She did not fit into his world, and she never would. Not after what had happened tonight. Even if his mother never found out, Carly would always be a liability in Ryan's life, and he in hers.

*

Carly closed the backdoor behind her, pressing her full weight against the cool polished oak. She took a deep breath in and out, releasing the tension from the role she'd been forced to play, both with Harrison and for Ryan. It was dark in the mudroom, but she didn't switch on the overhead light. She needed a few minutes to prepare a reasonable explanation for her presence. Mom knew about the banquet, which meant that everyone else knew, too. And Carly had confided to Joe her anxieties about attending the fundraiser. He would be able to tell the second he saw her face that something had gone terribly wrong.

Maybe coming here was a mistake. She could call a taxi and head back to Sarah's, if she had enough cash in her wallet. But that wasn't happening. She'd left her wallet on her bedroom dresser. Her small evening bag contained a compact, a tube of lip gloss, her driver's license, and one five-dollar bill.

She opened the kitchen door to find Joe and her brother engrossed in a game of chess. Joe's back was to her, so Jared noticed her first. A second of brief eye contact was all it took for her brother to get her message. She wanted to talk to Joe alone but couldn't voice her request out loud without betraying Ryan.

“Hi, sis. We didn't expect to see you tonight.” He rose and pulled out a chair for her to sit, but she stood, frozen. Literally.

She couldn't feel her toes.

"Party over early?" Jared asked.

"For me it is."

"I see." Her brother moved toward the door, clearly intending to make a quick exit as she'd hoped.

Joe raised his eyebrows in surprise. He was probably shocked that Jared would bail on their game. They'd been equally matched in high school, and they were clearly still trying to best each other.

"We can finish this later. I just remembered I have a phone call to make."

A transparent excuse at best but Joe nodded.

Carly pushed in the chair Jared had pulled out for her because sitting beside Joe wouldn't be a good idea. She kicked off her wet shoes and sat in the chair her brother had vacated. Being careful to keep her legs covered, she tucked her feet beneath her and waited for Joe to ask the question burning in his blue eyes.

Instead, he poured her a mug of hot herbal tea that warmed her hands and her throat.

His trademark patient expression soothed her nerves. "I was right," she said simply.

"Who was it?" Joe rested his elbows on the table and leaned close to her.

She resisted the urge to reach for his hands. "No one you'd know. A man named Harrison. He offered me a full-time job as his mistress." She stared at the sharp contrast of her silver polished nails against the red Christmas mug. "I have to admit I didn't think I was worth that much," she whispered.

"You're worth more than you know."

"To God?"

"And to me." He captured her hands in his.

She pulled free of his tender grip. "Please don't say that."

*

"Why not?" He knelt beside her, and grasping her shoulders, urged her to face him. When she didn't resist, he lifted her chin with his index finger until she looked up. Tears pooled in her eyes then trickled past her cheekbones. The urge to kiss her coursed through him. Kissing her would make him feel better, but it would probably have the opposite effect on her. "I've always loved you, Carly. Nothing you've ever done or ever could do can change that."

She jumped from her chair and backed away from him until the sliding glass doors blocked her escape. Her lower lip trembled as she swiped at the tears trailing down her cheeks. "I know what you want me to say. But Ryan—"

"Isn't the man for you."

She averted her face. "If I'd known you were here, I wouldn't have come home tonight."

He resisted the urge to pull her into his arms. "I don't think that's true. You came here hoping to see me."

"How dare you!" she shouted, slapping her palms against his chest and shoving him off-balance. "I'm sick of men thinking they know how I feel or what I think. I'm going home. Jared will drive me. And I don't care what you do!"

She ran from the kitchen before he could say one word. Going after her wouldn't be wise. Not yet. He'd obviously misjudged how upset she was over her encounter with Harrison. Joe's emotions had short-circuited his normally on-target instincts. Of course, Carly was an emotional wreck. He should have let her save face. Instead, he'd made everything worse by making her feel disloyal to her boyfriend. *Stupid move, man.*

Joe typed a text to Jared. "Tell Carly I'm sorry for being a jerk."

A few seconds later, a reply beeped in. "She's crying. What

did you say to her? I can't get her to stop."

"Where are you?" Joe texted back.

"In the living room," was the immediate reply.

Praying for the right words, Joe strode down the hallway into the spacious front room, where Jared sat balanced on the arm of the couch, his hand on Carly's shoulder. "I don't think she wants to talk to you."

With her arms wrapped around her bent legs and her forehead pressed against her knees, Carly wrenched Joe's heart. He decided to try again. Maybe this time he wouldn't put his foot in his mouth. "Can you give us a few minutes, Jared?"

He scowled. "I don't think this is the best time."

No time was the best time for Joe and Carly. But he had no other choice but to play the hand he'd been dealt. "She needs a friend right now."

Jared nodded, leaving without further argument.

That took a lot of trust, more probably than Joe deserved, given the circumstances. He was always telling himself not to push Carly. Too bad he hadn't listened to his own advice tonight. Determined to set things right, he lowered his six-foot-three frame to the sofa, carefully maintaining a space between them. She raised her face to him. Her eyes were bloodshot from crying and red splotches covered her cheeks. "I really thought it would work out with me and Ryan."

Joe held his breath then released it in a whoosh. Listening was definitely his best option.

Carly unfolded her legs and got up from the couch. With her back to him, he couldn't read her expression, but he didn't need to. Sobs shook her shoulders. What could he say to make her feel better? "Tell me what I can do."

"Nothing." She was staring out the picture window, probably watching the fierce snowstorm. "I have to ... take care of this myself."

He ignored the need to go to her. "What do you want to do?"

"I have to tell Ryan it's over. I can't ever measure up. His mother, the congregation, everyone expects him to choose someone who's … who hasn't …"

Joe leapt to his feet, crossed the room, and pulled her into his arms. This time she collapsed against him, the weight of her grief pressing on his heart. He held her and let her cry. After a few minutes, he said, "You are perfect just the way you are. If Ryan doesn't know that, he doesn't deserve you."

"You have it all wrong. I don't deserve him."

What could he say? She believed the devil's lies.

"Or you," she murmured against his shirt. "Or any good man."

"That's not true." He cradled her head in his hand, stroking her silky hair the way he would soothe an inconsolable child. But she was not a child. She was the woman he loved more than his own life. Her body pressed against him was like coming home after years of loneliness. Taking a leap of faith, Joe declared, "I'd marry you tomorrow if you'd have me."

She stared at him, her eyes wide with disbelief. And then a flash of hope brightened her face.

They were meant for each other. Maybe it wouldn't be as difficult to convince her as he'd feared.

CHAPTER TWENTY-FIVE

Carly knew Ryan wouldn't let her go easily. Dreading the inevitable, she'd avoided his calls since he'd dropped her off after church on Sunday afternoon. On Friday morning, she'd sent him a brief text: "Can you come over today?" His text—equally brief—had simply said, "Busy today. Tomorrow at two?" She'd sent a one-word reply. "Okay." Surely, he'd suspected something when she hadn't said she missed him.

Now that she could see his face, the haunted, shocked look in his eyes declared he'd had no idea she wanted to end their relationship. What more could she say to convince him they could never be happy together?

"I'm not the right woman for you."

"That's not true," he repeated, sliding closer to her on the couch until their thighs touched. His pleading stare magnified the pain in her chest. "My mother likes you. Everyone at church loves you. No one's ever said one negative thing about you."

Carly doubted that, but she didn't want to argue. She inched away until her hip bumped the edge of the armrest. "That's because they don't know about my past."

"You're wrong, Carly. Your past doesn't matter. All Christians have something in their past, something they regret ..." His voice broke. "Something they're ashamed of. We're all new creatures in Christ, but the old things have passed away, and all things have become new."

His brown eyes clouded with pain, boring a hole in her heart. Telling him it was over three days before Christmas was a mistake. If only she could've waited until after New Year's. She'd made it through the Christmas program, but she couldn't pretend everything was fine with them. She really had changed. For years, the art of pretense had been as natural to her as breathing. No more. "Ryan, please. It would never work between us."

"That's not true. I've told you over and over, no matter what happens we'll handle it together. Don't you trust me?"

She hesitated, drawing in a deep breath and releasing it, all the while praying for strength to tell him the rest. "I don't ..." For a second, she closed her eyes tight against the tears that threatened to derail her resolve.

"You don't trust me?"

"I don't love you. Not the way a woman should love the man she hopes to marry. I tried. You've been so good to me. Better than I deserve, and I really thought we *could* make a life together. You're a good man, Ryan."

"But not the right man for you."

Hearing him use the same words Joe had said cinched the knot in her stomach. "I'm sorry. I never meant to hurt you. I hope you can forgive me."

He stood and reached for her hands. She let him pull her to her feet but resisted his attempt to ease her into his arms. Defeat dimmed his features. "If you ever change your mind, you know where to find me."

Not wanting to give him any false hope, Carly shook her head in denial.

He moved toward the door and shrugged into his coat. "If you need anything, you'll call me, right? Any time, day or night."

She nodded, praying God would forgive another lie, this

one unspoken.

"I suppose I won't see you on Sunday."

She pressed her lips together, tensing her jaw. "I'm moving back home with my parents until I can find another apartment of my own."

"I see."

There wasn't anything else left to say. Why didn't he just go? She hated long goodbyes. Why prolong the pain?

He bent low, leaning toward her. She turned her face slightly to deflect his kiss, which razed her cheek. "You're a fine woman, Carly Lawrence, and the man who marries you will be blessed beyond his wildest expectations. I'll never forget you."

She forced herself to smile. "Thank you for everything."

Ryan nodded, opened the door without returning her smile, and walked out into the snowy afternoon, his shoulders hunched against the bracing cold. She'd hurt him, but she couldn't erase the anguish she'd caused. God would have to do that. She allowed herself one last look at Ryan's retreating form, then sank onto the couch, and hugged her knees to her chest. So many men had said they'd never forget her. She prayed fervently that they would.

Carly trudged to the bathroom. Maybe, a long soak in a hot bath would clear her head. She started the water running, added her bubble bath, and lit a lavender-scented candle. Then she went to her room to retrieve her cell phone. She'd set the alarm to make sure she didn't fall asleep in the tub, which was a definite possibility. She couldn't remember when she'd felt so exhausted. She needed something to read, too—something to distract her from the self-pity swirling in her head. On her nightstand, the Christmas romance she'd been reading last night mocked her. Real life—at least hers, was so much more complicated. In a romance novel, the heroine always lived happily ever after with the hero, but then again, she'd never read a romance about a former prostitute finding her true love.

"Stop." Her thoughts would send her spiraling into despair if she didn't short-circuit them now. "Stop being negative." Determined, she picked up the novel. Her sins, no matter how disastrous, couldn't limit God's plans for her life. He promised to work all things for her good, and all He asked in return was her love.

Being miserable for the rest of your life is what you deserve. A home, a husband, and family are not God's plan for you.

Clutching the paperback to her chest, Carly shuddered at the icy chill knifing through her. Was that her thought? Or the enemy's?

That morning, she'd read Jeremiah 29:11, "I know the plans I have for you, to give you a future and a hope." How many times in the ten years she'd spent with Al had that Bible verse come to her mind, and she'd foolishly believed the words didn't apply to her? God had been calling, waiting for her to accept His grace and mercy.

She hurried back to the bathroom to shut off the water before the tub overflowed. She was in no mood to mop up a flooded floor. The water level was perilously close to the top. Carly sighed with relief as she twisted the faucet knobs, shutting off the torrent of water.

When she straightened to her full height, she caught her reflection in the bathroom mirror. Startled at the haunted eyes staring back at her, she declared, "I know God has good plans for me," but her voice sounded weak, her tone unsure.

Maybe after this life. But not now. You've crossed the line. You have to live with the consequences of your sins.

"Nothing can separate me from Your love, God." Saying it out loud made her feel stronger, less vulnerable to the shameful memories she longed to forget. "Thank You for wanting me, in spite of everything. For making me Your daughter."

From out of nowhere, a melody ran through her mind. Carly started to sing, "What can wash away my sins? Nothing but the blood of Jesus." Healing tears slipped down her cheeks. With every word she sang, a deeper understanding of the magnitude of His salvation chased the doubts from her mind. No matter what happened, she did *not* have to live with the consequences of her sins. Jesus had paid that price for her. He had redeemed her life and her future. But she did have a choice to make. Every day, she could brace herself, expecting God to continue to chasten her for her past mistakes. Or she could greet each day with joy and expectation, waiting to see how God would bless her.

All things—even her past—God had promised to work together for good. She wasn't sure how that could be, but she didn't need to know. She would put her hand and heart into His safekeeping, trusting in His perfect love for her.

Carly smiled. *God loves me. Me—the woman who sold herself to please a man who didn't love her at all.*

She sank to her knees on the bathroom carpet and closed her eyes. *Lord, whenever I'm tempted to label myself as a prostitute and a murderer, remind me that I'm Your daughter and I'm forgiven. Thank You for loving me.*

Peace wrapped her in a holy embrace. The fact that *she* was precious to God took root in her heart and settled her as no truth ever had before. She'd been a prostitute who'd killed her own child, but from this moment forward, she would live believing that she was God's precious daughter, forgiven and redeemed.

*

Jared moved his bishop, forcing Joe into check for the

third time in as many minutes. "Carly is moving back home. Temporarily."

Joe tamped down his excitement at the news that could only mean one thing. She'd broken it off completely with Ryan. Joe moved his rook into position to capture his friend's bishop, only to realize that he'd left his king defenseless against Jared's queen.

"Checkmate, pal." Jared grinned. He started placing Joe's pieces into the box.

"Aren't you going to let me challenge you to a rematch?"

"Nope. Your mind hasn't been in this game. Do you want to talk about what happened with you and Carly last Friday night?"

"Nothing happened between me and Carly." Joe pushed his chair back and carried his empty coffee mug to the counter. It was too late for a refill. Stalling, he rinsed his mug and filled it with water from the tap. Then he reached for a couple more of Mrs. Lawrence's delicious cut-outs. "She was upset and needed to talk to someone."

"And the person she chose is you. That means something, man." The weight of Jared's hand settled on Joe's right shoulder.

Not sure he was ready for this discussion, Joe turned to meet the other man's scrutinizing gaze.

"For the record ..." Jared grinned. "Telling her you'd marry her tomorrow is not nothing."

"You were listening?"

Jared's face went red. "No, I was heading upstairs from the kitchen." He backed up until he knocked into the table. The few chess pieces left on the board teetered and fell. "I happened to be in the hallway just in time to hear you propose to my sister."

Joe's brow scrunched in a frown. "I did not propose."

"You didn't? Then do you mind explaining what exactly I did hear?"

Joe ate a star-shaped cookie in two bites. Then, stalling for time, he pushed a second cookie into his mouth and gobbled it down as quickly as the first. How much could he say without betraying Carly's confidence? "She said she didn't deserve a good man. I told her she was wrong. End of story. If you want more details, you'll have to ask your sister. The rest is her business to share. Or to keep to herself."

Nailing Joe with a glare meant to intimidate him, Jared said, "So you're not going to tell me what happened between her and Edgar."

Joe squared his shoulders. "I don't *know* what happened between her and Edgar."

Carly hadn't called him, not once since their distressing conversation on Friday night. It rankled that she hadn't confided in him. He'd figured she'd let him know as soon as she decided what to do. But he'd been wrong about that.

*

Instead of going to church, Carly spent Sunday morning packing her clothes, shoes, boots, and books into boxes. Her camera case and equipment she'd carry herself. She wasn't taking any chances with her new Nikon. She walked through the rooms of the house that had been her sanctuary. She hadn't left anything behind. Except her guilt and shame. They reared their ugly heads at weak moments, but she wasn't afraid of shadows lurking around the corners anymore. She'd stood up to Harrison. God had shown her that with His help, she would deal with the backlash of her choices and come out stronger, more grateful for God's awesome grace and mercy.

Her father was picking her up at three o'clock. It would be good to be home for a while. Her only regret was not being able to say goodbye to Sarah. The dear lady was going directly from church to the airport. Sarah's former college roommate was getting married on New Year's Day, a pleasant but unexpected blessing. Finding out Sarah wouldn't be alone during the holidays alleviated Carly's regret over moving out on such short notice. Sarah, always understanding, agreed that continuing to attend church together would be uncomfortable for both Carly and Ryan, so moving back to Lancaster was a good short-term plan until she could find her own place. Moving back to her apartment in North Buffalo held no appeal. Maybe, she could find a place close to school.

Once she'd stacked the four boxes and three suitcases near the front door, Carly decided it was time for lunch. The toast and peanut butter she'd scarfed down hadn't been much of a breakfast, and her stomach grumbled its complaint. A quick perusal of the refrigerator declared her limited options. Leftover roast beef or tuna. Neither sounded particularly appealing, especially since the only bread available was marble rye. Carly scooped the roast beef and gravy into a container and made a spot for it in the freezer. The tuna wouldn't keep. She'd eat that with the last slice of American cheese. She filled the teakettle with water, put it on the stove to heat, and stood watch over her sandwich. She'd still eat it if she burned one side, but it definitely tasted better if both sides were grilled to a golden brown.

A few minutes later, she flipped her sandwich then poured boiling water over two tea bags in the pretty Christmas teapot. She'd be spending Christmas with her family for the first time in ten years. God was so good. Outside the kitchen window, snow swirled and danced in the subzero wind, but inside she was snug and warm. Grateful for the hospitality Sarah had extended to her for the past four months, Carly thanked God for the safe haven to heal physically, emotionally, and spiritually.

But she still had a long way to go. She regretted missing church, but it wouldn't be fair to Ryan to have to preach with her sitting in the congregation. She'd join her parents at their home church next Sunday. To satisfy the hunger in her heart today, she'd have to settle for studying the Bible over lunch. When she bowed her head to thank the Lord for her food, she also thanked Him for another fresh start. Opening to the Gospels, she picked up reading in Matthew 18 where she'd left off the night before. Ryan often touched on God's commandment to Christians to forgive others, but the story of the man who'd been forgiven a huge debt but refused to forgive another man who owed him far less weighed on her heart. She finished her sandwich and tea as she reread the passage, trying to figure out why she was so disconcerted.

Unease morphed into full-blown anxiety as she read the last verse aloud. "So likewise shall my heavenly Father do also unto you, if ye from your hearts forgive not every one his brother their trespasses."

Carly bowed her head and closed her eyes to pray. "Lord, is there someone *I* need to forgive?"

Al's angry face immediately filled her mind. Fear ricocheted through her as images of that last day assaulted her peace. She jumped, backed into a corner. Covering her head with her hands, she sank to the linoleum floor. Tears erupted from the deep wound in her heart. Her body shook with sobs, and her stomach contracted with the memory of his relentless kicks. She jerked her hands from her head and clutched her stomach, trying in vain to protect her unborn child. "Stop!"

A warmth like the presence of a man's hand rested on her shoulders. *It's over.*

She was safe. Al couldn't hurt her anymore.

"What do You want me to do, Lord?" Carly pressed her

hand to her pounding heart, hoping the pressure would stop the painful palpitations.

Forgive him.

"Forgive Al?" She jerked, scooting backward until her shoulder bumped the wall. "I can't. How can You ask me to forgive the man who killed my baby, killed both of my babies?"

I forgave you.

Ashamed and resistant, Carly wanted to hide, but there was nowhere to hide from God. *But I … I hate him. I wish …*

Forgiving will set you free.

*

On Monday, Christmas Eve morning, Joe rose an hour later than his usual 5 a.m. He and his partner were working the third shift. Joe didn't mind. Guys with kids needed the time off more than he did. But today his plate was full of extra responsibilities. His mom was being released from the hospital, and even though Maureen kept urging Mom to stay with her and Bob, Joe had intervened. Their mom would have her own room at his place, and that meant privacy and quiet to continue recuperating, neither of which she would have with five grandkids underfoot. Addie preferred to go immediately to her own tiny apartment, but neither Joe nor Maureen would tolerate any discussion of their mother recovering with no one to care for her.

After his 45-minute workout, a quick shower, and a protein-packed breakfast of eggs and sausage, he wrapped the rest of the Christmas gifts—every one in plain red foil paper because that's all he had left. He should have bought more kids paper, but he didn't have time to stop at the store. Joe shrugged into his down jacket, and bracing himself against the cold, he headed out to pick up his mother. The sun shone brilliantly against the snow-covered fields, a rare occurrence in western New York in winter, but with the wind chill, 25° F felt like 10° below. Joe started the truck engine and reached in the door compartment for his sunglasses just as his cell phone rang out with "God Rest Ye Merry Gentlemen." Carly's name appeared on his screen. As long as he kept the conversation short, he could still get to Roswell on time. "Hi, beautiful," he said, hoping this wasn't one of those days when she'd deflect all his compliments.

"Hi, Joe. I know it's Christmas Eve, and you're probably busy, but I need a favor."

He suppressed his gut reaction—that he would do anything for her as long as it wasn't illegal. "I'm on my way to pick up my mother at the hospital. After I get her settled in, I could be free for a few hours. I'm on at eleven tonight."

The silence on her end of the line wasn't good. Whatever she wanted, she believed he'd say no. "Carly, are you still there?"

"Will you drive me to Attica?"

"What? You can't mean—"

"I need to see Al."

"That's the worst idea I've heard in my entire life." Grinding out the words, Joe resisted the urge to slam his fist into the dashboard. "The guy almost killed you. He did kill your baby. And now you want to go visit him on Christmas Eve. Forget it. I'm *not* driving you."

"Then I'll go by myself."

"You will not. I forbid it."

"You forbid it?" Her anger crackled across the satellite connection. "Last I looked I wasn't wearing your wedding ring, so you have no right to tell me what I can and can't do."

Her words were a slap to his face. Didn't she realize he only wanted to protect her?

"Carly, that didn't come out right, but please listen to reason. The man is a monster. I can't let him hurt you again.

I don't even know why you want to see him. You should have gotten the restraining order last month like I told you to. I thought you never wanted to see him again. You were so grateful that you didn't have to testify."

There was no reply. She had hung up.

*

Carly couldn't believe Joe wouldn't let her explain. Ryan would have understood.

She wanted to scream or cry or both. She did neither. She knelt beside her bed, bowed her head, and prayed for God's direction. She had no intention of getting up from her knees until she had a clear answer. "That was You, Lord, wasn't it? Telling me I needed to forgive Al. In person. It wasn't just my imagination, was it?"

She waited for confirmation that she was following His plan and not her own. Several minutes passed as she quieted her mind and her breathing slowed to an even pace. Then she remembered a Bible verse about living in peace with others. Jesus said the peacemakers would be blessed, and they'd be called children of God. But if she tried to make peace with Al, Joe would be mad at her.

Was there some way she could help him understand that forgiving Al was the next step in moving forward with her life? She rose from her knees. "I love You, Lord. I just didn't think serving You would be this hard."

A knock reminded her that she was rarely alone in her parents' house.

"Breakfast is ready, Carly," Jared said through the closed door. "Mom's outdid herself."

Carly sighed. She needed a few more minutes to be sure of her plan, but keeping everyone waiting would be rude. "Coming."

She exited her room and bumped straight into her

brother. "Hey!"

"Hey, yourself. Joe just texted me about some crazy idea you have. He said I should make sure you stayed put until he got here. What's up with you two, anyway?"

Carly scrunched her brows. How dare her brother take that tone with her? "Nothing is up with us, and if he doesn't give me some space, nothing ever will be! And you can tell *your* friend that for me."

Jared raised his hands, palms open, and backed up several steps. "Did I ask to be caught between you? Why can't you both figure it out?"

"Figure what out?"

"Whether or not you're a couple."

Maybe they should be, but Carly had no intention of letting a man micromanage her life. She'd been there and done that with disastrous results. "Let's drop this for now. By the delicious smells coming from the kitchen, Mom's worked really hard to make this breakfast special, and she'll be upset if we don't eat it while it's hot."

Jared's scowl relaxed into acceptance. "Agreed."

During breakfast, Joe shot her two more texts. The first said, "I'm sorry for being a jerk. Please call me." The second said, "Please. Before you leave."

She ignored both messages. Fighting with Joe would make it harder for her to see Al, and if she was going to drive alone, she needed to be at her best.

Going alone was apparently not God's plan. After agreeing to let her borrow his car, her father insisted at the last minute on driving her himself. Dad was backing out of their driveway when Joe pulled up. He signaled her to stop, but Carly deliberately turned her face away from the window and urged her father to keep going. She needed all of her energy for her conversation with Al. Arguing with Joe would sap her strength. Or take so long that it would be too late to make the 30-minute drive. Visiting hours ended at three o'clock, and who knew how long she'd have to wait, what with it being Christmas Eve.

Her cell rang out the first notes of "Joy to the World." Of course, it was Joe. Should she answer it? If he understood her even a little bit, he should have realized how much she wanted *him* to go with her. She typed a text message. "Dad offered to take me. I'll call you tomorrow."

*

Joe pulled into the Lawrences' driveway, threw the car in park, and opened Carly's text. Five minutes sooner and he might have been able to stop her. *Why does she think she needs to see this guy? Why now?*

What if she still had feelings for him? Even after all Rutledge had put her through, did she still care about the man? Sometimes women in her situation developed an emotional attachment with the perpetrator. Joe shook his head. He was being a complete idiot. Carly showed no signs of being unable to separate from the man who had nearly killed her. She'd been angry and understandably bitter, but by the end of October, she'd put those negative emotions behind her and embarked on a new relationship with Ryan Edgar.

A relationship that had ended badly. And Carly had said she didn't deserve a good man. Was she going back to Rutledge because she didn't believe she deserved better?

*

As Dad held the door open for her, Carly stepped out of the warm car into the bitter cold. The steadily falling snow would accumulate rapidly. Her dad didn't mind driving on snowy roads, but Mom would worry about the treacherous conditions if they weren't home before dark. From the parking lot, the face of Attica's front gate looked more like a medieval castle than a prison. She shuddered, knowing the impenetrable walls were designed to keep dangerous prisoners in, rather than to protect the occupants from threats from without. Attica was a maximum security prison, housing the worst criminals, or so she assumed. She couldn't begin to guess how tall the concrete walls were, and the guard towers strategically placed around its perimeter made the structure all the more imposing.

Fear skittered through her nervous system like an electric shock, followed by complete panic. What was she doing here? The urge to flee threatened her determination, but her legs felt like heavy fence posts. *Lord, help me. I'm afraid.*

At her father's questioning look, Carly almost said *let's go home.*

"You don't have to do this."

The concern in his eyes strengthened her resolve. "It's the right thing to do."

"You don't have to see him. Write him a letter."

Frowning, she tried to adjust her coat as the wind whipped her hood off her head. She snagged it, then snapped it securely under her chin the way a child would. "Dad, I have to do this in person." They hadn't said much in the car, but she'd tried to explain her conviction that God expected her to tell Al that she forgave him for everything. Her eyes watered … from the wind. She would not cry.

"What can I do?"

Carly swallowed around the lump lodged in her throat. "Pray. I don't want to cry in front of him." She took her father's hand as they headed toward the main entrance. In a low voice, she added, "Crying always set Al off, and if he's angry, he won't let me finish."

When she'd called to enquire about visiting, she'd been surprised to learn Al had listed her as a potential visitor.

Perhaps, he hoped she'd come to her senses and want to renew their relationship. It didn't matter what he thought. She was just relieved she wouldn't have to postpone her plans. She might not have the courage if she had to wait.

No one understood her sense of urgency. Even she wasn't absolutely sure about talking to Al today, on Christmas Eve. But the coming new year made her want to start completely fresh, and the first step toward doing that would be obeying God.

Would Al even care that she forgave him? Wouldn't accepting her forgiveness require him to admit his guilt? More than likely, Al would refuse to take any responsibility. He hadn't shown any remorse at the trial. At least, that's what her lawyer, unable to mask his disgust, kept saying. Even though it made no sense, the fact that Al wasn't sorry he'd hurt her pained Carly more than the physical injuries he'd caused. She couldn't believe she'd actually planned to marry him someday.

As she and her dad crossed the lot, Carly stamped her feet to keep the blood circulating in her toes as the snow whirled around her face. *Lord, I just want to get this over with.*

As her dad opened the door into the prison wall, she was struck by the bleak surroundings. Directly to their right was a bathroom. To their left two guards sat at a desk checking photo IDs. In a matter of minutes, she and her dad were seated on a metal bench waiting to go through the metal detector. Thank goodness she'd checked the prison website for visitors' guidelines. The sports bra she wore under her thick sweater felt strange, but it was better than being forced to remove her bra and carry it in a clear plastic zip bag, the routine consequence for a woman wearing an underwire bra. After they'd successfully made it through the metal detector, gotten their hands stamped with a substance visible only under ultraviolet light, and signed in with another guard, she and her dad reclaimed a spot on the metal benches and waited to be called. A moment later, the guard's gruff voice startled Carly into motion. She willed her legs not to wobble as the door slid opened revealing a narrow space in front of which was yet another sliding door. A wave of nausea hit her as the first door closed behind them. She swallowed the bile, and the second door slid open. Trembling, she stared at the older guard shining his ultraviolet scanner over her hand. He scanned her father's hand, clearing them to pass through a second pair of sliding doors.

This time her claustrophobia stole her breath. Dad reached for her hand, his strong grip infusing her with strength.

The last door opened to reveal not the prison but outside. To her right behind a high, chain link fence were rows of trailers, probably for conjugal visits. Disgust filled her. What if Al thought that was why she came? No, he was smarter than that.

Overwhelmed by the need to stay alert, she refocused her attention on her surroundings.

She was shocked by the level of security. Above her head, coiled barbed wire made escape over the wall impossible. On either side, chain link fencing boxed them in. A quick glance revealed perpendicular rows of fences placed about a hundred yards apart all along the space between the prison building and the wall. Coiled barbed wire topped every inch of fencing. Instead of making her feel secure, the fencing and barbed wire roused another wave of claustrophobia that made her want to flee.

But before she could change her mind, another guard led them into the prison itself, down a bleak hallway and into the visitors' waiting area. The packed room was unusually quiet.

A few people talked in soft, anxious voices, but most waited silently to be called for their turn.

Shaken by the oppressive atmosphere, Carly wiped her clammy hands on her jeans and prayed for strength to revisit the darkest moments of her life. Before she felt ready, her name was called. Her dad squeezed her hand and whispered, "I'll be praying for you."

Thanking him, she rose on unsteady legs and followed a tall guard into the visiting room.

The huge room was filled with more tables and people than Carly could count. Oddly, every table had chairs on only three sides, which puzzled her until she realized that all of the prisoners sat on the far side of the tables, facing the guards. Strikingly beautiful Disney murals painted by former inmates adorned the wall behind the prisoners. Some of the scenes weren't exactly suitable for children's eyes. Repulsed, she turned away. On a stage directly to her left, three correction officers stood watch. Just beyond them, vending machines featured the usual snacks and beverages. The room looked more like a cafeteria than a prison visitation area. She'd imagined a more private setting for this painful discussion. The guard who'd escorted her into the room led her to a table at the far end, along a bank of windows that revealed an overflow room where several prisoners and visitors talked.

The second Al spotted her and locked eyes with her, the urge to run and never look back surged through Carly. His penetrating gaze unnerved her and unclothed her. Her breath caught in her throat, her hands shook, and she laced her fingers together.

"Are you all right, miss?" the guard asked.

She nodded, but she couldn't turn away from the flash of sadness that dimmed Al's fiery blue eyes to a washed out slate gray. He stared at her, his expression uncertain then hard. At the guard's nod, she sat down with only a table separating her from the man who had tried to kill her. Her heart pounded with a wave of fear. What was she doing here? For a nanosecond, she couldn't remember.

"Why are you here?" he asked flatly, then reached diagonally across the table for her hand. When she inched her chair back, he scowled and folded his hands. "You didn't come all this way to wish me a Merry Christmas, did you?"

Run. You don't have to do this. He doesn't deserve your forgiveness.

She started to stand but forced herself to sit again. She had to see this through. "I came … to tell you that I forgive you."

Al leaned forward, crowding into her physical space. He smirked, his eyes sardonic and menacing. "You forgive me? Don't you think it should be the other way around? You should be asking me for my forgiveness. After all, it's your fault that I'll be in here for the next 10 years. Maybe less if I make parole."

The hatred in his tone flashed her back to the day he almost killed her. Fear pulsed through her veins. She raised her gaze, checking to be sure the guards remained alert at their posts. "I forgive you for almost killing me, for killing our baby. I … I forgive you for forcing me to have an abortion."

"I did *not* force you to do anything. You killed your baby."

Merciless and relentless, his words ground her spirit like mortar and pestle.

"You made your choices and now you want to blame me because you feel guilty." He grabbed her hand, and she winced.

Carly struggled against his strength, but he wouldn't release her. Couldn't the guards see?

"You're hurting me." Al was crushing the bones in her hand. Screaming in pain, she jumped up, but he didn't let go.

She lurched forward, nearly falling across the table.

Through her pain and panic, she heard, "Visiting Room One to area supervisor. Need your assistance immediately."

Two guards raced to their table. "Let her go," the taller, dark-haired guard commanded.

Al squeezed her wrist harder. He stared at her with murderous loathing, and she started to shake.

"Let the lady go," the second guard ordered, stepping between her and Al to separate them. Having a guard standing between them offered some protection, but Al twisted her wrist, and she cried out. The first guard gripped Al's arms, and he instantly relaxed his iron grip, letting her go at last.

Blinking back tears, she massaged her throbbing, bruised hand. Her head was spinning. Was she going to faint? Here, in front of all these strangers?

"She's no lady," Al muttered as the guards guided his body to the table and handcuffed him. "She's nothing but a common whore."

"That's enough, Rutledge. Visit's over," the first guard said.

Al let lose a string of curses. "I didn't ask her to come. She's nothing to me. Nothing but a whore."

Carly clasped the edge of the table to keep from collapsing.

A moment later, under the watchful eyes of the supervisor, the two guards escorted Al from the visiting room. As one guard pulled the door closed, Al yelled back, "Expensive and gorgeous but still a whore. That's all you'll ever be."

People stared, some with shocked, sympathetic expressions, others judging her, and for that brief moment, she was once more Elise, one of the highest-priced call girls in western New York. But she straightened her shoulders and found the strength to stride out of the visitation room with her head held high.

The visit was over. Had she accomplished what she'd come to do?

CHAPTER TWENTY-SIX

Carly held back her tears until her dad pulled out of the prison parking lot. Then, hunched over as much as the seatbelt would allow, she covered her face with her hands and sobbed. Her dad didn't say a word. He just reached over and patted her arm a few times before heading the car in the direction of home.

Isolated in her grief, she prayed, *God, what went wrong? I did exactly what You told me to do. Now, I feel worse than I did before.*

You did Your part. Trust Me to do Mine.

I don't understand, Lord.

Trust My love.

She closed her eyes and leaned back against the headrest, utterly exhausted.

*

"Carly, honey, we're home."

She stirred from sleep, opened her eyes, and stretched her legs. "How long have I been asleep?"

"For the whole ride. Except maybe the first five minutes or so."

Two trucks were parked in the driveway. Her brother's and Joe's. Would that man never learn to give her some space?

"Dad, can I use your car?"

Her father shot her a quizzical look. Until he glanced at the trucks, and added one plus one and came up with Joe. "I get it."

Leaving the engine running, Dad exited the car, and she climbed over the console into the driver's seat.

"What should I tell your mother?"

"Tell her I had some last minute shopping to do and not to wait dinner for me."

"And what should I tell Callahan when he asks when you'll be home?"

She almost said, when he leaves, but she couldn't be that mean to Joe. "Tell him I'm not ready to talk to him yet."

"You got it, babe."

"Thanks, Dad."

He shut the driver's door, and she backed out of the driveway before anyone in the house could have time to come outside and try to stop her from leaving. She hadn't recovered from the shock of Al's violent reaction. No matter how much she cared about Joe, Carly couldn't muster any strength for another confrontation today. She feared he'd still be angry. She needed him to be an unconditional friend, not a protector.

*

Joe had waited more than two hours for Carly to get home, only to have her leave without even coming into the house. He was no dunce. She obviously didn't want to see him, but he had to know where they stood. Before her dad could even say hello, Joe asked, "Did Carly give you a message for me?"

The sympathetic look on the older man's face didn't bode well. "Yep, she said she's not ready to talk to you yet."

Mrs. Lawrence patted his arm. "Let me send you home with a container of chicken noodle soup for your mother. I'm sure Carly will call you later."

And with that he was dismissed.

Jared only shrugged. No help there. Joe didn't blame him. Jared's first loyalty should be to his sister.

This day wasn't turning out like Joe had planned at all.

He'd been imagining sitting in the Christmas Eve service with Carly beside him. Now, even calling her to ask how her visit at the prison had gone was out of the question. How had he messed things up so badly? All he'd wanted to do was protect her. Something he'd failed miserably at in the past. Apparently, he was still clueless about what she needed.

*

After three stops, Joe finally found a florist willing to deliver flowers today. He ordered a dozen long-stemmed roses arranged with pine greens in a crystal vase. At first, the shop girl was reluctant, but when he laid two extra twenties on the counter, the young woman—Amanda, according to her nametag—shrugged her shoulders and smiled. "One's for you, and the other is for your delivery person." He covered the bills with his hand. "If you can promise to deliver the flowers today."

She glanced twice at the address that he scrawled on the back of one of the shop's fliers—Flowers by Amanda. This was her flower shop.

She smiled, clearly noticing the moment he made the connection. "I'll drop them off myself after I close up at six."

Joe breathed a sigh of relief, then wrote a quick message on a holly-edged card. He handed it to the young woman. "Thank you, Amanda. You may be helping to save my future."

She nodded as though she'd heard the same thing before. How many guys pleaded for forgiveness with flowers? Probably countless.

"No problem. Do you want to stay while I put together the arrangement?"

He shook his head. "No, but I want four red, four pink, and four white roses."

"Are you sure? Most women prefer red." She smiled to temper her criticism of his choice.

"Not Carly. She likes mixed bouquets." He'd almost said, not my girl. But she wasn't his girl. Not yet. "Thanks again for delivering them today. I really appreciate it. Merry Christmas."

Heading out the door, Joe braced himself against the biting cold. Fighting the fierce wind, he kept his head down as he strode to his car, praying Carly would accept his apology and give them the chance they'd never had before. He'd do whatever it took to convince her that she could count on him.

*

Carly paid for her coffee at the drive-thru window. Now where should she go? She didn't have any more shopping to do. She hadn't meant to lie. She prayed for forgiveness and then decided to make things right by picking up an extra gift for her mother. Braving traffic at the mall was absolutely out of the question. Perhaps a centerpiece for their Christmas table. As she pulled up to what was possibly the only florist still open, she spotted Joe coming out of Flowers by Amanda. The strong wind was practically pushing him in the direction of his car, which was parked within sight of hers, so there was no way he could not notice her. Still, Carly slid off the seat and onto the floor until her head was below the window.

She stayed scrunched in that awkward position until her left leg started to cramp up. The bone ached enough in this cold without twisting herself like a pretzel. "What are you doing?" Climbing back onto the seat, she laughed out loud at herself. If Joe had seen her, she wouldn't have been rude to him. Running off without talking to him had been childish. So why was she hiding in the car?

She'd done nothing to be ashamed of. Even though Al had refused to accept her forgiveness, telling him she forgave him was the right thing to do. She's been blindsided by his rage, but his reaction was definitely not out of character. Why hadn't she been more careful, more prepared? Thank goodness the guards had intervened in time. Carly tested her fingers, wiggling them a bit. Despite the pulsating pain and the peculiar purple overtaking her wrist, nothing was broken, though Al had certainly tried to crush her bones.

He hated her, but thanks to the Lord working in her life, to her amazement, she no longer hated Al. She pitied him.

Right there in her car, she prayed for him, for God to forgive him and to change him, and in that moment, the agony of the abortion and the heartbreak of the miscarriage diminished. Miraculously, God rooted out the bitterness. In its place sadness lingered. Thinking about her babies might always hurt, but torturing herself with memories couldn't change what had happened.

Could she redeem the past? God had shown her that she was precious to Him. She did not have to label herself a murderer and a prostitute anymore. That part of her life was dead and buried, and with God's help, eventually, she would stop digging up the horrible memories. She sighed and hugged her arms to her chest. Feeling precious was amazing beyond words, and something she had given up ever experiencing years ago.

If only she could tell Joe how she was feeling, he could rejoice with her.

If he decided to trust her. His reaction today showed that he still doubted her, even now that she'd given her life to God. Maybe, he didn't believe her commitment to Christ was sincere.

Carly was tired of paying the price for Joe's mother's mistakes. Shouldering the weight of her own past had been difficult enough.

*

When she opened her parents' front door to find a florist

standing on the porch, clutching a vase of flowers in her gloved hands, Carly frowned in confusion. This was the same girl who had made Mom's centerpiece. And she was here with another arrangement? Why? "Can I help you?"

The young woman's easy smile testified to the many times she'd been greeted with surprised disbelief. "If your name is Carly Lawrence, these are for you," she said, holding the flowers out at arms' length.

Carly took the heavy vase and wished the florist a Merry Christmas.

Grateful that her parents were washing dishes together in the kitchen, and her brother had disappeared after dinner to wrap his last minute purchases, Carly set the vase on the end table. Heart pounding, she removed the layers of plastic and tissue paper until a stunning arrangement of red, pink, and white roses accented with baby's breath, Scotch pine, and holly leaves came into view. For one paralyzing moment, she feared they were from Al. Inhaling a strengthening breath, she dismissed her groundless anxiety. Al would never send her flowers. She removed the card from the envelope, and read the message. "Carly, please forgive me. I don't want to spend another Christmas without you. If you're ready to talk before I go to work, I'm on 11 to 7 tonight. Love, Joe."

She closed her eyes and sighed. *Lord, Joe and I have been on this roller coaster for so long that I don't know how we'll ever get off.*

You forgave Al. Now, forgive Joe.

For several minutes, Carly waited, but no matter how hard she tried, she couldn't deny God's still small voice. He'd given her clear direction.

She wanted to believe Joe had changed. That he'd see the woman she was today, not the girl who had run off to chase empty dreams. Not the girl who reminded him way too much of his wanderlust mother.

Carly sat cross-legged on the couch and swiped her thumb across her phone screen. No texts. *Silly, girl. He's waiting to hear from you first.* "It's your move."

Her parents' laughter alerted her to their arrival. When they came through the doorway, Dad was actually holding Mom's hand. Carly ignored the tight pang in her chest. Would she ever have a constant love like theirs? She didn't want to end up like Addie Callahan. How horrible to be sick and alone. What if her family hadn't forgiven her? Carly shuddered, remembering how closed off Joe had become, refusing to accept anything or anyone at face value. How much of that was an occupational hazard she couldn't begin to guess.

Finally forgiving his mom was a good sign. A sign that maybe … maybe what? What did Carly want from him? His forgiveness. And his love.

She keyed in the password on her phone. She should at least thank him for the flowers. Just to be polite. But he wanted more than polite. He expected an invitation to Christmas dinner. That would give her parents and Jared the clear impression that she and Joe were definitely a couple.

The trouble was … trusting each other.

Dad bent to slip a DVD into the player, and she moved to the recliner so her parents could have the couch. Before the DVD even loaded, Carly imagined the opening scene of *It's a Wonderful Life.* She didn't exactly feel like her life was wonderful.

Until she remembered how she'd spent last Christmas Eve.

Suffocating shame heated her cheeks. But self-condemnation was counterproductive. God was good. He had good plans for her, free of disgrace and despondency. Whether or not that included the man she loved.

Could she give Joe another chance? Clearly, he still didn't trust her. Otherwise, he wouldn't have freaked out over her wanting to see Al. If only she and Joe could have a conversation—one where he didn't see her as a younger version of his wayward mother.

Hiding her struggle behind a bright smile, Carly made eye contact with each member of her family in turn. "Does anyone else want hot chocolate?" She needed a few minutes to collect herself, to put today in perspective. "With Christmas cookies?"

"I do." Her brother came up behind her and leaned over the couch to stick his nose in her bouquet, which occupied a prime spot near the front door where every person entering the house could enjoy its beauty. Jared pivoted, nailing her with his big-brother-knows-best look. "Did you call him yet?"

Dad glared at Jared. "Leave your sister alone. It's her first Christmas Eve home in more than ten years, and it *will* be a peaceful Christmas in the Lawrence house."

Jared frowned but didn't say a word.

He didn't have to. Her brother was thinking that she should cut the guy some slack, while Dad was obviously thinking cut your sister some slack.

"It's all right, Dad. I realize Jared is caught in the middle."

Alone in the kitchen, while the milk simmered on the stove, she almost called Joe. Three times. Joe said he'd marry her in a heartbeat. Had he been serious? She keyed in two text messages but didn't send either of them. What could she say? *I love you, but until I know you trust me, we can't be together?* Fighting the tears welling up, she swallowed around the tight feeling in her throat as she whisked the cocoa mix into the warm milk.

Two hours later, the minute the movie was over, Carly headed upstairs to draw herself a hot bath. The bathroom clock read ten fifteen when she finally dragged her wrinkled self from the tepid water. Joe would be getting ready for work. Should she call him? And say what? *Let's talk? Come over for breakfast and stay for the day? Stay with me forever because you're the only one for me?*

*

Disappointed, Joe set his phone to silent.

Harris shot him a sympathetic look. "So, she didn't call or text. That doesn't mean she won't forgive you. It just means she needs a little more time. When a woman thinks you don't have faith in her judgment, it takes more than flowers to convince her to give you another chance."

Joe started the engine. It would be a long night. "You're right. I messed up, and as soon as this shift ends, I'm going to tell her in person."

But Joe didn't stop checking his phone until about 3 a.m. So much for keeping his head in the job. Fortunately for him, it was an uncharacteristically quiet night, especially for a holiday.

*

After a quick shower, Joe put on jeans and blue thermal shirt, then frowned at himself in the mirror. The Lawrences always dressed up for Christmas dinner. Should he change? No. Carly wouldn't be impressed by anything he wore. Today, she'd be looking straight past his clothes to his heart. And that's what he was counting on.

He sent a quick text to Carly's mother, asking if she had room for two more at her Christmas table. Within minutes, Mrs. Lawrence replied, "Of course."

Joe knocked on the guest room door. "Mom, are you up? I have a favor to ask you."

From behind him, Addie called out, "I'm in the kitchen."

Joe headed that way. His plan was radical and designed to convince Carly once and for all that he trusted her with his heart. Completely. He was sure his mother would approve.

Bathed in rays of morning light, she looked healthier than he'd seen her since he was a kid. She kissed his cheek. "Merry Christmas, Joe."

Joe met his mother's smiling gaze. "Merry Christmas, Mom."

"Something's happened. Something more than just your joy over spending Christmas with your mother."

He reached for her right hand. On her ring finger, she still wore the square-shaped ruby that had been his great-grandmother's engagement ring. "Remember when you told me the story of this ring, and how it had been worn by three generations of women in our family?"

"Of course, I remember. Your father gave me this ring. I tried to give it back to him, that last time I left, but he insisted it belonged to me." She blinked back tears.

"Mom, don't." He couldn't bear her blaming herself for things that couldn't be changed. He'd blamed her enough for the both of them.

With a knowing smile, she swiped the moisture from her cheeks. "When you were ten, I promised you that someday the ring would be yours to give to the love of your life." She slid the gold band off her finger, placed it on his palm, and then closed his fingers over the sparkling jewel. "It's a perfect Christmas gift for Carly."

He smiled. That wasn't exactly what he had in mind.

Joe pulled his mother into a quick hug. "Thank you for letting me take care of you for a while."

"I've been meaning to talk to you about that." She leveled him with her no-arguments look. "I want to be back in my own place before New Year's Eve."

Joe studied her determined features. "I thought you'd stay a little longer, until you got your strength back."

She patted his arm. "Being near my family is the best medicine in the world, and I've enjoyed your fussing over me, but I want to start painting again, and for that, I need solitude."

"I get it, Mom." It made perfect sense. All of the women in his life needed their space, some more than others. "I'm off the day after tomorrow, so I can help you get settled and take you grocery shopping, whatever you need."

"That's very thoughtful." She poured two mugs of coffee and handed one to him. "Are you heading over to the Lawrences' for breakfast?"

"Not unless you're ready to go."

His mother frowned. "Oh, my. Didn't I tell you that Bob was picking me up right after the kids opened their presents? Maureen wanted me to sleep over last night, but I had this feeling I needed to be here with you this morning." Her face glowed with happiness. "Now, I know why."

Joe patted the ring in his pocket, a ring he hoped would soon be on the hand of the woman he loved.

*

Carly stretched in her bed. Never again would she take such simple movements for granted. The sounds of "Joy to the World" floated up the stairs and under her door. Her mother was probably up listening to Christmas music, having her coffee, and reading her Bible in her favorite chair while she waited for the rest of the family to awaken. Carly savored the memories of Christmases past and the sheer joy of being home again. God had restored so many of her abandoned dreams. Her new dream of standing beside Joe before the altar made her hug herself and smile. Maybe next year by Christmas they'd be living in a home of their own.

Her red velour dress hung waiting on the closet door.

Feeling festive, she dressed quickly, then fussed with her

hair until the auburn curls behaved to her satisfaction. She missed her blonde hair. How long would it take to get it back to its natural color? She chuckled at her foolishness. Changing her hair hadn't protected her from Harrison. God had done that by giving her the courage to face her fear.

Eager to focus on today, she looked with longing at the black satin heels but settled instead for the sensible ballet flats. To her delight, the swirling folds of the A-line dress complemented the shoes perfectly. Assessing herself in the full-length mirror, Carly made peace with her slender shape. Placing her hand on her flat stomach no longer made her want to scream with anger and grief. She was only twenty-nine. She still had plenty of time. She would trust God's timing. Someday her arms would cradle a baby of her own.

Would it ... could it be Joe's, too?

*

After they'd exchanged their Christmas gifts, Carly helped her mother in the kitchen while her brother set the table for brunch. Dad had ducked outside to try out his new snow blower. With only an inch or two of new snow, clearing the driveway and sidewalk shouldn't take more than twenty minutes or so. By that time, the food would be ready.

The sound of stamping feet in the mudroom made Carly turn just as the door opened to reveal not her father but Joe. She drew in a startled breath. She shouldn't be surprised that he was here so early, but she was. He hadn't slept. The lines around his eyes declared his exhaustion, but the determination in his blue gaze quickened her pulse.

Her feet were glued to the linoleum.

"Good morning, Joe," her mother said, as if she'd expected him sooner. "Carly, why don't the two of you go into the living room and talk? I'll turn down the oven to keep the casserole warm while we wait for your father. If I know him, he'll want to do the neighbors' sidewalks, too, so you two take your time."

"Thank you, Mrs. Lawrence," Joe said, his eyes still studying Carly, waiting for a sign of encouragement.

She reached for him. The instant their palms touched warmth sparked a blush in her cheeks. Smiling, he squeezed her hand and led her from the room.

The smell of pine filled the air. Sunlight played with the Christmas tree lights, illuminating an eclectic collection of ornaments.

"I see you got my flowers." Joe lowered himself to the couch and patted the cushion beside him.

Carly sat cross-legged, her whole body turned toward him, so she could read his eyes. "They came last night around seven. I should have called you, but ..." She searched his face for evidence she'd hurt him, but his impassive cop look hid his thoughts. "Joe, I'm sorry I got so mad."

"I'm sorry, too. I should have listened to you, instead of jumping to conclusions. I'm sorry for running roughshod over you. I promise, I'll never try to control you like that ever again. Can you forgive me?"

"Of course, I forgive you, but if you'd given me a minute to explain, I would have told you that I was doing what God wanted me to do."

Joe opened his mouth to speak, but she put her finger over his lips. "I needed to tell Al that I forgive him." She paused, praying Joe would understand. "For everything."

Joe's gaze dropped to the purplish black bruises on her hand and wrist. A scowl furrowed his brow.

She resisted the urge to hide the damage.

He lifted her hand from her lap and cradled it gently in his own. "Rutledge did this to you? Where were the guards?"

"Watching. They stopped him before he could break any bones."

The glint in Joe's eyes was a mix of frustration, hurt, and suppressed anger. "This is exactly why I didn't want you to go."

He was furious with Al, but was Joe angry at her, too? Tears pricked her eyes, and her throat tightened with her effort to keep from crying. She swallowed. "I forgive you for not coming with me. Not in the visiting room, but to the prison. I needed to know you trusted me. I needed your support. Talking to Al would have been so much easier if I'd known you were waiting for me."

"I know. And I let you down. Maybe, if I could forgive myself for letting you go off with him in the first place—"

"What? What are you talking about it? It wasn't your fault I couldn't see the real Al underneath all that charm."

Joe moved closer to her until her knees pressed against his thigh. "If I'd told you I loved you, helped you to believe it, your whole life would have been different." His grim expression was weighed down with crushing guilt.

She cupped his face, her fingers caressing his cheekbones. A single tear dropped on one of her fingers. "Is that what you think? What you've thought all of these years? You can't possibly blame yourself for my mistakes."

His eyes clouded with anguish.

"You do, don't you? Just like you blamed yourself for your mother leaving. *You* didn't do anything wrong, Joe, so you need to forgive yourself, once and for all. I love you and your mother loves you. She's always loved you."

Joe's lips parted into a slow smile. "You love me?" He leaned close, his cinnamon breath caressing her face.

"I do. I love you, and I forgive you for not trusting me, and if you want to try—"

He covered her mouth with a kiss as he pulled her to her feet. She stood on her toes and encircled his neck with her arms. He deepened the kiss, and her pulse soared to match his. His hand on the small of her back felt right, but her mother's and brother's voices reminded her that she and Joe could be interrupted at any moment. She broke off the kiss and wriggled out of his embrace.

He reached into his pocket.

She couldn't breathe.

He opened his hand. A sparkling, two-carat ruby lay in his palm.

"That's your mother's ring." Tears tracked down Carly's face, and she sobbed. "It's been in your family forever."

"I told you I'd marry you tomorrow, if you said yes." Reaching for her left hand, he slid the ring onto her finger. "It fits perfectly. Just like you. You and I are a perfect fit."

"You really believe that?"

"With all my heart. Will you marry me, Carly, and make me the happiest man on earth?"

She swiped futilely at the flood of tears. "Yes, I will marry you, Joe Callahan, tomorrow, if you'll have me."

A grin split his face. "I was thinking maybe Valentine's Day. That way I'll never forget our anniversary."

She laughed, and the sound of baritone laughter reached her ears.

"It's about time," Jared declared. "Mom and Dad are waiting in the dining room. If you, two are done making up, let's eat before breakfast gets cold."

Carly allowed Joe to wrap his arm around her waist and pull her close to his side where she belonged. They followed her brother into the dining room, the table laden with their traditional holiday breakfast. In the center, two red candles flanked her mother's centerpiece. Grinning with joy, her parents were seated at each end of the festive table. As Carly and Joe took the chairs opposite her brother, a joyous peace settled in her heart. She was home at last, surrounded by the people she loved the most, and by God's grace, nothing would separate her from their love or His love ever again.

Dear Reader,

I hope reading the story of Carly's journey back to God has blessed you. When she first appeared in my imagination, her brokenness gripped my heart. As her life unfolded on these pages, time and again, I saw evidence that so many others like her believed they had gone too far for God to want them anymore. But absolutely nothing can separate you from His perfect love. It is my prayer that this truth resonates in your heart and mind—that God will not let you go, that His love will restore all you have lost, no matter how far you have drifted from Him, no matter how you came to be there. Like the prodigal son, may you run into your heavenly Father's open arms. He is waiting especially for you. His Son died on the cross to wash away your every sin. "Though your sins be as scarlet, they shall be as white as snow; though they be red like crimson, they shall be as wool" (Isaiah 1:18). The life God has planned for you is more wonderful than you can possibly imagine.

I would be happy to hear from you. Please contact me at authorlaurahervey@gmail.com.

Yours truly,

Laura Hervey

If you enjoyed this book, please consider giving me a review on Amazon, Goodreads, or your favorite book review site.

About Laura Hervey

Laura Hervey writes inspirational romance. She is also the author of a variety of short works, including articles, opinion pieces, poetry, short stories, and devotionals. *Scarlet Tears* is her first published novel. Visit Laura at her author website, www.laurahervey.com.

Laura lives in western New York. She attends the Bible Tabernacle, a non-denominational Christian church and is a member of American Christian Fiction Writers. She teaches English Language Arts. When she isn't writing or teaching, she enjoys spending time with her two children and her grandchildren. She shares her home with two dogs, a German shepherd and a miniature Dachshund.